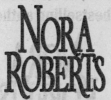

NORA ROBERTS

THE MacGREGORS
SERENA~CAINE

Published by Silhouette Books

America's Publisher of Contemporary Romance

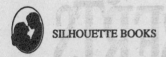

SILHOUETTE BOOKS

THE MacGREGORS: SERENA~CAINE

Copyright © 1998 by Harlequin Books S.A.

ISBN 0-373-48388-0

PLAYING THE ODDS
Copyright © 1985 by Nora Roberts

TEMPTING FATE
Copyright © 1985 by Nora Roberts

Printed in U.S.A.

CONTENTS

THE MacGREGORS

Daniel Duncan MacGregor
m.
Anna Whitfield
(THE MacGREGORS: Daniel~Ian, Silhouette Books, 4/99)

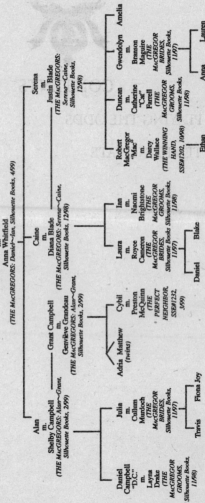

Alan
m.
Shelby Campbell
(THE MacGREGORS: Alan~Grant, Silhouette Books, 2/99)

- Daniel Campbell "D.C."
  m.
  Layna Drake
  (THE MacGREGOR GROOMS, Silhouette Books, 11/98)
  - Travis
  - Fiona Joy
- Julia
  m.
  Cullum Murdoch
  (THE MacGREGOR BRIDES, Silhouette Books, 11/97)

Grant Campbell
m.
Geneviève Grandeau
(THE MacGREGORS: Alan~Grant, Silhouette Books, 2/99)

- Cybil
  m.
  Preston McQuinn
  (THE PERFECT NEIGHBOR, SSE#1232, 3/99)
- Adria Matthew
  (twins)

Caine
m.
Diana Blade
(THE MacGREGORS: Serena~Caine, Silhouette Books, 12/98)

- Laura
  m.
  Royce Cameron
  (THE MacGREGOR BRIDES, Silhouette Books 11/97)
  - Daniel
  - Blake
- Ian
  m.
  Naomi Brightstone
  (THE MacGREGOR GROOMS, Silhouette Books 11/98)

Serena
m.
Justin Blade
(THE MacGREGORS: Serena~Caine, Silhouette Books, 12/98)

- Robert MacGregor "Mac"
  m.
  Darcy Wallace
  (THE WINNING HAND, SSE#1202, 10/98)
  - Ethan
- Duncan
  m.
  Catherine "Cat" Farrell
  (THE MacGREGOR GROOMS, Silhouette Books, 11/98)
- Gwendolyn
  m.
  Branson Maguire
  (THE MacGREGOR BRIDES, Silhouette Books, 11/97)
  - Anna
  - Lauren
- Amelia

PLAYING THE ODDS

Chapter One

There was always a great deal of confusion, more noise, and a touch of panic to flavor the arrival of embarking passengers. Some were already a bit travel weary from their flight into Miami, others were running on the adrenaline of anticipation. The huge white ocean liner, the *Celebration*, waited in port—their ticket to fun, relaxation, romance. When they crossed the gangway, they would no longer be accountants, assistant managers, or teachers, but pampered passengers assured of being fed, spoiled, and entertained for the next ten days. The brochures guaranteed it.

From the rail of the Observation deck, Serena watched the flow of humanity. At that distance she could enjoy the color and noise, which never lost its appeal for her, without being caught in the inevitable tangle of fifteen hundred people trying to get to the same place at the same time. The cooks, the bartenders, the cabin stewards, had already begun the orgy of work that would continue, virtually uninterrupted, for the next ten days. But she had time. Serena relished it.

These were her idle moments—before the ship pulled out of port. She could remember her first experience with a cruise liner. She'd been eight, the youngest of the three children of financial wizard Daniel MacGregor and Dr. Anna Whitefield MacGregor. There had been first-class cabins, where the steward had served her hot buns and juice in bed. Serena had enjoyed it the same way she enjoyed her tiny cabin in the crew's quarters now. They were both an adventure.

Serena remembered, too, the day she had told her parents of her plans to apply for a job with the *Celebration*. Her father had huffed and puffed about her throwing away her education. The more he had huffed, the more pronounced his soft Scottish burr had become. A woman who had graduated from Smith at the tender age of twenty, who had then gone on to earn degrees in English, history, and sociology didn't swab decks. And even as Serena had assured him that wasn't her intention, her mother had laughed, telling Daniel to let the child be. Because at six foot three and two hundred and twenty pounds, Daniel MacGregor was helpless against what he called his females, he did just that.

So Serena had gotten her job and had escaped from what had become endless years of study. She'd traded her three-room suite in the family mansion in Hyannis Port for a one-room broom closet with a bunk on a floating hotel. None of her coworkers cared what her I.Q. was, or how many degrees she'd earned. They didn't know her father could have bought the cruise line lock, stock, and barrel if he'd had the whim, or that her mother was an authority on thoracic surgery. They didn't know her oldest brother was a senator and the younger a state's attorney. When they looked at her, they saw Serena. That was all she wanted.

Lifting her head, she let the wind take her hair. It danced on the breeze, a mass of blond, the rich shade of gold one found in old paintings. She had high, slanting cheekbones and a sharp, stubborn jaw. Her skin refused to tan, remaining a delicate peach to contrast with the violet-blue of her eyes. Her father called them purple; a few romantics had called them violet. Serena stubbornly termed them blue and left it at that. Men were drawn to them because of their uniqueness, then to her because of the elegant sexuality she exuded without thought. But she wasn't very interested.

Intellectually, Serena thought a man was a fool if he fell for a shade of irises. It was a matter of genetics after all, and had little to do with her personally. She'd listened to accolades on her eyes for twenty-six years with a kind of detached wonder. There was a miniature in her father's library of his great-grandmother, another Serena. If anyone had asked, she could have explained the process of genetics that resulted in the resemblance, down to the bone structure and eye shade—and the reputed temper. But the men she met were generally not interested in scientific explanation, and Serena was generally not interested in them.

Below her, the crowd flowing up the gangway was thinning. Shortly the calypso band would be playing on the Lido deck to entertain the passengers while the ship prepared to sail. Serena would enjoy staying outside, listening to the tinny, rhythmic music and laughter. There would be a buffet laden with more food than the well over one thousand people could possibly eat, exotic drinks, and excitement. Soon the rails would be packed with people wanting that last glimpse of shore before all there would be was open sea.

Wistfully, she watched the last stragglers come on board. It was the final cruise of the season. When they returned to Miami, the *Celebration* would go into dry dock for two months. When it sailed again, Serena wouldn't be on it. She'd already made up her mind that it was time to move on. When she'd taken the job on the ship, she had been looking for one thing—freedom from years of study, from family expectations, from her own restlessnes. She knew she had accomplished something in the year on her own. Serena had found the independence she had always struggled for, and she had escaped the niche so many of her college friends had been determinedly heading for: a good marriage.

And yet, though she'd found the freedom and independence, she hadn't found the most important ingredient: the goal. What did Serena MacGregor want to do with the rest of her life? She didn't want the political career both her brothers had chosen. She didn't want to teach or lecture. She wanted excitement and challenges and no longer wanted to look for them in a classroom. They were all negative answers, but she knew whatever it was that would fill the rest of her life wouldn't be found by floating endlessly in the Bahamas.

Time to get off the boat, Rena, she told herself with a sudden smile. The next adventure's always just around the corner. Not knowing what it would be only made the search more intriguing.

The first long, loud blast of the horn was her signal. Drawing back from the rail, Serena went to her cabin to change.

Within thirty minutes she entered the ship's casino dressed in the modified tux that was her uniform. She had pulled her hair back in a loose bun at the nape of her neck so that it wouldn't tend to fall all over her face. Her hands would soon be too busy to fool with it.

The chandeliers were lit, spilling light onto the red and gold art deco carpet. Long curved windows allowed a view of the glassed-in Promenade deck, then the blue-green stretch of sea. The remaining walls were lined with slot machines, as silent as soldiers waiting for an attack. Fussing with the bow tie she could never seem to get quite right, Serena crossed to her supervisor. As with any sailor, the shifting of the ship under her feet went unnoticed.

"Serena MacGregor reporting for duty, sir," she said crisply.

Turning, a clipboard in one hand, he looked her up and down. Dale Zimmerman's lightweight boxer's build skimmed just under six feet. He had a smooth, handsome face he dedicatedly tanned, winning crinkles at the corners of his light blue eyes, and sun-bleached hair that curled riotously. He had a reputation, which he assiduously promoted, of being a marvelous lover. After his brief study of Serena, his grin broke out.

"Rena, can't you ever get this thing right?" Tucking the clipboard under his arm, Dale straightened her tie.

"I like to give you something to do."

"You know, lover, if you're serious about quitting after this run, this is going to be your last chance for paradise." Tugging on her tie, he lifted his eyes to grin into hers.

Serena cocked a brow. What had begun a year ago

as an ardent pursual on Dale's part had been tempered into a good-humored joke about Serena's refusal to go to bed with him. They had become, more to his surprise than hers, friends. "I'm going to hate to miss it," Serena told him with a sigh. "Did the little redhead from South Dakota go home happy?" she asked with a guileless smile.

Dale's eyes narrowed. "Anybody ever tell you that you see too much?"

"All the time. What's my table?"

"You're on two." Taking out a cigarette, Dale lit it as she walked away. If anyone had told him a year before that a classy number like Serena MacGregor would not only hold him off but make him feel fraternal, he'd have recommended a good psychiatrist. With a shrug he went back to his clipboard. He was going to regret losing her, Dale reflected, and not only because of his personal feelings. She was the best damn blackjack dealer he had.

There were eight blackjack tables scattered throughout the casino. Serena and the seven other dealers would rotate from position to position through the rest of the afternoon and evening, with only a brief, staggered dinner break. Unless the playing was light, the casino would stay open until two. If it was heavy, a few tables might stay open until three. The first rule was to give the passengers what they wanted.

Other men and women clad in tuxedos went to their stations. Beside Serena the young Italian who had just been promoted to croupier stood at table two. Serena gave him a smile, remembering that Dale had asked her to keep an eye on him.

"Enjoy yourself, Tony," she suggested, eyeing the

crowd that already waited outside the glass doors. "It's going to be a long night." And all on our feet, she added silently as Dale gave the signal to open the door.

Passengers poured in. Not in a trickle—they rarely trickled in the first day of a cruise. The crowd would be thin during the dinner hours, then swell again until past midnight. Dress was casual—shorts, jeans, bare feet—the uniform for afternoon gambling. With the opening of the door Serena heard the musical sound effects of arcade games already being fed on the Promenade deck. Within minutes the sound was drowned out by the steady clatter of slots.

Serena could separate the gamblers from the "players" and the players from the "lookers." There was always some of each group in any batch of passengers. There would be a percentage who had never been to a casino before. They would simply wander around, attracted by the noise and the colorful equipment before they exchanged their bills for change for the slots.

There were some who came for fun, not really caring if they won or lost. These were the players—they came for the game. It usually took little time for the looker to become the player. They would shout when they won and moan when they lost in much the same way the arcade addicts reacted.

But always, there were the gamblers. They would haunt the casino during the trip, turning the game of win and lose into an art—or an obsession. They had no specific features, no particular mode of dress. The mystique of the riverboat gambler could be found in the neat little grandmother from Peoria just as it could be found in the Madison Avenue executive. As the tables began to fill, Serena categorized them. She smiled at the five people who had chosen her table, then broke the seal on four decks of cards.

"Welcome aboard," she said, and began to shuffle.

It took only an hour for the scent of gambling to rise. It permeated the smoke and light sweat that drifted through the casino. It was a heady scent, tempting. Serena had always wondered if it was what drew people more than the lights and green baize. The scent, and the noise of silver clattering in the bowls of the slot machines. Serena never played them, perhaps because she recognized the gambler in herself. She'd decided long ago not to risk anything unless the odds were on her side.

During her first shift she changed tables every thirty minutes, making her way slowly around the room. After her dinner break it began again. The casino grew more crowded after the sun set. Tables were full and the roulette wheel spun continuously. Dress became more elegant, as if to gamble in the evening required glamor.

Because the cards and people always changed, Serena was never bored. She had chosen the job to meet people—not the cut-out-of-the-same-affluent-cloth people she'd met in college, but a variety. In that she'd accomplished her goal. At the moment she had a Texan, two New Yorkers, a Korean and a Georgian at her table, all of whom she'd identified by their accents. This was as much a part of the game for her as the cards she slid onto the baize. One she never tired of.

Serena dealt the second card around, peeked at her hole card, and was satisfied with an eighteen. The first New Yorker took a hit, counted his cards, and gave a disgusted grunt. With a shake of the head he indicated

that he'd stand. The Korean busted on twenty-two, then
rose from the table with a mutter. The second New
Yorker, a sleek blonde in a narrow black dinner dress,
held with a nine and a queen.

"I'll take one," the man from Georgia drawled. He
counted eighteen, gave Serena a thoughtful look, and
held.

The man from Texas took his time. He had fourteen
and didn't like the eight Serena had showing. Considering the possibilities, he stroked his chin, swilled some
bourbon, then motioned Serena to hit him. She did, a
tad too hard with a nine.

"Sweetheart," he said as he leaned on the table,
"you're just too pretty to take a man's money that
way."

"Sorry." With a smile she turned over her hole card.
"Eighteen," she announced before she settled the bet-
ting.

Serena saw the hundred-dollar bill on the table before she realized someone had taken the Korean's vacant stool. Glancing up, she met a pair of green eyes—
cool, depthless, direct. She stared, trapped in that instant of contact into seeing nothing else. Cool green,
with amber rimming the iris. Something like ice skidded down her spine. Forcing herself to blink, Serena
looked at the man.

He had the lean face of an aristocrat, but this was no
prince. Serena sensed it instantly. Perhaps it was the
long, unsmiling mouth, or the rough sweep of black
brows. Or perhaps it was simply the inner warning that
went off in her brain. A ruler yes, but not royalty. This
was the type of man who planned ruthless coups and
succeeded. His hair flowed over his ears thick and black

and down to the collar of a white silk shirt. The skin stretched taut over the long bones of his face was as tanned as Dale's, but Serena didn't think he worked on the tone like her supervisor. This man faced the elements without a thought for fashion.

He didn't slouch like the Texan or lounge indolently like the man from Georgia, but rather sat like a sleek, patient cat, always coiled to spring. It wasn't until one rough brow rose slightly in question that Serena realized she'd been staring.

"Change a hundred," she said briskly, annoyed with herself. With deft movements she slipped the bill into the slot of the table, then counted out chips. When the bets were placed, she dealt the cards.

The man from New York glanced at the ten Serena had showing and hit on fourteen. He broke. The new player held on fifteen with a wordless gesture of his hand. She broke the other New Yorker and the Georgian before the Texan held on nineteen. Serena turned over a three to go with her ten, dealt herself a deuce, then broke with twenty-three. The man with the dangerous face drew out a thin cigar and continued to play silently. Serena already knew he was a gambler.

His name was Justin Blade. His ancestors had ridden swift ponies and hunted with bow and arrow. Serena had been right about the aristocracy, though his bloodline wasn't royal. Part of his heritage came from simple French immigrants and a dash from Welsh miners. The rest was Comanche.

He hadn't known a reservation, and though he had brushed with poverty in his youth, he was well accustomed to the feel of silk against his skin. Accustomed enough so that like the very wealthy, he rarely noticed

it. His first stake had been won in the backroom of a
pool hall when he'd been fifteen. In the twenty years
since, he'd played more elegant games. He was, as Serena had sensed, a gambler. And he was already figuring the odds.

Justin had entered the casino with the notion of passing a few hours with a mild game. A man could relax
with small stakes when he could afford to lose. Then
he'd seen her. His eyes had passed over other women
in sleek dinner dress, the gleam of gold and sparkle of
jewels, and came to rest on the blonde in the mannish
tuxedo. She had a slender neck which her hairstyle and
the ruffled shirtfront accentuated, and a carriage that
shouted breeding. But what was more, what he had
sensed in the loins, was a blatant sexuality that required
no movement, no words on her part. She was a woman
a man would beg for.

Justin watched her hands as she dealt. They were
exquisite—narrow, long-fingered, with delicate blue
veins just under the surface of creamy skin. Her nails
were oval and perfect, with the gleam of clear polish.
They were hands suited to fragile teacups and French
pastries. The kind of hands a man burned to have on
his skin.

Lifting his eyes from them, Justin looked directly
into hers. With the faintest of frowns, Serena stared
back. Why was it, she wondered, that this dark, silent
man brought her both discomfort and curiosity? He
hadn't spoken a word since he'd sat down—not to her
nor to any of the others at her table. Though he'd been
winning with professional consistency, he didn't appear
to gain any pleasure from it. He didn't appear to be
paying any attention to the game if it came to that, she

told herself. All he did was stare at her with that same calm, watchful expression.

"Fifteen," Serena said coolly, indicating the cards in front of him. Justin nodded for the hit and took a six without the slightest change of expression.

"Damn if you don't have the luck, son," the Texan stated jovially. Glancing at his own meager pile of chips, he gave a quick grimace. "Glad somebody does." He wheezed as Serena dealt him the card that eased him out at twenty-two.

Turning over twenty for the house, she collected chips, then slid two twenty-five dollar markers to Justin. His fingertips covered hers over them. The touch was light, but potent enough to have her eyes flashing up to his. Watching her steadily, he made no move to take his hand from hers. There was no pressure, no flirtatious squeeze, but Serena felt the response shoot through her as though their bodies rather than their fingers had pressed together. Calling on all her control, she slowly brought her hand back to her side.

"New dealer," she said calmly, noting with relief that her shift at that station was finished. "Have a nice evening." She moved to the next station, swearing to herself she wouldn't look back. Of course she did, and found her eyes pinned to his.

Infuriated, she allowed herself a slight toss of her head. Her expression became challenging. For the first time that evening she saw the long mouth curve in a slow smile—a smile that barely shifted the angles and planes on his face. Justin inclined his head, as if accepting the challenge. Serena turned her back on him.

"Good evening," she said in a clear voice to the new set of players.

* * *

The moon was still high, cutting a swath of light across the black water. From the rail Serena could see the white tips of waves as the ship moved in a fast sea. It was after two A.M., and the deck was deserted. She liked this time of the morning, while the passengers slept, before the crew began its early shift. She was alone with the sea and the wind and could imagine herself in any era she chose.

She breathed deeply, inhaling the scent of salt spray and night. They'd be in Nassau just past dawn, and while in port the casino would be closed. She would have the morning free to do as she chose. She preferred the night.

Her mind drifted back to her working hours, to the silent gambler who'd sat at her table, winning and watching. She thought he was a man women would be drawn to but wasn't surprised that he'd been alone. A solitary man, Serena mused, and strangely compelling. Attractive, she admitted as she leaned farther out to let the wind whip at her face. Attractive in a dangerous sort of way. But then, it was in her blood to look on danger as a challenge. Risks could be calculated, percentages measured, and yet...And yet Serena didn't think the man would follow the neat path of theory.

"Night suits you."

Serena's hands tightened on the rail. Though she'd never heard him speak, though she hadn't even heard his approach, she knew who stood behind her. It took all her effort not to gasp and whirl. While her heart hammered she turned to watch him come out of the shadows. Wanting her voice to be steady, she gave herself a moment while he stopped to stand beside her at the rail.

"Did your luck hold?" she asked.

Justin kept his eyes on her face. "Apparently."

She tried, and failed, to place his origin through his accent. His voice was deep and smooth and without inflection. "You're very good," she stated. "We don't often get a professional in the casino." There seemed to be a quick flash of humor in his eyes before he drew out a slim cigar and lit it. Smoke stung the air, then vanished in the wind. Serena relaxed her fingers on the rail, one at a time. "Are you enjoying your trip?"

"More than I anticipated." He took a slow, thoughtful drag on the cigar. "Are you?"

Serena smiled. "It's my job."

Justin leaned back against the rail, resting his hand beside hers. "That's not an answer, Serena," he pointed out.

Since there was a name tag on her lapel, she only lifted a brow at his use of her name. "I enjoy it, Mr.—"

"Blade," he said softly as he ran a fingertip down her jawline. "Justin Blade. Remember it."

Serena refused to back up though the lightning response of her body to his touch surprised her. Instead, she regarded him steadily. "I've a good memory."

With a trace of a smile he nodded. "Yes, that's why you're a good dealer. How long have you been doing it?"

"A year." Though he removed his fingertip, her blood didn't cool.

Surprised, Justin took a last drag on his cigar, then crushed it under his foot. "I would have thought longer from the way you handle the cards." Taking her hand from the rail, he studied the back, then turned it over to look at the palm. Soft, he thought, and steady. An interesting combination. "What did you do before?"

Even as her brain told her retreat would be wise, Serena allowed her hand to remain in his. She sensed strength and skill in the touch, though she wasn't certain of the aspect of either. "I studied."

"What?"

"Whatever interested me. What do you do?"

"Whatever interests me."

She laughed, a low sultry sound that whispered along his skin. "Somehow I think you mean that quite literally, Mr. Blade." She started to remove her hand, but his fingers closed over it.

"I do," he murmured. "It's Justin, Serena." His eyes skimmed the deserted deck, then the dark, endless sea. "This isn't the place for formality."

Common sense told her to tread carefully; instinct drove her to provoke. "There are rules for the crew when dealing with passengers, Mr. Blade," she said coolly. "I need my hand."

When he smiled, the moonlight glittered in his eyes, like a cat's. "So do I." Lifting it, he pressed his lips deep in the center of her palm. Serena felt the aftershock of the kiss in every pore. "I take what I need," he murmured against her flesh.

Her breathing had quickened without her being aware of it. On the dark, empty deck he was barely more than a shadow with a voice that might have been pressed through honey, and dangerous eyes. Feeling her body yearning toward him, Serena restrained it with a quick flash of temper.

"Not this time. I'm going in, it's late."

Keeping her hand firmly in his, Justin reached up to

pull the pins from her hair. As it tumbled over her shoulders, he tossed them into the sea. Stunned by his audacity, Serena glared at him. "Late," he agreed, combing his fingers from the crown to the tips of the thick, blond mane. "But you're a woman for the dark hours. I thought so the moment I saw you." With a movement that was too quick and too smooth to be measured, he had Serena trapped between his body and the rail. Her hair flew toward the sea, pulled by the wind, her skin pure as marble in the moonlight. Justin discovered the need was stronger that he had realized.

"Do you know what I thought?" Serena demanded, struggling to keep her words from jerking. "I thought you were rude and annoying."

He laughed, a rich quick sound of amusement. "It seems we were both right. Should I tell you it very nearly distracted me from my game, wondering how you tasted."

Serena became very still. The only movement came from the rich strands of gold that danced around her face. Then her chin rose; her eyes darkened with challenge. "A pity," she said quietly as she curled her hand into a fist. Passenger or no passenger, she determined, she was going to give him a good swift punch, just the way her brothers had taught her.

"It's rare for anything or anyone to interfere with my concentration." As he spoke he leaned closer. Serena tensed her muscles. "You have the eyes of a witch. I'm a superstitious man."

"Arrogant," Serena corrected steadily. "But I doubt superstitious."

She saw the smile in his eyes only as his face dominated her vision. "Don't you believe in luck, Serena?"

"Yes." And a good right jab, she added silently. She felt his fingers slide beneath her blowing hair to cup the base of her neck. His mouth lowered toward hers. Somehow the warm flutter of his breath caused her lips to part and her concentration to waver.

One hand still held hers, and he circled the palm with a finger as if to remind her of the feel of his lips on her flesh. Fighting the growing weakness, Serena drew back, aiming for his vulnerable, unsuspecting stomach.

Less than an inch away from her target, her fist was captured in a hard grip. Frustrated, she struggled, only to hear his quiet laugh again. "Your eyes give you away," he told her, holding her still. "You'll have to work on it."

"If you don't let me go, I'll..." The threat trailed off as his lips brushed hers. It wasn't a kiss, but a temptation. Her tongue came out to moisten her lips as if in anticipation of something darkly sweet and strictly forbidden.

"What?" he whispered, touching his mouth to hers again with a lightness that had the blood pounding in his head. He wanted to crush and devour almost as much as he wanted to savor. Her lips were damp and she smelled faintly of the sea and summer. When she didn't answer, Justin traced the shape of her mouth with his tongue, committing it to memory while he absorbed the flavor and waited.

Serena felt the thick, liquefying pleasure seep into her. Her lids were too heavy and fluttered closed; her muscles relaxed. The fist still curled in his hand went limp. For the first time in her memory her mind went blank—a clean slate on which he could have written anything he desired. She felt the tiny arousing pain as he nipped into her full bottom lip, and her mind filled again. But not with thoughts.

His body was against hers, hard and lean. His mouth was so soft, softer than she thought any man's could be, like the brush of fine silk against naked flesh. There was the faint scent of tobacco, something rich and foreign, and the smell of him without the interference of cologne. He whispered her name as she had never heard it spoken before. The boat listed, but he swayed with it as easily as she as he gathered her closer. With no more thoughts of resisting, Serena let her arms curve around his neck, her head dropping back in invitation.

Justin felt an almost savage need to plunder as he gripped her hair in his hand. "Open your eyes," he demanded. While he watched, the heavy lids opened to reveal eyes misted with pleasure. "Look at me when I kiss you," he murmured.

Then his mouth crushed hers, ruthless, ravaging. He could hear his own heartbeat raging in his chest as he plunged deeper. He discovered tastes, endless flavors, in the recesses he explored as her tongue answered with equal urgency. His eyes were only slits while he watched the misty pleasure in hers smolder into passion then become opaque. On a moan they closed, and his own vision blurred.

Serena felt desire grip her as if it had claws. Wants, needs, secrets, were exposed in one tumultuous explosion. Even as she hungered to fulfill them she realized he was a man who could strip her to the soul. And she knew nothing of him. Frightened, she struggled to free herself, but he held her close, his lips clinging until he was done. In some sane portion of her brain she realized he would always take without regard for willingness.

When she was free, Serena took time to catch her breath. Justin watched her again with that strange ability he had for absolute stillness and absolute silence. There would be no reading his eyes. In a habitual defense Serena turned her fear into anger.

"If you read your brochure, you'll see that your passage fee doesn't include your pick of the crew."

"Certain things have no price, Serena."

Something in his tone made her tremble. It was as if he'd already put his mark on her, a mark she wouldn't easily erase. She backed into the shadows. "Stay away from me," she warned him.

Justin leaned back on the rail, keeping his gaze on her silhouette. "No," he said mildly. "I've already dealt the cards, and the odds always favor the house."

"Well, I'm not interested," she hissed. "So deal me out." Turning, she clattered down the stairs that led to the next deck.

Slipping his hands into his pockets, Justin jingled change and smiled. "Not a chance."

Chapter Two

Serena slipped into a pair of khaki shorts, then crawled under her bunk to find her sandals. According to her calculations, most of the passengers who would disembark for the day on Nassau would have already done so. There was little chance of being caught in the crush or of having to weave her way through the waiting cab drivers and tour guides on the docks. Since it would be her last trip there, Serena wanted to play tourist herself and pick up a few souvenirs to take home to her family. Cursing the sandal which had somehow tucked itself into a far corner, she squiggled farther under the bunk.

"You'd think I'd learn to be neat after living in a closet for a year," she muttered, wiggling back out again.

She lay full length, she could touch each side wall of the cabin. In the other direction she had about two feet to spare. Beside the bunk there was a tiny mirrored dresser bolted to the floor and a cubbyhole that passed for closet space. She'd often thought it was a lucky thing she didn't suffer from claustrophobia.

Still on the floor, she pushed the sandals on her feet, then began to check the contents of the tote bag she would carry. A wallet and sunglasses. Well, she couldn't think of anything else that was necessary, Serena reflected as she jumped lightly to her feet. Briefly she considered asking one of the other dealers if they wanted to join her, then rejected the idea. She wasn't in the best of moods, and it wouldn't take anyone who'd worked closely with her long to notice it, and perhaps ferret out the reason.

The last thing Serena wanted to discuss was Justin Blade. In fact, she added smartly as she pulled a khaki tennis cap over her hair, the last thing she wanted to even *think* about was Justin Blade with his cool green eyes, long, unsmiling mouth, and ruthless good looks.

When Serena realized she *was* thinking about him, she left her cabin in an even poorer mood. Only nine more days, she reminded herself as she ignored the elevator and marched up the steps. She could put up with anything for nine days.

With a smirk Serena remembered the salesman from Detroit who had haunted her table throughout a cruise the previous spring. He'd gone so far as to follow her down to the crew's quarters and try to talk his way into her cabin. She'd dispatched him by claiming her lover was the chief engineer, a swarthy Italian with biceps like cinder blocks. Serena's smirk faded. Somehow she didn't think that tactic would work with a man like Justin Blade.

As she climbed upward, the threadbare carpet of the crew's decks was replaced by the bold red and gold pattern that graced the rest of the ship. Ornate light fixtures lit the landings rather than the plain glass shields of belowdecks. Coming out on the main level, she exchanged a quick word of greeting with other members of the crew still on board.

Two men lounged on either side of the gangway— one in the crisp white uniform of the first mate, the other in casual cruise wear. As usual, they were arguing intensely but without heat. Serena caught the eye of the cruise director first, a small Englishman with sandy hair and boundless energy. She winked at him, then planted herself in between the two men.

"What diplomat put the two of you on gangway duty together?" she asked with a mock sigh. "I suppose I'll have to play referee again. What is it this time?"

"Rob claims that Mrs. Dewalter is a rich widow," Jack, the Englishman, began in his rounded tones. "I say she's divorced."

"A widow," the first mate started again, folding his arms. "A beautiful rich widow."

"Mrs. Dewalter," Serena mused.

"Tall," Jack began. "Short, sculptured red hair."

"Built," Rob added.

"Philistine," Jack put in mildly, then addressed himself to Serena. "A rather gamine face."

"Okay," Serena said slowly, getting the picture of a woman she'd seen briefly in the casino the night before. "Widowed or divorced?" she inquired, well used to the picky arguments between the two men. "What about rings?"

"Exactly." Rob pounced on the question with a smirk for his associate. "She wore rings. Widows wear rings."

"So do bubble-brained first mates," Jack pointed out with a glance at the signet ring on Rob's hand.

"The point is," Serena interrupted before Rob could retort. "What sort of rings? A gold band? A jeweled circle?"

"A chunk of ice as big as a hen's egg," Rob told her, giving Jack another satisfied sneer. "Rich widow."

"Divorced," Serena disagreed, bursting his bubble. "Sorry, if we go with the percentages, Rob, that's the most likely answer. Hen's eggs are rarely worn for sentimental value." After patting his cheek in consolation, she gave him a snappy salute. "Permission to go ashore, sir!"

"Get out of here." He gave her a quick nudge. "Go buy a straw mat."

"My plans exactly." With a laugh, she jogged down the narrow iron steps to the dock.

The sun was brilliant, the air moist and balmy. Serena bargained with a few boys who loitered on the docks hawking shell necklaces and decided it wouldn't be such a bad day after all. She had hours before her to do as she chose in one of the prettiest tourist spots in the Bahamas.

"Three dollars," the lean-limbed black boy told her, holding out handfuls of dark-shelled necklaces. He wore only a pair of shorts and a medallion that was slowly oxidizing. His partner held a small portable radio to his ear, moving lithely to the scratchy reggae beat.

"You pirate," Serena said good-naturedly. "One dollar."

The boy grinned, sensing a true haggler. "Oh, pretty lady," he began in his high, sing-song voice. "If I could, I would give you the necklace for only your smile, but then my father would beat me."

Serena lifted a brow. "Yes, I can see how abused you are. One dollar and a quarter."

"Two-fifty. I gathered the shells myself and strung them by the light of a candle."

With a laugh Serena shook her head. "The next thing you'll tell me is you fought off a school of sharks."

"No sharks near our island, my lady," he said proudly. "Two American dollars."

"One and a half American dollars because I admire your imagination." Digging into her tote, she drew out her wallet. The money was out of her hands and into the pocket of his shorts in the blink of an eye.

"For you, pretty lady, I will risk a beating."

Serena chose her necklace, then found herself giving him another quarter. "Pirate," she murmured as he grinned at her. Slinging her tote over her shoulder, she started to walk away.

It was then that she saw him, standing alone on the dock behind her. Serena wasn't as surprised as she thought she should've been. But then somehow she'd known she'd see him. He wore a plain beige T-shirt that made his skin seem nearly copper, and a faded pair of cutoffs that accentuated his lean, muscular thighs and rangy build. Though the sun was glaring fiercely, he wore no tinted glasses or other protection. He didn't seem to need it. Just as she was debating whether she should simply walk by him, he came toward her. He moved lightly, with the grace of a hunter—a man, she thought for no specific reason, who was more accustomed to sand or grass than asphalt.

"Good morning." Justin took her hand as though the meeting had been arranged.

"Good morning," she returned frostily, refusing to

give him any satisfaction by tugging on her hand. "Didn't you sign up for any of the tours?"

"No. I don't care to be directed." He began to walk toward town with Serena in tow.

Biting back words of fury, she spoke in a calculatedly pleasant voice. "Several of the tours are very worthwhile. They're really the best way to see the island in the limited amount of time we're in port."

"You've been here before," he said easily. "Why don't you show me?"

"I'm off duty," Serena stated crisply. "And I'm going shopping."

"Fine. Since you've already begun," he said, glancing down at the necklace she still held in her hand, "where do you want to go next?"

She decided to give up diplomacy altogether. "Will you please go away? I plan to enjoy myself today."

"So do I."

"Alone," she said pointedly.

Stopping, he turned to her. "Ever hear about Americans sticking together on foreign soil?" he asked as he took the necklace from her fingers and slipped it over her head.

"No," she returned, wishing she didn't want so badly to smile.

"I'll explain it to you while we take a carriage ride."

"I'm going shopping," she reminded him as he led her toward town.

"You'll have a better idea where to buy what after a ride."

"Justin." Serena matched his stride because it was better than being hauled. "Do you ever take no for an answer?"

He appeared to think this over before he shook his head. "Not that I remember."

"I didn't think so," she muttered, then stood eyeing him stonily.

"All right, let's try it this way. Heads we go for a ride, tails you go shopping." Reaching into his pocket, he drew out a coin.

"Probably has two heads." Serena frowned suspiciously at the quarter.

"I never cheat," Justin said solemnly as he held the coin between his forefinger and thumb for her inspection.

She could refuse and simply walk away, Serena considered, but she found herself nodding. The odds were even. With a practiced flick of the wrist, Justin sent the coin spinning in the air, nabbed it, then flipped it over on the back of his hand. Heads. Somehow she'd known it would be.

"Never bet against the house," Serena mumbled as she climbed into a carriage.

As the horse began its meandering clip-clop down the street, Serena thought about maintaining a dignified silence—for about thirty seconds. Knowing herself well, she was forced to admit that if she hadn't wanted to get into the carriage, she wouldn't have gotten into it. Not without a fuss. So instead of a dignified silence, Serena dropped her tote bag on the floor of the carriage, ignoring the charm of the narrow little street, and stared at her companion.

"What are you doing here?"

He tossed an arm over the seat, his fingers skimming over her hair. "Enjoying the ride."

"No smart answers, Justin. You wanted my company

and you've got it unless I decide to scream assault and jump out of the carriage."

He eyed her for a moment, first in curiosity, then in admiration. She'd do just that. He dropped his fingers to the nape of her neck. "What do you want to know?"

"What are you doing on the *Celebration?*" Serena demanded, shifting away from the pleasure his fingers brought her. "You don't strike me as the type of man who'd go on a relaxing tropical cruise."

"A friend recommended it. I was restless, he was persuasive." His fingers brushed her neck again. "What are you doing on the *Celebration?*"

"Dealing blackjack."

His brow rose at her answer. "Why?"

"I was restless." In spite of herself, Serena smiled.

The driver started his monologue on the highlights of the island, but noted that the couple wasn't interested in anything but each other. He clicked his tongue at the horse, then remained silent.

"All right, where are you from?" Serena asked, looking for a starting point. "I have a habit of placing people in regions, and I can't place you."

Justin smiled enigmatically. "I travel."

"Originally," she persisted, narrowing her eyes at the evasion.

"Nevada."

"Vegas." Serena nodded. "You've spent some time there. I imagine it's a good town for people with the right skills." When he only shrugged, Serena studied his profile. "And that's how you make your living? Gambling?"

Justin turned his head until his eyes met hers. "Yes. Why?"

"There were only two gamblers at that table last night," Serena mused. "You and the man from Georgia, though he was a milder sort."

"And the others?" Justin asked, curiosity piqued.

"Oh, the Texan just likes the game; he doesn't put that much thought into it. The blonde from New York thinks she's a gambler." Because the gentle swaying of the carriage was soothing, Serena smiled a little and relaxed. "But she can't keep up with the cards or the odds. She'll end up dropping a bundle or winning on sheer luck. The other man from New York watches the cards but doesn't know how to bet. You have the concentration that separates a gambler from a player."

"A very interesting theory," Justin reflected. With a fingertip he slid Serena's sunglasses down the bridge of her nose so he could see her eyes without interference. "Do you play, Serena?"

"Depends on the game and the odds," she told him, pushing the glasses back up. "I don't like to lose." From the look in his eyes she realized they hadn't been speaking of cards, but a more dangerous game.

Smiling, he leaned back again, gesturing toward the right with his hand. "They have beautiful beaches here."

"Hmm."

As if on cue, the driver began his spiel again, giving a running commentary on the island until he brought them back to their starting point.

The streets were filled with people now, the majority of them tourists with bulging shopping bags and cameras. Both sides of the road were lined with little shops, some with their doors open, all with their windows crowded with displays. "Well, thanks for the ride."

Serena started to climb down, but Justin circled her waist with his hands and lifted her lightly.

He held her an inch above the ground for a moment while she gripped his shoulders for balance. Her lightness surprised him, making him realize that her sexuality and style had blinded him to how small she was. His fingers became abruptly gentle as he set her on the ground.

"Thanks," Serena managed after she'd cleared her throat. "Enjoy your day."

"I intend to," he told her as he took her hand again.

"Justin…" Serena took a deep breath. The time had come, she decided, to take a firm stand. That brief instant when he had held her had reminded her how foolish she had been to relax even for a moment. "I took your carriage ride, now I'm going shopping."

"Fine. I'll go with you."

"I'm looking for souvenirs, Justin," she said discouragingly. "You know, T-shirts, straw boxes. You'll be bored."

"I'm never bored."

"You will be this time," she told him as he began to meander down the street, his fingers laced with hers. "I promise."

"How about an ashtray that says Welcome to Nassau?" Justin suggested blandly.

Valiantly she swallowed a chuckled. "I'm going in here," Serena stated, stopping on impulse at the first shop they came to. And, she determined, she would stop at every shop on Bay Street until she successfully drove him crazy.

By the time her tote bag contained musical key chains, assorted T-shirts, and shell boxes, Serena had forgotten she had wanted to be rid of him. He made her laugh—the gentlest seduction. For a man she had instinctively termed a loner, Justin was easy company. Before long Serena had not only stopped being resentful, she'd stopped being wary.

"Oh, look!" She grabbed a coconut shell that had been fashioned into a grinning head.

"Elegant," Justin stated, turning it over in his hands.

"It's ridiculous, you fool." Laughing, Serena fished out her wallet. "And perfect for my brother. Caine's ridiculous too...Well, not all the time," she added scrupulously.

The aisles of the straw market were crammed with people and merchandise, but not so crowded that Serena couldn't worm her way through in search of treasures. Spotting a large woven bag overhead, she pointed. Justin obligingly lifted it down to her.

"It's nearly as big as you are," he decided as she took it from him.

"It's not for me," Serena murmured, studying it minutely. "My mother does a lot of needlework; this should be handy for carting it around with her."

"Handmade." Serena glanced down at the large dark-skinned woman in a rocking chair, smoking a little brown pipe. "Myself," she added, patting her generous bosom. "Nothing made in Hong Kong at my stall."

"You do beautiful work," Serena told her, though the woman already interested her more than the bag.

Lifting a large palm fan, the islander nodded majestically and began to stir the sultry air. Serena was fascinated to see a ring on every thick finger. "You buy something pretty for your lady today?" she asked Justin with a flash of white teeth.

"No, not yet," Justin said before Serena could speak. "What do you suggest?"

"Justin—"

"Here." The old woman cut Serena off, turning to push back some cloth at her right. With a few wheezes and grunts she pulled out a cream-colored dashiki-style tunic with a border of bold rainbow stitches. "Special," the woman told Justin, pushing it into his hands. "Lots of purple here, like your lady's eyes."

"Blue," Serena began, "and I'm not—"

"Let's see." Justin held it up in front of her, surveying the effect through narrowed eyes. "Yes, it suits you," he decided.

"You wear it for your man tonight," the woman advised, already folding it into a bag. "Very sexy."

"An excellent idea," Justin agreed as he started to count out bills.

"Wait a minute," Serena pointed at him with the hand that still held the straw bag. "He is not my man."

"Not your man?" The woman went into peals of laughter, rocking back and forth in the chair until it screeched in protest. "Honey, this is your man for sure, you can't trick a seventh daughter of a seventh daughter. No indeed. You want the bag too?"

"Well, I…" Serena stared down at the straw bag as if she hadn't a clue how it had gotten into her hand.

"The bag too." Justin peeled off more bills. "Thank you."

The money disappeared into her huge hand as she continued to rock. "You enjoy our island."

"Now, wait—"

But Justin was already pulling her along. "You can't

argue with a seventh daughter of a seventh daughter, Serena. You never know what curse she'll toss at you.''

"Nonsense," she stated, but glanced cautiously over her shoulder to where the big woman sat rocking. "And you can't buy me clothes, Justin. I don't even know you."

"I already did."

"Well, you shouldn't have. And you paid for my mother's bag."

"My compliments to your mother."

She sighed, squinting as they emerged into daylight. "You're a very difficult man."

"There, you see? You do know me." Taking her sunglasses from the top of her hat, he slid them back in front of her eyes. "Hungry?"

"Yes." The corners of her mouth twitched, so Serena gave up and smiled. "Yes, I am."

With his eyes on hers he slowly circled her palm with a fingertip. "How about a picnic on the beach?"

It wasn't a simple matter to ignore the tingling that was now racing up her arm, but she managed a casual shrug. "If you had food, and if you had transportation, and if you had some cold island concoction to drink, I might be interested."

"Anything else?" Justin asked as he stopped to lean on the hood of a Mercedes.

"Not that I can think of."

"Okay, let's go then." Pulling keys out of his pocket, Justin walked around to unlock the passenger door of the car.

With her tote bag dangling from her fingers, Serena stared. "Do you mean this is your car?"

"No, this is the car I rented. There's a cooler in the trunk. Do you like cold chicken?"

When he tossed the bags into the backseat, Serena put her hands on her hips. "You were awfully damn sure of yourself, weren't you?"

"Just playing the odds," he claimed, then cupped her chin in his hands and brushed her lips with his. "Just playing the odds."

Serena dropped into the passenger seat not certain if she admired or detested his sheer nerve. "I'd like to know what cards he has up his sleeve," she muttered as he rounded the hood to join her.

She noticed Justin drove as he did everything else, with the arrogant ease of control. He seemed acclimated to driving on the left side of the road as if he did so daily.

They passed under the fat leaves of almond trees, beside thick green grapes which would be purple in another month. Branches laden with the bright orange blossoms typical of the island danced in the breeze as they drew nearer to the sea. He didn't speak, and again she noticed he had that oddly admirable capacity for silence. Yet it wasn't soothing, but exciting.

It occurred to her as they drove by the graceful colonial homes of the wealthy toward the public beaches that true relaxation was something not often experienced around a man like Justin Blade. Then the thought came quickly—too quickly—that relaxation was something she rarely looked for.

Turning in her seat, Serena exchanged the tropical beauty of Nassau for Justin's handsome, almost hawkish features. A gambler, she mused. A shipboard acquaintance. Serena had too much experience with the two to trust in any deep, lasting relationship. Still, she thought that if she were careful, she might enjoy his companionship for a few days.

What harm could there be in getting to know him a bit better? In spending some of her free time with him? She wasn't like some of her coworkers in the casino who fell in and out of love with each other or lost their hearts to a passenger only to be miserable and desolated at the end of a cruise. When a woman had managed to keep her heart in one piece for twenty-six years, she wasn't about to lose it in ten days...was she?

Justin turned to give her one of his cool, unsmiling looks. Butterflies fluttered in her throat. She'd be very careful, Serena decided, as if she were walking through a minefield.

"What are you thinking?"

"About bombs," she answered blandly. "Deadly, camouflaged bombs." She gave him a quick, innocent grin. "Are we going to eat soon? I'm starving."

With a last brief look, Justin pulled off to the side of the road. "How's this?"

Serena gazed out over the white sand to the intense blue of the ocean. "Perfect." Stepping from the car, she took a deep breath of blossoms and sea and hot sand. "I don't do this often. When the ship's in port I usually catch up on my sleep or my reading, or give another shot at getting a tan on deck. I've lost count of the number of times I've been docked at this island."

"Didn't you take the job on the ship to travel?" He took a small cooler and a folded blanket from the trunk.

"No, it was the people really. I wanted to find out just how many kinds of people there were in the world." Serena slipped off her sandals to feel the warm

sand on her feet. "We have more than five hundred in
the crew, and only ten Americans. You'd be amazed at
the variety of people you meet. It's like a floating
U.N." Taking the blanket from under his arm, Serena
snapped it open, then let it billow onto the sand. "I've
dealt cards to people from every continent." She seated
herself Indian fashion on the edge of the blanket. "I'll
miss that."

"Miss it?" Justin dropped down beside her. "Are
you quitting?"

Tossing her hat aside, Serena shook back her hair.
"It's time. I want to catch up with my family for a
while before I do anything else."

"Anything else in mind?"

"I've been thinking about a hotel-casino." She
pursed her lips in thought. It was a project she intended
to discuss with her father soon. He'd know the best
way to go about financing property and a building.

"You've had the experience," Justin mused, believ-
ing she was considering applying for a job as a dealer.
"The only difference would be you'd be on dry land."
An idea germinated in his mind, but he decided to wait
before approaching her with it. "Where's your family?"

"Hmm? Oh, Massachusetts." Her gaze fell on the
cooler. "Feed me." When he opened the lid she noticed the napkins and cutlery came from the ship.
"How'd you manage that?" Serena demanded. "The
kitchen has a policy against making up picnic
lunches."

"I bribed them," he said simply, and handed her a
drumstick.

"Oh." She took a healthy bite. "Good thinking. What'd you get to drink?"

For an answer, Justin drew out a thermos and two plastic glasses with the ship's logo. "How's the chicken?"

"Terrific. Eat." She accepted the cup of dark pink liquid he handed her and sipped cautiously. It was richly fruity, smoothed with island rum. "Oh-oh, the *Celebration*'s speciality." She gave the drink a dubious look. "I usually make it a policy not to get within a yard of one of these."

"You're on shore leave," Justin reminded her, plucking a piece of chicken from the cooler.

"And I want to live to tell about it," she murmured. For the moment she concentrated on the chicken and the pleasure of having no more to do than enjoy the breeze off the ocean.

"I would've thought the beaches would be more crowded," Justin commented.

"Mmm." Serena nodded as she drank again. "Most of the tourists who aren't shopping are on guided tours or scubaing on the other side of the island. It's off season too." She gestured with the drumstick before she dropped it onto a napkin. "The beaches aren't so quiet during the rush. But there's really a lot to see and do in Nassau besides swimming and sunbathing."

"Mmm." He watched her brush some sand from her thigh. "So our carriage driver said."

"I'm surprised you didn't ferry over to Paradise Island to the casinos for the day."

"Are you?" Leaning over, he took her hair in his hand. "It isn't the only game in town."

Justin touched his lips to hers, intending to give her

a light, teasing kiss. But the intention evaporated at the warm, ripe taste. "How could I have forgotten how badly I want you?" he murmured, then drowned her muffled response with hard, unyielding pressure.

His tongue eased between lips he parted expertly as he pressed her back against the blanket. Feeling the muscled ridges of his body against hers, Serena started to object, but her arms were already around him, pulling him closer, her mouth was already searching, moving avidly under his.

The sun filtered through the leaves of the palm they lay under, flickering light over her closed lids until it was only a red mist dancing in front of her eyes. He kissed her as she'd never been kissed before, with lips and teeth and tongue, nibbling then devouring, seducing, then possessing. Mouth clung to mouth in a taste more potent than the rum they'd sampled.

A gull soared toward the sea with a long, wailing cry neither of them heard, then with a flick of a wing he was gone as if he'd never been. When Justin ran his hands down her arms, Serena felt his touch over every inch of her body. Her breasts ached from it; her thighs trembled. Longing for the imaginary to be real, she moaned and moved under him in invitation.

Ripping his mouth from hers, Justin pressed it against her throat as he struggled to cling to the fine edge of reason. He wanted her, wanted to feel her soft skin grow hot and moist under his hands. He wanted to touch every subtle curve and dip, feel every pulse hum and taste and taste until they were both raging.

Desire clawed at him with a sharpness he'd never experienced before as her hands moved over his back, pressing and kneading while he fought to remember they were not alone in a dark, quiet room. Had a woman ever taken him so far with only a kiss? He could only think of how much further she would take him when he was free to have all of her.

Nibbling and sucking, he ran his mouth up to her ear. "Come back with me now, Serena." He licked the lobe before he caught it between his teeth. "Come back to my cabin with me. I want you."

His words seemed to float into her consciousness, almost drifting away before their meaning penetrated her passion. "No." Hearing her own weak protest, Serena fought to strengthen it. "No," she repeated, struggling away from him. Sitting up, she hugged her knees until her breathing leveled. "No," she said for a third time. "You have no right to—to—"

"To what?" Justin demanded, grabbing her face in his hands and jerking it back to him. "To want you or to show you that you want me?"

His eyes weren't cool now, but light and angry. Serena remembered her own first impression of ruthlessness and forced back a shudder before she pushed his hands away. "Don't tell me what I want," she tossed back. "If you're interested in a little shipboard fling, go find somebody else. You shouldn't have any trouble." Springing up, she strode furiously toward the sea. Justin caught her arm and spun her around.

"And don't tell me what I'm interested in," he ordered curtly. "You didn't even know where we were. I could have taken you on a public beach in broad daylight."

"Really?" She threw her head back, infuriated that he spoke no less than the truth. "Well, if you're so sure of that, why didn't you?"

"Normally, I like my privacy, but keep pushing and I'll make an exception."

"And pigs fly," she said evenly as she turned toward the surf a second time. She'd no more than gotten her toes wet when he grabbed her again. For a moment Serena thought she had miscalculated. The rage in his eyes was nothing to tamper with, but she'd never had much luck controlling her temper once it had gotten beyond a certain point. When Justin dragged her against him, she cursed him.

He wanted to crush that hot, furious mouth again. Desire was raging through him as quickly as his temper, and one fed the other. Knowing what the outcome would be if he gave in to the first, Justin gave in to the second. Serena landed on her bottom in the shallows.

Shock covered her face first, then utter fury. "You— you *animal!*" Scrambling up, she launched herself at him, intent only on revenge. But when he grabbed her arms to ward her off, he was grinning.

"Would you believe you look beautiful when you're angry?"

The dip in the water hadn't cooled her temper. "You're going to pay for that one, Justin Blade." With her arms hampered she compensated with a kick but only ended up back in the water, tangled with him. "Get your hands off me, you jerk!" She shoved, submerged, and came up sputtering. "Nobody pushes a MacGregor around and gets away with it!"

In his attempt to prevent her from drowning both of them, his hand connected with her breast. The next moment he found that his mouth had covered hers again while his hand caressed through her wet, clinging shirt. Though he felt her moan of response, she continued to struggle, taking them both under again. He tasted salt, and her lips; he felt the slender thighs pressed against his as he rolled her over with the next wave. With a muffled laugh he heard her swear at him again as she gulped in air. Then the water tossed their bodies together. The surf sprayed and ebbed, shifting the sand and shells beneath them. They lay, half covered with water, breathing hard.

"MacGregor?" he repeated suddenly, shaking his head to clear it. Drops of water from his hair splattered on her face. "Serena MacGregor?"

She pushed her own dripping hair out of her eyes and tried to think. Her body was throbbing with the potent combination of anger and desire. "Yes. And the moment I remember some of those wonderful Scottish curses, I'm going to dump them all on you."

For the first time she saw pure surprise on his face. It had the effect of draining her anger and replacing it with bewilderment. Then his eyes narrowed on an intense study of her features. Still panting, Serena stared back, only to become more confused when the smile spread slowly over his face. Dropping his forehead on hers, Justin chuckled, then roared with laughter.

The sound was appealing, but as she started to respond to it, Serena concentrated on the uncomfortable lump of sand and shell digging into her back. "What's so funny?" she demanded. "I'm soaking wet and full of gritty sand. I've little doubt that my skin's been slashed by shells and I never even finished my lunch!"

Still laughing, he lifted his head, then gave her a brotherly kiss on the nose. "Ask me again sometime. Come on, let's rinse off and eat."

Chapter Three

Serena MacGregor. Justin shook his head as he reached into the narrow closet for a shirt. It was, he decided, the first time he'd been completely confounded in years. When a man made his living by his wits, he couldn't afford to be taken by surprise often.

Strange that he hadn't noticed the family resemblance, but then, she had little in common physically with her large, broad-featured, red-haired father. She was more a modern version of the little painted miniature Daniel kept in his library. How many times had he been to that fortress in Hyannis Port over the years? Justin wondered. Rena, as the family called her, had always been away at school. For some reason he had developed a picture of a scrawny, bespectacled scholar with Daniel's flaming hair and Anna's eccentric dignity. Yes, Serena MacGregor was quite a surprise.

Odd, he thought, that she would take a job that would do little more than pay her room and board when she was reputed to have an I.Q. that rivaled her father's weight and enough capital to buy an ocean liner for her personal pleasure yacht. Then again, the MacGregors were a strange, stubborn lot, prone to the unexpected.

For a moment Justin stood, naked from the waist, his shirt hanging forgotten from his fingertips. His torso was dark and lean, the skin stretched taut over his rib cage, where on the left it was marred by a six-inch scar. He was remembering.

The first time he had met Daniel MacGregor, Justin had been twenty-five. A run of luck had given him enough money to buy out his partner in their small hotel on the Strip in Las Vegas. Justin wanted to expand and remodel. For that he needed financing. Banks were usually dubious about lending large sums of money to men who made their living with a deck of cards. In any case, Justin didn't care for bankers, with their smooth hands and dry voices. And the Indian in him had little faith in a promise made on paper. Then he heard of Daniel MacGregor.

In his own fashion, Justin checked out the stock wizard and financier. He gained a picture of a tough, eccentric Scotsman who made his own rules, and won. Justin contacted him, diddled around by phone and letter for over a month, then made his first trip to the fortress at Hyannis Port.

Daniel worked out of his home. He didn't care for office buildings where one had to depend on elevators and secretaries. He'd purchased his plot of land near the sea with the wealth he had earned first with his back, and then with his mind. Daniel had realized early that he could earn more, very satisfactorily, with his mind. Then he had built his home and his empire—to his own liking.

It was a huge barn of a house, with massive corridors and enormous rooms. Daniel didn't like to be crowded. Justin's first impression of him as he was led into the tower room that served as his office was of bulk…and wit.

"So you're Blade." Daniel drummed his fingers on the surface of a desk that had been carved from a giant California redwood.

"Yes. And you're MacGregor."

A grin creased the broad face. "That I am. Sit down, boy." Daniel noticed no change of expression at his use of the term, and folded his hands over his chest as Justin sat. He liked the way Justin moved; he'd judged men on less. "So, you want a loan."

"I'm offering an investment, Mr. MacGregor," Justin corrected him coolly. The chair was designed to swallow a man. Justin sat in it with an ease that only accentuated the readiness to spring. "With my property as collateral, of course."

"Umm-hmm." Daniel steepled his hands as he continued to study the man across from him. Not a simple man, he concluded, observing the aristocratic features. Cool, controlled, and potentially violent. Comanche blood—warrior's blood—but not a brawler. Daniel came from good warrior stock himself. "Umm-hmm," he said again. "What are you worth, boy?"

An angry retort sprang to Justin's mind and was left to smolder. Reaching down, he brought up a briefcase. "I have the financial papers, the appraisals, and so forth."

Daniel gave a gusty laugh and waved them away. "You think you'd have gotten this far if I didn't know all the figures you have in there? What about you?'' he demanded. "Why should I lend my money to you?''

Justin set the briefcase back on the floor. "I pay my debts.''

"Wouldn't last long in the business if you didn't.''

"And I'll make you a great deal of money.''

Daniel laughed again until his blue eyes watered. "I've got money, boy.''

"Only a fool doesn't want more," Justin said quietly, and Daniel stopped laughing.

Leaning back in his chair, he nodded. "You're damn right.'' Then he grinned, slapping his wide palm on the desk. "You're damn right. How much to fix up that little hole in the wall of yours?''

"Three hundred and fifty thousand,'' Justin answered without blinking.

Daniel reached into his desk and drew out a bottle of Scotch and a deck of cards. "Stud poker.''

They played for an hour, speaking only to bet. Justin heard the reverberating gong of a grandfather's clock from somewhere deep in the house. Once someone knocked on the door. Daniel bellowed at them, and they weren't disturbed again. The scent of Justin's cigar mixed with the aroma of whiskey and the ripe fragrance of the overblown roses on the windowsill. After dropping fifteen hundred dollars, Daniel leaned back in his chair again.

"You'll need stockholders.''

"I've just gotten rid of a partner.'' Justin crushed out the butt of his cigar. "I don't want another.''

"Stockholders, boy.'' Daniel pushed the cards aside. "You want to make money, you've got to spread it around first. A man who plays like you do already knows that." With his pale blue eyes on Justin's, he considered a moment. "I'll lend you the money and buy in for ten percent. You're smart, you keep sixty and spread the rest around." After swirling the Scotch, he drained his glass and grinned. "You're going to be rich."

"I know."

Daniel's gusty laugh shook the windowpane. "Stay for dinner," he said, heaving himself out of his chair.

Justin stayed for dinner, and became rich. He renamed his hotel Comanche, then made it into one of the finest hotel-casinos in Vegas. He bought a dying property in Tahoe and repeated his success. Within a decade he had five thriving gambling hotels and interests in a variety of enterprises throughout the country and Europe. In the ten years since their meeting in the tower room, Justin had been to the MacGregor home dozens of times, entertained Daniel and Anna in his own hotels, and fished with their sons. But he'd never met the daughter.

"Bright girl," Daniel would say of her from time to time. "But won't settle down. Needs a good man—you should meet her."

And Justin had steered clear of the not so subtle matchmaking attempts. Or so he'd thought.

"The old devil," he murmured, shrugging into the shirt.

It had been Daniel who had pushed him into the cruise. Get away from the pressure, he'd insisted. Nothing like good sea air and half-naked women to relax a man. Because he'd been restless, Justin had considered it, then had been trapped when Daniel had mailed him the tickets with a request for a case of duty-free Scotch.

So the old pirate was still wheeling and dealing, Justin thought, amused. Daniel would have known that Justin would spend time in the casino on board, and left the rest to chance. With a quick laugh Justin began doing up the buttons of his shirt. Chance, he reflected, with a stacked deck. What would the old man have to say if he knew his friend and business associate had been wrestling with his daughter that afternoon with the predominant notion of getting her into his bed? Exasperated, Justin ran a hand through his hair. Daniel MacGregor's daughter. Good God.

Justin grabbed his jacket from the closet, then closed it with a bang. It would serve the cagey devil right if he had seduced his daughter. It would serve him right if he avoided her for the rest of the trip and never uttered a word about meeting her in the first place. That would drive the Scotsman up the wall. Justin caught his own reflection in the mirror, a dark lean man in black and white.

"And if you think you can stay away from her, you're out of your mind," he muttered.

When he walked into the casino, Serena was standing near the small black and white monitor talking to the blond man Justin recognized as her supervisor. She laughed at something he said, then shook her head. Justin's eyes narrowed fractionally as Dale ran a finger down her cheek. He knew what it would feel like—soft and cool to the touch. Dale grinned, then straightened her bow tie as he spoke to her in undertones. Even recognizing the emotion as petty jealousy, Justin had trouble controlling it. In a matter of days Serena had made him feel desire, fury, and jealousy—emotions he normally kept in perfect balance. Cursing her father, he walked over to her.

"Serena." He caught the quick stiffening of her shoulders before she turned. "Not dealing tonight?"

"I've just come on from my break." She should have known the twenty-four hour respite wouldn't last. "I didn't see you in here last night, I thought perhaps you'd fallen overboard." Hearing Dale's sharp indrawn breath, Serena turned back to him. "Dale, this is Justin Blade. When I didn't fall for his charm at the beach in Nassau, he tossed me into the water."

"I see." Dale extended his hand. "I've never tried that one. Did it work?"

"Shut up, Dale," Serena said sweetly.

"You'll have to excuse her," Dale told Justin. "Sea life makes some of us surly. Are you enjoying your trip, Mr. Blade?"

"Yes." Justin glanced at Serena. "It's been quite an experience so far."

"You will pardon me," she said with exaggerated politeness. "I have to relieve Tony." Turning, she stalked over to table five. Because gritting her teeth hurt her jaw, Serena forced the muscles to relax. She gave the three players at the table a professional smile which iced over as Justin took a vacant stool. "Good evening. New deck." Breaking the seals, Serena shuffled the cards together, doing her best to ignore Justin's calm, steady stare. He stacked what she estimated to be two hundred dollars worth of chips in the slot in front of him, then lit a cigar. After giving the cards a final snap, she determined to see if she could clean him out.

"Cut?"

Justin took the thin sheet of plastic she offered. As

Serena slipped the cards into their clear holder, he pushed a twenty-five-dollar marker forward. She checked the table to see if all bets were placed, then began.

At one point Serena had him down to three chips and was feeling a grim satisfaction. Then she dealt him double sevens, which he split, counting twenty on one hand and twenty-one on the other. Steadily, he built the five chips to ten. When it came time to rotate her table, he infuriated her by moving with her. Serena renewed her vow to clean him out.

For the next twenty minutes she hardly noticed the other players. She could see only Justin's unfathomable green eyes or his hand as he stood pat or took a hit. Though she was determined to beat him, his chips gradually multiplied.

"I got blackjack!" The shout from the college student at the end of the table broke her concentration. Serena glanced over to see him grinning. "I won three dollars!" he told the casino at large, holding up the three light blue chips like a trophy. He was, Serena concluded, pleasantly drunk. "Now..." He slapped the three chips back on the table, then rubbed his palms together. "I'm ready to gamble."

Laughing, she reached for the cards again, but her eyes met Justin's. She saw humor, the first expression she'd seen in them for hours, and warmed to it. For a moment she wanted to reach across the table and touch him, run her fingers through the thick soft hair that surrounded his lean face. How could the simple light of laughter in his eyes make him seem so important?

"Hey!" The college student lifted his beer in a toast. "I'm on a streak."

"Yeah, of one," his girlfriend said dryly.

The interruption cleared Serena's head. Lifting her chin, she reached for the cards. One smile wasn't going to make her forget she was here to beat him. "Possible blackjack," she said as she flipped over an ace for herself. "Insurance?" The college student's girlfriend plunked down a chip. Justin didn't move. Turning up the tip of her hole card, Serena was satisfied with a three. It would give her plenty of room. "No blackjack." She glanced at Justin's cards, pleased to have dealt him a poor count. "Sixteen. Hit or stand?" He merely motioned with his forefinger for a card. Serena had to bit back an oath as she turned over a four. "Twenty." He passed a hand over the cards to indicate he was satisfied.

And so you should be, she thought resentfully, turning up a jack to break the next player. Just freak luck, she told herself, bumping the college student up to eighteen. "Four or fourteen," she announced as she turned over her card. With her eyes on Justin's, she pulled another. "Six or sixteen," she said as if to him alone. She bit back another oath as she drew the three of clubs. "Dealer stands on nineteen," she stated, knowing Dale would throw her overboard if she took another hit. "Pays twenty."

Raking in all the chips but Justin's, she then slid another twenty-five-dollar marker over the baize. She thought she caught another glimpse of laughter in his eyes as he dropped it into his slot, but this time it didn't warm her.

Smoke hung in the air, too thick to be completely banished by the cooling system. Serena didn't need to glance at her watch to know she'd been standing on her feet for nearly ten consecutive hours. Gradually, the clatter from the slots began to lessen, the first indication that the late shift was almost over. The couple at the end of the table, looking heavy-eyed, began discussing the stopover in Puerto Rico the next day. Between them they cashed in five dollars worth of chips before they left.

A quick glance around showed Serena that all but three of the tables were empty. There were only two players left at hers, Justin and a woman she identified as the Mrs. Dewalter who had captured Jack's and Rob's attention. The redhead was paying a great deal more attention to Justin than to her cards. Feeling spiteful, Serena decided the diamond on her hand was vulgar, and nearly grinned when she broke her at twenty-three.

"I guess this isn't my game," the redhead said with a sulky pout. She shifted toward Justin so that her considerable cleavage was in full view. "You seem to be tremendously lucky. Do you have a system?" Running a finger down his sleeve, she smiled. Serena wondered how she would like her nose pressed into the green baize.

Amused at the obvious tactic, Justin allowed his eyes to roam up from the deep plunge of her bodice to her face. "No."

"You must have some secret," she murmured. "I'd love to hear it...over a drink?"

"I never drink when I play." He blew a stream of smoke past her shoulder. "One interferes with the other."

"Bets?" Serena said just a tad too sharply.

"I believe I've had enough cards this evening." Letting her thighs brush Justin's, she rose, then dropped a hundred dollars worth of chips into her purse. Serena had the small satisfaction of knowing she'd started with four. "I'll be in the lounge," she told Justin with a last lingering smile before she turned away.

"Better luck next time," Serena said before she could stop herself. She turned back to find Justin grinning at her.

"Cash me in?"

"Certainly." Then he'll go chasing after that redhead with the size 38C personality, she thought furiously. Quickly, she stacked and counted his chips. Seven hundred and fifty dollars, she calculated, and only became more angry. "Dale's busy, I'll take care of this myself."

Watching her stride away, Justin tried to remember her father. It wasn't easy.

Serena came back with a stack of crisp bills and a white slip attached to a clipboard. Swiftly, she counted the money out, then passed it across the table. "You had a profitable evening." After slipping the paper into the compartment under the table, she reached for the cards. Justin took her wrist.

"Another hand?" he asked, enjoying the quick jump of her pulse beneath his fingers.

"You've already cashed in," she pointed out, and tried to tug away. He tightened his grip.

"A different bet, between you and me."

"I'm sorry, it's against the rules to have side games with the passengers. Now, if you'll excuse me, I have to close up the table."

"No money." He watched her eyes narrow in fury

and smiled. "A walk on the deck if I win," he said smoothly.

"Not interested."

"Not afraid to go one on one, are you, Serena?" The hand that attempted to remove his from her wrist paused. "You still have house advantage," he said quietly.

"If I win," she began, then carefully removed his hand, "you'll keep away from me for the rest of the cruise?"

He considered the question. It was, after all, a much wiser course than the one he was pursuing. Taking a last puff on his cigar, he crushed it out. It wouldn't be the first time he left his fate to the cards. "Deal."

He glanced at the two and five in front of him, then at the ten Serena had showing. Nodding for a hit, he drew a queen. His first thought was to stand, but another glance at Serena showed him she looked entirely too pleased with herself. He'd have bet every dollar in his pocket she had an eight or better in the hole. Keeping his eyes on hers, he gestured for another card.

"Damn!" She tossed down the four of diamonds and glared at him. "I swear, Justin, one day I'm going to beat you." Disgusted, she turned over the jack she had in the hole.

"No." He rose, slipping his hands into his pockets. "Because you're trying to beat me, not the cards. I'll wait for you outside."

Dale glanced over to see his best blackjack dealer sticking her tongue out at the back of a passenger.

Leaning back against the wall, Justin watched Serena through the glass doors of the casino. He thought he could almost see the combination of annoyance and frustration simmering around her. He felt much the same way himself. With a shrug he reminded himself that he had left it up to chance. The bet could have been as easily lost as won.

Idly, he fingered a twenty-five-dollar chip still in his pocket. Some might say he'd had an unusual run of luck. Then again, he mused, it might have been luckier to have lost that final bet. If he continued to see Serena, his life wasn't going to be uncomplicated.

He might have been able to ignore the feeling of having Daniel MacGregor looking over his shoulder if he could have convinced himself that taking her to bed would get her out of his system. But those were very long odds. She was the first woman Justin had ever known who had threatened to become a permanent part of his thoughts.

And what would she say, he wondered, if I told her her father had arranged the entire scenario from his fortress in Hyannis Port? A smile curved the corners of his mouth. She'd skin the old man and hang him up to dry, he concluded. Watching Serena walk toward the doors, Justin decided to save that little bombshell for another day.

"I suppose you have a right to smile," Serena said coolly as she let the door close behind her. "You're on quite a winning streak."

Justin took her hand, and in an unexpectedly courtly gesture kissed her fingers. "I intend for it to go on a lot longer before it's broken. You're really quite beautiful, Serena."

Disconcerted, she stared at him. "When I'm angry," she finished, struggling not to be charmed.

He turned her hand over and kissed her palm, watching her. "Really quite beautiful."

"Don't try to throw me off by being nice." Unconsciously, she laced her fingers with his. "There's nothing nice about you."

"No," he agreed. "Let's go out. I imagine you could use some fresh air."

"I agreed to take a walk." Together they began to climb the stairs. "That's all I agreed to."

"Umm-hmm. And the moon's nearly full. How'd you do tonight?"

"The casino?" When he opened the door the wind rushed in, delightfully warm and clean. "Better than usual. We've been operating at a loss since spring."

"Too many nickel slots—cuts your profit margin." He slipped an arm around her waist as Serena looked up at him. "You'd make more at the tables if some of your dealers were sharper."

"It's hard to stay sharp when you work up to sixty hours a week for peanuts," she said ruefully. "Anyway, the turnover's constant. Most of them have six weeks training tops, working up from cashier to croupier, and a large percentage of them don't stay more than a couple of runs because they find out it's not the floating vacation they thought it was." Without realizing, she hooked her arm around his waist as he matched his stride to hers. "This is my favorite part."

"What?"

"Late at night when the ship's quiet. You can't hear anything but the sea. If I had a porthole in my cabin, I'd leave it open all night."

"No porthole?" His hand began to move rhythmically up and down her back.

"Only passengers and officers have outside cabins." She arched against his hand, sighing as it soothed her tired muscles. "Still, I wouldn't trade this past year for anything. It's been like finding a second family."

"Your family's important to you?" he asked, thinking of Daniel.

"Of course." Because she found it an odd question, Serena tilted her head back to look at him. As he angled his to meet her eyes, her lips nearly skimmed his jaw. "Don't do that," she murmured.

"What?" And the word, soft and quiet, whispered over her parted lips.

"You know very well what." Dropping her arm, she moved away from him toward the rail. "My family," she said more steadily as she turned, resting her arms across the wood, "has always been the most important part of my life. The loyalty is sometimes uncomfortably fierce, but necessary to all of us. What about you?"

She looked totally and unconsciously intriguing, her soft curves hidden, yet enhanced by the mannish tux, her once tidy hairstyle being whipped apart by the wind. Her face was tilted back so that a splash of moonlight marbleized her skin.

"My family..." Struggling to pick up the thread of the conversation, he moved to stand in front of her. "I have a sister, Diana. She's ten years younger; we've never been close."

"Your parents?"

"They died when I was sixteen. Diana went to live with an aunt. I don't think I've seen her in practically twenty years."

Serena's automatic wave of sympathy was immediately quelled. "That's disgraceful!"

"My aunt's never approved of my profession," he said dryly. Though she never questions the money for Diana's support, he mused, moving his hands to the buttons of Serena's jacket. "It was easier for Diana if I didn't interfere."

"What right does your aunt have to approve or disapprove?" Serena demanded, too inflamed to notice how deftly he was unbuttoning her jacket. "She's your sister."

"My aunt's a firm believer that gambling is the devil's work. She's a Grandeau, from the French part of the family."

Serena shook her head at his logic. "So what are you?"

"Blade." His eyes locked on hers. "Comanche."

His face was very close, closer than she had realized. Though she felt the wind flutter through the thin fabric of her shirt, she didn't yet understand what he had done. Serena found herself swallowing as his eyes held hers. Had there been a threat in those two words, or had it been her imagination?

"I should have known," she managed. "I suppose I let your eyes throw me off."

"From the drops of French and Welsh blood that slipped through. My father was almost pure, and my mother descended from the line of a Comanche brave and a French settler." Slowly, his eyes never leaving hers, he pulled loose the tie at her throat. Serena swallowed again, but didn't move. "The story goes that one of my ancestors saw a woman with golden hair alone near a creek bed. She had a basket of laundry and was singing as she washed. He was a fierce warrior who had killed many of her people to protect his land. When he saw her, he wanted her." Justin released the buttons of her blouse, one by one. "So he took her."

"That's barbaric," she managed over a suddenly dry throat. "He kidnapped her, stole her away from her family—"

"A few days later she sunk a knife into his shoulder, trying to escape," Justin continued quietly. "But when she saw his blood on her hands, she didn't run. She stayed and nursed him and gave him green-eyed sons and daughters."

"Perhaps it took more courage to stay than to use the knife."

Justin smiled, noting the tremor in her voice and the steadiness of her eyes. "He gave her a name that translates to Prize of Gold and never took another woman. So it's a tradition, when one of my people sees a woman with golden hair who he wants—he takes."

His mouth crushed down on hers, whirling her quickly into passion. With his hands he dove into her hair, dislodging pins that danced in the wind before they fell into the waves below. Serena grabbed his shoulders, almost afraid she would follow them, plunging down into the dark, fast water. For surely this was how it felt to spiral down, helpless, from a high point toward the unknown. Her heart was racing even before his palm covered it, a contact of hard flesh against soft—man against woman.

On a moan she tightened her grip, as if he were a life line in the sea that had gone suddenly from calm to tumultuous. Forgetting her smallness, he took her into his hand, abandoning both gentleness and reason. No man had ever dared touch her that way; perhaps that was why she allowed it. He dared, without request, without practiced words of seduction. It was a force, consuming them both—an impulse too old and too basic to be denied.

Her body throbbed to be touched. While her thoughts tangled, it took over, showing them both what she needed. The wild, ruthless kisses that raced down her throat only made her crave more. The warm, smoothing breeze from the sea became like small flames to heighten her fever. She drew the moist air into her lungs and felt it turn to fire.

The hand at her breast kneaded, tormented, while the other slipped up her naked back to find some tiny point near her spine. A press of his finger turned her legs to jelly. She gasped as she arched against him while waves of unbelievable pleasure ran through her.

"No." Serena's voice sounded thin and far off. "No, don't."

But he pressed his lips to hers to devour her trembling protests. Her mouth was too hungry to heed the warning that had sounded in her brain. It clung to his, relishing the light flavor of salt spray. Whatever magic his fingers held, it dominated her now. She would give anything he asked, so long as he never stopped touching her. Digging her hands into his hair, she dragged him closer without noticing the fine mist of dampness that lay on it.

When her lips were free, with his buried at her throat, she could do no more than breathe his name. The moistness on her face went unfelt; all her senses were bound up in what his hands and lips could bring her. Then he was moving, and she swayed as he took her away from the rail. Weak with desire, Serena leaned against him while he stroked her hair.

"You're getting drenched," Justin murmured, but couldn't prevent his lips from brushing over the damp crown of her head, couldn't prevent himself from breathing in its fragrance. "Let's go in."

"What?" Dazed, Serena opened her eyes and saw the fine curtain of rain. "It's raining?" As the cool water revived her she shook her head. She felt she had been in a dream, to be wakened by a brisk slap in the face. "I—" Pushing away from him, she ran a hand through her hair. "I..."

"Have to get some sleep," he finished. He had come too close, Justin discovered, to taking her, like a maniac, where they had stood.

"Yes." Feeling raindrops on her bare flesh, Serena clutched her jacket together. "Yes, it's late." Her eyes were still clouded and confused as she glanced around the deck. "It's raining," she repeated.

There was something about her abrupt vulnerability that made Justin want her more than he had moments before, and made it impossible to take her. Sticking his hands into his pockets, he balled them briefly into fists. Damn Daniel MacGregor, he thought fiercely. The Scotsman set a fine trap with prime bait. If he took her now, it would almost certainly destroy his relationship with a man he'd come close to loving. If he didn't, he would only go on wanting her. If he waited...well, that was a gamble.

"Good night, Serena."

She stood irresolute a moment, wanting to race inside to sanity, wanting to fall into his arms and madness. Taking a deep breath, she clutched her jacket tighter. "Good night."

Serena went quickly, knowing it took only a moment to change a mind.

Chapter Four

Because she thought it would be deserted, Serena chose the Veranda deck aft. Anyone still on board would more likely opt for the larger pool area, with its proximity to the Lido Bar and Grill, for sunning. Most of the passengers would be seeing the sights in San Juan, walking the brick streets in the historical section, exploring forts, snapping pictures of the surrounding mountains. Anyone who dribbled back during the day wasn't likely to disturb her on the quiet rear deck.

She'd nearly overslept, forgetting she was slated to help Dale figure last night's take. Because it had been dawn before Serena had finally drifted off, she'd managed only four hours sleep before the alarm had shocked her awake. With her work finished for the morning, she'd come to lie in the midday sun and bake the tiredness from her body.

Serena didn't want to think, as she had during those long quiet hours between three A.M. and dawn. She knew she was too weary to dwell on what had happened the previous evening, but even as she stretched out on a deck chair, everything came back to play in her head. What was it that happened to her every time Justin's lips touched hers? Whatever it was, Serena had sworn she wouldn't let it happen again, then had been helpless to prevent it. What was it about him that kept pulling her along, dragging her closer to the edge of something fatal? Each time it became more difficult to remember to back away.

Serena released the halter strings to the top of her bikini and settled back. It might be smarter all in all, she decided, to give the whole business some serious thought rather than to dance around it. If there was one common thread running through the MacGregor clan, it was that they were realists. Face a problem head-on and mow it down. That, Serena thought with a quick grin, should have been their clan motto. So, for the problem of Justin Blade.

He was dangerously attractive. Dangerous, Serena concluded, because the attraction had hit her in the first instant and hadn't abated in the least. And it wasn't merely his looks, she mused, adjusting her sunglasses. Looks could easily be discounted. It was that strength and the sex, and the quietly domineering style. All three challenged her to match him, point for point. It was, very simply, an irresistible combination to a woman who rarely chose the easy path.

Did she like him? Serena gave an automatic snort, then became thoughtful. Well, she asked herself again, *did* she? The answer came with the memories of an easy afternoon in Nassau, that quick, shared joke in the casino, the natural way her hand fit with his. Perhaps she did like him, Serena admitted uncomfortably. A little. But, she pushed her sunglasses more firmly on her nose and shut her eyes, that wasn't the point. The point was, what was she going to do about him for the next five days?

She couldn't hide. Even if it had been physically possible while they were both on the same ship, Serena's pride would never have allowed it. No, she would have to deal with him...and with herself. The idea that she could spend some time with him, learn to know him a bit better, could no longer be classified as harmless. If she were honest, Serena would have to admit that she had known from the outset that there was nothing harmless about Justin Blade. That took her full circle, back to the basic attraction. And this, she decided as she rolled over onto her stomach, wasn't solving anything.

She had only a few more days aboard the *Celebration* before she headed home for an extended visit. Unemployed. Wrinkling her nose, she shifted until she was comfortable with the thick plastic strips of the lounge. With the rest of her life to decide upon, what to do about an encounter with an itinerant gambler should hardly take precedence in her thoughts. It was only, Serena concluded, because she was allowing it to. Now that she had admitted that she found Justin both attractive and interesting, that should be the end of it.

Her course was really quite simple—treat him as she would treat any other passenger. Polite and friendly. Well, she amended, dropping her sunglasses on the deck, not too friendly. And no more side bets, Serena added firmly before she shut her eyes. The man's luck was phenomenal.

And the sun was much too warm, the deck much too

quiet to think about complications. Sighing, she pillowed her head on her hands and slept.

Warm and soothing…These sensations drifted through her, causing Serena to sigh again. Hazy thoughts of floating naked on a raft while the sun stroked her skin brought a small sound of pleasure to her lips. She could have floated endlessly, without destination. She felt a freedom—no, an abandonment. She was alone in a blue sea, or perhaps in a dense green jungle. A secret, solitary place where there were no restrictions. There the sun caressed her body like lover's hands.

She could feel its stroking, bringing hot, sleepy pleasure…languid fingers of sunlight…lazily arousing…delicately seducing…

The brush of a butterfly against her ear made her smile. Serena lay still, not wanting to disturb it. Soft as dew, it fluttered to her cheek, resting a moment, as though it had found a pungent blossom. With a final sweep of wings it whispered her name at the corner of her mouth.

How strange, she thought with a tiny moan of pleasure, for a butterfly to know her name. Shifting her shoulders toward the gentle caress on her back, Serena commanded her eyes to open, wanting to see the colors of those soft wings. She saw only the cool depthless green of Justin's eyes.

For a moment Serena stared into them, too content to be confused. "I thought you were a butterfly," she murmured as she closed her eyes again.

"Did you?" Smiling, Justin touched his lips to the corner of hers a second time.

"Mmm-hmm." It came out as a long, lazy sigh. "How did you get here?"

"Where?" Enjoying her gentle stretching beneath his palm, he continued to stroke her back.

"Wherever we are," Serena murmured. "Did you float on a raft?"

"No." He knew from the rhythm of her breathing, by that brief look into her dark, misty eyes, that she was already aroused, disoriented enough to be completely pliant. Her absolute vulnerability touched off twin urges to take and to protect. As each one fought for supremacy, Justin brushed a kiss over her bare shoulder. "You've been dreaming."

"Oh." Serena didn't see why it mattered as long as those wonderful, warm caresses continued. "It feels good."

"Yes." Justin traced a fingertip down her spine. "It does."

The touch brought a quick shudder, a more concentrated arousal. Serena's eyes flew open. "Justin?"

"Yes?"

Abruptly awake and throbbing, Serena lifted herself up on her elbows. "What are you doing here?"

Briefly, his eyes passed over the small swatch of material that tenuously clung to her breasts. "You already asked me that. With your skin you shouldn't lie in the sun unprotected." He slid his hand down her back, spreading the cream he'd applied. When his fingers pressed near the base of her spine, she caught her breath.

"Stop it!" she demanded, furious that her voice was shaky.

"You're very sensitive," he murmured. The desire

in her eyes had flared quickly, darkening and widening even as she struggled against it. "It seems a pity we're never at the appropriate spot at the appropriate time."

"Justin." Serena shifted away from his hand, barely remembering to hold the top of her bikini in place. "I really wish you'd let me get some rest." As she sat up, she meticulously tied her halter strings behind her neck. "I had to get up early this morning, and the casino opens as soon as we leave port tonight." Stretching out again, she dismissed him. "I want a nap."

"I want to talk to you." He shifted lightly on the balls of his feet where he had crouched beside her, then rose.

"Well, I don't—" She broke off as her gaze traveled up long muscular legs to narrow hips encased in brief black trunks, to a hard, lean torso. It was a body that hinted at strength and sinew and speed. Quickly, Serena averted her gaze, reaching behind her to adjust the back of the deck chair. "I don't want to talk to you," she finished, popping her sunglasses back on her nose. "Why don't you go visit San Juan like everyone else?"

"I have a proposition."

"I bet you do."

Without waiting for an invitation, Justin nudged her legs over and sat on the end of the chair. "Business."

Serena slid her legs farther away so that her skin wouldn't rub against his and distract her. "I'm not interested in your business. Go get your own chair."

"Isn't there a rule about crew being rude to passengers?"

"Report me," she invited him. "It's my last week on the job."

"That's what I want to talk to you about." Justin ran a lotion-slick palm along her thigh.

"Justin—"

"Good." He smiled at her furious face. "I have your attention."

"You're going to have a fractured nose if you don't leave me alone," she told him, exasperated.

"Do you always have such a difficult time concentrating on a business discussion?" Justin asked mildly.

"Not a legitimate one."

"Then we shouldn't have any problem."

Flopping back on the chair, Serena eyed him from behind the tinted glasses. She spotted the jagged white scar along his ribs. "That looks as if it was nasty," she said with a cool smile. "A present from a jealous husband?"

"A bigot with a knife." His answer was as cool as her question, devoid of emotion.

A pain shot into her, sharp and unexpected. It caught with a gasp in her throat as she could almost see the blade slicing into flesh. "That was a stupid thing to say. I'm sorry." She glanced at the scar again, nearly sick from her own careless words. "It must've been serious."

Justin thought of the drugged two weeks in the hospital ward, then shrugged. "It was a long time ago."

"What happened?" She couldn't prevent herself from asking, perhaps because some intimate part of her shared the pain without knowing the cause.

Justin studied her for a moment. He didn't think about the incident anymore. Perhaps he hadn't given it more than a cursory thought in fifteen years. Still it was, like the scar, a part of him. It might be better if she knew. Taking a towel from the deck, he wiped his hands.

"I was in a bar in eastern Nevada. One of the regulars didn't care to breathe the same air as an Indian. I had a beer to finish, so I suggested he breathe somewhere else." A very cold, mirthless smile touched his mouth. "I was young enough to find some enjoyment in the prospect of a brawl. At eighteen a fistfight relieves a lot of frustrations."

"But you didn't get that scar from a fistfight," she murmured.

Justin lifted a brow in acknowledgement. "Most things tend to get out of hand when liquor's involved. He was drunk and feeling mean." Almost absently, he ran a finger down the line of the scar in a habitual gesture he thought he'd conquered years before. "It started predictably enough—words, shoves, fists—then he had a knife. He was probably too drunk to realize what he was doing, but he had it into me."

"Oh, God." Automatically, Serena reached out to take his hand. "That's horrible. Why didn't someone call the police?"

It flashed through his mind that despite the wealth, the extensive education, and traveling, she'd lived a sheltered life—perhaps because of it. "Things aren't always done that way," he said simply.

"But he *stabbed* you," she said with a mixture of logic and revulsion. "He must have been arrested."

"No." Justin's gaze remained as calm and steady as his voice. "I killed him."

At the flat statement, Serena's hand went limp in his. Justin could see her eyes grow wide and shocked behind the tinted glasses. He felt her instant, automatic withdrawal. Then just as quickly, her fingers tightened on his again. "Self-defence," she said with only a trace of a tremor in her voice.

He said nothing. All those years ago he had needed that kind of simple, unquestioning faith—during the pain of his hospital days, the cold, solitary fear in his cell awaiting trial. There'd been no one then to believe in him. No one to give him back any portion of the hope and trust he had lost during those endless, empty days. As she cupped his hand between both of hers, something moved inside him and crept out of a long-closed lock.

"I grabbed for the knife," Justin said at length. "We fell. The next thing I knew I was waking up in the hospital, charged with second-degree murder."

"But it was his knife." There was quick outrage in her voice and no question. "He attacked you."

"It took a while for that to come out." Justin could remember every hour, every minute of the waiting— the smell of the cell, the faces in the courtroom. The fear and fury. "When it did, I was acquitted."

With how many other scars? Serena wondered. "No one wanted to testify for you," she said instinctively. "The others in the bar that night."

"I wasn't one of them," he said flatly. "But they stuck to the truth when they were under oath."

"It must have been a frightening experience for a boy to go through." When Justin only lifted a brow, Serena tried to find a smile. "My father would say that a man's not a man until he's thirty, or maybe it's forty. He isn't always consistent."

How well he knew, Justin thought. He was tempted to tell her then and there about his relationship with

Daniel, but made himself stick with his original plan. Justin Blade was consistent. "I told you about this because if you accept my offer, you'd probably hear snatches of it anyway. And I'd rather you had it from me all at once." He saw that he had her curiosity now, which was better than her attention.

"What kind of offer?" she asked warily.

"A job."

"A job?" Serena repeated, then laughed. "What do you want to do, set up a floating blackjack game with me as dealer?"

"I had something a bit more stationary in mind," Justin murmured as his eyes drifted down. "Just how secure are those skinny little strings?"

"Secure enough." She barely resisted the urge to tug at them. "Why don't you tell me exactly what you have in mind, Justin…. Straight."

"All right." Abruptly, the humor left his eyes. They were cool again and level on hers. "I've watched you work. You're very good. Not just with the cards, but with people. You're a quick judge of the players, and your table is nearly always full, while some of the others thin out regularly. In addition to that, you know how to handle a player when he's annoyed with the cards or had a bit too much to drink. All in all," he added in the same impersonal tone, "you've got a lot of style."

Not certain what he was leading up to, and not wanting to be too pleased by his words, Serena moved her shoulders carelessly. "So?"

"So. I've a use for someone with your talents." His expression didn't change when her eyes narrowed. Justin merely folded his legs under him and watched her, looking, Serena thought, a bit too much like his infamous kidnapping ancestor must have looked.

Pushing her glasses on top of her head, Serena stared straight back at him. "What sort of use?" she asked coolly.

"Managing my casino in Atlantic City." He had the satisfaction of seeing incredulity cover her face.

"You own a casino in Atlantic City?"

Without seeming to move at all, Justin rested his hands lightly on his knees. "Yes."

Serena frowned at him through narrowed eyes. He thought, amused, that her trust didn't come as easily this time, then slowly she let out a breath. "Comanche," Serena murmured. "There's one in Vegas, too, and in Tahoe, I think." Leaning back, she closed her eyes. So the itinerant gambler turned out to be a very wealthy, very successful businessman. "I should have known."

Even more amused by her reaction, Justin relaxed. He'd first thought of offering her a job during the morning in Nassau. Then it had been part whim, part business. Studying her strong, elegant face, he knew it was already more than that, more than it should be. That was something he would deal with—after he'd arranged things.

"I fired my manager just before I left," Justin went on, not waiting for Serena to open her eyes again. "A bit of trouble with the take."

She opened them now, her brows arching. "He cheated you?"

"Tried," Justin corrected her mildly. "No one cheats me."

"No," Serena agreed. "I'm sure they don't." She

drew her knees up so that they would no longer be touching, then wrapped her arms around them. "Why do you want me to work for you?"

Justin had the uncomfortable feeling she knew it was more than he'd said, even though he himself wasn't certain of all the reasons. He was only sure that he wanted her in his world where he could see... and touch her. "I've told you," he said simply, too cautious to stroke her skin again.

"If you have three successful hotels—"

"Five," he corrected her.

"Five." She gave him a slight nod. "Then I can't imagine you as a man who runs his business on impulse." Or anything else on impulse, she added silently. "You must know that managing a casino like yours is a long way from dealing cards on a cruise liner. You probably have twice the tables we do, and a take that would make our little profit look like bubble-gum money."

Justin allowed himself a smile. It was true enough. "Of course, if you don't think you can handle it—"

"I didn't say I couldn't handle it," she retorted, then scowled at him. "You're very clever, aren't you?"

"Think about it," he suggested, hooking his finger around one of hers. "You said yourself you have no definite plans after this cruise."

No definite plans, she mused. Just a vague notion about opening her own place. She still wanted her own place, but wouldn't it be logical to manage someone else's until she learned a bit more? "I'll think about it," Serena said slowly, hardly noticing that Justin's thumb was moving lightly up and down the length of her finger.

"Good." With his free hand he reached up, idly plucking a pin from her hair. "We can have dinner in San Juan and discuss the practicalities." Letting the first pin drop, Justin drew out another.

"Will you stop that." Annoyed, Serena grabbed his wrist. "Every time I see you, you're tossing my pins away. I won't have one left by the end of the cruise."

"I like it down." He ran his fingers through the loosely secured bun and scattered the rest of the pins. "I like to see it fall down."

Shoving his hand away, Serena scrambled up. When he used that tone, a smart woman kept her distance. "I'm not having dinner with you in San Juan or anywhere else." She snatched up the dashiki she'd worn over her suit. "And I believe I've thought long enough about your proposition."

"Afraid?" Unfolding his legs, Justin rose in a smooth, catlike movement.

"No." She met his eyes calmly, so that he would understand she spoke the truth.

"Good." Pleased with the strong, stubborn look, he cupped his hands around the base of her neck. Fear was too ordinary and too easily defeated. "But take a few days to think this over. The business offer is exactly that. It has nothing to do with you and me being lovers."

The firm kneading of his fingers at the back of her neck had nearly seduced her into relaxing. His words had her eyes flashing. "We're not lovers."

"We will be," he said, holding her still with one hand as he stepped closer. "Soon. We're both people who take what we want, Serena. We want each other."

"Why don't you put your ego down for a while,

Justin. It must be getting heavy." When his hand went to her lotioned back to press her closer, she remained stiff, unwilling to struggle, unwilling to lose.

"Gamblers believe in fate." Though her back was straight and unyielding, he felt the soft give of breasts against his chest. Only a narrow band of material separated flesh from flesh. "You're as much a gambler as I am, Serena MacGregor." Lowering his head, he nibbled along her jawline. "We've both got to play with the hand we were dealt."

How long could she resist that honeyed tone and clever mouth? Already Serena could feel the hammer of her heart against her ribs and the heavy fluid weakness in her limbs. If she resisted, she would lose. Perhaps...Her brain began to cloud, and frantically she forced the silken mists away. Perhaps this time she would play the game his way and earn a draw. Fighting her own need to surrender, she took a dangerous gamble.

Slowly, softly, she ran her hands up his naked back, letting her fingernails lightly rake his skin. When his mouth pressed against her throat, her knees nearly buckled, but she bit down hard on the inside of her lip. Pain would help her keep control. She rubbed against him sinuously, while her fingers crept up to trace patterns on the base of his neck. His heartbeat began to thud, racing with hers.

His mouth grew hungry, but she turned so that his lips fell anywhere but on hers. If he kissed her, locked her in one of those deep, mindless feasts of mouth on mouth, she'd be lost. His breath raged unsteadily over her ear, wrenching a moan from her. Serena squeezed her eyes tightly, struggling not to feel all the things he could so effortlessly make her feel. She pressed her lips to his throat, telling herself that it wasn't for the taste of him but only the next step in the game. She wouldn't be weakened by the dark male flavor, by the feel of muscle taut and strong under her hands. This time— this time, she promised herself, she'd bring him to his knees.

She heard him groan, felt the light quiver run through him as he crushed her against him. Too astonished by the newly discovered power to be pleased with it, Serena merely clung. He whispered something low, in a primitive tongue she didn't understand, before he buried his face in her hair.

Her heart urged her to stay as she was, warmed flesh to warmed flesh. Could it feel so right if she didn't belong there? If her body had not been fashioned for this, could they fit together so unerringly? If her mouth had not been made for his, would it heat at even the thought of a kiss?

No. Serena caught herself before the weakness could spread too far. She wouldn't let herself be ruled by a need...or by a man.

She pushed firmly away, knowing she was free only because she'd caught him off guard. Slowly, praying her legs would hold her, she bent down to retrieve the dashiki which had fallen to the deck. Without a word Serena slipped it over her head. It gave her a moment, just a moment, to brace herself before she looked at him.

She saw desire—a reckless desire that had her heart thudding painfully—in his eyes. And she saw the wariness. It strengthened her to know he'd been no more prepared for the attack on the senses than she had been. Because of it, she had the edge.

"If and when I decide I want to make love with you, you'll know." She said it calmly, then turned and walked away without a backward glance. Her knees were shaking.

Justin watched her. Oh, he could drag her back, he thought as his hand curled into a fist. He could drag her to his cabin and have her within a matter of moments. He could say the hell with the game plan and assuage this gnawing hunger that seemed to be eating him from the inside out. If once, just once, he was truly alone with her... With care, Justin unclenched his hand. It never paid to let emotions rule your moves. That was something he'd learned too many years ago to forget now.

Bending, he picked up the bottle of lotion Serena had left beside her chair. She'd been intrigued with his offer, he mused, absently tightening the cap. And while she might try to shrug it off, the idea had been planted. After a year of following orders, the notion of giving them would appeal to her. Having come fresh from a victory, she would consider herself well able to handle him on the personal front. He counted on there being enough MacGregor in her to make a challenge irresistible.

A slow, cool smile touched his mouth. Justin was just as susceptible to a challenge as Serena. He'd made his bid, he decided. For the moment, he'd let it stand.

Serena's room was completely dark when the phone beside her bunk shrilled. Blindly, she groped about, fumbling for the button of the alarm. When this did nothing to stop the ringing, she pushed at it in annoyance, then knocked the receiver from the phone. It conked her smartly against the temple.

"Ouch, damn it!"

"Good morning, little girl."

Hazy with sleep and rubbing her head, she cradled the receiver against her ear. "Dad?"

"How's life on the high seas?" he asked in a booming, cheerful voice that made her wince.

"I—um…" Running her tongue over her teeth, Serena struggled to wake up.

"Come on, girl, speak up."

"Dad, it's…" She pushed at her alarm again until she could read the luminous dial. "It's barely six A.M."

"A good sailor's up with the dawn," he told her.

"Uh-huh. Good night, Dad."

"Your mother wants to know when you'll be home."

Even half asleep, Serena grinned. Anna MacGregor had never been a mother hen, but Daniel… "We'll be in Miami Saturday afternoon. I should be home by Sunday. Are you going to have a brass band?"

"Hah!"

"One Highland chief with a bagpipe?"

"You were always the sassy one, Rena." He tried to sound stern, and ended up sounding proud. "Your mother wants to know if they're feeding you proper."

She swallowed a giggle. "We get a whole loaf of barley bread a week and salt pork on Sundays. How is Mom?"

"Fine. She's already gone to the hospital to cut somebody open."

"Alan and Caine?"

Daniel gave a snort. "Who sees them?" he demanded. "It breaks your mother's heart that her children've forgotten their parents. Not one grandchild to bounce on her knee."

"Inconsiderate of us," Serena agreed dryly.

"Now, if Alan had married that pretty Judson girl…"

"She walked like a duck," Serena reminded him bluntly. "Alan'll pick his own wife when he's ready."

"Hah!" Daniel said again. "Got his nose buried down in D.C., Caine's still sowing oats he should've been done with, and you float around on some boat."

"Ship."

"Your poor mother will never live to hold her first grandchild." With a heavy sigh he lit one of the fat cigars Anna hadn't managed to confiscate.

"Did you wake me up at six A.M. to lecture me about the procreation of the MacGregor line?"

"That's nothing to curl your lip at, little girl. The clan—"

"I'm not curling my lip," she assured him, wanting to avoid a long, passionate diatribe. "And I plan to stay home awhile, so you can start bullying me after Sunday."

"Now, is that any way to talk?" he demanded, offended. "Why, I've never so much as raised my hand to you."

"You're the best father I've ever had," she said soothingly. "I'll buy you a case of Scotch in St. Thomas."

"Well, now." Pleased with the idea, he softened, then remembered another promised case of Scotch and his main purpose for the predawn call. "Met any interesting people on the cruise, Rena?"

"Mmm, I could write a book. I'm really going to miss the rest of the crew."

"What about passengers?" he persisted. Daniel puffed on his cigar and tried his hand at smoke rings. "Get any real gamblers?"

"Now and again." Her thoughts drifted to Justin, just as Daniel's did.

"I suppose you've had your hands full with the men." She gave a noncommittal grunt and shifted to her back. One man anyway, she mused. "'Course there's nothing wrong with a bit of romance now and then," he added in a jovial voice. "Providing the man's got good blood and some starch. A true gambler has to have a sharp brain."

"Would you feel better if I told you I was planning to run off with one?"

"Which one?" he demanded, narrowing his eyes.

"No one," Serena returned firmly. "Now, I'm going back to sleep. Be sure to get rid of all that cigar ash before Mom gets home." Daniel scowled at the phone, then at the butt in his hands. "I'll see you and Mom Sunday. And by the way, I love you, you old pirate."

"Eat a decent breakfast," he ordered before he hung up.

Thoughtfully, Daniel leaned back in his massive chair. Rena had always been a tough egg to crack, he mused. As for Justin, well, if Justin Blade hadn't made it his business to spend a tropical evening or two in her company, then he wasn't the man Daniel thought he was. He tapped out his cigar, reminding himself to dispose of the evidence before Anna came home.

Damned if he was wrong about Justin Blade! Daniel MacGregor knew the make of a man. He gave himself a moment's pleasure speculating about a black-haired, violet-eyed grandchild. A boy first, he decided. Though he wouldn't carry the MacGregor name—and that was a pity—he'd carry MacGregor blood. They'd name him after his grandfather.

In a fine mood, Daniel picked up the phone, thinking he might as well badger his other children while he was at it.

Chapter Five

As much as she told herself it wasn't any of her business, Serena couldn't help wondering what Justin was up to. For two days she hadn't had a glimpse of him. During that time he hadn't set foot inside the casino. Nor had he been on the port side of the Promenade deck indulging in one of the private games, at least not when she just happened to stroll out there during her break.

What, Serena demanded of herself as she prepared for her last free day of the cruise, was he doing? A gambler was supposed to gamble, wasn't he? He wasn't the kind to settle for a bingo game in the lounge.

He's doing it on purpose, she decided as she buttoned up her scarlet romper. He's trying to get to me. She wouldn't have been the least surprised if while she had been working and wondering, he had spent his time lazing in the sun somewhere, knowing it. Infuriating. He'd probably had that cozy little drink with Mrs. Dewalter, too, she concluded, and grabbed her brush. Taking it through her hair in hard, quick strokes, Serena scowled at herself in the small mirror.

"So what?" she said aloud. "If he's nipping around her ankles, he's not nipping around mine." The last thing she'd wanted on her final days on the ship was a constant battle, verbal or otherwise. So it was just as well that he'd found something else to keep him occupied; that saved her the trouble of ignoring him.

He stirred her up when he was around. He stirred her up when he wasn't around, too, she thought, and tossed the brush back on the dresser. Where was the justice? I won't think about it, Serena decided, flopping down on the floor to slip on her sandals. I'm going to do some snorkeling, buy some trinkets—a case of Scotch—and, she added grimly, I'm going to enjoy myself. I won't give him another thought.

It's deliberate, she thought, slapping a sandal against her palm. He dangled that business about managing his casino in front of my nose, then disappeared. He knew it would drive me crazy, she decided with fresh frustration. Well, two can play, Serena reminded herself as she wiggled her foot into the sandal. I'll stay out of his way for the next couple of days if I have to claim seasickness and lock myself in my cabin. And that, she determined, would be a lesson to him.

Serena continued to frown when the knock sounded on her door. "It's open," she called shortly.

The last person she'd expected to see in her doorway was Justin. The last thing she'd expected to feel was pleasure. Oh, my God, she realized, I've missed him.

He saw the quick smile light in her eyes before she successfully turned it into a glare. "Morning."

"Passengers aren't permitted on this deck," she told him in a tone that was both cool and prim.

"Oh." He stepped inside, shutting the door behind him. Ignoring her hiss of annoyance, Justin glanced around the tiny cabin.

It should have been drab and colorless, with its plain bunk and white walls, but she'd given it an odd sort of style with only a few touches. A flashy painting of sailboats, a bottle-green free-form bowl filled with crushed shells, a boldly striped needlepoint pillow that reminded him of Anna. The pantry in Hyannis Port, he mused, was larger.

"No wasted space," he ventured, letting his eyes roam back to her.

"It's *my* space," Serena reminded him. "And it's strictly against the rules for you to be in here. Would you go away before you get me fired?"

"You've already quit." Easing between her and the bunk, Justin took a closer look at the painting. "This is very good—the harbor here in St. Thomas?"

"Yes." Serena stayed seated deliberately, knowing it was next to impossible for two people to stand in the cabin without touching. "I'm sorry I can't entertain you, Justin, but I'm just on my way out."

With an absent sound of agreement, he sat on the bunk. "Sturdy," he commented, nudging a reluctant smile from her. It was hard as a rock.

"It's great for the back." They sat eyeing each other for a moment as she fought off the simple pleasure of having him with her. "I thought I was rid of you."

"Did you?" Lifting the flimsy teddy she'd slept in, Justin ran the lace through his fingers. Without any effort he could picture her in it, picture the thin, creamy material sliding over her skin as he slipped it off of her.

"Put that down." She leaned over to snatch it out of his hands, going across his body to do so.

"So you have a taste for silk and lace," he stated, letting the lingerie slip back to the bed before Serena could grab it. "I've always admired women who wear things like this, then sleep alone." Justin looked down at her as Serena knelt on the floor, frustrated. "It shows a certain independence of spirit."

Her brows furrowed. "Is that a compliment?"

"I thought so." With a smile he leaned forward to wrap the ends of her hair around his fingers. "Why did you think you were rid of me?"

"I wish you wouldn't be nice, Justin; it throws me off." Sitting back on her haunches, Serena sighed. "You haven't been in the casino."

"There are other entertainments on board."

"I'm sure." Her voice chilled. "Like explaining your system to Mrs. Dewalter?"

"Mrs. who?"

Her feathers ruffled, Serena got up and began to search for her tote bag. "The divorced redhead with the hen's egg."

"Oh." Amused and baffled, Justin watched her rummage under the bunk. "Looking for something?"

"Yes."

As he watched, Serena squirmed under the bunk on her stomach. "Would you like some help?"

"No. Damn it!" She swore as she rapped the back of her head on the bottom of the bunk. When she wiggled back out, Justin was sitting on the floor beside her. Without speaking, he smiled and brushed her mussed hair away from her face. "Justin…" Serena turned away and dumped the contents of the bag on the bunk. "I really hate to say this."

Accustomed to her sharp tongue, he shrugged. "Go ahead, say it anyway."

"I missed you."

Looking back, Serena saw surprise on his face for the second time. "I told you I hated to say it." When she started to rise, he took her arm and held her still.

Three words. Three words that brought on a torrent of conflicting emotions that he'd never experienced. He'd been prepared for her annoyance, her coolness, her fury. But not for those three simple words. "Serena." He laid his hand on her cheek in a rare gesture of complete gentleness. "That's a dangerous thing to tell me when we're alone."

She touched her hand to his briefly, then carefully drew it away from her skin. "I didn't intend to tell you at all. I don't think I realized it myself until you walked in here." Her sigh was both puzzled and wistful. "I just don't understand it."

"I wonder why it is we both feel we need to," he said half to himself.

Abruptly, she jumped up and began dropping what she thought she'd need into the tote bag. "I'm going to the beach for snorkeling and sightseeing," Serena told him. "Would you like to come with me?"

She didn't hear him move—he didn't make a sound—but she knew he'd risen to stand behind her. For the first time in a year, Serena felt the light panic of claustrophobia.

Justin placed his hands on her shoulders and turned her to face him. Those eyes, he thought. That impossibly rich color. It seemed he had only to look into them for the need to spread to his. "A truce?" he asked.

She saw, with relief, that he wasn't going to press the advantage she'd given him. "What fun would that be?" Serena retorted. "You can come with me if you want, but no truce."

"Those seem like reasonable terms," he mused. When he slipped his hands around her waist, Serena stuck the tote bag between them. Justin glanced at it, then at her. "That's hardly an obstacle."

"The offer was for sightseeing," she reminded him. "Take it or leave it."

"We'll go with that." With a hesitation so slight it went unnoticed, Justin dropped his hands. "For now."

Accepting this, Serena turned and opened the door. "Ever been on a glass-bottom boat?"

"No."

"You're going to love it," she promised, and reached for his hand.

Her skin was wet and warm and glistening in the sunlight. Two tiny scraps of material clung to the curves of her breasts and hips. As she stretched out her legs on the blanket, Serena gave a contented sigh.

"I like to think of the pirates." She looked out over the magnificent blue water and could almost see the Jolly Roger fluttering in the breeze. High green mountains rose around them, as if floating on the sea itself. "Three hundred years ago." Shaking back her wet hair, she smiled over at Justin. "Hardly any time at all, really when you think of how long these islands have been here."

A few droplets of water glistened on his dark skin.

"Don't you think Blackbeard might be a bit upset if he saw all this?" He gestured to indicate the people dotting the white sand beach and splashing in the turquoise water. Laughter rose with the scent of suntan lotion. "Unlike the rest of us, I don't think he'd consider these beaches unspoiled."

She laughed, both refreshed and exhilarated from their hour of snorkeling. "He'd find another place. Pirates have a knack for it."

"You sound as though you admire them."

"It's easy to romanticize after a couple of centuries." Serena leaned back on her elbows, enjoying the sensation of drying in the sun. "And I suppose I've always admired people who lived by their own rules."

"At any price?"

"Oh, you're going to be practical." Serena tilted her face toward the sun. The sky was as blue as the water, and cloudless. "It's too beautiful here to be practical. There's as much barbarism and cruelty today as there was three hundred years ago, and not nearly as much adventure. I'd love a ride in H. G. Wells's time machine."

Intrigued, Justin picked up the comb she had discarded and began to run it through her hair. "Where would you go?"

"Arthur's Britain, Plato's Greece, Caesar's Rome." She sighed, finding the sensation of Justin drawing the comb through her hair both sensual and soothing. "Hundreds of other places. I'd have to meet Rob Roy in Scotland or my father would never forgive me. I'd like to have seen the West before the settlers discovered it, but then, I suppose I'd've been on the first wagon to Oregon." Laughing, she tilted her head back farther so that she had upside-down view of his face. "It would've been worth the risk of being scalped by your ancestors."

Justin weighed her hair in one hand. "It would have been quite a prize."

"I'd just as soon have kept it," Serena admitted wryly. "What about you?" she asked. "Wouldn't you like to go back a couple of centuries and play Red Dog in a Tombstone saloon?"

"They didn't welcome Comanches."

Reaching back, she brushed damp hair from his forehead. "You're being practical again."

His eyes held hers a moment. "I would have been in the war party, attacking your wagon train."

"Yes." She looked out to sea again. It was foolish to forget who and what he was, even for a moment. He was different. It only added to the attraction. "I suppose you would have. We would have been forging new frontiers, you would have been defending what was already yours. The lines get misted and you wonder if either side was wrong in the beginning. Do you ever feel cheated?" she wondered aloud. "Your birthright?"

Justin drew the comb slowly through her hair. As it dried he could see all the subtle shade variations that merged together for the rich gold. "I prefer making what I own rather than thinking of inheritances."

She nodded, because the words so exactly expressed her own feelings. "The MacGregors were persecuted in Scotland, forced to give up their name, their plaid, and their land. If I'd been there, I would have fought. Now it's just a fascinating story." She gave a low laugh as her mood shifted. "One my father will tell again and again at the least provocation."

A toddler, racing across the sand to escape her mother, landed like a plump ball in Serena's lap. Giggling, she tossed her arms around Serena's neck and clung as if they were in the conspiracy together.

"Well, hello." With a laugh Serena returned the hug, then she tilted the child's head back enough to see fun-filled brown eyes. "Making a break for it, are you?"

The girl grabbed a handful of Serena's hair. "Pretty."

"What a bright child," she commented, looking over her shoulder at Justin. To her surprise, he hoisted the child onto his own lap and touched a finger to her button nose. "You're pretty too." With another peal of giggles she pressed a wet kiss to his cheek.

Before Serena had gotten over her surprise at the ease with which he accepted the damp greeting, a woman in a trim black maillot rushed to the trio breathlessly. "Rosie!" The frazzled mother held a plastic pail and shovel while her cheeks grew pink. "Oh, I'm so sorry."

"Pretty," Rosie claimed again, giving Justin another kiss. This time Serena burst into giggles.

"Rosie!" Exasperated, the mother ran a hand through her hair. "I really am sorry," she repeated. "She heads everywhere at a dead run. No one' safe."

"When you run there's more time to play once you're there, isn't there, Rosie?" Serena stroked the warm brown hair as she smiled her reassurance at the mother. "She must keep you busy."

"Exhausted," the woman admitted. "But really, I—"

"Don't apologize." Gently Justin brushed the sand from the child's hand. "She's beautiful."

Obviously pleased, the mother relaxed, then held out her hand to her daughter. "Thank you. Do you have children?"

It took Serena a moment to realize they were being addressed as a couple. Before she could recover, Justin was already answering. "Not yet. I don't suppose this one's for sale."

Hefting Rosie on her hip, the young woman beamed down at him. "No, though there are times I'm tempted to rent her out. She's a handful. Thanks again. Not everyone appreciates being attacked by a two-year-old tornado. Say good-bye, Rosie."

"'Bye!" Rosie waved a chubby hand over her mother's shoulder before she made a valiant effort to scramble down again. Serena could hear high, delighted giggles as the mother and daughter moved across the beach.

"Really, Justin." Serena brushed away the sand Rosie had brought with her. "Why did you tell that woman we didn't have any children yet?"

"We don't."

"You know very well what I mean," she began.

"Now who's being practical?" Before Serena could retort, he wrapped his arms around her waist and pressed his lips to her shoulder. Instead of resisting, she leaned back against him a moment, enjoying the closeness.

"She was sweet."

"Most children are." He pressed a kiss to her other shoulder. "They've no pretensions, no prejudices, and very little fear. Soon her mother will teach her not to talk to strangers. Necessary, but rather sad."

Serena drew away so that she could turn around and look at him fully. "I wouldn't have believed you'd give children a moment's thought."

Justin started to tell her that the moment with the child that they had shared had awakened urges in him, a need for family he'd almost forgotten he had. A woman beside him, a child reaching up for a kiss. Then he brushed the thought away even as Serena brushed away sand. It was best to tread lightly on ground you didn't know, he thought. "I started out that way myself," he said at length.

She noticed his hesitation, but found her own emotions strangely muddled. "Are you sure?" Smiling, she rested her hands on his shoulders.

"Reasonably."

"I'm going to tell you something," Serena said solemnly, leaning a bit closer.

"Yes?"

"I don't think you're pretty."

"Children have a clearer outlook than adults."

"You don't even have a pretty nature," she insisted, but found the urge to press her lips to his too difficult to resist.

"Neither do you." Running his hands up her back, Justin deepened the kiss. His lids had lowered as hers had, but neither closed. She felt something creep out of her while her bones were softening, something small and vital that was hers one moment and his the next. Serena yielded to him in a kiss that held more promise than passion.

"I never intend to have one," she murmured.

"Thank God." His hand tightened in her hair suddenly, briefly, though his mouth remained gentle on hers.

Serena drew away. Something had changed. There was no clear explanation why, no idea what, but something had changed. There was a need to put things back on a solid footing until she had the time to decipher it. Her body felt soft and weak and alien.

"We'd better go," she managed. "I have some things to pick up in town before I'm due back at the ship."

" 'Time and tide wait for no man,' " he mused.

"That's about it." Rising, she shook loose sand from her romper before she slipped it over her suit.

"You won't always have that excuse." Justin stood beside her, halting the hands that worked the buttons.

"No," Serena agreed, then began to fasten the romper again. "But I have it now."

It took some artful driving through the traffic of Charlotte Amalie, then a dash of luck to find an empty parking place. The streets were jammed with cabs, people, and small open-air busses with gaily patterned roofs. During this time both Justin and Serena were silent, occupied with their separate thoughts.

What had happened, she wondered, during that brief, almost friendly kiss on the beach? Why had it left her feeling like jelly inside, apprehensive and somehow delighted? Perhaps it had something to do with how touched she'd been to see Justin with the little girl. It was difficult to imagine a man like him, a gambler with those parallel streaks of coolness and ruthlessness, being a sucker for a twenty-pound brunette with sticky, salty hands. She simply hadn't given him credit for that quality of sweetness.

It could also be the fact that where she'd once thought she *might* like him, Serena now knew she *did*. But cautiously, she added, as if to reassure herself. It would never be wise to completely drop caution in dealings with Justin. And now that she could admit she liked him and enjoyed his company, the cruise was almost over. During what was left of it, Serena would be kept so busy by her shifts and duties in the casino that she wouldn't have a leisurely hour to spend with him, much less a leisurely day. For the rest of the trip they would be at sea, with the casino open sixteen hours a day.

Of course there was still the option of accepting his job offer. Frowning slightly, Serena glanced out the window to see a table on the sidewalk near Gucci covered with hats made from palm leaves. For the past two days she had deliberately blocked the proposition out of her head—first from temper, then from the sensible notion that it would be better to consider it after there was some distance between them. Atlantic City would be an adventure. Working with Justin would be a risk. Perhaps one was the same as the other.

Why did the sudden softening of her attitude worry him? Justin wondered. That had, after all, been one of his goals. He wanted her, just as he had wanted her the first moment he had seen her. Yet, the days of contact, of arguments, laughter, and passion had added some new aspect to what should have remained a basic need.

It wasn't as simple as it had once been to attribute his conflicting emotions to the machinations of her father. In truth, he hadn't thought of her as Daniel

MacGregor's daughter in days. As he pulled into an empty space, Justin decided it might be wise to think of her that way again...at least for the moment.

"More key chains that play *Für Elise?*" he asked as he switched off the ignition. Despite what he had just told himself, Justin drew her closer to taste her lips again.

"I never repeat myself," she retorted, but she didn't move away.

"Just this once," he murmured, "make an exception."

On a low laugh she increased the pressure until they both forgot they were in a parked car in the middle of a crowded city. Tonight, she thought, as her fingers ran up his cheek on their journey to his hair. The time had come to stop pretending and take what she wanted.

"Serena." It was half sigh, half moan as he drew her away.

"I know." For a moment she rested her head against his shoulder. "We seem destined to find ourselves in public places." She took a quick, audible breath and scooted out of the car. "Since we spent so long at the beach, I won't have time for anything but the most disciplined shopping." Justin walked around to her to take her hand. Serena smiled, then with a quick glance up and down the narrow, crowded street, she pointed. "I should be able to pick up a few souvenirs and the liquor I need in there."

Before she could reach her destination, the window display at Cartier's stopped her. Her long sigh was part appreciation and part desire. "Why is it an intelligent woman can find herself coveting a bunch of shiny rocks?" she wondered aloud.

"It's natural, isn't it?" Justin moved to stand beside her, letting his gaze roam over the sparkle of diamonds, the gleam of emeralds. "Most women are attracted to diamonds—most men too."

"Pressurized carbon," she mused, then sighed again. "Hunks of rock dug out of caves. Centuries ago we used them as amulets to ward off evil spirits or bring good luck. The Phoenicians traveled to the Baltic countries of Europe for amber. Wars have been fought over them, countries exploited…and somehow that makes them more attractive."

"Don't you ever indulge yourself?"

Serena turned away from the window and smiled at him. "No, it gives me something to look forward to. I've promised myself that the next time I travel it'll be strictly for relaxation. Then I'm going on a binge that may put a serious hole in my bank account. For now—"she gestured toward the next shop—"I need to pick up some more traditional sort of souvenirs for a few cousins, and a case of Chivas Regal."

Justin walked into the store with her, where Serena immediately became caught up in a flurry of picking, choosing, and buying. She generally disliked shopping, but once committed, did so with a vengeance. When Justin wandered off she paid little attention, engrossed as she was in a selection of embroidered table linen.

With the souvenirs purchased and wrapped, Serena went to the counter where bottles of liquor, liqueurs, and wines were displayed in profusion. A quick glance at her watch showed her she had nearly two hours before she was due on board. "A case of Chivas, twelve year."

"Two."

At Justin's voice, Serena turned her head. "Oh, I thought I'd lost you."

"Did you find what you wanted?"

"And more," she admitted with a grimace. "I'm going to hate myself when it comes time to pack." The clerk slid the two boxes of Scotch onto the counter. "I'd like mine delivered to the *Celebration*." Drawing out her credit card, she waited for the clerk to fill out the form.

"And mine," Justin added, counting out bills.

Serena pondered his case of Scotch while he relayed the necessary information. Strange, she mused, she hadn't thought him the kind of drinker to buy Scotch by the case. He never drank when he gambled. It had been one of the first things she'd noticed. Throughout the cruise, she'd seen him with a drink in his hand only once, during the picnic at Nassau. She decided perhaps he bought it in lieu of souvenirs, but it seemed odd he'd buy so much of one brand. After signing her name to the credit slip, Serena stuffed the receipt into her bag.

"I suppose that's it." Slipping her hand into his, she walked toward the exit. "Odd that we both bought the same brand of Scotch."

"Not when you consider we bought it for the same person," he returned mildly.

With a puzzled smile, Serena looked up at him. "The same person?"

"Your father doesn't drink any other brand."

"How do you..." Confused, she shook her head. "Why would you buy my father a case of Scotch?"

"He asked me to." He guided her by a clutch of teenagers.

"Asked you to?" Hampered by another crowd of shoppers, Serena had to wait until she'd plowed her way through. "What do you mean he asked you to?"

"I've never known Daniel to do anything without a catch." Justin took her arm to guide her across the street as she was looking at him and not the cars. "A case of Scotch seemed reasonable at the time."

Daniel? Serena thought, noting the easy use of her father's name. For a moment her mind concentrated on that small point until unanswered and uncomfortable questions began to leak through. Disregarding the flow of pedestrian traffic, she stopped dead in the center of the sidewalk.

"Justin, you'd better tell me exactly what you're talking about."

"I'm talking about buying your father a case of Scotch for his thoughtfulness in booking my passage on the *Celebration*."

"You've got something mixed up. My father isn't a travel agent."

He laughed just as uproariously as he had the day he'd learned her last name. "No, Daniel's many things, but he's not a travel agent. Why don't we go down here and sit."

"I don't want to sit." She gave her arm a jerk as he led her to one of the cool courtyards. "I want to know why the hell my father would have anything to do with arranging your vacation."

"I think he had my life in mind, actually." Finding an empty table, Justin gave her a nudge into a chair. "And yours," he added as he sat.

She could smell the freshly made delicacies from the bakery across from them, hear the chatter from the little bookstore next door. Because she suddenly wanted to punch something, Serena folded her hands on the table. "What the hell are you talking about?"

"I met your father about ten years ago." Calmly, Justin drew out a cigar and lit it. Serena was reacting precisely the way he had expected. The predictability eased the tension he'd been fighting since that moment on the beach when he'd felt something slipping away from him. "I came to Hyannis Port with a business proposition," Justin began. "We played some poker and have been doing business off and on ever since. You've quite an interesting family." Serena made no comment, but her fingers clenched tighter.

"I've grown quite fond of them over the years," he continued blandly. "You always seemed to be in school when I visited, but I heard quite a bit about...Rena. Alan admires your mind, Caine your right cross." Though her eyes smoldered, Justin couldn't prevent a small smile from curving his lips. "Your father nearly erected a monument when you graduated from Smith two years ahead of schedule."

Serena repressed the urge to swear, repressed the urge to scream. The man had been privy to her life for a decade without her knowledge or consent. "You've known," she began in a low, furious voice. "You've known who I am all this time, and you've said nothing. Playing games when you only had to explain—"

"Wait a minute." As she started to rise he took her arm in a forceful grip. "I didn't know the blackjack dealer named Serena was Daniel's Rena MacGregor, the paragon I've heard about for the last ten years."

She flushed, both in fury and embarrassment. Most of her life she had found her father's bragging as amusing as it was endearing. Now it served as a cold, hard slap in the face. "I don't know what your game is—"

"*Daniel's* game," Justin interrupted again. "It wasn't until that day on the beach when you were shouting at me about MacGregors not being pushed around that I realized who you were and why Daniel had been so persuasive about my taking this trip."

Because she could remember the expression of utter shock on his face, Serena relaxed fractionally. "He sent you the tickets and didn't mention the fact that I worked on the *Celebration?*"

"What do you think?" Justin countered, tapping his cigar in a plastic ashtray as he watched her. "When I found out your full name, I realized I'd been maneuvered by an expert." He grinned, amused all over again. "I'll admit it gave me a moment or two of discomfort."

"Discomfort," Serena repeated, unamused. Her brief telephone conversation with her father played back in her head. He'd been pumping her, she realized, wondering if his little scheme had borne fruit. "I'm going to murder him," she said quietly. Her eyes, dark with barely controlled fury, came back to Justin's. "As soon as I'm done with you." She gave herself a moment because the need to scream was building again. "You could've told me days ago."

"Could have," Justin agreed. "But as I figured your reaction would be essentially what it is, I chose not to."

"You chose," she said between her teeth. "My father chose. Oh, what marvelous egomaniacs you men are! Perhaps it didn't occur to you that I was on the chess board too." Anger flooded her face. "Did you think you'd get me into bed to pay him back for those moments of discomfort?''

"You know better than that." Justin spoke so mildly, Serena had to bite back a new retort. "For some reason I had a difficult time remembering whose daughter you were every time I put my hands on you."

"I'll tell you what I know," she said in the same dangerously low voice. "The two of you deserve each other. You're both arrogant, pompous, overbearing fools. What right do you have to intrude on my life this way?"

"Your father instigated the intrusion," Justin told her evenly. "The rest was strictly personal. If you want to murder the old devil, it's your business, but don't stick your claws into me."

"I don't need your permission to murder him!" she tossed back, her voice rising enough to cause a few heads to turn.

"I think I just said that."

She sprang up, casting about futilely for something to throw at him. Since it was physically impossible for her to lift him and heave him bodily through the plate glass window of the bookstore, she only smoldered. "I'm afraid I lack your sense of humor," she managed after a moment. "I happen to think what my father did was insulting and demeaning." With as much dignity as she had left, Serena reached for her bags. "I'd appreciate it if you'd stay out of my way during the rest of the trip. I'm afraid I'd find it extremely difficult to restrain myself from throwing you overboard."

"All right. If—" Justin added before she could speak again, "you promise to let me know in two weeks about the position in Atlantic City." Even as her eyes widened and her mouth flew open to pour out abuse, he held up a hand. "Oh, no. Deal's off if you give me your answer now. Two weeks."

Stiffly, she nodded. "You'll get the same answer then, but I can postpone it. Good-bye, Justin."

"Serena." Smoldering, she turned back to glare at him. "Give Daniel my best before you murder him."

Chapter Six

The first thing Serena noticed during the drive from the airport were the trees. It had been some time since she'd seen oak and maple and pine touched with fall. It was barely September, but the feel of autumn was in the air, with all its strength and color. Even while she appreciated it, she seethed.

If it hadn't been indoctrinated into her to finish a job once it was started, she would have caught the first plane out of St. Thomas after Justin's revelation. Instead, she'd gone about her duties with an outward smile and inward rage. Rather than cooling off during the interim, Serena had grown more angry and frustrated, and felt more misused. Perhaps because Justin had kept his part of the bargain and steered clear of her for the remainder of the cruise, all of Serena's temper was fully focused on one man: Daniel MacGregor.

"Oh, you're going to be sorry," she muttered, causing the cabbie to glance quickly in his rearview mirror.

Nice-looking lady, he mused. Mad as a hornet. He

began the gentle ride along Nantucket Sound in discreet silence.

The first view of the house had the effect of distracting Serena from plans of revenge. The gray stone glistened with minute pieces of mica in the late afternoon sun. It had been built to Daniel's fancy, and with its twin towers, as nearly resembled a castle as he could manage. There were large stone balconies, roughly carved, and tall, mullioned windows. A lush bed of flowers flowed in a semi-circle around the front—in place, Serena had always thought, of the moat he would have preferred.

From the main structure two lower stone buildings spread out. One was a ten-car garage, which with Alan and Caine away would be only half full. The other held a heated pool. Daniel might prefer a primitive style of architecture, but he appreciated comfort.

The cab pulled up in front of the granite steps, interrupting Serena's survey of the home she'd grown up in. Leaving the two suitcases and Scotch to the cab driver, she gathered together the sundry packages from her shopping sprees, and started up the steps.

Following an old habit, she looked at the massive oak door, where the MacGregor crest was carved into a brass knocker. Under the crowned lion's head was the Gaelic motto, which translated to "Royal Is My Race." As always, when reading it, she smiled. Her father had insisted they learn to say it in Gaelic, if they learned nothing else.

"Just set them there, thank you." Still smiling, Serena paid off the driver, then turned to thud her family crest against the door. It would reverberate through the house, she thought, like the sound of approaching cannon.

The door was swung open on its well-oiled hinges by a tiny scrap of a woman with iron-gray hair and pointed features. Her mouth fell open, accentuating the sharp chin. "Miss Rena!"

"Lily." Serena embraced the small, bony woman with all the exuberance of youth. In addition to her duties as housekeeper, Lily had been surrogate mother whenever Anna had been busy at the hospital. She had handled the three unruly children expertly, patching wounds and allowing squabbles to run their course. "Did you miss me?" Serena demanded, giving Lily a final squeeze before she drew the older woman away.

"Hardly noticed you were gone." Lily gave her a welcoming smile. "Where's your tan?"

"In my imagination."

"Lily, wasn't that the door?" Holding a piece of needlepoint in one hand, Anna MacGregor poked her head out of a doorway down the long hall. "Rena!" She came forward, her arms outstretched. Serena raced into them.

Anna was soft and strong. Both qualities flowed through Serena, along with a hundred memories. She took a deep breath, inhaling the scent of apple blossoms her mother had worn as long as she could remember.

"Welcome home, darling. We weren't expecting you until tomorrow."

"I caught an earlier plane." Serena pulled back, tilting her head so that she could study her mother's face. The skin was still creamy, with only a few fine lines betraying her age. There was a youthful softness about Anna's face that Serena thought she would never lose.

Her eyes were calm, reflecting the nature that had refused to change through years of operating rooms and death. Her hair waved gently, a rich brown dashed with gray. "Mom." Serena pressed her cheek against her mother's again. "How do you stay so beautiful?"

"Your father insists on it."

Laughing, Serena pulled away, grasping one of her mother's strong, skilled hands. "It's good to be home."

"You look wonderful, Rena." Anna studied her with an easy mixture of maternal pride and professionalism. "Nothing better than moist sea air for the complexion. Lily, please tell Cook that Miss Rena's home; we'll have our welcome-home dinner a day early. I want you to tell me all about your travels," she continued, turning back to her daughter. "But if you don't go up to see your father first, I'll never hear the end of it."

Abruptly, Serena remembered her mission. Anna watched her eyes narrow, and recognizing the sign, lifted her brows. "Oh, I intend to go up and see him, all right."

"Anything you'd like to tell me about?"

"Afterward." Serena drew a deep breath. "He's going to require medical attention when I'm through with him."

"I see." Knowing better than to question her daughter, Anna smiled quietly. "I'll be in the parlor then. We'll have a nice long talk when you're finished yelling at your father."

"It won't take long," Serena muttered, and started up the wide, curved staircase.

At the first landing she glanced down the corridor to her left. This was where the family slept, with Serena's childhood room three doors down on the left. The wing was a maze of twists and turns and shadowy corners. She could remember her brother Caine hiding behind a three-foot-high urn, then jumping out and scaring her nearly to death.

Serena had chased him for nearly thirty minutes until her temper had been defeated by the sheer joy of the chase. He'd let her catch him eventually, on the east lawn, where he had tossed her to the ground to wrestle until she was weak with laughter. How old had she been? Serena wondered. Eight, nine? Caine would have been eleven or twelve. Suddenly, she missed him with a purely physical ache of kinship.

And Alan, she mused, continuing her climb. He'd always protected her in an offhanded way. Perhaps because he was six years her senior, they had never indulged in the hand-to-hand combat she and Caine had been prone to. As a boy Alan had been scrupulously honest, where Caine had used the truth to suit himself. Never lying, Serena remembered with a faint smile. Just evading masterfully. Yet, in his own way, Alan had always worked circumstances to his own favor. She decided it was a basic MacGregor trait. Glancing at the narrow stairway that led to the tower room, Serena vowed that there was one MacGregor who'd be sorry for it.

Daniel leaned back in his chair and listened to the precise, boring voice on the phone. Bankers, he thought maliciously. It was a curse to deal with them. Even owning controlling interest in the bank didn't protect him from them.

"Give them a thirty-day extension on the loan," he ordered finally. "Yes, I'm aware of the figures, you just gave me the figures." *Dunderhead,* he added to himself. Impatiently, he drummed his fingers on his desk. Why was it bankers couldn't see beyond two plus two? "Thirty days," he repeated. "With the standard penalty rate of interest." He heard the loud thump at his door and was about to bellow at the intruder when it swung open. Annoyance was immediately flooded by pleasure. "Do it," he barked into the phone before he slammed it down. "Rena!"

Before he could heave himself from his chair, she had advanced on him. Planting herself in front of the desk, she slapped her palms down on it and leaned over.

"You old goat."

Settling his bulk back in the chair, Daniel cleared his throat. The fat, he concluded, was in the fire. "You look well, too."

"How...dare...you." She spaced the words slowly and evenly—the next danger signal. "How dare you dangle me in front of Justin Blade like a piece of prime beef?"

"Beef?" Daniel gave her an incredulous look. Pretty girl, he thought proudly. A true MacGregor. "I don't know what you're talking about," he went on. "So, you met Justin Blade. Fine boy."

She made a sound deep in her throat. "You set me up. Hatching your little plot right here in this room like some mad king with a surplus daughter on his hands. Why didn't you just draw up a contract?" Serena demanded as her voice rose. "It's no less than I expect from you. Daniel Duncan MacGregor hereby trades his only daughter to Justin Blade for a case of twelve-year-old Scotch." She smacked her hand on the redwood. "You could even have put in provisions about the number of progeny you expected me to provide to carry on the family name. I'm surprised you didn't offer him a dowry!"

"Now, listen here, little girl—"

"Don't you little-girl me." She stalked around his desk and swung his chair around to face her. "It was despicable. I've never been so humiliated in all my life!"

"I don't know what you're talking about. I persuaded a friend to take a relaxing cruise."

"Don't you try to weasel out of it." She poked a slim finger into his massive chest. "You sent him on my ship hoping we'd trip over each other enough times so your investment would pay off."

"You might never have met him at all!" he thundered. "It's a big boat."

"Ship!" she thundered back. "It's a big ship and a small casino. You knew damn well the odds were in your favor."

"Well, what's the harm in that?" he wanted to know at the top of his lungs. "You met a young friend of mine. You've met hundreds of friends of mine."

The sound came from her throat again. This time Serena whirled away. There was a huge bookshelf along the east wall. Stomping to it, Serena pulled out a volume entitled *Constitutional Convention*. She flipped it open, revealing the hollow where six cigars were secreted. Watching her father, she scooped them out and then broke them in half.

"Rena!" he said in quiet horror.

"It's the next best thing to poisoning you," she told him, dusting off her fingers.

Holding a hand to his heart, Daniel rose. His broad-featured face was wreathed in gloom. "It's a dark day when a daughter betrays her own father."

"Betrays!" she shouted, advancing on him again. "You have the nerve, the utter gall, to talk to me of betrayal?" Sticking her hands on her hips, she glared up at him. "I don't know how Justin feels about it, but I can tell you, I'm insulted by your little scheme."

He bristled, but noted her use of Justin's first name. Perhaps things were not as bad as they seemed. "That's the thanks I get for caring for my daughter's happiness. There's nothing sharper than the tongue of an ungrateful child."

"The butcher knife I was considering is."

"You said poison," he reminded her.

"I'm flexible." Then she smiled slowly. "Well, just so you won't think your money went for nothing, I suppose I should tell you what I've decided about Justin."

"Well, then…" Daniel went back to his desk, thinking she would be more reasonable now that she'd shouted and raged a bit. A pity about the cigars though. "He's a fine boy, good brains, integrity, pride." He folded his hands over his stomach, prepared to be magnanimous and forgiving.

"Oh, yes, I quite agree," she said in dulcet tones. "He's also very, very attractive."

Daniel smiled, pleased. "I knew you were a sensible girl, Rena. I've had a strong feeling about you and Justin for some time."

"Then you'll be happy to know I've decided to become his mistress."

"I can't—" Daniel broke off, confused, then stunned, then outraged. "*The hell you are!* The day my daughter takes herself off to be—to be *kept* is the day I take a strap to her for the first time in her life! Aye, a strap, Serena MacGregor, grown woman or no.''

''Ah, so I'm a grown woman now, am I?'' While he blustered she gave him a long, hard look. ''Remember this, a grown woman decides whom she'll marry, when she'll marry, and if she'll marry. A grown woman doesn't need her father arranging outrageously complicated blind dates. Just think about how this whole business could have blown up in your face before you stick your nose in next time.''

Frowning, he studied her face. ''You're not thinking of becoming his mistress, then?''

Serena gave him a haughty look. ''If I choose a lover, I'll choose one, but I won't be any man's mistress.''

He felt a flash of pride along with a twinge of discomfort. It only took an instant for him to concentrate on the pride. Daniel pushed at a gold pen and pencil set on his desk. ''Did you remember my Scotch?''

She tried to glare again, but the twinkle in his eyes undermined her. ''What Scotch?''

''Aw, Rena.''

Walking to him, Serena curled her arms around his neck. ''I'm not forgiving you,'' she murmured. ''I'm only pretending to forgive you. And I want you to know I never missed you at all.'' She pressed her lips to his cheek.

''Always were a disrespectful brat,'' he stated, hugging her fiercely.

When Serena went down to the parlor she found her mother sitting in her favorite rose-patterned armchair,

working on her latest needlepoint project. On the rose-
wood tea tray beside her sat a dainty porcelain tea service dotted with tiny violets. Glancing at the scene,
Serena marveled again that a woman who could be so
happily domesticated on one level could be such a dedicated and brilliant surgeon. The hands that created the
fragile pattern with needle and yarn would wield a scal-
pel on Monday.

"Oh, good." Anna glanced up as Serena entered. "I
thought I had timed well when I ordered the tea. Toss
another log on the fire, dear, then come tell me about
it."

As Serena moved to obey, Anna set her needlework
on the piecrust table beside her. The fire was already
crackling in the stone fireplace but roared at the addition of fresh wood. Serena watched the oak catch, then
breathed deeply. Until that moment she hadn't realized
how much she had missed the scent of burning wood.

"And a tub bath," she said aloud. Smiling, she
turned to her mother. "Isn't it strange that just now I
realize what an utter luxury it would be to soak in a
bath for as long as I wanted? After twelve months of
standing in a bucket that passed for a shower stall!"

"And you loved every minute of it."

Laughing, Serena sat on the hassock at Anna's feet.
"You know me so well. It was hard work and great
fun. But I'm glad to be home." She accepted the cup
and saucer Anna passed to her. "Mom, I know I'd
never have met so many people, so many different
kinds of people in my life if I hadn't done it."

"Your letters were always full of them. You should
read them over yourself one day to bring it all back."
Anna curled her legs under her and chuckled. "You'll

never know how hard it was to talk your father out of taking an ocean cruise.''

"When will he stop worrying?" Serena demanded.

"Never. It's part of the way he shows his love.''

"I know." With a sigh Serena sipped her tea. "If he'd just relax and let me take care of my life my own way…"

"Why don't you tell me what you thought of Justin." When Serena glanced up sharply, Anna only smiled. "No, I hadn't the faintest idea what your father was up to. He knew better than to tell me. Your…ah, discussion with him was quite penetrating.''

"Can you believe it!" Incensed all over again, Serena rose with the cup in her hand. "He actually duped Justin into that trip, hoping that I'd come home with stars in my eyes and orange blossoms in my brain. I've never been so furious, so *embarrassed.*''

"How did Justin take it?"

Serena gave her mother a disdainful look. "I think he found the whole thing very amusing after his initial shock. He had no idea who I was until we were arguing on the beach one day and I said my full name.''

Arguing on the beach, Anna mused. To conceal a smile, she sipped her tea. "I see. Your father thinks very highly of him, Rena. So do I. I suppose Daniel just couldn't resist the temptation.''

"He's infuriating.''

"Who?"

"Justin—both of them," she amended, setting down her cup with a snap. "He didn't tell me until the cruise was nearly over, and then in the most careless of ways. Why, I was actually beginning to…'' Trailing off, she turned away to stare at the fire.

"Beginning to?" Anna prompted gently.

"He's very attractive," Serena muttered. "I suppose it has something to do with his unapologetic ruthlessness and that damned charm that sneaks up on you." Wisely, Anna remained silent, speculating. "Even when he made me furious he stirred things up inside me that would have been more comfortable left alone. I've never felt that kind of passion before. I'm not certain I ever wanted to." Turning back, she found her mother watching her calmly. "We spent the last day together in St. Thomas. I would have gone to bed with him that night—until he told me about Dad's little scheme."

"How do you feel now?"

Serena looked down at her hands, then let out a long breath. "I still want him. I don't know if it's any more than that. How could it be when we knew each other less than two weeks?"

"Rena, do you really trust your instincts so little?" Her brow creased, Serena looked back up at her mother. "Why should emotions require a certain time pattern? They're as individual as the people they belong to. When I met your father I thought he was a conceited, loud-mouthed ox." At Serena's appreciative chuckle, Anna grinned girlishly. "Of course he was. I fell for him anyway. Two months later we were living together, and within a year we were married." She made a wry smile at the obvious shock on her daughter's face. "Passion and premarital sex aren't the exclusive property of your generation, my love. Daniel wanted to get married; I was determined to finish medical school first. The only thing we both agreed on was that we couldn't, and wouldn't live without each other."

Serena considered her mother's words while the fire snapped violently behind her. "How did you know it was love and not just desire?"

"Of all my children, you've always asked the most difficult questions." Leaning forward, Anna took her daughter's hands. "I'm not certain you can separate the two when it concerns a man and a woman. You can feel one without the other, but not when it's real love, not when it's real desire. Passion that comes quickly and then fades with time is only an echo. No substance, simply a result. Do you think you've fallen in love with Justin, or are you afraid you have?"

Serena opened her mouth, closed it, then tried again. "Both."

Anna gave Serena's hands a squeeze. "Don't tell your father; he'd be entirely too pleased with himself." This drew another reluctant laugh from Serena before Anna sat back again. "What do you intend to do about it?"

"I haven't thought about it. Rather, I've refused to think about it." She brought up her knees to rest her chin on them. "I suppose I've known all along that I'd have to see him again. He offered me a job."

"Oh?"

Serena moved her shoulders restlessly as ideas began to shift and sort in her mind. "Managing a casino in Atlantic City. It's a coincidence, because I'd decided to consult Dad about the possibility of opening my own gambling hotel."

"If Justin offered you a position like that, he must have a great deal of faith in your skill."

"I developed a knack for handling people," Serena mused as a thought focused.

"You developed it when you were two," her mother informed her.

"I've got a feel for the business," she went on with a hint of a smile on her lips. "I learned more than dealing cards this past year. In essence, the *Celebration* is one of the best run hotels I've ever seen, and though the casino's small-scale, all the basics are there. There wasn't any part of it I didn't learn from the inside out." She grew silent again as her smile widened. Anna recognized the look.

"What are you hatching, Rena?"

"I'm thinking of raising the bet," she answered. "Win, lose, or draw."

After tipping the bellboy, Justin stripped and headed for the shower. The maid could deal with the unpacking in the morning, and the casino could run another night without his attention. For now, he would have dinner in his suite while he made all the necessary phone calls to his other properties. With luck there would be no problems that couldn't be handled long distance. He had other things on his mind.

He adjusted the shower dial so that the water came out in pulsing jets. Serena would be home by this time, he reflected. And, if he knew her, Daniel would already be paying the price. Justin's grin came quickly, naturally. He'd have given a lot to have been within earshot during the reunion. It would almost make up for those last two long, boring, frustrating days aboard the *Celebration.*

Keeping his end of the bargain had been more difficult than Justin had imagined. To know she was within reach—dealing cards in the sophisticated tux, sleeping in that narrow bunk wearing only a flimsy handful of silk—had nearly driven him mad. But he'd stayed away because a deal was a deal—and because he had recognized that beneath her anger was a keen embarrassment that only time would lessen. The two weeks he'd given her should make her easier to negotiate with.

Even if she refused his offer, as he expected her to do initially, Justin didn't plan to leave it at that. He calculated he could taunt her to Atlantic City if necessary, and after she was there, he'd have house advantage. Flipping off the shower, he reached for a towel.

He needed a sharp manager downstairs. He needed a woman on the top floor. Serena was the only one who could fill both requirements. With the towel hooked around his waist, Justin walked into the bedroom.

Like the rest of the owner's suite, the room was spacious and sophisticated. The carpet beneath his bare feet was a thick, soft pewter. Long vertical blinds covered the glass doors to the balcony, and the touch of a button would swing them open, revealing a view of the Atlantic. He glanced at the wide bed covered in deep blue silk. How many women had slept in it? Justin neither knew nor cared. A night's mutual pleasure, they'd meant nothing more, nothing less.

From the closet he drew out a robe, letting the towel fall as he slipped into it. There had been years when he had lived in places smaller than this one single bedroom. He'd still had women. If he wanted one tonight, he had only to choose a number from his book and dial the phone. His body ached for one. Yet he knew that for the first time in his life just any woman wouldn't do.

Frustrated and restless, he roamed through the suite. He'd had good reason to base himself in the East. The Atlantic City operation was his newest, and the newest always required the most attention. It had never mattered to Justin where he lived. Over the years he'd grown used to the convenience of a hotel where his slightest wish would be seen to by the push of the right button. Now he found himself thinking about a home— something permanent, with grass to be tended and air that wasn't being shared with hundreds of other people.

Running a hand through his hair, Justin wondered why he should feel this vague dissatisfaction when he had everything he'd ever wanted. But his plans had never included wanting one woman. Was it because of her that he'd felt the lack of warmth when he'd entered his rooms again? If she were here, the echoing emptiness wouldn't be. She would fill it with temper and laughter. With passion.

Why had he given her two weeks? Justin asked himself angrily, stuffing his hands into the pockets of his robe. Why hadn't he badgered her into coming back with him, dragged her back so that he wouldn't be alone now, aching for her? He needed some contact with her—her voice over the phone. No, Justin thought more calmly, not her voice. That would only make matters more complicated. Going to the phone, he dialed Daniel MacGregor's private number.

"MacGregor."

"You old bastard," Justin said mildly.

"Ah, Justin." Daniel cast his eyes up at the ceiling,

knowing he was in for his second tongue-lashing of the day. "How was your trip?"

"Educational. I take it Serena's already spoken to you?"

"Thrilled to be home," Daniel stated, glancing wistfully at the broken cigars on his desk. "Speaks very highly of you."

"I'll bet she does." With a grim smile Justin sat on the plump sofa. "Wouldn't it have been simpler to have told me Serena worked on the ship?"

"Would you have taken the trip?"

"No."

"There, then," Daniel stated reasonably. "And I'm sure it did you a world of good. You've been tense, boy, restless." He contemplated trying to light one of the mutilated cigars. "And don't worry, I'll talk to Rena for you, calm her down a bit."

"No, you won't. I'm holding a case of Scotch hostage, Daniel, until I'm certain you'll stay out of it."

"Now, now, there's no need to do that. It's just parental concern for both of you." These two certainly knew where to stick the needle, he mused glumly. "Why don't you extend your vacation a few more days, Justin, pay us a visit here."

"Serena's going to come to me," he answered flatly.

"Come to you?" The wide forehead creased. "What do you mean by that?"

"What I said."

"All right, boy." His chest expanded. "You'd better tell me what your intentions are."

"No." Some of the tension eased from Justin's muscles. Enjoying himself, he leaned back.

"What do you mean no?" Daniel roared. "I'm her father."

"You're not mine. You dealt me this hand, Daniel, I'm playing it out."

"Now, listen here—"

"No," Justin said again, just as calmly. "I'm telling you to fold, Daniel. Serena and I are going double or nothing."

"You hurt that girl and I'll skin you alive."

Justin laughed. "If ever there was a woman who could take care of herself, it's Serena MacGregor."

"Aye." Pride swelled his heart and distracted him. "The girl's a pistol."

"Of course, if you think she's going to make a fool out of herself…"

"No child of mine makes a fool of herself!" Daniel snapped, making Justin grin.

"Fine, then you'll keep out of it."

Daniel ground his teeth and scowled at the receiver.

"Your word, Daniel."

"All right, all right. I wash my hands of it, but the minute I hear that you've—"

"Good-bye, Daniel."

Justin hung up, satisfied that he had paid back his benefactor in spades.

Chapter Seven

Justin kept his office suite on the ground floor of the Comanche, connected by a private elevator to his penthouse rooms. He found the arrangement convenient, his working hours were sporadic and there were times when he had no desire to pass through the public rooms of the hotel. The elevator was a practicality, as were the small television monitors in the far corners, and the two-way glass concealed behind the mahogany paneling on the side wall.

Because he demanded complete privacy in his own offices Justin worked in a large room without windows and with only one entrance. His experience in a cell had given him a long-standing aversion to closed-in places, so to compensate, he'd decorated his working area carefully. The furniture was light-colored—maize, oatmeal, biscuit—to give the appearance of airiness. The paintings were large and full of color. A desert scene caught in the last dying streaks of sun, the stark unforgiving peaks of the Rockies, a Comanche brave in full gallop on a war pony. The color, and the lack of it, gave Justin an illusion of freedom that counteracted the restlessness he sometimes felt when he found himself trapped behind a desk.

At the moment he was reviewing a stockholders' report that would please anyone holding shares in Blade Enterprises. Twice Justin caught himself reading and retaining nothing, and forced himself to begin again. Serena's two weeks were up, and so, he discovered, was his patience. If she didn't phone within the next twenty-four hours, he'd be on his way to Hyannis Port to hold her to her end of the bargain.

Damn, he didn't want to go chasing after her, Justin thought as he tossed the report back onto the desk. He'd never chased after a woman in his life, and he'd already come uncomfortably close to doing so with Serena since the beginning. He played his best game when his opponent made the offensive moves.

Opponent, Justin mused. He'd rather think of her that way. It was safer. But no matter how he thought of her, he went on thinking of her. No matter what he struggled to concentrate on, she was always there, just at the back of his mind, waiting to slip through the guards. Every time he thought of having a woman, Serena was on his mind, almost close enough to touch, to smell. Desire for her completely obliterated desire for anyone else. Frustrated, hungry, Justin had told himself to wait it out. Now, he decided, he'd waited long enough. Before the night was over he would have her.

As Justin reached for the phone to arrange for transportation north, a knock sounded at his door. "Yes."

Warned by the tone in the one syllable, his secretary

poked only her head through the doorway. "Sorry, Justin."

With an effort he directed his temper away from her. "What is it, Kate?"

"Telegram." She entered, a sleek, willowy brunette with a low-toned voice and sculptured features. "And Mr. Streeve's been hanging around outside. He wants you to extend his credit."

Justin took the telegram with a grunt. "What's he in for?"

"Five," she said, meaning five thousand.

As he tore open the envelope, Justin swore softly. "Jackass doesn't know when to quit. Who's on the floor?"

"Nero."

"Tell Nero Streeve's good for one more, then he's cut off. With luck he'll recoup a couple of thousand and be content with it."

"With his luck he'll be trying to trade his shares of AT&T for chips," Kate retorted. "Nothing worse than the spoiled rich who're temporarily short of fluid cash."

"We're not here to moralize," Justin reminded her. "Tell Nero to keep an eye on him."

"Okay." With a shrug Kate shut the door behind her.

Absently, Justin reached for the button that would slide the paneling clear of the two-way mirror. It would be wise if he kept his eye on Streeve as well. Before he could press it again, Justin's gaze fixed on the message line of the telegram.

Have considered your offer. Will arrive Thursday af-
ternoon to discuss terms. Please arrange for suitable
accommodations.

S. MacGregor

Justin read the brief message twice before a smile
tugged at his mouth. How like her, he thought. Short,
to the point, and beautifully vague. And well timed, he
added, leaning back. It was already past noon on Thursday. So, she was coming to discuss terms, he considered. Some small knot of tension unwound at the base
of his neck. Drawing out a cigar, Justin lit it thoughtfully. Terms, he reflected. Yes, they'd discuss terms,
keeping that area coolly businesslike.

He'd meant everything he had said to her when he'd
offered her the position. In his opinion, Serena was well
qualified to handle his staff and customers. He needed
someone on the floor who could make independent decisions, leaving him free to travel to his other opera-
tions when it became necessary. With the rest of the
hotels to oversee, he couldn't afford to spend all of his
time supervising the casino. Blowing out a thin stream
of smoke, Justin decided to make the job worth Serena's while. And once that was settled...

Once that was settled, he thought again, she'd have
to deal with him on a personal level. His eyes became
opaque, his long, thin mouth set. This time there'd be
no Daniel MacGregor playing the benevolent third
party with an ace up his sleeve. Tonight he and Serena
would begin a very private two-handed game. Justin's
eyes cleared with a quick laugh. Winning was his business.

Picking up the phone, he punched the button for the

front desk. "Front desk, Steve speaking. May I help you?"

"This is Blade."

The clerk automatically came to attention. "Yes, sir."

"A Miss MacGregor will be checking in this afternoon. Serena MacGregor. See that her bags are taken to the guest suite on my floor. She's to be brought directly to me."

"Yes, sir."

"Have the florist send some violets to her room."

"Yes, sir. A card?"

"No."

"I'll take care of it personally."

"Good." Satisfied, Justin hung up. Now all he had to do was wait. Picking up the stockholders' report again, he gave it his complete attention.

Serena handed the doorman her car keys and took her first long look at the Comanche. Justin hadn't gone for flashy or opulent, but had managed an excellent happy medium. The hotel was an open, V-shaped tower done in a drab adobe shade that brought a touch of the West to the East Coast. Serena approved the architecture, noting that nearly all the rooms had a view of the ocean. The drive circled around a two-level grottolike pool with its own miniature waterfall. Coins glistened in the bottom. Obviously there were plenty who were willing to risk some loose change for good luck.

Beside the main door was a lifesize Comanche chieftain in full headdress. No dime-store Indian, Serena mused, but an exquisite sculpture in black-veined white marble. Giving in to the urge to touch it, she ran a fingertip down the smooth stone chest. How like Justin not to choose the ordinary, she thought as she let her eyes drift up to the marble face. Was it her imagination, or was there some resemblance there? If the eyes were green... Shaking her head, Serena turned away.

While her bags were being unloaded, she used the time to take a look at the boardwalk.

Famous names in huge letters on white billboards, bold neon signs, quiet in the late afternoon light, huge hotel after huge hotel, fountains, traffic, noise. But it wasn't the same as Vegas, she decided. And it was more than just the absence of mountains and the sound of the sea in her ears. There seemed to be more of a carnival flavor here. This was still a resort, she concluded, with a beach at the back door. One could smell the gambling, but it carried the moist salt spray of the Atlantic with it, and the laughter of children building sand castles.

Adjusting the strap of her shoulder bag, Serena followed her luggage inside. There was no red carpet or glistening chandeliers, but rather subtle mosaic tile and indirect lighting. Both surprised and pleased, Serena noticed huge leafy plants in pottery jugs and wall hangings that clearly depicted the life and culture of the Plains Indian. Justin's heritage was more a part of him than he realized, she thought as she wandered toward the registration desk. She could hear the familiar sound of slot machines muted by distance and the click of her own heels on the tile floor. Passing a bill to the doorman, she turned to the desk clerk.

"Serena MacGregor."

"Yes, Miss MacGregor." He gave her a quick welcoming smile. "Mr. Blade is expecting you. Take Miss

MacGregor's bags to the guest suite in the penthouse," he told the bellhop, who was already hovering at her side. "Mr. Blade would like you to come right to his office, Miss MacGregor. I'll show you the way."

"Thank you." Nerves began to jump in her stomach, but Serena ignored them. She knew what she was going to do, and how she was going to do it. She'd had two weeks to work out her strategy. During the long drive from Massachusetts to New Jersey, she had gone over everything again and again. Once or twice she'd nearly given in to the urge to turn the car around and drive back north. She was taking an enormous risk with her future, and with her heart. Sooner or later she was going to be hurt. That was inevitable. But there was something she wanted in Atlantic City—and his name was Justin Blade.

She pressed her hand to her stomach once quickly, as if to push the nerves away as the desk clerk opened one of a pair of thick wooden doors marked Private. The brunette at an ebony desk glanced up in inquiry before her eyes rested on Serena.

"Miss MacGregor," the clerk announced.

"Yes, of course." Kate rose with a nod. "Thank you, Steve. Mr. Blade's expecting you, Miss Mac-Gregor, just let me tell him you're here."

So this was why the boss had been on a short fuse, Kate concluded, giving Serena a cool, appraising look as she lifted the interoffice phone. She took in the long golden hair swept back at the temples with two ivory combs, the strong, elegant features accented by large violet eyes, the slim figure in a raw silk suit a few shades darker than irises. Very classy, Kate decided,

and as Serena met her stare without flinching, added—
and no pushover.

"Miss MacGregor's here, Justin. Of course." She
cradled the receiver, giving Serena a smile that stopped
just short of friendly. "Right this way, Miss Mac-
Gregor." Leading the way, Kate opened another door.
Serena paused beside her.

"Thank you, Miss..."

"Wallace," Kate responded automatically.

"Thank you, Miss Wallace." Serena took the door
handle herself and gently closed it behind her. Kate
stared at the knob a moment, realizing she had been
expertly dismissed. More intrigued than annoyed, she
went back to her desk.

"Serena." Justin leaned back in his chair. Why had
he expected something to change? he wondered
quickly. Somehow he had thought he'd be prepared for
the onslaught of feeling simply seeing her brought to
him. Every hour of the past two weeks vanished in one
instant.

"Hello, Justin." She prayed he wouldn't offer his
hand, as her own palms were damp. "You have quite
a place here."

"Sit down." He gestured to the chair in front of his
desk. "Would you like something? Coffee?"

"No." With a polite smile she crossed the room to
sit in a chair of buttery buckskin leather. "I appreciate
your taking the time to see me right away."

He only lifted a brow at this. They'd circled each
other for a while, he mused, like a pair of boxers studying defenses in the early rounds. "How was your
flight?"

"I drove," she answered. "It was something I

missed doing this past year. The weather was lovely,"
she added, determined to keep the trite conversation
going until her nerves settled.

"And your family?"

"My parents are fine. I wasn't able to see Alan or
Caine." Serena gave her first hint of a genuine smile.
"My father sends his best."

"He's still among the living then?"

"I found more subtle ways of revenge." With grim
pleasure, Serena thought of the broken cigars.

"You're adjusting to land life?" Unable to resist the
urge, Justin dropped his gaze to her mouth for a moment. It was untouched by lipstick and faintly moist.

"Yes, but not to unemployment." She could feel the
brush of heat across her lips and the answering warmth
that kindled in the pit of her stomach. She found herself
wanting to go to him, to take whatever he would give
on whatever terms he offered. Just to be held again, to
have those lean, clever hands touch her. Carefully, she
folded her own in her lap. "That's what I want to talk
to you about."

"The position of casino manager's still open," he
said easily, though he took his time bringing his eyes
back to hers. "The hours are long, though I don't think
you'll find them as all-consuming as on the ship. Generally, there's no need for you to be on the floor before
five, though naturally you can adjust that from time to
time if you need an evening off. There's a certain
amount of paperwork, of course, but for the most part
you'd be directing the staff and handling the customers.
You'd have your own office on the other side of the
reception area. When you're not needed on the floor,

you can supervise from there. There are monitors," he continued, gesturing. "And a more direct view."

Justin pressed a button, releasing the paneling. Serena glanced through the glass to watch the crowd in the casino, gambling, talking, wandering, in silent movie effect. "You'll have an assistant," Justin went on. "He's competent, but not authorized to make independent decisions. A suite of rooms is included in your salary. When I'm away from the hotel you'll have complete authority over the casino...within my framework of rules."

"That seems clear enough." Unclenching her hands, Serena made herself relax. She gave Justin a mild, friendly smile. "I'd consider taking over the managerial duties of the casino, Justin...as your partner."

She saw a flicker, but only a flicker of surprise in his eyes before he leaned back. With anyone else it would have been a gesture of relaxation. With Justin it seemed a preparation for action. "My partner?"

"In the Atlantic City Comanche," she returned calmly.

"I need a manager for the casino, Serena; I don't need a partner."

"And I don't need a job, or a salary for that matter," she countered. "I'm fortunate enough to have financial independence, but I'm not of a nature to stay idle. I took the job on the *Celebration* as an experiment, I don't need to take another job for the same reasons. I'm looking for something I have a bit more of a stake in."

"You said once you were considering looking for work in a casino when you left the ship."

"No." She smiled again and shook her head. "You

misunderstood me. I was thinking of opening my own place.''

"Your own place?" With a quick laugh he relaxed again. "Do you have any idea just what that involves?"

Her chin came up. "I think I do. I've just spent a year of my life working and living on what was essentially a floating gambling resort. I know how a kitchen's run to accommodate over fifteen hundred people, how housekeeping keeps ahead of the linen supply, and how to stock a wine cellar. I know when a dealer's feeling under par and needs to be relieved and how to convince a customer to find another game before he gets nasty. There was little more for me to do on that ship than learn. And I learn very quickly."

Justin considered the coldly furious tone of her voice, the hard, determined light in her eyes. She could probably do it successfully enough, he decided after a moment. She had the guts, the drive, and the bankroll. "Taking all of that into consideration," he began slowly, "why should I take you on as a partner?"

Rising, Serena walked over to the glass. "Do you see the dealer on table five?" she asked, tapping a finger against the window.

Curious, Justin rose and joined her. "Yes, why?"

"She has excellent hands—fast, steady. It looks to me as though she's worked out a very comfortable rhythm without appearing to rush the players along. She doesn't belong working midweek afternoons. You need dealers like that during the heavy traffic. The croupier at the crap table looks bored to death. He needs to be fired or given a raise."

"Clarify that one for me."

Because there was a touch of humor in his voice,

Serena grinned up at him. "Given a raise if he takes the hint to be a bit more personable. Fired if he doesn't. Your casino staff should reflect the same attitude as the rest of the hotel staff."

"A good point," he admitted. "And a good reason for wanting you as my casino manager. It doesn't cover your partnership."

Serena turned her back on the silent world behind the glass. "A few more reasons then. When you're needed out west, or in Europe, you'll know you're leaving someone in charge who has a vested interest—not only in the casino, but in the whole operation. I did a bit of research," she added. "If Blade Enterprises continues to grow at its current rate, you'll have to have someone help shoulder some of the responsibility. Unless, of course, you chose to work twenty-four hours a day making money without any time to enjoy your success. The money I'm willing to invest would give you enough fluid cash to sweeten your bid on that casino in Malta."

Justin's brow rose. "You have done your research," he commented dryly.

"We Scots never do business blindfolded." She gave him a satisfied smile. "The point is I have no intention of working *for* you or anyone else. For half interest I'll run the casino, *and* pick up the slack in other areas when necessary."

"Half," he murmured, narrowing his eyes.

"Equal partners, Justin." She met his eyes on level. "That's the only way you'll get me."

Silence came quickly and completely, and Serena forced herself to control her breathing to a slow, even rate. She wouldn't let him know how nervous she was or let herself think how easy it would be to forget pride and run into his arms. What had begun the last time they had been together had been quietly accomplished during their separation. She'd fallen in love with him when he hadn't even been around to tempt her. But he wouldn't know—she wouldn't allow him to know—until she was ready.

"Suppose you take some time to think it over," she said at length. "My plans are flexible," Serena went on as she walked to retrieve her purse from the chair. "I'd intended to look into some property here while I'm in town."

When Justin's fingers curled around her arm, Serena made herself turn slowly. He was going to call her bluff, she was certain of it. And when he did, she'd have the choice of folding, or riding it out.

"Anytime during the first year that I decide it isn't working, I can buy you out."

She struggled against a shout of laughter. "Agreed," she told him quietly.

"I'll have my lawyer draw up a draft of an agreement. In the meantime you can get your feet wet in there." He jerked his head toward the casino. "You should have a week or so to change your mind."

"I have no intention of changing my mind, Justin. When I make a decision, I stick to it." Their eyes met again in a long, cautious stare. Serena held out her hand. "A deal then?"

Justin glanced at her hand, then slowly closed his over it. He held it, as though making a pact, then brought it to his lips. "A deal, Serena," he said. "Though we might both be sorry for it."

"I'll go up and change." She drew her hand away from his. "I'll work the casino tonight."

"Tomorrow's soon enough." Justin moved ahead of her to the door, closing his fingers over hers on the knob.

"I'd rather not waste time," she said simply. "If you could introduce me to my assistant and a few of the croupiers, I should manage from there."

"Whatever you want."

"Give me an hour to change and unpack then." Wanting to break contact, Serena twisted the knob.

"We have other things to talk about, Serena."

The words seemed to flutter along her skin. Aching with need, she turned back to him. "Yes," she said quietly. "But I'd rather we cleared up the business preliminaries first, so it's clear one thing has nothing to do with the other."

Watching her, Justin caught the collar of her suit between his thumb and forefinger. "I'm not sure that one hasn't very much to do with the other," he murmured. "And that both of us aren't fools for pretending otherwise."

The pulse at the base of her throat began to hammer visibly. But even as he noted it, her voice became strong and clear. "We'll both find out soon enough, won't we?"

With a slow smile, Justin dropped his hand. "Yes, we will. I'll see you in an hour."

It was going to be hard work, Serena discovered quickly. Every bit as hard as her work on the *Celebration*. But this time, she mused as she glanced around the crowded, noisy casino, she had her own stake. She signed her name to a cash receipt one of the croupiers brought her and felt a small glow of pleasure. Part of the life pulsing around her at that moment belonged to her.

Adjustments would take time, she reminded herself as she noted a few speculative glances aimed her way. When Justin had introduced her as his partner, Serena had almost heard the wheels turning inside each brain. She would simply have to prove herself qualified for the position no matter what happened between her and Justin personally. Rule number one was confidence. Rule number two was tenacity. When applied together, Serena considered them an unbeatable combination— not unlike the formula she used to handle her father.

Her assistant, Nero, was a big, quiet black man, who had taken the news of Serena's interest in the hotel with a silent shrug. She learned that he had worked in Justin's first casino as a bouncer, and in one capacity or another, had worked in all of Justin's properties. With as few words as possible he took Serena through the casino, gave her the basic routine, then left her alone. He was one man, she concluded, who wouldn't be won over easily.

Catching a signal from one of the dealers, Serena crossed the room. Before she was halfway to the table she heard the angry raised voice. It took only a glance to determine the man in question was very unlucky and more than a little unhappy about it.

"Excuse me." Giving the players at the table a general smile, Serena moved to stand beside the croupier. "Is there a problem?"

"You bet there is, sweetheart." The man on the end leaned over and took her wrist. "Who are you?"

Serena allowed her eyes to lower to his hand, then brought them slowly back to his face. "I'm the owner."

He gave a quick laugh before he drained his glass. "I've seen the owner, lady. He doesn't look anything like you."

"My partner," Serena informed him with an icy smile. Out of the corner of her eye she caught Nero's movement toward her, and imperceptibly shook her head. "Is there something I can help you with?"

"I've dropped a bundle at this table tonight," he told her. "My friends here'll vouch for that."

The other players ran the gamut between looking bored or annoyed. All of them ignored him.

"Would you care to cash in the rest of your chips?" she asked politely.

"I want a chance to make some back," he countered, setting down his empty glass. "This joker won't raise the limit."

Serena glanced at the poker-faced croupier and saw the dregs of fury in his eyes. "Our dealers aren't authorized to raise the table limit, Mr...?"

"Carson, Mick Carson, and I'd like to know what kind of operation this is where a man can't have a chance of getting even."

"As I said," Serena returned calmly, "the dealers aren't authorized to up the limit, but I am. How much did you have in mind, Mr. Carson?"

"That's more like it," he said, and signaled for another drink. Serena gave a small shake of her head to the roaming cocktail waitress. "Five thousand on the hand." He sent Serena a hard grin. "That should balance things out. I'll sign for it."

"All right. Bring Mr. Carson his tab, Nero," she ordered, sensing he stood within earshot. "You can play the single hand for five thousand, Mr. Carson." Serena shot him a level look. "And if you lose, you call it a night."

"All right, honey." He took her wrist again, letting his eyes travel down the length of the sleek ruby dress. "And if I win, why don't you and I go and have a quiet drink somewhere?"

"Don't press your luck, Mr. Carson," Serena warned him with a smile on her face.

Chuckling, he took the clipboard Nero brought to him, then scrawled his name. "Never any harm in trying, honey. Oh, no," he added when Serena stepped aside. "You deal."

Without a word Serena took the croupier's place. It was then she caught sight of Justin standing to the side, watching her. *Damn!* She met his eyes briefly, wondering if she had let her annoyance get in the way of judgment. With another glance at Carson she told herself it would be worth the five thousand to get rid of him peacefully.

"Bets?" she asked, letting her eyes skim the other players as she counted out Carson's chips. By unanimous consent the others at the table abstained.

"Just you and me," Carson said, sliding his chips forward. "Deal."

Silently, Serena dealt him a seven and a two. A glance at her hole card revealed twelve with nine showing.

"Hit," Carson ordered, reaching absently for his empty glass. She turned up a queen. "Stand," he said, and sent her a wide, mirthless smile.

"Stand on nineteen." Serena turned up her hole card. "Twelve...fifteen," she continued as she turned up a three. Without pausing she drew out a five. "Twenty." Carson let out his breath in an oath. "Come back again, Mr. Carson," she said coolly, and waited for him to stand.

He eyed her a moment as she calmly raked in his chips, then rising, walked out of the casino without a word.

"I apologize for the inconvenience." Serena smiled at the other players before she nodded to the dealer.

"You did that real smooth, Miss MacGregor," Nero mumbled as she walked past him.

Stopping, Serena turned back. "Thank you, Nero. And it's Rena." She had the pleasure of seeing him flash her a smile before she walked to Justin. "Were you ready to have me committed?" she asked him quietly.

Justin looked down at her, then idly twirled the end of a lock of hair around his finger. "You know, I wanted you here for a variety of reasons. That was one of them."

Pleased, she laughed. "What if I'd lost?"

Justin shrugged. "Then you'd've lost. You'd still have handled a potentially uncomfortable situation with the minimal of fuss. And with style," he murmured, scanning her face. "I do admire your style, Serena MacGregor."

"Strange." She could feel the change inside her even as it happened—the softening, the heating. The wanting. "I've always admired yours."

"You're tired." Justin ran a thumb lightly under her eyes where the faintest of shadows was forming.

"A little," she admitted. "What time is it?"

"Around four."

"No wonder. The trouble with these places is that you lose track of day and night."

"You've already put in more than your share," he told her as he began to lead her through the casino. "What you need is some breakfast."

"Mmm."

"I take it that means you're hungry."

"I hadn't noticed, but since you mention it, I think I'm starving." Serena looked back over her shoulder as he nudged her through the doors of his outer office. "But isn't the restaurant the other way?"

"We'll have breakfast up in my suite."

"Oh, wait a minute." With another laugh she pulled up short. "I think the restaurant'll be a lot smarter."

Justin studied her a moment, then reached into his pocket.

"Oh, Justin—"

"Heads, my suite, tails the restaurant."

With lowered brows she held out her hand. "Let me see that coin." Taking it from him, Serena examined both sides. "All right, I'm too hungry to argue. Flip it."

With a deft movement of his thumb, he did. Serena waited until it lay on the back of his hand, then let out a sigh. "We'll take the elevator up," Justin said blandly.

Chapter Eight

I'm still going to beat you one of these days," Serena said with a yawn as Justin pressed the button for the penthouse. "And when I do, it's going to be worth more than breakfast." She glanced around at the smoky mirrored walls. "You know, I hardly noticed the elevator when I was in your office."

"It's an escape route," he said, then gave her a small smile when she looked at him. "We all need one occasionally."

"I don't suppose I thought you would." She remembered the two-way glass in his office and sighed. "Do they crowd you at times, Justin? All those people only a thin wall away?"

"More lately than they used to," he admitted. "I suppose you felt the same way on the boat occasionally. Isn't that why you went out on deck when everyone else was asleep?"

She answered by lifting her shoulders. "Well, I'll have to get used to it if I'm going to be living here. In any case, I've always seemed to live in a crowd." When the doors slid open, Serena stepped through. "Justin, this is really lovely."

He used bolder colors in his personal rooms, slashes of indigo in the cushions of a low, spreading sofa, the flash of chartreuse in the shade of a glass lamp. For balance there were sketches in pastel chalks and a beveled mirror in a gilt frame.

"You can relax here," Serena decided, picking up a carved figure of a hawk in mid-dive. "It hardly seems like a hotel at all with your personal things around."

Oddly, when he saw her with her hands on what was his, Justin felt his first intimacy with the room. To him, it had always been a living arrangement, nothing more, nothing less. A place to go when he wasn't working. He had similar rooms in other hotels. They were comfortable, private and, he realized suddenly, empty. Until now.

"Of course, my suite is very nice," Serena went on, roaming at will to touch or examine whatever came to hand. "But I'll feel more settled in once I spread some of my own things around. I think I'll have my mother ship me my writing desk and a few other pieces." Turning, she found him watching her in the still, silent manner he could so easily slip into. Suddenly nervous, Serena set down a small glass bowl of cobalt blue.

"What sort of view do you have?" Serena moved toward the window, and had taken the first step up onto the small raised platform in front of it before she noticed that the glass table was already set. Lifting the cover from one of the plates, Serena saw a hearty Mexican omelet, a rasher of bacon, and a corn muffin. With a tilt of the lid on a silver serving pot, the aroma of fresh coffee filled the room. Beside the table was an ice bucket of champagne.

"Well, imagine that," Serena murmured as she slipped the single rosebud from its crystal vase. "Look what the good fairy left, Justin. Amazing!"

"And they say miracles are a thing of the past."

"You want to hear a miracle?" Serena asked him, passing the bud under her nose. "It's a miracle I don't dump this coffee over your head."

"I prefer to take it internally," he murmured as he crossed the room to join her. "Do you like your rose?"

"This is the second time you've made my eating arrangements before consulting me," she began.

"You were hungry last time, too," he reminded her.

"That's not the point."

"What is?"

Serena took a deep, frustrated breath and was assaulted by the aroma of hot food. "I knew what it was a minute ago," she muttered. "How did you manage to have it here, all hot and ready?"

"I called room service before I came out to the casino to see if you needed rescuing." Draping a cloth over the bottle, he deftly removed the champagne cork.

"Very clever." Surrendering to hunger, Serena sat. Propping her elbows on the table, she set her chin on her folded hands. "Champagne for breakfast?"

"It's the best time for it." Justin filled two glasses before he joined her.

"*If* I decide to overlook your arrogance," Serena considered as she cut into the omelet, "this is really very nice of you—in an underhanded fashion."

"You're welcome," he murmured, lifting his glass.

After the first bite, Serena closed her eyes in silent

appreciation. "And it's easy to overlook arrogance on an empty stomach. Either I'm starving, Justin, or this is the best omelet every made."

"I'll give the chef your approval."

"Mmm. I'll have to take a look at the kitchen tomorrow, and the nightclub," she added over another mouthful. "I noticed you have Chuck Rosen for a week run. There shouldn't be an empty seat."

"I have him signed for an exclusive two-year contract." Justin broke a muffin in half. "He's a guaranteed sellout in all the hotels."

"That was a wise investment," Serena mused. "You know..." Lifting her wine, she studied him over the rim. "You're exactly what I thought you were when you sat down at my table the first time, and yet, you're nothing like I thought you were."

Sipping, Justin returned her gaze. "What did you think I was?"

"A professional gambler—which, of course, was accurate. But..." Serena trailed off and drank again. Justin was right, she mused. Champagne had never tasted better. "I didn't see you as a man who could build up and run a chain of places like this."

"No?" Amused, he toyed with his meal as he watched her. "What then?"

"I think I saw you as sort of a nomad. Which again is partially accurate because of your heritage, but I didn't consider you as a man who'd want the sort of responsibility hotels like these require. You're an interesting mix, Justin, of the ruthless and the responsible; the hard and"—she picked up the rosebud again—"the sweet."

"No one's ever accused me of being that before," Justin murmured as he filled her glass again.

"Of what?"

"Of being sweet."

"Well, it's not one of your dominating virtues," she mumbled into her wine. "I suppose that's why it throws me off when it comes through."

"It gives me great pleasure to throw you off." His finger trailed down the back of her hand to her wrist. "I've found a certain…weakness for vulnerability."

Determinedly, she took another swallow of wine. "I'm not vulnerable as a rule."

"No," he agreed. "Perhaps that's why it's all the more rewarding that I can cause you to be. Your pulse jumps when I touch you here," he whispered, grazing a finger over the inside of her wrist.

A bit unsteadily, Serena set down her glass. "I should go."

But he rose with her, and now his fingers were laced with hers. His eyes, when hers met them, were very calm and very confident. "I made myself a promise this afternoon, Serena," he told her quietly. "That I'd make love with you before the night was over." Taking a step closer, Justin captured her other hand. "We still have an hour before sunrise."

It was what she wanted. Every pore of her body seemed to be crying out with need. Yet if his hands hadn't held hers so firmly, she would have backed away. "Justin, I won't deny that I want you, but I think it would be best if we gave it some more time."

"Reasonable," he agreed as he drew her into his arms. "Time's up." He stopped her protesting laugh with his lips.

There was no food to stop this hunger. His mouth was hard, devouring, before Serena could respond or struggle away. Yet she knew as he crushed her body to his that this time he would permit no struggle. She tasted his lips, and tasted urgency. She felt the firm, long lines of his body and felt need.

When his tongue sought hers there was no easy teasing, no gentle testing, but a desperate demand for intimacy. *Now,* he seemed to say to her. *There's no turning back.* What had begun weeks before with a long, cool meeting of eyes would reach its culmination. It would happen, Serena thought dizzily, because neither of them wanted any other answer.

Through those first urgent stirrings of passion she felt a quiet joy. She loved. And love, she realized, was the ultimate adventure. Placing her hands on either side of his face, she carefully drew her lips away from his, then looked into his eyes, warmer now with need for her. She wanted a moment, only a moment to clear her head, to say what she wanted to say without the heat of passion racing through her. Gently, she traced her fingers over the long, strong bones of his face. His heart thudded against her breast as hers began to calm. A smile touched the lips that were warm and aching from his.

"This," she told him quietly, "is what I want, what I choose."

Justin said nothing as he stared down at her. The simple words were more seducing than her soft summer scent, than the hot pulsing taste. They weakened him, exposing vulnerabilities he'd never considered. Suddenly, there was more than passion raging through him.

Bringing his hand to hers, he slid it to his mouth, pressing his lips against the palm.

"I've thought of nothing but you for weeks," he said. "Wanted no one but you." He ran a hand down the length of her hair before his fingers closed over it in a fist. Need—good God, when had he ever felt such need? "Come to bed, Serena, I can't do without you any longer."

Her eyes were calm as she offered him her hand. Without words, they walked to the bedroom. The room was in shadows, accented by the faint light that signals the end of night. And it was silent, so silent that Serena could hear her own breath as it began to quicken. When she felt Justin move away from her she stood resolute, suddenly tingling with nerves.

He wouldn't be gentle, she thought as she remembered the feel of his mouth and hands on her. As a lover he would be equally thrilling and terrifying. She heard a sharp scrape, then saw the flare of a match as he held it to the wick of a candle. The shadows danced.

Her eyes were drawn to him. In the flickering yellow light his face held a dangerous beauty. He seemed to belong more to his Indian ancestors now than to the world she understood. And she knew at that instant why the captive woman had fought against, then remained willingly with her captor.

"I want to see you," Justin murmured, reaching out to bring her into the candlelight. With surprise he felt the quiver run through her. Only moments before she had seemed so strong, so sure. "You're trembling."

"I know." She took a deep breath and exhaled quickly. "It's silly."

"No." He felt a streak of power, sharp and clean.

Serena MacGregor wasn't a woman to tremble for any man. But for him, even as the fire lit in her eyes, her body shuddered. Taking her hair in his hand, Justin drew her head back. In the shifting light his eyes glistened with fierce, almost savage, desire. "No," he said again, then crushed her mouth to his.

She seemed to melt into him. Justin thought he could feel her bones soften, liquefy, until she was totally pliant in his arms. For the moment he would accept surrender, but soon he would have more, much more. With his mouth still avid on hers he began to undress her. Forgetting the fragile material, he tugged, pausing only to mold, inch by inch, the flesh he uncovered. She was shuddering now, pulling at the buttons of his shirt as her dress slid down to pool at her feet.

He'd known she would wear something soft and filmy. With a fingertip Justin nudged the thin straps of her camisole off her shoulders. But he didn't remove it—not yet. He wanted the pleasure of feeling silk between them. He tormented her, running hot, nibbling kisses over her face as she struggled to undress him. Her fingers touching his flesh wrenched a groan from him that he muffled against her throat.

Then she was beneath him on the bed, with only a fragile wisp of material separating them. He felt a madness, a driving need to take her swiftly that he had to fight back. Her breasts were small and firm in his hand, straining against the silk as he rained kiss after savage kiss on her lips. Consumed by her, Justin drove her mercilessly to the first peak with only his hands and mouth. Swallowing her gasps, he pressed his body down on hers so that her frantic movements blended into him. Then ruthlessly, he slid down to capture her silk-clad breast in his mouth.

Struggling for air, Serena arched against him. Her body shuddered from a hundred unexpected sensations. She was trapped in a world of silk and fire. At her every movement, the bedspread caressed her naked back and legs, whispering of dark promises. Her flesh was seared wherever he had touched, as though he'd carried the tiny gold flame of the candle in his fingers. As he wet the silk above her straining nipple with his tongue, she felt the fire leap into her. Like a voice from a distance she heard him murmuring her name, and more she couldn't understand.

As if he'd lost patience with any barrier, Justin drew the chemise down to her waist so that he could feast on her naked skin. Serena pressed him closer, her hands now as demanding as his. Though her mouth ached for the taste of him, her body thrilled to the desperate race of his lips over her skin. She knew only pleasure now, the steamy pleasure of unrelenting passion. Gone were restrictions and rules; here was the abandonment she had glimpsed briefly in a dream.

It was only now that she realized there was so much she didn't know, so much she'd never felt. Second by second there were new discoveries. As his mouth tarried just above the line of silk, she felt a hunger deeper than any she'd ever experienced. Her imagination ran wild, thoughts of him inside her, filling her, dreams of a pleasure so acute they brought a tug of pain between her thighs. Delirious, she clutched at his shoulders.

"Take me," she demanded on a ragged breath. "Justin, take me now."

But he continued driving her higher, as if he hadn't

heard her plea. He drew the silk down, caressing the newly exposed flesh with his lips—over the flat, quivering stomach, over the smooth curve of hip, to the taut, arching muscles of her inner thigh.

She arched, crying out, thrown swiftly into the river of passion. He was relentless, as terrifying a lover as she had feared, as thrilling as she'd dreamed. She was all that he wanted—soft and moist and out of control. Desperate, demanding, she clutched at him, scraping his flesh with those sleek, elegant nails. He could hear her moans, her incoherent words rasping out of her throat as he drove her further and further toward madness. Her skin was damp, beaded with passion, while her hips thrust her need toward him again and again. Now she was his, mindlessly his. And he knew, somehow, that no one had ever taken her more completely. Fighting to hold the power a moment longer, he ranged himself above her. Serena gripped his hips, urging him on.

In the first touch of daylight her face was like porcelain. Her eyes were closed, her lips parted as each breath trembled through them. Half crazed with need, he vowed no man would ever see her as he saw her at that moment.

"Look at me," Justin demanded in a voice harsh with passion. "Look at me, Serena."

She opened her eyes, and they were glazed with pleasure, dark with need.

"You're my woman." He slipped inside her and nearly lost control. "There'll be no going back for you now."

"Or for you." Her eyes lost focus as the two of them began to move together.

Justin struggled to comprehend what she had said, but she was moving faster. Burying his face in her hair, he swirled toward the madness.

Dawn streamed through the wide window in a flood of rose-gold light. With Justin's head still nestled at her throat, Serena watched it play over the length of his back. It looked like what she felt like, she discovered. Bright and rich and new. Was there a better way to watch the sunrise than with your lover's body warm on yours? Sleep...She felt no need for it. She knew she could lie like this for hours with the sun growing brighter and the sound of his breathing gentle in her ear. With a sigh sweetened by contentment, she ran her hands up his back.

At her touch Justin lifted his head. With their faces close he looked at her, letting his eyes roam feature by feature until there was nothing in his mind but her face, flushed and soft from loving. Without a word he lowered his mouth to hers in the butterfly touch he used so rarely. Gently, almost reverently, he brushed kisses over her eyelids, her temples, her cheeks, until Serena felt unexpected tears rise in her throat. Beneath his her body felt fluid and free.

"I thought I knew what it would be like," he whispered, touching his lips to hers again. "I should have realized with you, nothing's as I expect it." Raising his head again, he traced a fingertip under her eye. "You should sleep."

She smiled and brushed at the hair on his forehead. "I don't think I'll ever sleep again. I know I never want to miss another sunrise."

He kissed her lightly, then, rolling from her, brought her close to his side. "I want you with me, Serena."

Content, she snuggled closer. "I am with you."

"I want you to live with me," he corrected her, tilting her chin up so that he could see her eyes. "Here. It's not enough to know you're in a room down the hall." Then he paused, running his thumb over her lips. "There'll be talk downstairs, speculation."

Resting her head on his shoulder again, Serena began to trace a finger across his chest. "Talk won't stop downstairs once your name's linked with Daniel MacGregor's daughter," she told him.

"No." She heard the change in tone and knew that if she looked, his eyes would be unfathomable. "The press would find the relationship interesting, considering my background and reputation—as opposed to yours."

"Justin..." She trailed a finger down the center of his torso, then back up again. "Are you asking me to live with you or warning me not to?"

For a long moment he was silent while Serena continued to trace lazy patterns over his chest. "Both," he answered at length.

"I see. Well"—she turned her head so that she was free to nibble on his neck—"I suppose I should think about it." She felt a quiver of response as her hand ran low over his stomach. "Weigh the pros and cons," she continued, working kisses up his jawline. Shifting, she lay across him, her face just above his. "I don't suppose you could run through the pros and cons for me." With a smile she pressed her lips to his. "Just to refresh my memory."

"In the interest of helping you make an intelligent decision," he began, sliding a hand down to her hip.

"Mmm-hmm." But even as he sought to deepen the

kiss, she moved, finding the vulnerable spot below his ear. "Did you know I was captain of the debate team my senior year at Smith?"

"No." His eyes shut as the heady sensation of being seduced took over.

"Give me a subject," she said, sliding her fingertips down his ribs, "and the time for…research," she added as she nipped gently at his throat. "And I can argue either side of the issue. Now, as I see it…" She gave a sigh of pleasure as she pressed her lips to the fast, jerky pulse at the base of his throat. "Living with you entails a great many inconveniences." His hand roamed over her hip, slipping between her thighs. Serena slid farther down his body, frustrating him.

"Serena—"

"No, I have the floor," she reminded him, then flicked her tongue over his chest. "I'd lose my privacy, and a great deal of sleep," she said, reveling in the quickening of his breath as she boldly explored his body. "I'd risk the inevitable gossip and speculation of my new employees as well as the press."

As muscles bunched and flowed under her hands, beneath her seeking lips, she lost her train of thought. Like the marble sculpture of the chieftain, she thought hazily as her blood began to pound. "You'd be impossible to live with," she concluded, lost somewhere between her own initiative and the savage beauty of his naked body. "Demanding, infuriating, and because I find you so incredibly attractive, I'd never have a moment's peace of mind."

She moved back up him, letting her body please itself by rubbing sinuously against his on the journey. Her smile was slow and seductive as she saw his eyes were fixed on her face. "Give me one good reason why I should, after considering all that, live with you."

His breathing wasn't steady, but he couldn't control it. The hand that grabbed her hair wasn't gentle, but he couldn't stop it either. "I want you."

Serena lowered her lips until they were an inch from his. "Show me," she demanded.

Even as her mouth came down to his, Justin was rolling her over roughly, beyond reason. He thrust into her quickly, wrenching a cry from her that turned to gasping moans as he drove her harder and faster. With mindless, grasping greed he took and took, but the hunger only seemed to feed upon itself, growing and swelling as her legs and arms tangled around him. He was drenched with sweat, trapped in those soft white limbs, unable to breathe, unable to break free. And it was her name that shouted over and over in his mind.

His body seemed to shake with the sound, threatening to explode with the desperate repetition of her name. Then the word shattered into tiny fragments. He knew he would never be rid of them, then he knew nothing but the shuddering relief of fulfillment.

Dazed, he slept, with his body and mind tangled with her.

The phone woke him barely four hours later. Beside him, Serena stirred, sighed, and mumbled an oath. Keeping one arm around her, Justin stretched out the other and plucked up the receiver.

"Yes?" Glancing down, he saw that Serena had opened heavy eyes to stare at him. He brushed the top of her head with his lips. "When?" Seeing him tense, she pushed up on her elbow. "Have they evacuated? No, I'll handle it...I'll be down in a few minutes."

"What is it?"

Justin was already out of bed and heading for the closet. "Bomb threat in Vegas." He grabbed the first thing that came to hand—jeans and a cashmere sweater.

"Oh, God!" Serena was scrambling up, searching for her lingerie. "When?"

"The phone call said it would detonate at three thirty-five Vegas time unless we deliver a quarter of a million in cash. That doesn't give us a hell of a lot of time," he muttered, snapping his jeans. "They're still evacuating."

"You're not going to pay." Fury in her eyes, Serena pulled the chemise over her head.

Justin watched her in silence for a moment, then smiled—as cold and sharp as a knife. "I'm not going to pay."

As he strode into the next room, Serena dashed after him. "I'll be down as soon as I change."

"There's nothing for you to do."

The elevator doors were already opening as she grabbed his arm. "I'll be with you."

For an instant his features softened. "Hurry then," he told her, giving her a quick, hard kiss before he stepped into the car.

In less than ten minutes Serena was rushing through the reception area into Justin's office. He glanced up as she entered, but gave her no more than a nod as he continued talking in quiet tones into the phone. Kate stood beside the desk, her hands clenched, her usually composed face strained. "Miss MacGregor," she said curtly without taking her eyes from Justin.

"Could you fill me in, please?"

"Some nut claims he has a bomb rigged somewhere in the Vegas hotel. He's supposed to have a remote device that will set it off in"—she glanced at her watch—"an hour and fifteen minutes. They're evacuating, and the bomb squad's sweeping the place, but..."

"But?" Serena prompted.

"Do you have any idea how big that hotel is?" Kate demanded in a shaking voice. "How small and deadly a bomb can be?"

Saying nothing, Serena walked to the bar at the far end of the room and poured a snifter of brandy. She brought it back to Kate, pushing it into her hands. "Drink this," she ordered.

With a shudder, Kate tilted the snifter back until it was empty. "Thank you." She pressed her lips together a moment, then looked back at Serena. "I'm sorry. My husband lost an arm in Vietnam—a booby trap. This..." She let out a long breath. "This brings it all back."

"Come on, sit down," Serena said more gently as she urged her onto the sofa. "There's nothing to do now but wait."

"Justin's not going to pay," Kate murmured.

"No." Serena shot her a surprised look. "Do you think he should?"

Kate dragged a hand through her hair. "I'm not objective about things like this, but"—she brought her eyes to Serena's again—"he has so much to lose."

"He'd lose more than money if he paid." Turning, Serena ranged herself behind Justin. She touched him only once, briefly, a hand on his shoulder. As Kate looked on he reached up and caught Serena's fingers in his. The gesture told her more than a thousand words.

Why, he loves her, Kate thought, stunned. It had never occurred to her that Justin Blade would be vulnerable to any woman. Even as Kate studied his face, she wondered if he knew he was.

"He set off a charge in one of the basement storage rooms." Justin let the phone drop to his shoulder a moment.

"Oh, God, was anyone hurt?"

He looked up at Serena with eyes that told nothing of his thoughts. "No. There's damage, but it's fairly minor. He called in to tell the police that one was just a bonus to prove he wasn't bluffing. He wants the money dropped off at three-fifteen, Vegas time."

Serena dropped a hand to his arm. "What are you thinking, Justin?"

"I'm thinking he's cutting it very fine for someone who's after a quarter of a million. I'm wondering if that's all he's after. When he called the hotel he asked for me by name."

Serena felt a new ripple of unease. "A lot of people know you own the Comanche," she began. "Or it's very likely someone who once worked for you, or knew someone that did."

He shifted the phone again. "We'll have to wait and see, won't we?" And there was something in the quiet words Serena recognized. A threat of violence, a promise of revenge. "How many more people left in there?" Justin demanded into the receiver. "No, I want to know the minute everybody's out."

"I'll get some coffee," Serena said.

"No." Rising, Kate shook her head. "I'll do it. You stay with him."

Serena looked at the trim gold clock on his desk. Ten forty-five. Moistening her lips, she gripped the back of Justin's chair and waited.

His eyes drifted to the clock as well. Less than an hour, he thought. And he was helpless. How could he explain that the hotel was more than concrete and stone to him? It had been the first thing he had owned, his first home after his parents had died. It symbolized his independence, his success, his heritage. Now he could only stand by and wait for it to be blown apart.

Was that the reason for the feeling in his gut that the threat was directed at him personally? Running a hand over the back of his neck, Justin decided that made more sense—and yet his instincts told him differently.

"It might be a bluff," Serena's voice came calm and strong from behind him. Justin felt the sharp wave of frustration pass. Holding out a hand, he waited for her to come around the chair and slip hers into it.

"I don't think so."

She pressed his hand between both of hers. "It would be wrong to pay. You're doing the right thing, Justin."

"It's the only thing I know how to do." He gave his attention to the voice over the phone. "Good. The guests and staff are out," he told Serena.

She sat on the arm of his chair while they both watched the clock.

Kate came back with coffee, but it sat untouched on the desk while they waited. As the minutes ticked by, Serena could feel the tension coming off Justin in waves. He sat silently, the phone in one hand. She tried to imagine the complexity of a search in a hotel the size of Justin's Vegas Comanche. How many hundreds of rooms, Serena wondered, how many thousands of closets and corners? She wondered helplessly if the sound of the explosion would carry through the receiver. And how many other times, she thought, has Justin's fate rested on the caprices of luck? This time, she told herself as she placed her hand back on his shoulder, fate would have to beat them both.

Because she was watching them, Serena saw the sudden rigidity in the fingers that lay on the desk.

"Yes."

To keep herself from asking questions, Serena bit her lip as Justin listened to the voice over the phone.

"I see. No, not that I'm aware of. Yes, I'll be there as soon as possible. Thank you." Hanging up the phone, he turned to Serena. "They found it."

"Oh, thank God." She dropped her forehead onto his.

"From what I was just told, it would have taken out the casino and half the main floor. Kate, book me on the first flight to Vegas."

"Justin." Serena stood from the arm of his chair and found her legs were oddly weak. "Do they have any idea who?"

"No." For the first time he noticed the coffee mug on his desk. Lifting it, he drank half of it down. "I have to go out, smooth over things in the hotel and talk to the authorities. I'll be back in a couple of days." He rose and took her by the shoulders. "It looks like my new partner's going to have a trial by fire."

"I'll be fine." Rising on her toes, she brushed a kiss over his mouth. "And I'll take good care of our hotel."

"I'm sure you will," he said, then drew her closer. "I don't like leaving you just now."

"I'll be here when you get back." She reached up to frame his face with her hands. "Don't worry, just come back soon."

He lowered his mouth to hers and lingered. "Go get some sleep," he suggested.

"Oh, no, this is my first full day on the job." His face was calm, but she could feel the tension in him. Instead of the endless questions she wanted to ask, Serena made herself smile and pull away. "I have quite a few things to do—tour the hotel, inspect the kitchen, go through the files in my office, arrange to have my things moved to our suite."

The *our* hit him forcibly, leaving him a little stunned. "Do that first," he demanded, taking her hands again. "I want to know you're in my bed, Serena, I—"

"You're on a plane in forty-five minutes, Justin," Kate interrupted, poking her head in the doorway. "You'll have to hurry if you want to make it."

"All right, have a car brought around."

"Justin." With a half laugh Serena tugged on her hands. "You're breaking my fingers." There was something in the look he gave her—part wary, part stormy—that had her smile fading. "What is it?"

Had he been going to tell her he loved her? he thought with a quick flutter of panic. Had he been going to say the words before they had fully registered in his mind? "It'll keep," he said at length.

"All right." And because she wanted to erase the tension from his face, she smiled again. Then, throwing her arms around his neck, Serena pressed her mouth to his. "Be miserable without me, please."

"I'll do my best. Kate has the number if you need me."

"Justin, your car's here."

"Yes, all right." He gave Serena a last, bruising kiss. "Think of me," he ordered before he strode away.

Taking a deep breath, she sat in the chair, still warm from him. "Do I have any choice?" she wondered aloud.

Chapter Nine

Over the next week Serena immersed herself in the routine of the Comanche. It was, she decided, her first major investment that hadn't been carefully chosen by her father, and one she was determined to understand intimately. She didn't mind a few speculative looks, the occasional murmured word behind a hand as she inspected the public rooms or pored over the books and files and records. She expected them. She spent her days learning the hotel from top to bottom, her evenings in the casino or her office in the capacity as manager. The nights she spent alone in Justin's suite.

Over the week she discovered two things. The Comanche was a slickly run organization that catered to people who had money to spend. It gave its clientele the best—for a price. And second, Justin's absence was a blessing in disguise.

She had little time to miss him with her hours packed with things to do. Only late at night when she found herself alone did Serena fully realize how much she'd grown to depend on him. For a word, a touch, his presence. But alone, she had the opportunity to prove to herself and to her staff that she was both competent and serious about running the hotel. Serena made the most of it.

Her background served her well. Over the years she'd become accustomed to patronizing fine hotels, and knew what a client looked for from check-in to check-out. Her year on the *Celebration* had given her another perspective. She understood the problems that plagued the staff—from fatigue to boredom to shortage in the linen count. The first day she had won over Nero and Kate. By the second, Serena had swayed the chef, the night manager, and the housekeeper. She considered each one a major victory.

Behind the trim pecan desk in her office, Serena went over the current week's schedule of her croupiers. Directly in front of her the panel was open, giving her a broad view of the casino. She found she enjoyed the twin feelings of isolation and companionship. Since the day had barely started by casino standards, she planned to give her paperwork another two hours, knowing if she were needed, the buzzer on her desk would sound, lighting up the location of the trouble. Then she'd work the floor. If she kept busy until weariness took over, she wouldn't be tempted to pick up the phone and dial Justin's number in Vegas.

He was a man who needed room, who didn't make promises or expect them. If she were to win in the end, Serena knew she couldn't forget that. If she were patient, there might come a time when he'd be comfortable loving her. With a quick laugh she shook her head.

She'd never be *comfortable* loving him. Nor did she choose to be.

Rubbing the back of her neck, Serena frowned down at the schedule. It could be made less complicated, she mused, if they hired one more croupier as a floater. That would make the hours a bit more flexible and...

"Yes, come in." Without glancing up, Serena continued to look over the list. With a floater to pick up the slack, she mused, she could juggle the shifts. Then suddenly a spray of violets landed on the paper in front of her.

"I thought that might get your attention."

Feeling her heartbeat speed, Serena looked up. "Justin!" She was out of her chair and racing into his arms before either of them expected it.

As his mouth came down to hers, he realized it was the first time he'd seen that spontaneous, unrestricted joy on her face. And it was for him. The fatigue of a long flight, the tension of a week, melted from him. "What is it about a woman," he asked her, "that makes it so good to hold one?"

Smiling, she tilted her head back. The closer study of his face brought concern. "You look tired." Her fingers rose to smooth away the lines of strain around his mouth. "I've never seen you look tired before. Was it very bad?"

"I've spent more pleasant weeks." He drew her back to him, wanting to fill himself with the feel of her, the scent. Later, he thought, he'd tell her of the neatly printed note he'd received. Another threat, without detail or reasons, just a promise that it wasn't over. "I did what you asked," he added, running a hand over the smooth flesh the low back of her dress exposed.

"Mmm. What?"

"I was miserable without you."

She didn't laugh as he had expected, but tightened her arms around his neck. Fighting back tears, she pressed her lips to his throat. "You didn't call. I waited for you to call," she whispered. Appalled by her words, Serena pushed out of his arms, swallowing tears and shaking her head. "No, I didn't mean that the way it sounded. I know you were busy." She lifted her hands, then helplessly let them fall. "And—and so was I. There were a million things…" She turned to shuffle papers on her desk. "We're both adults, and independent. The last thing we need is to start putting chains on each other."

"You ramble when you're nervous," Justin commented.

Whirling, Serena glared at him with hot, furious eyes. "Don't make fun of me."

"Odd that I would have missed that killing look," he said as he came to her. Taking her face in his hands, he held it gently, his eyes on hers. Serena felt her anger drain to leave her weak and pulsing. "Serena," he said on a sigh as his mouth closed over hers.

The tender kiss grew hungry quickly. She felt the need pour out of him to match her own as their lips clung, parting only to seek new angles, deeper pleasures. Longings of a week intensified so that there were two pairs of hot, avid lips searching, two pairs of urgent hands roaming. On a jerky breath Justin crushed her against him. No woman, he thought dimly, had ever made him suffer like this.

"Oh, God, I want you, Serena. I want you so that I can't think of anything but having you."

She pressed her cheek against his, but the movements behind the glass caught her eye. "This is silly," she admitted, "but I feel...exposed." On a shaky laugh she drew back, but the look in his eyes had her heart thudding again. "Why don't you close the panel," she whispered, "and make love to me." The knock on the door brought a groan from her.

On a long breath Justin drew her away until he held her lightly by the shoulders. "I forgot. I brought you a present."

"Tell them to go away," Serena suggested. "And give it to me later." She brought her hands to his. "Much later."

The knock came again. "Come on, Justin, you've had your ten minutes."

"Caine?" Justin watched surprise and pleasure race across Serena's face. "Caine".

Kissing her nose, he let his hands drop away from her. "Why don't you go let them in?"

Dashing to the door, Serena wrenched it open. "Caine! Alan!" With a whoop of laughter she launched herself at both of them. "What are you doing here?" she demanded, kissing them both. "Won't the state and federal governments collapse?"

"Even public servants need a few days off now and then," Caine retorted, then held Serena at arm's length.

He'd changed so little, she thought. Though both her brothers had inherited their father's height, Caine was lean and rangy. Nearly thin, Serena mused now with sisterly objectivity. Yet he had a fascinating face, all planes and angles, with a powerful grin he used to his advantage and eyes nearly as dark as her own. His hair waved carelessly around his face—blond with hints of red. Looking at him, she could easily see why it was reputed his skill with women equaled his skill as a lawyer.

"Hmm. She hasn't turned out too badly, has she, Alan?"

With an arched brow Serena turned to her oldest brother. "No," he answered, giving her the slow, serious smile that suited his dark, brooding looks. He looks more like Heathcliff, she thought, than a U.S. senator. "Though she's still a bit scrawny." He took her chin in his fingers, turning her face right and left. "Pretty girl," he stated in a perfect imitation of their father's burr.

"Maybe you should have married Arlene Judson after all," she said sweetly. Then, relenting, she wrapped an arm around each of her brothers. "Oh, I'm so glad to see you!"

Justin sat on the corner of Serena's desk and watched them. She looked very small between the two tall men, but for the first time, he noted the resemblance between her and Caine—the shape of the mouth, the nose, the eyes. Alan was a larger, rougher version of Anna, yet all three of them carried Daniel's stamp. It seemed so clear now, Justin wondered that he hadn't recognized it the first moment he'd seen her.

Perhaps it was seeing them as a family, picturing Serena as a sister. He thought of Diana and felt a twinge of regret. He'd done all he could there, Justin reminded himself. Still, he'd never known what it was like to have that basic, lifetime kinship any more than he'd ever have the place in Serena's heart that belonged to family.

"How long are you staying?" Serena demanded as she pulled them both inside the office.

"Just over the weekend," Alan told her as Caine took a quick, thorough study of her office.

"So you've taken yourself a partner after all," he said to Justin. "We were all a bit surprised after you'd turned Dad down so often."

"I was more persuasive," Serena said simply.

Caine shot Justin a look that didn't ask questions only because he already knew the answers. There was warning in it, subtle, but perfectly clear.

"You still haven't told me what you're doing here like this." She walked over to stand beside Justin as Caine folded himself into a chair and Alan moved to glance through the glass.

"We heard about the bomb threat in Vegas," Alan told her. "I gave Justin a call. He suggested you might enjoy a visit. And"—he turned with one of his rare grins—"Caine and I thought our coming might keep Dad from putting in an appearance for a while."

"Last time I talked to him," Caine said, "he was hinting he might enjoy a few weeks at the beach."

Serena made a sound that was somewhere between a groan and a laugh. "I suppose you heard about his last little plot."

"It seems to have worked out well enough," Alan stated as he watched Justin's hand come up to rest on the back of her neck.

"I was tempted to break more than a few cigars," she muttered, then glanced down at the buzzer on her desk as it sounded. "Table six. No," she said, touching Justin's shoulder as he started to rise. "I'll take care of it. Why don't the three of you go upstairs and relax?

I'll be up as soon as I'm sure everything is settled down here.''

"Is it unethical for me to gamble here now that you're half owner?" Caine wondered aloud.

"Not as long as you play as poorly as usual," Serena answered as she swept out of the door.

With a quick oath Caine stretched out his long legs. "Just because I used to let her beat me at poker."

"Let her win, hell," Alan said mildly. "She used to massacre you. You didn't say much on the phone, Justin," he continued as he turned away from the two-way mirror. "Can you discuss what happened in Vegas?"

With a shrug Justin drew a cigar out of his pocket. "It was a homemade bomb, very compact. It was under one of the keno tables. The F.B.I.'s running down the list of former employees, regulars who've dropped large amounts of money, any known extortionists with a similar M.O. I don't have too much faith in that. There were some threatening calls, but they couldn't trace them and I didn't recognize the voice. They don't have much to go on." As he lit the cigar his gaze wandered past Alan's shoulder to where Serena stood, talking to a customer. "It's impossible to trace everyone who's lost money in one of my casinos, even if that is the motive behind the bombing."

"You don't think it was?" Caine asked, and followed Justin's gaze out to his sister.

"Just a hunch," he muttered, then rose restlessly. "There was a threat delivered a couple of days ago— nothing specific, just enough to let me know he'd try something else."

"No wheres, whens, or hows?" Caine put in.

"No." Justin gave him a grim smile. "Of course I

could close down all of my hotels and wait him out."
He took a quick savage drag on the cigar. "I'm damned
if I will." With an effort he controlled the impotent
fury. He was being stalked. He knew it just as surely
as if he'd seen the shadow behind him. "I want Serena
to go home until this is resolved," he said briefly. "Between the two of you you should be able to convince
her."

Caine's answer was a short laugh. Alan gave Justin
a quiet look. "She'd go," he said, "if you went with
her."

"Damn it, Alan, I'm not going to go find a convenient hole and hide while someone plays with my life."

"And Serena would?" he countered.

"She has a half interest in one out of five of my
hotels," Justin said tightly. "If anything happens to this
one, the insurance covers her losses." His eyes were
drawn to the glass again. "I've more than an investment at stake."

"You're a fool if you think that's all Rena has,"
Alan murmured.

Justin whirled on him, giving way to all the pent-up
anger he'd harnessed for a week. "I tell you, I have a
bad feeling about this. Someone's after me, and she's
too close. I want her away, safe, where nothing can
happen to her. I'd think you'd understand that. For
God's sake, she's your sister!"

"And what is she to you?" Caine asked softly.

Furious, Justin turned on him, a hundred curses trembling on his lips. He met the dark, direct eyes, so much
like Serena's. "Everything," he breathed before he
turned back to the glass. "Damn it, she's everything."

"Well, that's settled," Serena said as she swirled

back into the office. "I just..." She trailed off as the tension rose up like a wall. Slowly, she looked from one man to the other, then walked by her brothers to Justin. "What is it?"

"Nothing." Forcing himself to be calm, he tapped out his cigar and took her hand. "Have you had dinner?"

"No, but—"

Deliberately, he looked past her to Alan and Caine. "We'll have something brought upstairs, unless you'd prefer the dining room."

"Actually, I think I'll try my luck outside." Caine rose casually. "Alan can keep me from dropping a month's pay. Got any tips, Rena?"

"Stick to the quarter slots," she said, and made her lips curve.

"O ye of little faith," he muttered, and tugged on her ear. "We'll see you tomorrow."

"Late tomorrow," Alan put in as he opened the door. "I'll never get him away from the tables before three."

Serena waited until the door shut behind them. "Justin, what's going on?"

"I'm tired," he said, taking her arm. "Let's go upstairs."

"Justin, I'm not a fool." He led her quickly through to his office and into the elevator. "It felt like something was about to explode when I walked in there. Are you angry with Alan and Caine?"

"No. It's nothing that concerns you."

The cold, flat answer had her stiffening in defense. "Justin, I'm not trying to pry into your personal business, but as it appeared to involve my brothers, I feel entitled to an explanation.''

He recognized the hurt, and the anger. He wanted to drive them both away, drag her into his arms and stop her questions in a way that would erase his own temper and tension. But as the elevator doors slid open, Justin forced himself to think coolly. He could use the anger and hurt for his own ends.

''It's nothing that concerns you,'' he repeated carelessly. ''Why don't you order something from room service. I want a shower.'' Without waiting for her answer he strode off.

Too stunned by his tone to react, Serena only stared after him. What had changed since that desperate, tempestuous greeting they had shared? Why was he treating her like a stranger? Or worse, she realized, like a comfortable mistress a man could take or brush aside at his whim. Standing in the center of the room, Serena tried to summon up fury but found only anguish. She'd known the risk she was taking. It seemed she'd lost the gamble.

No. Bunching her hands into fists, she shook her head. No, she wasn't so easily dismissed. Let him have his shower and his meal, she decided. Then she would...*explain* to him exactly what she expected. Calmly, she added to herself as she walked to the phone. She'd be very calm. With a vicious stab of her finger she punched the button for room service.

''This is Ms. MacGregor. I'd like a steak and salad.''

''Of course, Ms. MacGregor. How would you like your steak?''

''Burnt,'' she muttered.

''Pardon?''

With an effort she got herself under control. "It's for Mr. Blade," she explained. "I'm sure you know what he likes."

"Of course, Ms. MacGregor. I'll have his dinner sent up right away."

"Thank you." Everyone jumps for Justin Blade, she thought grimly as she replaced the receiver. Walking to the bar, she fixed herself a tall, stiff drink.

When Justin came out of the bedroom Serena was sitting on the sofa while the room service waiter arranged Justin's meal on the table across the room. Justin wore only a robe, which parted at the throat when he dipped his hands into his pockets. "Aren't you eating?" he asked with a nod toward the single place setting.

"No." She sipped her drink. "You go right ahead." Opening her purse, she drew out a bill, then held it out to the waiter. "Thank you."

"Thank you, Ms. MacGregor. Enjoy your meal, Mr. Blade."

When the door shut behind him, Justin took his seat. "I thought you hadn't had dinner."

"I'm not hungry," she said simply.

With a shrug Justin applied himself to the salad and tasted nothing. "Apparently there were no major problems while I was gone."

"Nothing I couldn't handle. Though I do have a few personal suggestions, I feel the hotel and the casino run very smoothly."

"You made a good investment." He sliced through the meat.

"You could look at it that way." Serena draped an arm over the back of the couch. Her beaded jacket shimmered in the quiet light. Looking at her, Justin wanted nothing more than to drag it off her, and the thin black silk she wore beneath, to lose himself in her again, the soft white skin, the masses of gold hair. He stabbed a piece of steak with his fork.

"The hotel seems to have gotten over the hump in this last year," he said easily. "It seems unnecessary for both of us to give it twenty-four hours a day." Unable to swallow any more, he poured coffee. "You might want to think about going back home."

She held the glass halfway to her lips. "Home?" she repeated dully.

"You're not needed here at the moment," he went on. "It occurred to me that it would be more practical for you to go home, or wherever you like, then come back and take over when I have to be away."

"I see." Blindly, she set the glass on the table in front of her and rose. "I've no intention of falling into the category of silent partner, Justin." Her voice was strong and clear, but from across the room he could see her eyes swim. "Nor do I have the intention of falling into the category of excess baggage. It's a very simple matter to go back to our original agreement and forget a one-night mistake." Because she could feel her hand begin to tremble, she reached for her drink again and drained it. "I'll pack my things and move back into my own suite."

"Damn it, Serena, I want you to go home." Watching her fight back tears, he felt something twist inside his stomach. In defense Justin pushed away from the table and strode down to her. "I don't want you here."

He heard her quick indrawn breath, but the mist in her eyes cleared with it. He found the dry-eyed, wounded look a hundred times worse. "There's no need to be cruel, Justin," she murmured. "You've made yourself clear. I'll get out of your rooms, but I own half this hotel, and I'm staying."

"I haven't signed the agreement yet," he reminded her.

She stared at him for a long silent moment. "You're that desperate to get rid of me," she murmured. "My mistake." Serena stared down at the empty glass in her hands. "If I'd been smarter, I wouldn't have slept with you until it was finalized."

Enraged, he grabbed the glass from her hand and hurled it across the room, where it shattered against the wall. "No!" Dragging her against him, he buried his face in her hair and swore again. "I can't do it this way. I won't let you think that."

Rigid with hurt, Serena didn't struggle. "Please let me go."

"Serena, listen to me. Listen to me," he repeated as he drew her away with his hands tight on her shoulders. "There was a letter delivered before I left Vegas. It was addressed to me, personally. Whoever planted that bomb wanted me to know he wasn't finished. He's going to hit me again—sometime, somewhere. There's more than money involved, I can feel it. It's personal, do you understand? You're not safe with me."

She stared at him as the words cut through the pain. "You said those things to me because you think I might be in some kind of danger if I stay?"

"I want you to be away from this."

Reaching up, Serena pushed his hands from her shoulders. "You're no better than my father," she said furiously. "Arranging my life with your little plots and schemes. Do you know what you did to me?'' Tears threatened again and she forced them back. ''Do you know how you hurt me? Did you ever consider just telling me the truth?''

''I've told you,'' he retorted, struggling against waves of guilt and need. ''Now will you go?''

''No.''

''Serena, for God's sake—''

''You expect me to pack my bags and run?'' she interrupted, shoving at him in frustration. ''To hide because someone *might* plant a bomb in the hotel *sometime?* Why don't you just ask me to find a nice little glass ball somewhere and take up residence? Damn it, Justin, I have as much at stake in this as you do.''

''The hotel's fully covered by insurance. If anything happened, you wouldn't lose your investment.''

She closed her eyes on a sigh. ''You idiot.''

''Serena, be reasonable.''

When her eyes opened, the fury was back in them. ''You're being reasonable, I suppose.''

''I don't give a damn if I'm being reasonable or not!'' he tossed back. ''I want you somewhere where I know nothing can touch you.''

''You can't *know* anything!''

''I know that I love you!'' He grabbed her again, shaking her. ''I know that you mean more to me than anything else in my life, and I'm not going to take any chances.''

''Then how can you ask me to go away!'' she shouted. ''People in love belong together.''

They stared at each other as each realized what had been said. Justin's grip gentled, then his hands dropped away. ''Do this for me, Serena.''

"Anything else," she answered. "Not this."

Turning, he paced to the window. Outside, the sun was sinking into the sea. Flashes of fire, streaks of gold—just like the woman behind him. "I've never loved anyone," Justin murmured. "My parents, my sister perhaps, but they've been out of my life a long time. I managed without them. I don't think I could manage without you. Even the thought that something might happen terrifies me."

"Justin." Going to him, Serena wrapped her arms around him and pressed her cheek to his back. "You know there're no guarantees, only odds."

"I've played the odds all my life. Not with you."

"I still make my own choices," she reminded him. "You can't change that, Justin. I can't let you. Tell me again," she demanded before he could answer. "And this time don't shout it at me. I'm as susceptible to romance as the next person."

When he turned back to her, Justin traced the curve of her lips with his fingertip. "I always thought *I love you* sounded so ordinary—until now." He replaced his fingertip with his lips, with the same gentle touch. "I love you, Serena."

She sighed as she felt him slip the jacket from her shoulders. "Justin," she murmured when he lifted her into his arms.

"Hmm?"

"Let's not tell my father. I hate it when he gloats."

Laughing, he lowered her to the bed.

He was going to love her gently. It seemed right somehow when he remembered the hurt in her eyes. She was precious to him, vital to his life, a permanent part of his thoughts. Soft and already warm, she drew him to her. He was going to love her gently, but she drove him mad.

Her hands were already pushing his robe aside, moving over his skin. Her lips were already racing over his face, nipping at his—teasing, tormenting, demanding. Justin swore as he pulled the dress down her body, and the sound of her low, husky laughter pushed him over the edge. Perhaps he hurt her; he couldn't control his hands. They were wild to touch, to possess. But she only arched beneath him, wanton, with abandon, until her blood roared like thunder in his ears. He murmured mindlessly in the tongue of his ancestors—threats, promises, phrases of love and war he could no longer separate.

Serena heard the harsh, quiet words—words both primitive and erotic when whispered against her skin. There was nothing of the smooth sophisticated gambler in him now, but something fierce and untamed. And he was hers, she thought wildly as his hands bruised over her. She smelled his rich male scent, a scent undiluted by colognes, and buried her face against his shoulder, wanting to absorb it. But his hunger would allow her no leisure. Hot and open, his mouth crushed down on hers, demanding not surrender, but aggression.

Desire me, he seemed to say. *Need me*. She answered with a torrent of passion that left them both gasping. She thought he'd shown her everything there was to know, everything there was to have, in their first night of loving. How could there be so much more with still a promise of secrets as yet undiscovered? He seemed to have a depthless well of energy and need. As he had from the very beginning, he challenged her to match it.

He touched her, and a hundred small, violent explosions erupted inside her. As her body shuddered from them, all her girlhood imaginings of lovemaking—the tender words, the soft touches—paled into insignificance. This is what she'd been meant for: the tempest and the fury.

With mouths desperately clinging, they joined into one wild, insatiable form.

With her eyes still closed, Serena stretched luxuriously. "Oh, God, I feel wonderful!" Even to her own ears her voice sounded like the purr of a contented cat.

"I've often thought so," Justin agreed, and ran a hand down the length of her.

With a laugh she sat up, stretching her arms high over her head. In the half light he watched her hair tumble over her naked back as it arched. "No, I really do…if it weren't for the fact that I'm starving."

"You said you weren't hungry," he reminded her. Reaching up, he hooked an arm around her waist and brought her falling back onto the bed.

"I wasn't." She rolled on top of him. "Now I am." After nibbling kisses over his face, she nipped at his lip. "Famished."

"You can have the rest of my steak."

"It's cold," she complained. With a sultry laugh she pressed her mouth to his throat. "Can't you think of something else?"

"I admire your spirit," he said, bringing her lips back to his. After running a hand down her hair, he cradled her head on his shoulder. "Want me to call room service?"

She let out a long, contented breath. "In a little while. I love you, Justin."

As he closed his eyes, his arms tightened around her. "I wondered if you'd get around to telling me that."

"Didn't I mention it?" Smiling, Serena propped herself on his chest. "How's this? I love you," she began, punctuating her words with kisses. "I adore you. I'm fascinated by you. I lust for you."

"It might do for a start." Taking her hand to his lips, he kissed her fingers slowly. "Serena—"

"No." Quickly, she pressed her hand over his mouth. "Don't ask me again. I'm not going anywhere, and I don't want to fight with you, Justin. Not now, not tonight." She touched her cheek to his. "It seems like I've waited all my life to feel like this. Everything up to this moment seems like a prelude. It sounds crazy, but I think I knew the first minute I looked up and saw you that everything was going to change." She laughed again and drew away. "And I thought I was much too intellectually sound to believe in love at first sight."

"Your intellect," he told her, "slowed things down considerably."

"On the contrary," she said with a haughty smile. "It moved them along beautifully. I came here with the idea of becoming your partner so that we could deal on equal terms while I convinced you you couldn't live without me."

"Did you?"

She grinned down at him. "It worked."

"You might be a bit too cocky, Serena." Giving her hair a tug, he rose from the bed.

"Where are you going?"

"To let a little air out of your balloon." Opening a drawer, Justin drew out a small box. "I picked this up for you in St. Thomas."

"A present?" Scrambling up on her knees, she held out her hand. "I live for presents."

"Greedy little witch," he said as he dropped the box into her outstretched hand.

Her chuckle faded into silence as she opened it. Twin pinwheels of amethysts and diamonds gleamed up at her, catching fire even in the dim light of dusk. She remembered how they had looked in the sunlit window where she had first seen them. Hesitantly, she touched one with her finger as if the heat were real and not just an illusion in the stones.

"Justin, they're gorgeous," she whispered as she raised her eyes to his. "But why?"

"Because they suited you, and you wouldn't indulge yourself. And"—he dropped a hand to her cheek—"I already decided I wasn't going to let you walk out of my life. If you hadn't come here, I'd have brought you."

"Willing or not?" she asked, with the beginnings of a smile.

"I warned you it's an old tradition in my family." He tucked her hair behind her ears. "Put them on. I've wondered how they'd look on you."

Serena took them out of the box and clipped them to her ears. Still kneeling on the bed, she caught her hair back in her hand. "I want to see." Justin stopped her with no more than a look.

Her skin was pale and flawless. Her hair, when her hand slowly dropped, tumbled wildly. Wearing no more than a glitter of jewels at her ears, she looked like an exotic fantasy. The flare of desire in his eyes touched off one in her own. As her lips parted, she held out her arms to him.

Chapter Ten

Serena stretched luxuriously and contemplated getting up. If Justin hadn't already gone downstairs, the idea of lazing away the morning in bed would have been more appealing. She lay in the center of the tangle of sheets—the spot they had shared, wrapped close, throughout the night.

He was still worried, she mused. Even though he'd whispered nothing more than a few foolish endearments into her ear before he had left her, Serena had sensed the controlled tension in him. As long as Justin was convinced the bomb planted in Vegas had been a direct threat against him personally, and a prelude of more, there was nothing Serena could do to soothe him. She could only stay close, trying to convince him she was in no danger, that she could look after herself.

Men, Serena thought with a small smile. No matter how liberal, they simply couldn't accept the fact that women could take care of themselves. The last thing she was going to do was sit in Massachusetts while the man she loved sat in New Jersey. It wasn't logical, Serena told herself as she pulled herself out of bed. She believed exactly what she had shouted at Justin the night before—people in love belonged together.

Justin wasn't likely to relax fully until the police caught whoever had planted the bomb, and that could take months—if indeed he were ever caught. He might have given up completely when his plans were ruined. Or he could wait—days, weeks, months—before striking again.

Taking a robe out of the closet, she considered that possibility, then shrugged off the unease. Whether they caught him or not, Serena didn't share Justin's certainty that the man would try again. The note had probably been sent out of frustration after the extortionist's plans had fallen apart. That made more sense than someone with a personal vendetta against Justin.

He wasn't being objective, Serena decided as she belted the robe. The hotels were so much a part of him, he couldn't see them as an outsider would—buildings worth a great deal of money. The man had played his hand and lost. He had to know the authorities would be investigating, and that Justin would tighten his own security. Cowards plant bombs, she told herself. A coward isn't going to risk getting caught. In time, Justin would see the logic.

When she heard the knock on the door, Serena automatically checked the bedside clock. Too early for the maid, she reflected as she walked into the living room. Now, who would be…Her hand paused on the knob as all of Justin's words of the night before ran through her head. *Someone's after me. You're not safe.*

Suddenly uneasy, Serena peered through the peephole. There, you see, she told herself as her nerves drained away. It's just foolishness. Opening the door, she grinned at her brother.

"You must have lost quickly last night if you're up this early," she commented.

Caine stared at her a moment before he stepped into the room. "It's not that early," he countered, glancing around. "I came up to see Justin."

"You've just missed him." Serena closed the door and tossed back her sleep-tumbled hair. "He went down to his office about fifteen minutes ago. Where's Alan?"

Caine's affection for Justin was warring with the fact that Serena was his sister. His *baby* sister, damn it, he thought. And she was standing in Justin's private suite wearing nothing but the short silk robe he'd given her last Christmas. "He's just having breakfast," Caine told her as he prowled around the room.

"Well, you were always the one to be up and about in the morning," Serena remembered. "I always thought it was a disgusting habit. Want some coffee? It's one of the few essentials stocked in the kitchen."

"Yeah. Sure." Still dealing with the shock of realizing he had harbored the illusion that his sister was exclusively *his* sister, Caine followed her.

The kitchen was roomy and striking. The floor and walls were white, the cabinets glossy black. Serena plugged in the percolator as she gestured toward the breakfast bar with her free hand. "Sit down."

"You seem to know your way around," Caine heard himself saying.

She sent him an infuriatingly amused look. "I live here."

Annoyed, Caine slid onto a stool at the bar. "Justin certainly works fast."

"That's quite a chauvinistic remark for the liberal state's attorney," Serena commented as she measured out coffee. "From another point of view it could be said I work fast."

"You met him only a month ago."

"Caine." Turning around, Serena cocked her head. "Do you remember Luke Dennison?"

"Who?"

"He was the local stud when I was fifteen," she reminded him. "You cornered him in the parking lot of the movie theater and told him if he ever put his hands on me, you'd break all the small, vital bones in his body."

She watched Caine's grin flash as he remembered. "He never did, did he?"

"No." Then she walked over to him and grabbed both his ears. "I'm not fifteen anymore, Caine, and Justin isn't Luke Dennison."

Leaning over, he grabbed her ears in turn, applying enough pressure to bring her closer. "I love you," he told her, and kissed her quick and hard.

"Then be happy for me. Justin's everything I want."

Releasing her, Caine sat back. "He said the same thing about you."

He saw the pleasure darken her eyes. "When?"

"Yesterday when he asked Alan and me to talk you into going home for a while." Caine lifted a hand as the pleasure turned to temper. "Don't go for the jugular, Rena; we both declined."

Serena let out her breath in a quick huff. "Justin's convinced whoever planted that bomb had more than extortion money as a motive. Because of that, he has it fixed in his head that I'm not safe with him." Frustrated, she gestured widely with both hands. "He just won't be logical or practical about the whole business."

"He loves you."

The storm around her stilled instantly. "I know. All the more reason for me to stay with him. Tell me," she leaned back against the counter to watch him, "what would you do?"

"If I were Justin, I'd do my damnedest to make you leave. If I were you," he continued smoothly before she could start to yell, "I wouldn't budge."

"Nothing worse than the analytical, legal mind," Serena murmured as the coffee perked. "Well, why don't you tell me what you've been doing with yourself? Any fascinating new ladies—or is your work cramping your style?"

"I manage to eke out a little time for recreation," he commented, and earned a snort as Serena took down two mugs. "I've decided to go back to private practice."

"You have?" Surprised, she turned back. "Isn't that rather sudden?"

"Not really." He accepted the mug of black coffee. "I've been thinking about it for some time. Alan's the politician. He's got the patience for it." Shrugging, Caine sipped at his coffee. "I miss the courtroom. Bureaucracy doesn't give me enough time for it."

"I always loved to watch you argue a case," Serena remembered, taking her seat on the opposite side of the bar. "There was something deadly about your style, like a wolf circling a fire and losing patience."

Caine laughed. "There's that flighty MacGregor imagination surfacing again."

"Casting aspersions on the family name?" Alan asked from the kitchen doorway.

Serena turned to him with a quick warm smile. The look altered subtly as she shifted her eyes to the man beside her brother.

"Alan complained that he'd been deserted," Justin commented. "Any more of that coffee?"

"I just made it." She held out her hand to him as he entered. Taking it, Justin brushed a kiss over her fingers before he moved to the coffeepot.

"Alan?"

He was looking at his sister. "Yes, thanks."

"Caine hasn't told me how much he lost last night," Serena began as Alan leaned on the counter.

"Oh, his luck wasn't all that bad." He sent his brother a shrewd look, which Caine returned blandly.

Serena arched a brow. "You better not have been trying your *luck* with any of my dealers," she warned Caine.

"The little blonde," Alan supplied with a flashing grin, "with the big brown eyes."

"*Caine!*" Serena sent him a look of astonished amusement. "She's barely twenty-one."

"I don't know what he's talking about." Calmly, Caine sipped his coffee. "Alan was busy trying to impress some redhead in half a dress with his views on foreign policy."

"Well." Serena turned to Justin as he brought over fresh coffee. "It seems to me that neither the staff nor the customers are safe if we let these two loose."

"You can keep an eye on them tonight at the dinner

show.'' Justin handed Alan a mug before he opened the refrigerator for cream.

"I should have warned you," Serena told her brothers as she linked her hand with Justin's. "He has a habit of making arrangements without consulting anyone. But I for one," she added, smiling at him, "would love to go to the dinner show. Lena Maxwell's opening tonight," she mused, looking down at her nails. "I suppose Justin could be persuaded to introduce her if you two would like to come."

"What time's dinner?" Alan and Caine asked together.

Laughing, Serena rose. "Pitiful. Dangle a sexy brunette in front of their noses and they'll follow you anywhere. I've got to shower and change." She stood on her toes and brushed Justin's mouth with hers. "I'll be downstairs in a half hour."

As she walked from the room, she heard Caine's question. "Just where is Lena Maxwell rehearsing this afternoon, Justin?"

While she showered, Serena found herself laughing. If Caine got it into his head to track down Lena Maxwell, he wouldn't need Justin's introduction to charm his way into a personal conversation with her. Caine MacGregor had more than his fair share of charm.

She thought again of his reaction when he found her in Justin's suite. It was rather endearing really, she decided. And she hadn't missed the long, quiet look Alan had given her when he had walked into the kitchen with Justin. As soon as her brothers were alone, she concluded, they would discuss her relationship with Justin, probably argue a bit about it, then give her their unqualified support. It had always been that way among the three of them.

For a moment, with the water streaming hot over her body, Serena felt a wave of regret for Justin. He had never really known the security, the bond, the frustration, of family ties. Perhaps with time he would let her show him. Perhaps one day they would have children.

Deliberately, Serena stuck her head under the spray. She was getting ahead of herself. Far ahead. He loved her, but that didn't mean he was looking for marriage and children. He'd been solitary for so long, and their love was so new. Children would mean a home, and he'd never chosen to make one. He'd chosen a lifestyle without permanence. And the nomad in him had been, and was, part of his attraction for her. It was foolish to start dreaming about changes when they'd barely lived forty-eight hours under the same roof.

Yet, he'd spoken of his sister twice, and both times Serena had sensed a hint of regret. Justin hadn't turned his back on his family, but had been forced by circumstances to do without. If one day he wanted one, Serena promised herself, she'd be there for him.

Stepping from the shower, Serena flicked on the overhead heat lamp, then wrapped her hair in a towel. She began to hum as she rubbed scented lotion over her skin. Briefly, she ran over the scheduling she'd outlined for herself that day and decided she could accomplish everything before she needed to change for the dinner show. But not if she stood loitering in the bathroom all day, she reminded herself as she slipped into her robe. Unwinding the towel from her hair, she walked back into the bedroom.

As the door from the living room swung open, she gasped in surprise. "Justin!" Dragging a hand through her hair, Serena let out her breath. "You gave me a start; I thought you'd gone."

Dipping his hands into his pockets, he looked at her slowly, from her toes to the crown of her head. "No."

Why was it, she wondered, that he's seen and touched every part of my body but he can look at me like that and turn me to jelly? "Alan and Caine?"

"Gone down to compete for Lena, I believe."

"Lord, I hate to miss that," she thought aloud as she walked to the closet."

"What are you doing?"

"Well, I'm getting dressed," she returned with a laugh. "What does it look like I'm doing?"

"Seems like a waste of time, since I'm just going to take whatever you put on off you again."

She sent him an arched look over her shoulder. "Somehow, I think Kate might find it odd if I walked into the office wearing my robe."

He gave her a slow, cool smile. "You're not getting out of this room."

"Justin, don't be ridiculous." With another laugh Serena began to poke through the clothes in the closet. "I have a dozen things to do before dinner, and—" The rest of the words caught in her throat, then came out as a whoosh of air as he tossed her onto the mattress.

Standing above her he nodded. "I like the way you look in a rumpled bed."

"Oh, really?" Serena pushed herself up to her knees. "Well, I'd like to know where you got the idea you could throw me around." As she stuck her hands on her hips, her loosened robe fell off one shoulder. "It's not the first time," she went on, remembering her dunking in the ocean, "but if you think you can make a habit—"

"I know, nobody pushes a MacGregor around," he murmured as he hooked a finger in the opening of her robe.

"That's right." She pushed his hand away and succeeded in widening the gap down her front. "So just remember that the next time you get a wild urge to toss me around."

"I will. Sorry." With an apologetic smile he held out his hand. Though wary, Serena accepted it as she started to climb back out of the bed. In an instant she was on her back, pinned under him.

"Justin!" Fighting against laughter, she pushed at him. "Will you stop? I have to get dressed."

"Uh-uh, you have to get undressed. Let me help you." With one long gesture of his hand he parted her robe completely.

"*Stop!*" Amused, frustrated, and aroused, she struggled against him. "Justin, I mean it! The maid could walk in here any minute."

"She won't be coming until this evening." He found a spot, low on her ribs, and felt a thrill of pleasure as she moaned. "I called housekeeping."

"You—" With a new spurt of energy she tried to wrest free. "You did it again!" She nearly managed to get her arms free before he pinned them. "Didn't it occur to you that I might have had plans? That perhaps I don't *want* to spend the afternoon in bed with you?"

"I figured the odds were good that I could persuade you," he countered easily.

"*Oh!*" She kicked out, tangling her legs with his as she wiggled under him.

"Okay, we'll wrestle first, best three out of five."

"This isn't funny," she said, swallowing a giggle. "I mean it."

"Deadly serious." He rolled her over until she was on top of him. "That's one apiece." Before she could catch her breath she was back under him. "And two for me."

"Oh, sure." Serena blew the wet hair out of her eyes. "A real even match when I'm half naked and you're fully dressed."

"You're right." He covered her face with quick, teasing kisses. "Why don't you do something about that. My hands are busy."

She moaned involuntarily as they ran down her body. "Foul," she said breathlessly. "Justin..."

"Stop?" he asked halfheartedly, his eyes intent on her face as he let his fingertips do the persuading.

"No." Tangling her fingers in his hair, she brought his mouth down to hers.

It was always the same, always unique. Every time his lips met hers, she felt that enervating shock of heat. Her bones would soften with exquisite slowness until she thought her body was one warm, fluid mass. Yet the thrill was always fresh, as though it were happening for the first time. Forgetting his request that she undress him, Serena went lax with the first flood of pleasure.

Justin felt her surrender, a surrender he knew was only a prelude to her breathless excitement and frantic demands. He enjoyed the brief, heady power of total control. She was his now, a strong, vital woman who for a few precious moments would be like putty in his hands. The knowledge made him gentle, so that he caressed with more tenderness than he had believed himself capable of. Did love make so much difference? he wondered as he ran long, lean fingers over her skin.

His lips touched hers, muffling her soft sound of enjoyment. Her eyes, not quite closed, met his. When he traced the shape of her mouth with his tongue, her lids fluttered. He rubbed his lips over hers, savoring the taste, then found that his hands had stilled. His whole being seemed focused on the meeting of mouth to mouth. The power he had felt became a vulnerability, no less of a surrender than Serena had given him. He felt weak with it, and fearless.

"I love you," he murmured against her mouth. "I didn't know how much." The kiss was deep and slow and more arousing than anything he'd ever known.

Then her tongue sought his, moving through his lips to draw in all the tastes and flavors. As a shudder passed through him, he knew her surrender was over.

Serena slipped the soft wool of his sweater up his torso, over his shoulders, so that their lips were forced to part, but only briefly. Her hands were busy, touching, rubbing, demanding. He could see them in his mind's eye, smooth and white against his darker skin, the glossy feminine nails scraping over him in excitement. He moved his lips to her shoulder to nip gently, and was assaulted by her scent. It made him think of sultry summer nights, wild loving in high green grass. He ran kisses, grown more desperate, to the inside of her elbow, where her rapid pulse only intensified the fragrance. As he buried his mouth against the pale blue-veined skin, her body arched, tossed by passion.

Serena rolled to him so that they were side by side, then locked her arms around him. She didn't feel the tangle of sheets beneath her, the cool silk of her robe that had slipped down to her legs. All she felt was his hard, hot body against hers and the moist, tingling path his mouth streaked over her.

As he slid down she urged him toward all the secret places he'd discovered for both of them. No one else would ever bring her this torrid, wanton hunger. It filled her, consumed her, made her strong. With a sudden burst of energy she was on top of him, her mouth greedy, her hands quick and clever. He groaned, gripping her wet, sleek hair. The sound only made her move over him more urgently. He's beautiful, so beautiful, was all she could think as she touched and tasted again.

A light film of sweat glistened on his dark skin. Serena could taste the saltiness of it as she roamed over the hard, smooth chest, the lean line of ribs marred by the jagged scar, the narrow, long-boned hips.

Then his hands gripped her, dragging her up until his mouth was fastened on hers. She drew in the mingling flavor of their tastes until her head swam with it. Her body seemed to act without her knowledge, sliding down until she took him inside of her. The sensation rocketed through her, causing her to cry out as she arched back. But he rose up with her, his hands still gripping her hair, his mouth still fused to hers. She couldn't breathe, but even as she fought for air, her body set up its own raging rhythm.

Her arms were locked around him, his around her. The mutual grip tightened convulsively as they reached the sharp, airless summit, then as one form they slid back to the bed to lay gasping.

"I can't seem to get enough of you," Justin managed in a whisper. "Never enough."

"Don't." Serena let her head slip limply to his shoulder. "Don't ever get enough."

They lay quietly as breathing settled and trembles eased. With her palm over his heart, she could feel the pounding beat become slow, strong, and steady.

"There's only you," Justin said, feeling the sudden fierceness of love. "There's only you in my life."

Serena lifted her head to look down at him. "'Love that is not madness is not love.'" Smiling, she traced the line of his cheekbone. "I never understood that until now. I know I never want to be sane again."

He brought her finger to his lips. "So the brainy Serena MacGregor chooses insanity."

Wrinkling her nose, she folded her elbows over his chest. "No need to bring my brain into it."

"It fascinates me," Justin told her. "And it's one part of you I haven't really explored. Just how smart are you?"

She lifted a brow. "That," she said primly, "is an abstract question."

"Ah, you're going to be evasive." Grinning, he brushed her hair away from her shoulders. "How many degrees do you have?"

"Your first question doesn't have anything to do with your second. How smart are you?"

"Smart enough to know when I'm getting the run-around," he said mildly. "No burning desire to go into law or politics like your brothers?"

"No. My only burning desire was to learn. Then I had a burning desire to be doing. Now"—she bit his lower lip—"I have more basic burning desires."

"Hmm." He allowed himself the pleasure of feasting on her mouth a moment. "Don't you feel that running a gambling hotel is a bit of a waste of your education?"

"Of course not. My education's mine, I'll always have it whatever I choose to do. What good are degrees if you're not enjoying life?" With a sigh she lay across his chest again. "I didn't study so that I could pile up little pieces of paper suitable for framing, but because I was curious. Why do you run hotels?"

"Because I'm good at it."

Serena grinned at him. "And that's the exact reason I nearly became a professional student. But it was becoming too repetitious and too easy. There're challenges here every day and a constant variety of people. And," she added smugly, "I'm good at it too."

"Nero thinks you have class."

Now Serena's smile was just as smug as her voice. "He's very perceptive. Why didn't you make him manager?"

"He wasn't interested." Justin began to run a hand up and down her spine. "He likes his position as unofficial troubleshooter. I'll be sending him to Malta next year."

"You've bought the casino then?"

"I will have soon enough." Thoughtful, he studied her face. "I was considering taking on a partner."

He saw the smile light in her eyes just before her lips curved. "Were you? Then I suppose I should put in my bid right away."

He cupped his hand around the back of her neck. "The sooner the better," he murmured as he brought her lips to his.

When the phone rang, he swore ripely. Serena laughed and nuzzled against his throat as he reached for it.

"Blade." Listening to Kate's quiet, shaking voice, he fought to keep the tension out of his body. Serena would feel it. "All right, Kate, I'll be down." After hanging up he kissed the crown of Serena's head. "Something's come up downstairs."

She gave a resigned sigh. "That's the trouble with living where you work." Rolling over, she stretched. "Well, I really should go down myself."

"You haven't had a day off in over a week." Dressing, Justin wondered if he was wiser to leave her there or to keep her with him downstairs. He decided she'd be better off in the penthouse. "Relax for a while, I'll be back up soon. Why don't you order some lunch?"

The thought of having him to herself all afternoon was too appealing. Serena closed her mind to the paperwork on her desk. "All right—an hour?"

"Yes, fine." Preoccupied, he headed for the elevator.

Kate was waiting for him when he stepped off. Silently, she handed Justin a plain white envelope.

"Steve found it lying on the front desk. As soon as

I saw it…'' She trailed off, then got control of herself. ''It's just like the one you got in Vegas, isn't it?''

''Yes,'' Justin answered flatly as he studied the carefully executed block letters that spelled out his name. He had a quick, savage urge to simply rip it into pieces, but he took a letter opener from his desk and carefully slit one edge. Sliding the note out, he unfolded it.

IT'S NOT OVER YET. YOU HAVE A PRICE TO PAY.

''Call security,'' he told Kate as he read the words a second time. Then he let out his breath on one violent oath. ''And the police.''

Chapter Eleven

Serena pulled a black angora sweater over her head. It would feel good to be lazy for a day, she decided, to lounge around the suite in comfortable clothes and do absolutely nothing. She and Justin hadn't spent a full day together since St. Thomas.

That made her think of the earrings Justin had given her. She'd wear them tonight, Serena mused as she opened the top drawer of the dresser to draw out the box. They're exquisite, she thought as she looked at them again. All the more exquisite because he had bought them for her then, before they had been lovers.

What a strange man he is, she reflected. So cool in some ways, so introspective, yet he was capable of such incredibly sweet gestures. The violets in her room the first day—champagne for breakfast. And underneath it all there was that latent, controlled streak of violence. All those aspects of him excited her.

How smart are you? Serena laughed as she remembered Justin's question. Smart enough to know I'm a very lucky woman, she answered silently. Reaching into the drawer again, she drew out a two-headed quarter she'd picked up while Justin had been in Vegas. With a grin Serena examined it, then slipped it into the pocket of her jeans. And smart enough to keep an ace up my sleeve, she added with a gleam of mischief in her eye.

As she glanced at her reflection in the mirror, Serena's grin turned to a look of astonishment. Her hair had dried in a tangled and unruly mop around her face. What a mess, she thought as she picked up her brush. Well, she'd do something about it before she called room service. It would serve Justin right if he had to wait for his lunch, she added as she tugged painfully at the knots in her hair. Bending from the waist, she let her hair fall forward, then gritted her teeth and brushed the underside.

"Ouch! Just a minute," she called out at the quick, quiet knock on the door. Either Caine or Alan had struck out with Lena Maxwell, she thought with a smirk as she headed for the door, still brushing her hair. "Don't expect me to fix you up with—oh."

"Housekeeping." A slim boy of about twenty gave her a shy smile.

Justin must have decided to have them clean before lunch, she concluded. Typical. He might have called to let me know.

"I can come back later if—"

"Oh, no, I'm sorry. I was thinking of something else." Serena gave him a smile as she opened the door wide enough for him to roll the maid's cart inside. "You're new, aren't you?"

"Yes, ma'am, this is my first day."

That explains the nervous swallowing, she decided, and made her smile warmer. "Just relax and take your time," she advised him. "I'll stay out of your way." Gesturing with her brush, she turned away. "Why don't you start in the kitchen while I—"

Something clamped over her mouth and nose. Too stunned to be frightened, Serena grabbed at the hand as she drew her breath to shout. She inhaled something strong and cloyingly sweet that made her head spin. Recognizing the scent, she began to struggle more frantically, fighting the mists that were whirling in front of her eyes.

Oh, God, no. Her arms dropped heavily to her sides, the brush slipped from her limp fingers. Justin...

"The desk clerk found it on the counter," Justin told Lieutenant Renicki. "Apparently, no one saw who put it there. It was during checkout time, and the desk staff was busy."

"Yes. Well, he's not a fool." The police lieutenant picked up the plain sheet of stationery by the corner and slipped it into a plastic bag. "I'll have to turn this over to the Bureau, I imagine, but for now I'll leave a few plainclothesmen in the hotel."

"I've my own security stationed in all the public rooms."

Lieutenant Renicki lifted both of his bushy, graying brows in acknowledgment. Doesn't like dealing with me, he decided. Oh, he's a cool one. He watched Justin light a cigar with rock-steady hands. Not much gets under that one's skin.

"Got any enemies, Mr. Blade?"

Justin shot him a mild look. "Apparently."

"Anyone specific you want to tell me about?"

"No."

"Is this the first threat you've received since you got back from Nevada?"

"Yes."

Lieutenant Renicki suppressed a sigh. Characters like Blade made him feel like a dentist yanking at a reluctant tooth. "Hired or fired anyone recently?"

For an answer, Justin pushed his intercom. "Kate, check with personnel. See who we've put on or let go in the last two months. Then get a printout from the rest of the hotels."

"Great things, computers," the lieutenant said when Justin hung up. "I got a teenager practically married to one." Getting no response, he shrugged his rounded shoulders. "I'm going to check your security myself. If he's going to plant a bomb, he has to get in first."

"He can get in," Justin reminded him, "by signing a name at the registration desk."

"True enough." Lieutenant Renicki watched the cigar smoke drift. "You can close down."

The only change in Justin's expression was a fractional narrowing of his eyes. "No."

"Didn't think so." Lieutenant Renicki hauled himself out of the chair. "My men will be discreet, Mr. Blade, but we'll make a routine search. I'll check back with you after I've interviewed the desk clerks."

"Thank you, Lieutenant." Justin waited until the door closed behind him, then crushed out his cigar with a force that snapped it in two. If he'd felt a stalking sensation before, now he felt breathing down his neck. He was here now—if not in the hotel, then somewhere close. Waiting. Serena was going back to Hyannis Port if Justin had to tie her up and dump her on a plane.

He sat very still for a moment until he was calm again. He wouldn't get through to Serena by shouting or threatening. The only way would be to make her see that her presence there made it impossible for him to be completely rational. If she were gone, he could think clearly enough and perhaps reason out who and why. Justin lifted the intercom again.

"Kate, I'll be upstairs. Pass my calls through to me up there." Rising, he went to the elevator. Maybe on the way up he would think of the best way to tell Serena he was kicking her—and her brothers—out of his hotel.

As he stepped into the living room, Justin glanced toward the picture window, half expecting to see her sitting there, already nibbling at lunch. He was only vaguely surprised to see the table empty—he'd taken a bit more than the hour he'd allotted. Thinking perhaps she'd fallen back to sleep, Justin walked into the bedroom. The rumpled bed didn't bring on a twinge of desire this time but a feeling of unease. Calling her name, Justin walked toward the bathroom.

The faintest wisp of her scent clung to the air. Because the room was empty, it only made Justin's unease sharpen. Don't be an idiot, he told himself. She isn't tied to this suite. She could have gone out for a hundred reasons. But she was expecting me. She would have phoned down. How did he know? As he walked back out into the living room, Justin reminded himself that they hadn't been together long enough to be sure of the other's habits. She could have run down to the boutique for a dress.

Bending, Justin picked up the small, enamel-handled brush from the rug. For a moment his mind went blank, and he could do no more than stare at it. He shook himself clear. He was being an alarmist—she'd come walking back in any moment. It was like her to leave her things all over the suite. To be untidy, he mused mercilessly. Not careless. Picking up the phone, Justin punched a number.

"Page Serena MacGregor."

He held the brush as he waited. Her beaded jacket hung over the back of the sofa. He could remember slipping it from her shoulders the night before. Sometime during the morning she had picked it up and tossed it there. Then why would she have left her brush on the floor?

"Ms. MacGregor doesn't answer the page, sir."

Justin felt the knot in his stomach tighten. He gripped the handle of the brush until it threatened to snap. "Page Alan or Caine MacGregor." Glancing at his watch, Justin saw that it was thirty minutes past the time he had told Serena to expect him.

"Caine MacGregor."

"It's Justin. Is Serena with you?"

"No, Alan and I were—"

"Have you seen her?"

"Not since this morning." It was the first time in the ten years he had known Justin, Caine realized, that he'd heard a hint of panic in that controlled voice. Something like ice rippled down his back. "Why?"

Justin found his throat closed and stared down at the brush in his hand. "She's gone."

Caine felt the receiver grow wet under his palm. "Where are you?"

"Upstairs."

"We'll be right there."

Within minutes, Justin opened the door to admit Serena's brothers. "She might've gone out for something," Caine said immediately. "Did you check to see if she took her car out?"

"No." Justin cursed himself and picked up the phone again. "This is Blade. Has Ms. MacGregor taken her car out?" He waited, angry, impatient, while Caine prowled the room and Alan watched him. Justin listened to the answer from the garage, then hung up without speaking. "Her car's still there."

"She might have gone for a walk on the beach," Alan suggested.

"She was expecting me here a half hour ago," Justin said flatly. "She was supposed to order some lunch, but I've checked; she never called down. I found this near the front door."

Alan took the brush from Justin's hand. He remembered giving the antique vanity set to Serena for her sixteenth birthday. It was one of the few things she owned that she took meticulous care of.

"Had you been arguing?"

Justin whirled on Caine as his control slipped another notch.

"Justin," Caine said quickly. "Rena has a wicked temper. If she were angry, she could have stormed out without a word to anyone. She'd stomp around on the beach until she'd cooled off."

"No, we hadn't been arguing," Justin said tightly. "We'd been making love." He stuck his hands in his pockets because he wanted to ball them into fists. "I got a call from downstairs. An envelope had been left for me at the front desk. It was another threat.''

Alan set Serena's brush down carefully on the table. "Justin." He waited until the angry green eyes met his. "Call the police."

Like an exclamation point at the end of his words, the phone rang. Justin grabbed for it. "Serena," he began.

"Looking for her already?" The voice was muffled and sexless. "I've got your squaw, Blade." The connection broke with a soft click.

Justin stood still as stone for a full ten seconds. He tasted copper in his mouth and recognized it as fear. "He's got her," he heard someone say, then realized the voice was his own. On a blind wave of fury he ripped the phone out of the wall and threw it across the room. "The son of a bitch has her."

Lieutenant Renicki glanced around the living room of Justin's suite and decided it was warmer than he would have expected. The man he had met downstairs seemed suited to cold colors and straight lines. His eyes rested on the phone that lay drunkenly against the east wall. Well, still waters run deep, he supposed.

The tall blond man staring out of the window was Caine MacGregor, the hotshot young lawyer who was currently serving as state's attorney in Massachusetts. The dark man sitting in the chair staring at the hairbrush in his hands was Alan MacGregor, U.S. senator, a bit of a left winger with a glib tongue. The lieutenant looked at Justin again.

"Suppose you run through it once more."

Justin's eyes leveled on Lieutenant Renicki's, full of

fury and icy control. "I went downstairs to check out
the envelope that had been left for me at the front desk.
I left Serena here; it was just past noon. We made arrangements to have lunch here in the suite an hour later.
I was late, and when I came back, she wasn't here. I
was concerned, then when I found her hairbrush lying
on the floor by the front door I had her paged. When
she didn't answer, I paged her brothers. Fifteen minutes
ago I received a call."

"Yes, apparently from a kidnapper," Renicki put in,
not certain if he was pleased or annoyed with Justin's
cool recital. "You haven't told me precisely what he
said."

Justin gave the lieutenant a long, intense look. "He
told me he had my squaw."

Ready to explode, Caine whirled away from the window. "Damn it, this isn't getting us anywhere! Why
aren't you looking for her?"

Lieutenant Renicki watched him with tired, patient
eyes. "We're doing just that, Mr. MacGregor."

"He'll call again," Alan said quietly. He looked up
from the hairbrush to meet the lieutenant's gaze. "He
must know that between Justin and our family we can
raise any amount of money to get Rena back." He let
his eyes drift to Justin's and hold. "If his motive is
money."

"We'll have to work on that premise for now, Senator," Lieutenant Renicki stated in a no-nonsense
voice. "We'll be putting a tap on your phone, with your
permission, Mr. Blade."

"Do whatever it takes."

Caine looked at Justin then, looked at him for the
first since the phone call. "Where's the brandy?"

"What?"

"You need a drink." When Justin merely shook his head, Caine let out a quiet oath. "Well, I'm going to have one—before I call Mom and Dad."

Justin felt a fresh twinge inside his stomach and gestured. "In that cabinet."

From opposite ends of the suite the phone rang. Without waiting for Lieutenant Renicki's yes or no, Justin went into the kitchen to answer. He couldn't bring himself to go into the bedroom. "Blade." Closing his eyes, he fought frustration, then held out the receiver. "It's for you," he told the lieutenant.

When he came back into the living room Justin found Alan and Caine standing in the center of the room, speaking quietly. "Alan's going to call our parents," Caine told him. "They'll take it better from him. They'll want to be here."

Justin struggled not to let the panic through, or the grief. "Of course."

As Lieutenant Renicki came into the room, he waited until all three pairs of eyes were on him. "My men found an abandoned maid's cart down in the garage. The lab will go over it thoroughly, but they found a rag soaked with ether inside. Apparently, that's how he got her out without anyone seeing her." Watching closely, Lieutenant Renicki saw Caine's knuckles whiten on his glass, saw the wave of terrified anger in Alan's eyes. He saw no change in Justin's expression. "We have your description of Miss MacGregor, Mr. Blade, but a picture would be helpful."

Justin stared as pain sprinted from his stomach to his throat. "I don't have one."

"I do." Numb, Alan reached for his wallet.

"We'll have the trace on the line right away, Mr. Blade," Lieutenant Renicki went on, glancing at the picture Alan handed him. "We'll be recording everything that's said. The longer you keep him on the line, the better. Whatever demands he makes, insist on speaking to Miss MacGregor before you agree to anything. We have to establish that she is indeed with him." And alive, he added silently.

"And if he refuses?" Justin demanded.

"Then you refuse to deal."

Justin forced himself to sit down. If he stood, he would pace—if he paced, he would lose control. "No," he said evenly.

"Justin," Alan interrupted before Renicki could speak again. "The lieutenant's right. We have to be certain Rena is with him and unharmed." *It's Rena,* he thought wildly as he struggled to keep his voice even. *Our Rena.* "If you make it clear there won't be a ransom unless you hear her voice, he'll put her on the phone."

You have a price to pay. The words flashed through Justin's mind. Not Serena, he thought desperately. God, not Serena. "And after I've spoken to her," Justin began, "I'll agree to any terms he asks. I won't bargain, and I won't stall."

"It's your money, Mr. Blade." Lieutenant Renicki gave him a thin smile. "I'd like you to listen to his voice very carefully when he phones back. Chances are he has it disguised, but you might recognize a phrasing, an inflection."

There was a brisk knock on the door which the lieutenant answered himself. As he stood talking in undertones to one of his men, Caine again approached Justin with the offer of brandy. For the second time Justin shook his head.

"They're going to catch him," Caine said, just needing to hear the words aloud.

Slowly, Justin lifted his eyes. "When they do," he said calmly. "I'm going to kill him."

Feeling groggy and sore, Serena woke, moaning. Had she overslept? she wondered. She'd miss class if she didn't—no, no, it was her shift in the casino and Dale...Justin—no, Justin was coming up for lunch and she hadn't even called room service.

She had to get up, but her eyes refused to open and there was a light, rolling sense of nausea in her stomach. Sick, she thought hazily. But she was never sick. How...the door, she remembered. Someone at the door. Nausea swelled again, and with it, fear. Drawing all her strength together, Serena opened her eyes.

The room was small and dim. Over the one window a shade was drawn. There was a cheap maple bureau against one wall with a mirror streaked with dust and a small, straight-backed rocking chair. There was no lamp, only a ceiling fixture overhead. Because it was off and some light filtered through the shade, Serena knew it was still day. But her sense of time was so distorted, she had no idea which day.

Someone had once painted the walls an airy yellow, but the color had faded so that they now seemed more like the pages of a very old book. Serena lay in the middle of a double bed on top of a worn chenille spread. When she tried to move her right arm, she discovered that it was handcuffed to the center bedpost. That's when the fear overcame the grogginess.

The boy from housekeeping, she remembered. *Ether*. Oh, God, how could she have been so stupid! Justin had warned her...Justin, she thought again as she clamped down on her bottom lip. He'd be frantic by now. Was he searching for her? Had he called the police? Perhaps he thought she'd just gone out on an errand.

I have to get out of here, Serena told herself desperately and scrambled closer to the headboard to tug on the handcuffs. The boy must have had something to do with the bombing in Vegas. It seemed incredible. He looked barely old enough to shave. Old enough to kidnap, she reminded herself grimly, yanking uselessly at the metal cuffs. When she heard his footsteps, she sat very still and waited.

He'd planned it perfectly, Terry thought as he hung up the phone. Snatching the woman from under Blade's nose had been risky, but, oh, so worthwhile. Better than the bomb, he decided as he drummed his fingers against the table. He'd had to give them too much time and they'd found the bomb because he hadn't wanted to hurt anyone. Just Blade. But this—this was perfect.

She was beautiful, he mused. Blade would pay to get her back. But before he paid, he'd suffer. Terry was going to make sure of it. To relieve his own tension he reminded himself how clever he had been. Even while Justin had been in Vegas, Terry had been on his way to Atlantic City. At the time he'd been annoyed with himself for not choosing the East Coast hotel in the first place. But it had all worked out.

He'd noticed Serena the first night he'd hung around the casino—then he'd learned she was Justin's partner. It had only taken a few casual questions in the right places to learn she was much more than that to him. Then Terry had outlined his plan.

At first he'd been frightened. Getting a woman out of a hotel was trickier than getting a small bomb in. But he'd watched. No one looked twice at the people in the plain white housekeeping uniforms. After a couple of days of watching Serena's movements, he concluded there was a private entrance from the offices to the living quarters. Probably an elevator, he had reasoned. That was the way the rich did things. He'd been patient, spending most of his time at the slot machines, waiting.

When he'd seen Justin come back, he knew it was time to move. Stealing the uniform had been easy, as easy as planting the letter. No one took any notice of a young, harmless-looking man in plain clothes. The minute he had seen the desk clerk deliver the envelope to the offices, Terry had begun to move. He'd had to force himself to go slowly. He'd told himself to give Justin a full ten minutes to get downstairs. On the third floor he'd changed his clothes in a storage closet, then he'd simply walked off with one of the maid's carts that sat in the hallway.

He remembered how his heart had been pounding as he had wheeled into the service elevator. There was a chance that she wouldn't be there, that she'd gone down with Justin and he'd have to start all over again. When she had opened the door and smiled, he'd almost lost his nerve. Then he'd remembered Blade. The rest was easy.

It had taken him less than five minutes to cover her unconscious body with linen and wheel the cart down to the garage where his car was waiting. With Serena

in the backseat, covered with a blanket, he'd simply
driven away. But she'd been unconscious for a long
time. Maybe he'd used too much ether, or...Then he
heard her moan. Terry got up to fix her a cup of tea.

When he opened the door, Serena was sitting back
against the headboard, staring at him. But she didn't
look as frightened as he'd imagined she would. He
wondered if she was in shock. He expected she'd start
screaming any minute.

"If you yell," he said quietly, "I'll have to gag you.
I don't want to do that."

Serena saw that he was holding a cup, and that it
shook in his hand. A nervous kidnapper, she thought
quickly, would be more dangerous than a calm one. She
swallowed any urge to scream. "I won't yell."

"I brought you some tea." He came a little closer.
"You might be feeling a little sick."

He was approaching her, Serena thought, as one approached a cornered animal. He expects me to be terrified, she realized. Well, he wasn't far off. It might be
more to her advantage to let her control slip outwardly.
Inside she'd force herself to be calm. The first thing
she had to know was where he kept the keys for the
handcuffs.

"I do. Please"—she let her voice tremble—"can I
use the bathroom?"

"Okay, I'm not going to hurt you." He spoke soothingly as he set the tea aside and came to her. Taking a
key from the pocket of his jeans, he fit it into the wrist
lock. "If you try to run away or start yelling, I'll have
to stop you." He paused as his hand replaced the metal
on her wrist. "Do you understand?"

Serena nodded. He was stronger, she discovered, than he looked.

Silently, he led her into a small bathroom. "I'm going to be right outside the door," he warned. "Just be smart and nothing'll happen to you."

Nodding, Serena went inside. Immediately, she looked for means of escape and was frustrated. There wasn't even a window. A weapon. A rapid search turned up nothing more than a towel bar that wouldn't budge. She bit down on her lip as fear and helplessness began to take over. She'd have to find another way. She *would* find another way.

Running cold water in the sink, she splashed it on her face. She had to stay calm and alert. And she couldn't underestimate the man outside the door. He was dangerous because he was every bit as frightened as she was. So she'd be more frightened, she decided. She would cower and weep so that he wouldn't know she was watching, waiting for the opportunity of escape. First, she had to find out exactly what his plans were.

Opening the door, Serena let him seize her wrists again. "Please, what are you going to do?"

"I'm not going to hurt you," Terry said again as he pulled her toward the bed. "He'll pay to get you back."

"Who?"

She saw the fury in his eyes. "Blade."

"My father has more," she began quickly. "He—"

"I don't want your father's money!" At his fierce explosion, Serena didn't have to simulate a shudder. "It's Blade. He's going to pay. I'm going to bleed him dry."

"Were you—were you the one who planted the bomb in Vegas?"

Terry handed her the tea. Serena considered throwing it into his face, then decided against it. If it were hot enough to burn him, he'd probably leap back and the key would be out of her reach.

"Yeah."

She watched him. There was angry color in his face now and a look in his eyes that had her stomach rolling. "Why?"

"He killed my father," Terry told her, then strode out of the room.

Why doesn't he call! Justin thought as he drank yet another cup of coffee. If he's hurt her— He looked down to see that he'd snapped the handle cleanly away from the mug. Setting them both down, he drew out a cigar. Behind him, in the dinette, two detectives played gin. Caine paced while Alan was already on his way to the airport to pick up Daniel and Anna. The living room extension had been repaired and was now attached to a recording device. But still they waited.

It was growing darker as clouds moved in. There'd be rain before the night was over. For God's sake, where was she! Why did I leave her alone? Justin wanted to bury his face in his hands. He wanted to hit something, anything. He sat perfectly still and stared at the wall. Why did I think she'd be safe here? he demanded of himself. I would have made her go away if I hadn't wanted her with me so badly. I could have made her go away. If anything happens to her...

He pushed the thought aside. If he were going to stay in control, he couldn't even allow himself the luxury of guilt. The only sounds in the room were the desultory conversation of the detectives and the hiss of Caine's lighter as he lit another cigarette. If the phone didn't ring, Justin was certain he'd go mad.

When it did, Justin lunged for it. "Keep him on the line as long as you can," one of the detectives ordered curtly. "And tell him you have to talk to her before you deal."

Justin didn't even acknowledge the instructions as he picked up the receiver. The recorder was running silently. "Blade."

"Want your squaw back, Blade?"

It was a young voice, Justin realized. And frightened. The same voice he had heard on the police recordings in Las Vegas. "How much?"

"Two million, cash. Small bills. I'll let you know when and where."

"Serena. Let me talk to Serena."

"Forget it."

"How do I know you have her?" Justin demanded. "How do I know she's..." He had to force the words out. "Still alive."

"I'll think about it."

And the line went dead.

Serena huddled under the blanket. She was cold. Scared, she corrected herself brutally. The chill she was feeling had nothing to do with her thin sweater or bare feet. *He killed my father.* The flat statement ran over and over in her head. Could this be the son of the man who had attacked Justin all those years ago? He'd have been little more than a baby at the time. If he'd been harboring hate all those years...Serena shivered again and drew the blanket over her shoulders.

She shouldn't have doubted Justin's instincts. He'd known somehow that someone was after him personally. How far would the boy go for revenge? she asked herself. Be objective, she ordered. This is real.

She'd seen his face. Could he take the chance of letting her go when she could identify him? Yet, he didn't seem like a cold-blooded killer. He'd planted a bomb in a crowded hotel, she reminded herself. Oh, God, she had to get away!

Closing her eyes, Serena put all her concentration into listening. It was quiet, no sounds of traffic. She thought, but couldn't be sure, that she heard the ocean. It might've been the wind. How far out of town were they? she wondered. If she threw the teacup through the window and screamed, would anyone hear? Even as she weighed the odds, Terry came back into the bedroom.

"I brought you a sandwich."

He seemed more agitated this time, or perhaps, she reconsidered, excited. Make him talk, she told herself. "Please don't leave me alone." She grabbed his arm with her free hand and let her eyes plead with his.

"You'll feel better after you eat," he mumbled, and shoved the sandwich under her nose. "You don't have to be scared. I told you I wouldn't hurt you if you didn't try anything."

"I've seen you," she said, taking the chance. "How can you let me go?"

"I've got plans." Restless, he began to pace the little room. He wasn't big, she thought. If I could just get my hand free, I'd have a chance. "By the time I let them know where you are, I'll already be gone." He thought of Switzerland with grim pleasure. "They won't find me. I'll have two million dollars to help me hide in comfort.''

"Two million," she whispered. "How do you know Justin will pay?''

Terry laughed, turning to look at her. Her face was pale, her eyes huge. Her hair tumbled wildly around her shoulders. "He'll pay. He'll beg me to let him pay before I'm finished.''

"You said he killed your father.''

"Murdered him.''

"But he was acquitted. Justin told me——'' The words slid back down her throat as Terry whirled.

"He murdered my father and they let him go!'' he shouted. "Let him go because they felt sorry for him. It was all politics, my mother told me. They let him go because he was a poor Indian kid. My mother said that his lawyer paid off the witnesses.''

His mother, Serena thought, had been warping his mind for years. It would take more than a few words from her to change it now. Had his mother told him about the scar along Justin's side? Had she told him his father had been drunk, or that the knife that had killed him had been his own? Serena studied Terry's set, frightened face and hating eyes. "I'm sorry," she said weakly. "I'm so sorry.''

"He's paying now," Terry told her, and tossed a hank of errant hair out of his eyes. "I wish I could take the chance of holding you for more than a couple of days.'' He gave a soft, wondering laugh. "Who'd have thought I'd make Blade crawl for a woman?''

"Please, what's your name?''

"Terry," he said briefly.

Serena struggled to sit up straighter. "Terry, you

must know Justin's called the police. They'll be looking for me.''

''They won't find you,'' he returned simply. ''I didn't start planning yesterday. I put a deposit down on this place six months ago, when Blade opened the hotel. I was thinking about squeezing him a second time after he'd paid off from Vegas.'' He shrugged as if the business in Vegas meant little. ''The old couple I rented this from are in Florida by now. They've never even seen me, just the check I sent them.''

''Terry—''

''Look, nothing's going to happen to you. Just eat and get some rest. Ten hours after Blade makes the drop, I'll call and let them know where to find you.'' He stormed out of the room, slamming the door before she could say any more.

''What are they doing to get her back!'' Daniel demanded as he strode around the living room of Justin's suite. ''Look at these two''—he tossed out a hand toward the two detectives—''playing cards while some maniac has my little girl.''

''They're doing everything they can,'' Alan told him quietly. ''The phone's tapped. He didn't stay on the line long enough last time to trace it. They're checking out all the fingerprints on the maid's cart.''

''Hah!'' Letting his panic take the form of anger, he rounded on his son. ''And what kind of a place is it where a man can dump my daughter in a basket and go off with her?''

''Daniel.'' From her place on the sofa beside Justin, Anna spoke softly. She said only his name, but the pain in her eyes had him cursing again and striding to the window. She turned to Justin, putting her hand over his. "Justin—"

But he shook his head, rising. For the first time in the six hours of fear, he knew he was going to fall apart. Without a word he walked into the bedroom and shut the door behind him.

Her robe was tossed over a chair where she had left it. He had only to pick it up to smell her. He balled his hands into fists and turned away from it. The jeweler's box with the earrings he'd given her sat open on the dresser. He could remember the way they had looked on her the night before—gleaming, catching fire in the dim light as she had knelt naked on his bed and held her arms out to him.

Fear and anger rolled around inside him until his skin was wet and clammy. The silence of the room weighed down on him. There was only the sound of rain, falling cold and steady outside the windows. Only a few hours before, Serena had filled the room with life—laughter and passion. Then he'd left her. He hadn't told her he loved her, or kissed her good-bye. He'd walked out with his mind occupied with his own business. Left her alone, he thought again.

"Oh, God." Running his hands over his face, he pressed his fingers hard against his eyes. At the soft knock on the door, Justin dropped his hands and struggled against the sensation of despair. Daniel came in without waiting for his answer.

"Justin." He closed the door behind him and stood, looking huge—and for the first time in Justin's memory—helpless. "I'm sorry for that."

Justin met his eyes as he balled his hands in his

pockets again. "You were right. If I hadn't been care-less—"

"No." Coming to him, Daniel gripped both his arms. "There's no blame here. Rena—he wanted Rena, he'd have found a way. I'm scared." The big voice quavered as his grip tightened. "I've only been scared once before in my life. When Caine took it into his head to explore the roof and we found him hanging on a ledge two stories up. I don't know where she is." His voice shook as he turned away. "I can't get a ladder to her."

"Daniel, I love her."

On a deep breath, Daniel turned back. "Aye, I can see that."

"Whatever he asks, whatever he wants me to do, I'll do."

Nodding, Daniel held out his hand. "Come, the family should wait together."

Chapter Twelve

She must have dozed because it was dark when Serena felt herself being shaken awake.

"You're going to make a phone call," Terry told her, then walked over to flip on the overhead light.

Serena tossed her arm over her eyes to shield them. "Who," she began.

"He should have sweated enough by now," Terry mumbled as he hooked the phone in the bedroom jack. "It's after one. Listen." He jerked her arm down so that she could look at him. "You're going to tell him you're all right, and that's all. Don't try anything." He began to dial. "When he answers, just tell him you're not hurt, and you'll stay that way as long as he pays. Understand?"

Nodding, Serena took the receiver.

Justin was on the phone in the first ring. A half cup of cold coffee tipped over on the table and dripped on the rug. "Blade."

Serena squeezed her eyes shut at the sound of his

voice. It was raining, she thought dimly. It was raining, and she was so cold and frightened. "Justin."

"Serena! Are you all right? Has he hurt you?"

Taking a deep breath, she looked directly into Terry's eyes. "I'm all right, Justin. No scars."

"Where are you?" he began, but Terry clamped his hand over her mouth and grabbed the phone.

"If you want her back, get the money together. Two million, small bills, unmarked. I'll let you know where to make the drop. And you'll make it alone, Blade, if you don't want her hurt."

He hung up the phone, then let Serena go. The sound of Justin's voice did what the hours of fear hadn't been able to. On a trembling sob, she buried her face in the pillow and wept.

"She's all right." Justin replaced the phone with studied care. "She's all right."

"Thank God." Anna grabbed both of his hands. "What next?"

"I get the cash together, take it wherever he tells me."

"We'll take photographs of the bills," Lieutenant Renicki stated as he stirred himself from his chair. "One of my men will tail you when you make the drop."

"No."

"Listen, Mr. Blade," he began patiently, "there's no guarantee he'll let Miss MacGregor go after he's been paid off. He's more likely to—"

"No," Justin repeated. "We play it my way, Lieutenant. No tails."

The lieutenant took a deep breath. "All right, we can

plant a bug in the case. That way, when he picks up the money, he might lead us right to her.''

"And if he spots it?" Justin countered. "No," he said again. "I'm not taking any chances."

"You're taking a hell of a chance by handing him two million dollars cold," Lieutenant Renicki tossed back. "Mrs. MacGregor." He turned to Anna, thinking a woman, a mother, would be more reasonable. "We want your daughter back healthy, the same as you. Let us help you."

She gave him a long, steady look while the hand in Justin's trembled lightly. "I appreciate your concern, Lieutenant, but I'm afraid I feel as Justin does."

"Photograph the money," Caine put in. "And go after him when Rena's safe. By God, I'd like to prosecute him myself," he added in a savage mutter.

"Then you'd better hope he'll be prosecuted for only kidnapping and extortion—not murder," Lieutenant Renicki added cruelly. "He'll keep her alive until he's got the money. After that, it's anyone's guess. Listen, Blade," he continued as his patience snapped. "You don't like dealing with cops, maybe because you had some trouble years back, but it's a hell of a lot smarter to deal with us than to deal with him." He tossed his hand toward the phone.

In an unconscious gesture Justin ran his hand over his ribs. No, he thought, he didn't trust the police. The memory of those endless questions while his wound was healing into a scar were ingrained in his memory. Maybe he was making a mistake. Maybe he should...His fingers froze abruptly. Scars. No scars!

"Oh, God," he murmured as his eyes dropped to his hand. "Oh, my God!"

"What is it?" Anna was standing beside him, her fingers digging into his arm.

Slowly, he brought his eyes to hers. "A ghost," he whispered. Then shook away dread as he faced Lieutenant Renicki. "On the phone Serena was trying to tell me something. She said, 'No scars.' The man I killed in Nevada put a knife in me. Serena knows the story."

The lieutenant was already heading for the phone. "Do you remember his name?"

Justin gave a mirthless laugh. Did you ever forget the name of a man when you were tried for his murder? "Charles Terrance Ford," he answered. "He had a wife and a son. She brought the boy to the courtroom every day." He had blue eyes, Justin remembered. Pale, confused blue eyes. A wave of sickness rose up, threatening to swallow him.

"This time, drink it," Caine ordered as he thrust a snifter of brandy into Justin's hands.

Looking down at it, Justin shook his head. "Coffee," he mumbled, and walked into the kitchen. But he couldn't think. Pressing his palms down on the counter, he tried to clear his head. Helpless, he realized. He felt the same raging helplessness he'd experienced so long ago in that narrow little cell. Seventeen years, he thought. Dear God, he's had seventeen years to hate me. What will he do to her because of me?

"If it's all you drink, then drink it," Caine said roughly as he pushed a cup of coffee across the counter. He was remembering Serena standing there only that morning, her eyes laughing at him while he dealt with the fact that she'd grown up while he wasn't looking.

"I knew," Justin said quietly as he stared into the

black coffee. "I knew someone was after me. I knew she wasn't safe, but I didn't make her go."

Caine sat down heavily on a stool. "I've known Rena all her life, loved her all her life. No one, absolutely no one makes her do anything."

"I could have." Justin picked up the coffee and drank without tasting. "All I had to do was go with her."

"And he'd have followed you."

Justin slammed the cup back down. "Yes." The anger cleared his head and dispelled the lingering sickness in his throat. "I'm going to get her back, Caine," he said with deadly calm. "Nothing in hell's going to stop me from getting her back."

"His name's Terry Ford," Lieutenant Renicki stated as he walked into the room and headed for the coffeepot. "Booked a flight out of Vegas five days ago, destination, Atlantic City. We'll have a description soon. We're checking all the hotels, motels, condos, beach rentals, but there's no telling whether he's kept her in town. I wouldn't bank on him renting a room in his own name," he added as he helped himself to the sugar bowl. "His mother remarried about three years ago. We're tracking her down."

It felt good to have something solid to work with— names, faces. With a satisfied grunt Lieutenant Renicki sat across from Caine. "We'll get him," he promised. "You both should try to get some rest," he advised. "Odds are he won't be calling again until morning." When neither of them answered, the lieutenant sighed. This family knows how to close ranks, he reflected. "All right, Mr. Blade, why don't you tell me what arrangements you've made for getting the ransom together?"

"The money will be in my office by eight o'clock."

Lieutenant Renicki's bushy brows rose and fell. "No problem getting that amount of cash together?"

"No."

"Okay, tell him nine. Then we'll have time to photograph it in your office. That way, if he slips by us, we'll be able to grab him once he starts to pass it. I'd like you to reconsider letting us put a tracer in one of the cases. I can show you how successfully it can be concealed. Remember," he added before Justin could speak, "our primary concern is the same as yours. To get Miss MacGregor back, safe."

For the first time, Justin noticed the fatigue in the lieutenant's eyes. It occurred to him that the policeman hadn't eaten or slept any more than he had himself. Under most circumstances, he would have trusted those eyes. "I'll consider it," he said at length.

The lieutenant only nodded and drained the rest of his coffee.

At six A.M. the phone rang again. Anna and Daniel woke from a half doze on the sofa. Alan came to attention in the chair where he had spent the night, awake and restless. Caine stopped in the doorway of the kitchen where he was returning with yet another cup of coffee. Justin's hand snaked out to the receiver. He'd been staring at the phone for more than an hour.

"Blade."

"Got the money?"

"It'll be here by nine."

"There's a gas station two blocks down from the

hotel on the right. Be in the phone booth there by nine-fifteen. I'll call you."

Terry hung up the phone so tied up with nerves, he nearly knocked the small table over. He hadn't been able to sleep even after Serena's weeping had quieted. She shouldn't have been able to make him feel sorry for her, he thought as he rubbed the heels of his hands over his eyes. After all, what kind of a woman was she to be living with a murderer?

His mother would have said she was a tramp, but he'd sensed something about her. Classy, Terry mused as he stretched his stiff and aching muscles. She'd even looked classy in that sweater and jeans when she'd opened the door for him. And last night…He sighed, glancing at the door to the bedroom. Last night she'd looked so small and helpless when she'd curled up on the bed and cried.

Well, he was sorry he had to scare her that way, but she was the best weapon he could use on Blade. She shouldn't have gotten mixed up with scum like him in the first place, Terry reminded himself. I'd kill him if I could, Terry thought, but knew he didn't have it in him. Planting a bomb in a building and drawing a knife or gun on a man were two different things. A bomb was remote, and he was forced to admit that he'd probably never have gotten up the nerve to detonate it. But the threat. Oh, the satisfaction of being able to keep the man who had killed his father shaking in his shoes. Then he'd have the money, and every dollar he spent would be revenge on Justin Blade.

He heard Serena stir and rose to check on her.

She was disgusted with herself. What good had crying done but to give her a throbbing head and swollen eyes? She needed to be planning a way out, not wallowing in self-pity. The arm that was attached to the bedpost ached and tingled from the lack of circulation. Shifting on the bed, she tried to rub the blood back into it. *Think!* she demanded of herself. There's always a way out.

When the bedroom door opened, her head spun around. Serena caught the quick regret in Terry's eyes as he looked at her. God, I must be a pitiful sight, she thought wearily. Then use it, Rena! a small voice ordered impatiently. Start using your head.

She allowed the fear to surface again while she clung to her inner strength desperately. "Please, my arm hurts. I think I wrenched it during the night."

"I'm sorry." He stood irresolutely in the center of the room. "I'll fix you some breakfast."

"Please," she said quickly before he could go. "If I—if I could just sit in a chair. I ache all over from lying like this. Where can I go?" she asked on a half sob as he hesitated. "You're stronger than I am."

"Look, I'll take you into the kitchen. If you try anything, I'll bring you back in here and put a gag on you."

"All right, just please let me get up for a while."

Terry pulled the key from his pocket and unlocked the handcuffs. Serena pushed down the urge to run, knowing she'd get no farther than the door. Clamping his fingers over her arm, he led her quickly through the house.

The shades were drawn. I could be in Alaska for all I know, she thought in frustration. If I could run, what direction would I go? Does he have a car? He must have a car—how else did he get me here? If I could get the keys…

"Sit down," he ordered, and nudged her into a rickety chair at the kitchen table. Quickly, he knelt and slipped the cuffs around her ankle and a table leg. Pushing his hair out of his eyes, he rose. "I'll get you some coffee."

"Thank you." Her eyes swept the room swiftly in search of a weapon within reach.

"You'll be out of here by tonight," Terry told her as he poured coffee without taking his eyes from her. "He's already getting the money together. I probably could have asked for twice as much."

"You won't be happy with it."

"He'll be unhappy," Terry countered. "That's what counts."

"Terry, you're wasting your life this way." He looked so young, she thought. Too young to have so much hate packed inside him. "It took brains to plan everything out the way you have. Brains and skill. You could be putting your mind to so much better use. If you let me go now, I might be able to help you. My brother—"

"I don't want your help," he said between his teeth. "I want Blade. I want him to crawl."

"Justin won't crawl," she said wearily.

"Lady, I heard him on the phone. He'd crawl to hell and back for you."

"Terry—"

"Shut up!" he shouted at her as his nerves threatened to snap. "I've spent all of my life working out how I was going to make Blade pay. I had to watch my mother scrimp and save and work in a sleazy diner while he got richer and richer instead of rotting in a cell. I'm entitled to the money, and I'm going to have it." Resigned, Serena dropped her gaze to the table. "Look, I'm going to fix something to eat. Are you hungry?"

She started to tell him no, then realized he'd just lock her back in the bedroom. Instead, she merely nodded, keeping her face averted while she tried to think.

Hearing him rummaging in the cupboard, she gave her leg a testing jerk. She was going to have to take a chance. When he took the cuff off this time, she'd fight. With luck, she could surprise him enough to at least get outside, get someone's attention. If there were anyone close enough to hear her shouting...

When she looked back up, Terry had a large cast iron skillet in his hand. Without giving herself a chance to think, Serena moaned and began to slip slowly toward the floor.

"Hey!" Alarmed, he rushed over, dropping the skillet beside her as he tried to lift her by the shoulders. "What is it?" he demanded. "Are you sick?"

"I feel faint," she said weakly as her fingers closed over the handle of the skillet. She made herself go limp until his face bent over hers. Using all of her strength, she crashed the skillet against the side of his head. He went down like a stone.

At first, Serena lay still, trying to catch the breath he'd knocked out of her when he'd landed across her body. Then she had a moment's terror that she'd killed him. Struggling, she wiggled out from under him and felt for his pulse.

"Thank God," she murmured as she felt the beat. Quickly, she shifted until she could reach into his pocket for the key. His mother was the one who deserved that blow, she thought as she released herself. Poor kid never had a chance.

Rising, she considered her options. She could run like hell, but the chances were that he'd come to and take off. No, she had to make sure he stayed put first.

Serena stuck the handcuffs into the back pocket of her jeans then began to drag him toward the bedroom. He wasn't a big man, but as she started across the living room, bent over and tugging him by the shoulders, she discovered her strength wasn't at its maximum. By the time she got him through the doorway, she was breathing hard and dripping with sweat.

Resting against the doorjamb, she decided she'd never be able to drag him onto the bed. Instead, she left him stretched out on the floor, attached to the footboard with the handcuffs.

She stumbled on the way to the phone with a faintness that wasn't contrived. It occurred to her that she'd barely eaten in two days. It would wait, she told herself, shaking her head to clear it. She wasn't about to pass out now. Quickly, she lifted the phone and dialed.

After a quick shower and change of clothes, Justin came back into the living room. Anna was urging Daniel to eat, though she wasn't touching anything on her own plate. She looked up as Justin entered.

"We'll have a family dinner tonight," she told him with a valiant smile. "Rena loves the fuss." He saw the tears swim into her eyes to be hastily blinked away.

For the first time since he had known her, Justin went to her and put his arms around her. "Why don't you go down and speak to the chef? He'll fix whatever you want.''

He felt her shudder as her fingers dug into his back. "Yes, I'll do that. Be careful," she whispered. "Be careful, Justin.''

When the phone rang she jerked, then drew away. Her face was a mask of control. "He wasn't supposed to call again.''

"He probably wants to make sure nothing's gone wrong.'' His head pounding, Justin picked up the phone. "Blade.''

"Justin.''

"Serena!'' He heard Anna's quick gasp behind him. "Are you all right?''

"Yes, yes, I'm fine. Justin—''

"Are you sure? He hasn't hurt you? I didn't think he'd let you call again.''

She controlled her impatience and spoke lightly. "He didn't have any choice,'' she told him. "He's unconscious and cuffed to the bedpost.''

"What?'' Caine grabbed at his arm, but Justin shook him off. "What did you say?''

"I said I knocked him out and cuffed him to the bedpost.''

Something rushed through him that he didn't recognize. It was relief. It came out in a burst of laughter. "God knows why I was worried about you,'' he said as he sunk onto the couch. Looking up, he saw four pairs of anxious eyes. "She knocked him out and cuffed him to the bedpost.''

"That's a MacGregor for you!'' Daniel exploded, and swung Anna into his arms. "What did she hit him with?''

"Is that my father?" Serena wanted to know.

"Yes. He asked what you hit him with."

"A cast iron skillet." She realized her legs were shaking and sat on the floor.

"A skillet," Justin relayed.

"That's my little girl!" Daniel kissed Anna lustily, then laid his head on her shoulder and wept.

"Justin, could you come and get me?" Serena demanded. "I've had a really dreadful night."

"Where are you?"

"I don't know." As reaction set in, she buried her face on her knees. Don't fall apart, she ordered herself. Don't fall apart now. She could hear Justin calling her name through the receiver and swallowed the tears. "Wait a minute, let me pull up the shades and see if I can get my bearings. Talk to me," she demanded as she rose. "Just keep talking to me."

"Your family's all here," he said, hearing the edge of hysteria in her voice. "Your mother wants to have a dinner tonight. What would you like?"

"A cheeseburger," she said as she flipped up the first shade. "Oh, God, I'd love to have a cheeseburger and a gallon of champagne. I think I'm east of town, near the beach. There're a few frame houses farther down the road. I've never been in this section." She bit down hard on her lip to keep her voice from breaking. "I just don't know where I am."

"Give me the phone number, Serena. We'll trace it." Justin scribbled it down quickly as she read it off. "I'll be there, just hang on."

"I will, I'm fine really." Somehow, letting the light into the room helped. "Just hurry. Tell everyone I'm all right, not to worry."

"Serena, I love you."

Tears welled up again. "Come and show me," she said before she hung up.

Justin handed the piece of paper to Lieutenant Renicki. "Find out where she is."

With a nod the lieutenant began to dial the phone. "Knocked him out with a skillet, eh?" He gave a quick, appreciative laugh. "Must be quite a woman."

"She's a MacGregor," Daniel told him, then heartily blew his nose.

"A little waterfront house east of town," Lieutenant Renicki said a few minutes later, and headed for the door. "Coming?" he asked Justin.

Justin sent him a mild look. "We're all coming."

Serena stood in the open doorway though she shivered in the brisk morning air. It had been less than twenty-four hours, she realized. She felt as though it had been days since she'd seen the sunlight. The grass was still wet from the night's rain. How was it she'd never noticed how many colors there were in a drop of water on a blade of grass?

Then she saw the cars. Like a procession, she thought, and wanted badly to weep again. No, she wouldn't greet Justin with tears running down her face. Straightening her shoulders, she went out on the stoop to wait.

He pulled up in front of two police cars. Even as the car stopped, he was out of the door and rushing toward her. "Serena." His arms were around her, lifting her off her feet as he crushed her against him. With her face buried against his throat, she heard him say her name again and again. "Are you all right?" he demanded, but before she could answer, his lips were fastened on hers.

Why, he's trembling, she realized, and clutched him tighter. As reassurance, she put all of the love and warmth she had into the kiss. "You're freezing," he murmured, feeling the chill of her skin under his hands. "Here, take my jacket." As he started to remove it, Serena caught his face in her hands.

"Oh, Justin," she whispered, and stroked the lines of strain on his face. "What did he put you through?"

"Here now, let me take a look at her." Daniel took her by the shoulders, then ran his wide hands over her face. "So you took him out with a frying pan, did you, little girl?"

Seeing the red-rimmed eyes, she kissed him fiercely. "It was handy," she told him. "Don't tell me you were worried about me?" she demanded as if insulted.

"'Course not." He sniffed loudly. "Any daughter of mine can take care of herself. Your mother, she was worried."

Lieutenant Renicki watched as Serena was passed from one family member to another. He intended to keep an eye on Justin when Terry Ford was brought out. "We'll need a statement from you, Miss MacGregor," he said, moving over casually to stand beside Justin.

"Not now."

He acknowledged Justin's words with a simple nod. "If you could come down to the station later today, after you've rested." He felt Justin tense, and bracing himself, looked over as Terry was brought out by two uniformed officers. "Easy, Mr. Blade," he murmured. "Your lady's been through enough for one day."

Terry jerked up his head. Justin remembered those eyes. The pale anxious eyes he'd seen every day in a courtroom. He'd been no more than three, Justin thought. A baby. He felt Serena's hand link with his as the anger drained out of him. As they led him to the car, Terry continued to watch Justin over his shoulder.

"I'm sorry for him," Serena murmured. "So sorry for him."

Justin gathered her into his arms. "So am I."

"Some of my men will be going through the house," Lieutenant Renicki said briskly. "If you'd come downtown at your convenience, Miss MacGregor."

"Come on, let's get the girl back," Daniel stated, and took a step toward her.

"Justin will bring her." Anna took his arm and steered him toward the second police car. "The rest of us will go back and plan that dinner."

"She doesn't even have any shoes on her feet," Daniel blustered as he was pushed into the car.

"She'll be all right," Alan commented as he dropped into the front seat. He realized he was starving.

"Sure, she'll be fine," Caine agreed, then leaned over to his father's ear. "I'll buy you a cigar if you go quietly."

Daniel shifted his eyes toward his wife and settled back. "She'll be fine," he decided.

"Come on." Justin buttoned his jacket up to Serena's throat. "I'll take you back."

"Let's walk on the beach." She hooked her arm around his waist. "I really need to walk."

"You're barefoot," he pointed out.

"It's the best way to walk on the beach. You haven't slept," she commented as they crossed to the sand.

"No. But it appears I could have rested easy." He wanted to crush her against him, be certain she was real. Trying to keep his arm light around her shoulders, he brushed his lips over the top of her head.

"I hated to hurt him," she mused. "But I couldn't be sure how he'd react once he had you face to face. So much hate locked up inside that boy, Justin. It's so sad."

"I took something vital from his life. He took something vital from mine." He stopped, holding her close to his side as he looked out to sea. "I'm surprised he asked for such a small amount of money."

"Small?" She cocked a brow at him. "In most circles two million is a hefty sum."

"For something priceless?" He took her face in his hands, then lowered his mouth to hers. Then with a shudder he dragged her close and savaged her lips. "Serena." His mouth raced over her face, coming to rest again on hers. "I wasn't sure I'd ever hold you again. All I could think about was what he might have done to you—what I'd do to him when I found him."

"He wouldn't have hurt me." The violence was bubbling in him again, so she soothed it with her hands and lips. "The reason it was so easy to get away was because he didn't wish me any harm."

"No, it was me—"

"Justin. Enough!" She drew him away, and her eyes were suddenly touched with anger. "You didn't cause this; I'm not going to listen to you try to take the blame. What happened today was started long ago with drink and bigotry. Now it's over. Let it rest."

"I wonder why I missed you shouting at me," he murmured, then drew her close again.

"Masochist. You know"—she cuddled against him a moment—"I've had some time to think about our relationship."

"Oh?"

"Yes, I think we need to redefine the ground rules."

Puzzled, he drew her away. "I didn't know we had any."

"I've been thinking." She walked toward the surf, then discovering the water was freezing, stepped back again.

"And?" Wary, he took her shoulders and turned her to face him.

"And I don't think the current situation is very practical."

"In what way?"

"I think we should get married," she said very coolly.

"Married?" Thoughtful, Justin stared at her. She was standing barefoot in cold sand, in a jacket several sizes too big for her, with her hair tangled and tossed, calmly telling him they should get married. An hour before she knocked out a would-be kidnapper with an iron skillet. It wasn't, he discovered, exactly as he'd pictured it. He'd imagined asking her himself when they were in some dimly lit room, warm and fresh from loving. "Married?" he repeated.

"Yes, I hear people still do it. Now, I'm willing to be reasonable."

"You are." He nodded, wondering just what she was up to.

"Since it's my suggestion, we'll settle it your way." Digging in her pocket, she pulled out a coin.

Justin laughed and reached out to take it from her. "Serena, really—"

"Oh, no, my coin, my flip. Heads we get married, tails we don't." Before he could say another word she spun the coin in the air, then snatched it. She slapped it onto the back of her hand, then held it out for him to see. "Heads."

He glanced at it. Dipping his hands into his pockets, Justin raised his eyes to hers. "Looks like I lose."

"Certainly does." Serena slipped the two-headed coin back into her pocket.

"How about the best two out of three?"

A flare of temper lit her eyes. "Forget it," she told him, and started across the sand. She let out a quick screech when Justin swooped her up into his arms. "If you think you're going to welsh," she began, then gave a sigh of pleasure as he silenced her.

"I never welsh," he promised, nipping at her lip as he started to carry her back to the car. "Let me take a look at that coin."

As she twined her arms around his neck, her eyes laughed into his. "Over my dead body."

* * * * *

TEMPTING FATE

Chapter One

She wasn't sure why she was doing it. Diana studied the cloud formations spreading beneath her and tried to reason out if the trip she was making had been impulse on her part or calculated. Though she was scheduled to land in less than thirty minutes, she still wasn't certain.

It had been nearly twenty years since she'd last seen her brother. When Diana thought of him, she thought of him as a remote, exciting, casually affectionate teenager. Diana had loved him with all the single-minded intensity that a six-year-old girl can have for a sixteen-year-old boy.

Her image of him was frozen in the past—a dark, rangy youth with sharp good looks and cool green eyes. She remembered an arrogant sort of pride and self-sufficiency. He'd been a loner. Even at six, Diana had understood that Justin Blade had gone his own way.

With a mild, humorless smile, she leaned back in the soft comfort of her first-class seat. Justin had certainly gone his own way twenty years before. When their parents had died, he had comforted her, Diana supposed. But she'd been too bewildered to understand. She had thought her parents had left because she'd made a fuss about going to school. If she behaved and was quiet and attentive in class, her parents would come back. Then Aunt Adelaide had come, and Justin had gone. For months she had thought he'd gone to heaven, too, tired of her tears and questions. Her aunt had taken her east, to a different world, a different life. Not once in the span of two decades had Justin contacted her.

So now he's married, Diana mused. Perhaps because she still saw him as an intense, rather brooding teenager, she couldn't picture Justin as a husband. Serena MacGregor. Diana ran the name over in her mind. Odd that she should find herself with a sister-in-law when she barely felt that she had a brother.

Oh, she knew of the Hyannis Port MacGregors. Aunt Adelaide wouldn't have considered Diana's education complete if she hadn't been made aware of the background of one of the country's leading families—particularly when they lived close enough to Boston to be considered neighbors. After all, monied dynasties were the only royalty America claimed.

Daniel MacGregor was the patriarch, a full-blooded Scot and financial wizard. Anna MacGregor, his wife, was a highly respected surgeon. Alan, the oldest son, was a United States senator earmarked for bigger things.

Caine MacGregor. Here, Diana stopped her mental list. Though he was barely thirty, she'd heard his name bandied about the hallowed halls of Harvard Law School. Both she and Caine had chosen law and she'd slaved over the books, studied under the same professors and walked the same corridors. At length, she'd passed the same bar. He'd graduated the year before she'd entered and had already begun what looked to be a brilliant career.

Once when Diana had been a freshman, she'd overheard two female upperclassmen talking about Caine MacGregor. And, she remembered with a smirk, they hadn't been discussing his mind. Obviously, the inestimable MacGregor hadn't spent all his time sweating over his books.

Then there was Serena. From all accounts, she was brilliant—it seemed to be in the MacGregor genes. She'd graduated from Smith with honors, Diana recalled, then had spent the next few years collecting degrees. She seemed an odd match for the Justin Blade Diana remembered.

For a moment, Diana considered whether she would have attended their wedding if she'd been in the country. Yes, she decided. She would have been too curious not to. After all, it was primarily curiosity that had her traveling to Atlantic City now. Then again, she thought ruefully, it would have been difficult to refuse the invitation Serena had sent her without being childishly rude. If there were two things Aunt Adelaide had taught her, they were never to be childish or rude—at least not to those considered your peers. Diana pushed her aunt's quaint double standards to the back of her mind and unfolded Serena's letter.

Dear Diana,

    I was terribly disappointed that you were in Paris last fall and unable to attend the wedding.

I'd often requested a sister, but my parents wouldn't oblige me. Now that I have one, it's frustrating not to be able to enjoy her. Justin speaks of you, but it's not the same as meeting you face to face—especially since his memories are of a little girl. After all these years, I can think of nothing he'd like better than to meet the woman you've become.

Taking a page out of his book, I'm sending you an airline ticket. Please use it and be our guest at the Comanche for as long as you like. You and Justin have a lifetime to catch up on, and I have a sister to meet.

                                        Rena

Diana arched a brow as she refolded the letter. Warm, open, friendly, she mused. Not the sort of woman she would have paired up with Justin. With a quiet laugh, Diana leaned back. She didn't even know a man named Justin Blade.

If there was a part of her that longed to know him, she'd buried it long ago. She'd had to, in order to survive in her aunt's world. Even now, if her aunt were to discover she was planning on spending time with Justin at a gambling hotel, the woman would be horrified. And, Diana added, the lecture on where and with whom a lady is seen would begin.

She gave her attention to the clouds again. It hardly mattered, she mused. She would meet her brother and his wife, satisfy her curiosity, then leave. The little girl who had idolized unquestioningly didn't exist any longer. She had her own life, her own career. They'd both been stagnant for too long. It was a new year, Diana reminded herself. The perfect time for beginnings.

She probably won't show, Caine thought as he walked toward the terminal. Since Diana Blade hadn't responded to Serena's letter, he didn't understand why his sister was so certain she'd be on the plane. He was less certain why he had allowed himself to be drafted as chauffeur.

Rena would have come if things hadn't gotten so busy at the hotel, he reminded himself. And since the hell they'd been through only a few months before, Caine found himself willing to indulge his sister's whims. Otherwise, he mused, he'd be spending his week off skiing in Colorado instead of walking a northern beach in January.

A gust of wind blew down the collar of his coat as he reached for the door at the terminal entrance. A blonde, wrapped in red fox, passed through, pausing long enough to run her gaze up Caine's body and over his face before her eyes met his. Caine took the brief, speculative look with a half-amused smile and waited for her to move by.

He had a lean, somewhat pale face with sharp, strong bones offset by eyes that edged toward violet. At a casual glance, he might be deemed a scholar—a longer one might reveal the recklessness that was far removed from academia. Because he was hatless, the wind tossed his burnished gold hair around his face. The smile added charm to what were intense, almost wolfish features. He was a man aware of his looks and comfortable with them.

Caine moved through the terminal in a quick, rangy stride, looking neither right nor left. He'd spent enough time in airports to ignore the sounds and crowds. With a brief glance at the monitor, he checked the gate for the incoming flight from Boston, then settled down to wait for a woman he didn't expect.

When the arrival was announced, Caine sat back in the black plastic chair and lit a cigarette. He'd wait until the last passenger had deplaned, then go back to the hotel. Serena would be satisfied, and he'd have an afternoon workout in the gym. Since completing his term as state's attorney and resuming his private practice, Caine hadn't had time for an hour's relaxation, much less a week's. When he relaxed, he believed in doing it as thoroughly as he worked.

The next seven days, he told himself, were going to be dedicated to doing nothing. He wouldn't think of the chaos of his office, the cases he was going to have to turn down because there simply weren't enough hours in the day, or the reams of paperwork.

Caine knew her the minute he saw her. The high, slashing cheekbones were so much like Justin's, as was the smooth, almost copper complexion. The Indian heritage they shared was perhaps even more apparent in the sister. Her eyes weren't the light, unexpected green of her brother, but a rich, dark brown. Camel eyes, Caine thought as he rose. Luxuriously lashed and heavy lidded so that they appeared sleepy. The nose was straight and aristocratic, the mouth passionate. Or stubborn, he mused. It wasn't a face a man could easily categorize—beautiful, appealing, sexy—but it wasn't one he'd easily forget. Caine knew he'd already memorized it, feature by feature.

As she shifted her flight bag to her other arm, Diana's thick raven hair swung, not quite brushing her shoulders. She wore it loose and nearly straight, so that the tips just curved under, with a fringe of bangs over her forehead. The style suited her, easy but cleverly and meticulously cut, as was the deceptively simple burgundy suit.

Unnoticed, Caine let his eyes trail up, taking in the slender, well-disciplined body, narrow-hipped, slim waist, strong, swimmer's shoulders. She walked like a dancer, confident, smoothly rhythmic, so that when he stepped in front of her, Diana paused in midstride without any show of awkwardness. Unlike the woman in the red fox, she scanned his face briefly and with no show of interest.

"Excuse me." The words were perfectly polite and left the unmistakable impression that he was in her way.

Interesting, Caine mused, and didn't bother to smile. "Diana Blade?"

Diana's left brow disappeared under the fringe of bangs. "Yes?"

"I'm Caine MacGregor, Rena's brother." Keeping his eyes on her face, Caine held out a hand.

So this is the deadly MacGregor, Diana mused, accepting the hand he offered. "How do you do?" She'd expected a smooth palm and was surprised to find her hand clasped against hard, callused skin. A faint prickling of pleasure crept up her arm. Diana acknowledged it, broke contact, then forgot it.

"Rena would have come herself," Caine went on, still studying her face minutely, "but there were a few minor emergencies at the hotel." Because he was a man who could be diplomatic or blunt depending on his mood, Caine spoke as he started to take the flight bag from her shoulder. "I didn't expect you to come."

"No?" Diana kept her hand on the strap of the bag, refusing to relinquish possession. "And your sister?"

Caine considered engaging in a brief tug-of-war over the bag. Something about those large sleepy eyes made him want to annoy her. With a shrug, he dropped his hand. "She was certain you'd come. Rena believes everyone has strong family feelings because she does." The fleeting smile softened his features before he took her arm. "Let's go get your bags."

Diana allowed him to lead her down the wide crowded corridor, while behind the deceptively lazy eyes her mind was active and sharply alert. "You don't like me, do you, Mr. MacGregor?"

Caine's brows lifted and fell, but he didn't even glance at her. "I don't know you. But since we're in the position of being family, so to speak, why don't we bypass the formalities?"

During the short speech, she had another clue why he was so successful in his field. His voice was gold— rich, mellow gold with a hint of steel beneath. "All right," she agreed. "Tell me, Caine, if you weren't expecting me, how did you know who I was?"

"Your bone structure and coloring are very much like Justin's."

"Are they?" she murmured as they stopped in front of the conveyor belt.

Caine studied her again with the same thorough, un-apologetic intensity as before. Her scent was something he couldn't quite identify, wild rather than floral, and very French. He wondered if it suited her as well as the smartly cut wool suit. "The family resemblance is there," he commented. "But I think it would be less apparent if you stood side by side."

"That's something I've had little opportunity to do," Diana returned dryly and indicated her bags with a gesture of her hand.

Used to servants, Caine concluded as he hefted the two leather cases. But self-reliant, he added, remembering their silent battle over the flight bag. "I'm sure Justin will be pleased to see you after so many years."

"Possibly. You seem very fond of him."

"I've known him for ten years. He was my friend before he became my brother-in-law."

She wanted to ask what Justin was like but swallowed the question. Diana had her own opinion. If she were to change it, it wouldn't be through Caine's influence or anyone else's. "You're staying at the Comanche?"

"For a week."

As they stepped out into the frigid January air, Diana automatically stuck her ungloved hands in her coat pockets. The sky was a cold, hard blue, the street slick and grimy with melted snow. "Isn't it an odd time of year to be vacationing at the beach?"

"For some." The wind whipped his hair into his eyes, but he didn't seem to notice. "Then again, a great many people come for the gambling. Weather doesn't matter when you're inside a casino.''

Because the top of her head was level with his shoulder, Diana tilted her face back to see his. "Is that what you come for?"

"Not particularly." He looked down and discovered the sun brought out the faintest hint of gold in her eyes. "I enjoy an occasional game, but Rena's the gambler in the family."

"Then she and Justin must be well suited."

Caine set down her bags and slowly drew the keys out of his pocket. "I'll let you decide that for yourself." Without speaking, he loaded her cases in the trunk, then unlocked the car. "Diana…" Caine put his hand on her arm before she could slide in.

She'd never known her name could sound like that— soft and smooth and vaguely exotic. When she turned large, puzzled eyes to his, he brushed at her bangs in a gesture that was completely natural to him. Because his touch surprised her as much as it disconcerted, Diana said nothing.

"Things aren't always as they seem," Caine said quietly.

"I don't understand you."

For a moment, they merely stood in the windy parking lot with the thunder of planes and smell of fumes. Diana thought she could almost feel the texture of his hard palm through the thickness of her coat. His eyes, she thought, were oddly gentle in such a strongly featured face. Briefly, she forgot his reputation as a demon in the courtroom—and the bedroom. She found herself wanting to reach out to him, for help, advice, comfort, before she was fully aware she needed any.

"You have a beautiful face," Caine murmured. "Do you have any compassion?"

Diana drew her brows together. "I'd like to think so."

"Then give him a chance."

The puzzled, vulnerable look dropped away to be replaced by something cool and guarded. It was a look, though she didn't know it, that her brother could adopt at a moment's notice. "Some might consider my coming a sign of good faith."

"Some might," Caine agreed, then walked around to slide into the driver's seat.

"But you don't," Diana let the door shut with a peevish snap.

"If I had to guess, I'd say you came primarily out of curiosity."

"It must be gratifying to be right so often."

He flashed her a grin, powerful and quickly gone. She almost wondered if she'd imagined it. "Yeah." The Jaguar roared to life when he twisted the key. "For the sake of our kin, why don't we try to be friends. How was Paris?"

Idle conversation, she decided. Turn off the brain and give all the standard, meaningless answers. Diana leaned back. She'd enjoy the ride. One of her secret weaknesses was for fast, well-constructed cars. "It was chilly," she began.

"There's a little café off the rue du Four," Caine remembered as he maneuvered the Jag through airport traffic. "The best soufflés on either side of the Atlantic."

"Henri's?"

He sent her a curious look. "Yes, you know it?"

"Yes." With a hint of a smile, Diana turned her attention back to the window. Henri's was a noisy little hole in the wall. Aunt Adelaide would have starved before she stepped over the threshold. Diana loved it and always made a point of slipping away for an hour or two when she was in Paris to enjoy a meal and the company. Strange that it would also be a favorite of Caine MacGregor's. "Do you get to Paris often?"

"No, not anymore."

"My aunt will be living there now. I've been helping her settle into her apartment."

"You're living in Boston. What part?"

"I've just moved into a house on Charles Street."

"The inevitable small world," Caine murmured. "It seems we're neighbors. What do you do in Boston?"

Flicking back the hair that fell across her cheek, Diana turned to study him. "The same thing you do." Caine lifted a brow as he twisted his head to look back at her. "You remember Professor Whiteman, I'm sure," she continued. "He speaks very highly of you."

Caine's grin was quick and off center. "Do the students still call him Bones behind his back?"

"Of course."

With a laugh, Caine shook his head. "So, Harvard Law. It appears we have more in common than we bargained for. Family, alma mater, career. Are you practicing?"

"I'm with Barclay, Stevens and Fitz."

"Mmm, very prestigious." He shot her a look. "And staid."

For the first time, Diana's features relaxed into a smile. It was both wry and stunning. "I get all the fascinating cases. Just last week I represented a councilman's son who has a habit of ignoring the posted speed limit."

"You can work your way up in fifteen or twenty years."

"I've other plans," Diana murmured. By the time she was thirty, she calculated, she'd be ready for the break. After four years with a respected, conservative firm, she'd have the experience and the backing necessary to start her own practice. A small, elegant office, a competent secretary and then...

"Which are?"

She brought herself back to the present. She wasn't a woman to lay all her cards on the table. "I want to specialize in criminal law," she said simply.

"Why?"

"A thirst for justice, human rights." Laughing, she swung her face back to his. "And I love a good fight."

Caine acknowledged this with a thoughtful nod. Perhaps she wasn't as polished and proper as the trim suit indicated. He should have gotten a hint of who she was from her choice of scent. "Are you any good?"

"A second-year law student could handle what I'm doing at the moment." Her chin angled as she rested her elbow on the back of the seat. "I'm much better than that...and I intend to be the best."

"An admirable ambition," Caine commented as he

swung off the Strip toward the Comanche. "I've already earmarked that spot for myself."

Diana gave him a long, cool look. "We'll have to see who gets there first, won't we?"

For an answer, Caine only smiled. Diana thought she could see something of the demon in him now, a hint of that volatile, dangerous energy that had already propelled him far up the ladder. Without speaking, she stepped out of her side of the car. She wasn't intimidated by wolfish grins or challenging eyes. If there was one area where Diana was completely confident, it was law. Caine MacGregor would be hearing her name over the years, she was certain. He'd remember what she'd said.

"Ms. Blade's bags are in the trunk," Caine told the doorman as he handed over a folded bill and his keys. "I'm sure Rena'd like to see you right away," he went on as he took Diana's arm again. "Unless you'd rather go to your own rooms first."

"No." Rena, not Justin, she noticed. She felt the quick jumpiness in her stomach again and struggled to ignore it.

"Good. Then we'll go right up."

"So…" Diana glanced around, taking in the understated elegance of the lobby. "This is Justin's."

"He only owns half of this Comanche," Caine corrected as they stepped into the elevator. "Rena bought in as a full partner late last summer."

"I see. Is that how they met?"

"No." When he laughed, she turned her head to eye him curiously. "It's a complicated family joke. I'm sure Rena will tell you about it—though perhaps you'd have to meet my father to completely understand." He gave her a long look, then twisted the ends of her hair around his fingers. "On second thought, I'd better see that you don't meet him, or I'm likely to find myself in a similar situation." He kept his eyes on hers, stirred by the wildly seductive scent she wore. Was that mouth as passionate as it looked? he wondered. "You really are very beautiful, Diana," he murmured.

It was the way he said her name, Diana told herself, that caused that odd, almost uncomfortable prickling along her skin. He was an expert at making women uncomfortable, she remembered. And making them enjoy it. She gave him a steady look from half-closed eyes. "You left quite a reputation behind you at Harvard, Caine," she said mildly. "Not all of it in the lecture halls."

"Is that so?" Apparently amused, he gave her hair a quick tug before he released it. "You'll have to tell me about it sometime."

"Some things are best left unsaid." When the doors opened, Diana stepped out, then glanced over her shoulder. "Though I've often wondered if the... incident in the law library was based on fact."

"Hmm." Rubbing a hand over his chin, he joined her. "Suppose I plead the Fifth on that, counselor."

"Coward."

"Oh, yeah." He started to stick the key Serena had given him into the lock of the penthouse door, then stopped. "Are they still talking about that?"

Diana struggled with a smile as she studied his face. He wasn't particularly embarrassed, she mused, more curious. "It's become the stuff legends are made of," she told him. "Champagne and passion between Massachusetts Criminal Law and Divorce Proceedings."

Caine gave a shrug as he turned the lock. "It was beer, actually. These things get blown out of proportion with time." He gave her a very charming smile. "You don't believe everything you hear, do you?"

Diana paused long enough to return the smile. "Yes." With this, she pushed open the unlocked door and stepped inside.

Diana didn't know what she'd been expecting. Whatever it had been, it had little to do with the warm elegance of her brother's suite. Muted tones accented with bold slashes of color, large expanses of glass with a panoramic view of the Atlantic, small, exquisite carvings, pastel sketches, low inviting furniture snuggled into plush carpeting.

Was this her brother's taste? she wondered, suddenly feeling more remote from him than ever. Or was it Serena's? Who was this man who shared parents and a heritage with her? Why was she here, looking, opening herself to emotions she'd locked out most of her life? They needed to stay locked out, she told herself frantically. That was survival. In a moment's panic, Diana turned toward the door but found herself face to face with Caine.

"Whom are you going to run from?" he asked as he lifted his hands to her arms. "Justin, or yourself?"

Diana stiffened. "This isn't any of your concern."

"No," he agreed, but his eyes dropped, of their own accord, to her mouth. She was tense, muscles tight. What would it be like, he wondered, to loosen her, to get beyond that finely drawn wall of control and elegance? He'd always preferred more flamboyant women—women who knew how to laugh and to love without undercurrents. But this, after all, would just be a test. It wasn't as if there were a chance of involvement.

There was a moment's temptation to satisfy his curiosity—bring her those few inches closer and taste. The fact that her response could fall anywhere between fury and passion only made it the more difficult to resist.

Diana felt the need come unexpectedly, and uninvited—to be held, driven, possessed. Somehow she knew he could bring her to that. There'd be no unanswered questions, no uncertainties, only floods of pleasure and passion. Mindless, no thought, no reason, no justifications—she could find that heady, forbidden world if only she reached for it. And for him.

For a moment, she swayed between temptation and rationality—that thin razor's edge understood by all lovers. It would be so easy....

A faint mechanical rumble snapped her back. Diana turned her head toward the doors of an elevator she hadn't even noticed. Without speaking, Caine slid his hands up to her shoulders and slipped her coat off as they opened.

Diana watched a woman walk through, small and blond and striking in a simple violet sheath that matched her eyes. "Diana." Serena walked to her, enveloping her in a hard, unselfconscious hug. "I'm so glad you came!" Serena slid her hands down until they gripped her sister-in-law's. "Oh, you're lovely," she said with a wide, welcoming smile. "And so like Justin, isn't she, Caine?"

"Mmm." Standing back, he watched the meeting as he lit a cigarette.

A bit overawed by the greeting, Diana retreated a step. "Serena, I want to thank you for the invitation."

"It's the last formal one you'll get," Serena told her. "We're family now. Caine, how about a drink? Diana, what would you like?"

Diana glanced from brother to sister and lifted her shoulders. "A little vermouth." Nervous and unwilling to settle, she wandered to the window. "The hotel's beautiful, Serena. Caine tells me you and Justin are partners."

"In this one, and the one we're rebuilding in Malta. I haven't wormed my way into the others as yet. I will." Accepting the glass Caine handed her, Serena took a seat on the sofa.

"It turns out Diana and I are neighbors." Caine crossed the room with another glass and offered it to Diana.

"Really?"

That strange moment had passed, Diana told herself. And it had been nerves, not needs, she thought as she took the drink from Caine. Then their eyes met, their fingers brushed. She wasn't as certain as she wanted to be. "Yes." Deliberately she turned away from Caine to face his sister. "It's quite a coincidence."

Caine smiled slowly as he let his gaze sweep up Diana's back. "Even more of a coincidence," he drawled as he walked back to the bar. "We have the same profession."

"You're a lawyer?" Serena watched Diana's eyes follow Caine. It appears my brother doesn't waste any time, she mused, then sipped thoughtfully at her drink.

"Yes, I was at Harvard a few years behind Caine." Diana switched her drink to her other hand and wished she hadn't asked for it. "But his presence was still felt," she added.

Serena threw back her head and laughed. "Oh, I don't doubt it. In most cases you should take stories with a grain of salt. In Caine's…" She trailed off, sending him a provocative smile. "I always wonder just how much was left out."

"Your faith in me is touching," Caine murmured.

They're close, Diana mused. They've shared years and know dozens of foolish things about each other. She stared down into her drink. What am I doing here? "Serena," she began. "I want you to know I appreciate the invitation. But I wonder…" Diana stopped and fortified herself with a sip of vermouth. "I wonder if Justin's any more comfortable about this than I am."

"He doesn't know you're coming." When Diana's eyes shot up, Serena went on quickly. "I wasn't certain you would, Diana. I didn't want him to be hurt if you refused."

"Would he be?" Diana murmured, then lifted her glass again.

"You don't know him," Serena returned. "I do." The cool, quiet look Diana sent her was so like Justin's that Serena's heart twisted. "Diana, I think I have some idea how you must feel." Setting her drink on the table, she rose. "Please don't shut him out. He's—"

At the sound of the elevator, Serena broke off. Damn

it, I need a few more minutes! She glanced at Diana to see her sister-in-law standing stiff and silent. Serena cast one helpless look at Caine and got a shrug for an answer. Diana watched the doors slide open.

"There you are." Justin strode directly to his wife. "You disappeared."

"Justin—" Serena found her words muffled against his mouth.

He's so tall, Diana thought numbly. Confident, successful, her mind went on as she could do nothing more than stare at him. How much was left of the moody, intense boy she'd known? Was this her brother? He'd lifted her on his shoulders once so that she could see over the crowd when a circus had come to town. Dear God, why should she remember that now?

"Justin," Serena began breathlessly when her mouth was free. "We have company."

He spared Caine a brief glance, then gathered Serena closer. "Go away, Caine, I want to make love to your sister."

"Justin." With a half laugh, Serena pressed her hands against his chest. When she glanced toward the window, Justin followed her eyes.

"Oh." Smiling, he ran his hand down his wife's hair but didn't release her. "I didn't realize Caine had brought a friend."

He doesn't even know me, Diana thought as her hands tightened on the glass. We're strangers, we'd pass each other on the street. At a loss, she stared back at him, struggling for words that wouldn't come.

Slowly, Justin's eyes narrowed. Serena felt his hand tighten on her hair, then release gradually until he was no longer holding her. "Diana?" In her name was recognition and incredulity.

Dry-eyed, she stood perfectly still. Her knuckles were white against the glass. "Justin."

He crossed to her, searching her face. The clock was spinning backward and forward so quickly it left him shaken and disoriented. He wanted to reach out, touch her, but didn't know how. She'd been so small when he'd left her, and pudgy with baby fat. Now she was a tall, slender woman with his father's eyes. His face was as expressionless as hers as they studied each other.

"You cut your pigtails," he murmured, and felt foolish.

"Several years ago." Diana called on every lesson in deportment Aunt Adelaide had ever drummed into her. "You look well, Justin," she said with a polite smile.

Whatever overture he might have made was smothered by that one, impersonal sentence. "And you," he said with a nod. "How's your aunt?"

"Aunt Adelaide's fine. She's living in Paris now. Your hotel's very impressive."

"Thank you." He gave her a wry smile as he slipped his hands into his pockets. "I hope you'll stay with us for a while."

"For a week." The ache in her hand told her to loosen her grip on the glass. Diana concentrated on doing so while his eyes stayed steady on hers. "I haven't congratulated you on your marriage, Justin. I hope you're happy."

"Yes, I am."

Finding the stilted conversation unbearable, Serena stepped forward. "Please, sit down, Diana."

"If you don't mind, I'd like to unpack, settle in a bit."

"Of course." Justin spoke before Serena could protest. "You'll join us for dinner tonight?"

"I'd be glad to."

"I'll show you to your rooms." Caine drained the rest of his drink, then set it down.

"Thank you." Diana crossed toward the door, pausing long enough to give Serena a brief smile. "I'll see you tonight, then."

There was faint, but unmistakable disapproval in the violet eyes. "Yes. Please let us know if there's anything you need. Does eight o'clock suit you?"

"I'll be ready." Without looking back, Diana walked through the door Caine already held open. Neither spoke as they moved down the hallway. In a few minutes, Diana thought frantically, she could untense her muscles, unstrap her emotions.

Silently, Caine drew the door key out of his pocket and slipped it into the lock. Diana walked through, then turned, intending to give him a brief thank-you. He closed the door behind him. "Sit down."

"If you don't mind, I'd really like to—"

"Why don't you finish that drink?"

Glancing down, Diana saw that she still held the glass. With a shrug, she turned away as if studying the room. "Very nice," she said without having the vaguest idea what she was looking at. "I appreciate you showing me to my room, Caine. Now I really have to unpack."

"Sit down, Diana. I'm not leaving while you're churned up this way."

"I'm not churned up!" Her voice was too sharp. In defense, she took another swallow of vermouth. "I am tired, though, so if you don't mind…"

"I was watching you." Firmly, Caine took her by the shoulders and pushed her into a chair. "If you'd stood in there another five minutes, you'd have keeled over."

"That's ridiculous." Diana set the glass on the table beside her with a click.

"Is it?" He took her hand between both of his, rubbing absently as he watched her face. "Your hands are like ice. You can lie with your eyes, Diana, not with your hands. Couldn't you have given him something?"

"No." The word wavered and she sucked in her breath to steady it. "I don't have anything to give him." Snatching her hand away, she rose. "Please leave me alone."

They were close now, so close she could see the fractional lift of his brow. "Stubborn," Caine murmured and absently traced the shape of her mouth with his thumb. "I thought as much when I saw you get off the plane. Diana…" With a sigh, Caine brushed the hair away from her cheeks. She felt everything slip out of focus. "You're hurting yourself by binding your feelings up this way."

"You don't know anything about my feelings." Her voice was low and unsteady as she fought to keep tears from misting her vision. She wasn't going to cry—not in front of him or anyone. There was nothing, absolutely nothing to cry about. "This is none of your business. My feelings are none of your business." She choked on a sob and pressed her hand to her mouth. "Leave me alone," she demanded, but found herself cradled against his chest.

"When you've finished," he murmured, and held her.

The wordless, unquestioning comfort was more than she could resist. Clinging, Diana let her emotions break loose in a storm of weeping.

Chapter Two

The water was slate gray with jagged crests of white-caps. It was angry, noisy and fascinating. Diana could smell the sea and the promise of snow. As she walked across it, the sand was brittle with cold, crunching quietly underfoot. She had her coat buttoned high against the wind but lifted her face to it, enjoying its slapping fingers. And the solitude. She reveled in the solitude that could be found on a winter's beach just past dawn.

So much of her life had been crowded with people. She'd never been alone in her aunt's house on Beacon Hill. Diana tossed back her hair and smiled ruefully. She'd never been *allowed* to be alone. Beneath Adelaide's fussing and lectures on deportment had been the fear that Blade blood, Comanche blood, would prove too strong and too wild to be controlled.

Diana had controlled it, because there was nowhere else for her to go. At first, Diana had done everything she was told, allowed herself to be molded into the quiet little lady her aunt had wanted. Everyone else had left her, and Diana had lived with the daily fear that she would be left again.

She'd learned to control the fear, but she'd never been able to alleviate it. It was the ability to control her emotions that had become her most successful defense against Adelaide's criticisms and her own insecurity. Even as a child Diana had understood that her aunt had taken her in because of a sense of duty. There was no love between them, despite the fact that the young girl had thirsted desperately for love.

Diana had been the offspring of Adelaide's half sister, a dark-haired, golden-skinned girl born of their father's second marriage to a woman of mixed blood. Comanche blood. And the half sister whom Adelaide had accepted out of duty had compounded their father's lack of judgment by marrying a Blade. Blood had called to blood, Adelaide had often said when she spoke of what she considered her half sister's betrayal of their name and heritage. With Diana, she'd been ruthlessly determined to correct her family's previous errors.

The Comanche strain was to be ignored—more, it was to be erased. Adelaide demanded perfection. She was a Grandeau. Diana was to be a mirror of her own values, opinions and wishes. The child learned to be cautious, to be obedient and to question only in her head. The wrong question, voiced aloud, could be met with tight-lipped impatience, or worse, another lecture on deportment.

Diana had accepted, then had excelled in her studies, in music, in poise. They'd been an escape that had fulfilled her quest to learn and her need to belong. Her calmly determined will to succeed had begun as a way of surviving. Over the years the cool, elegant demeanor she'd adopted had become second nature.

If there were moments when she'd longed for something more, something...exciting, unfathomable, she'd suppressed the needs. She'd come to believe that if she played by the rules, if she followed the steps carefully, she'd win in the end. So her rebellions had been very discreet and her dreams meticulously subdued.

Still, Adelaide would have been appalled to know that her niece enjoyed restaurants that didn't have a four-star rating and movies that didn't have strict cultural significance. And sports cars, Diana mused with a quiet laugh. Steamed crabs and beer. Stopping, she slipped her hands into her pockets and looked out to sea. And wild winter beaches, she reflected.

Is that why Justin seems to have settled here? Diana wondered as she turned to face the back of the hotel. Does he find himself drawn to the cold passion of a winter sea? Was the heritage they shared stronger than the years of separation—the years when he had gone his own way to gamble and win, and she had submitted and quietly rebelled?

Shaking her head, Diana continued to walk. She knew nothing of the man who'd sat across from her at dinner the night before. He was smooth and sophisticated with something like thunder just beneath the surface. They'd had little to say to each other. Even when Serena's eyes had pleaded with her, Diana could find nothing more than meaningless cocktail talk.

What did a woman like Serena MacGregor know of her feelings? Diana thought with quick resentment.

She'd grown up surrounded by family, love. She'd had a place and a lineage she didn't have to ignore. Just watching how easy she was with Caine...

Caine, Diana thought with a sigh. It was impossible to pin down what she thought about him, what she felt about him. She hadn't been prepared for the sensitivity he'd shown her when she'd fallen apart—or more, his insight in knowing how close she'd been to the edge. Yet he, like Justin, had a certain polish that seemed like a thin glaze over something very dangerous. When her weeping had run its course, she hadn't felt safe in his arms, though he'd done no more than stroke her hair as if she'd been a child.

He threatened to ignite some spark in her, like the reluctant flame that comes from rubbing two sticks together with steady, endless patience. A forest fire can be started that way, Diana reminded herself. She wasn't about to have her life interrupted by one.

"You're up early."

Diana whirled to find Caine behind her. He was dressed more casually now in a leather bomber jacket, jeans and sneakers. It occurred to her that he should be freezing, but he seemed perfectly comfortable as he scanned her face. "I wanted to watch the sun rise over the water," she began, then glanced up at the thick, lead clouds. "I didn't have much luck this morning."

"Let's walk." His hand closed over hers before she could answer. "Do you like the beach?"

Diana relaxed. He wasn't going to badger her about Justin or the strained dinner they had shared the night before. "I've never been much of a summer beach person," she began. "But I never knew how appealing it could be this time of year. Do you come often?"

"No, not really. Luckily both Alan and I were here a few months ago when Rena was kidnapped, but—"

"What?" Diana stopped, her fingers tightening on his.

Caine's eyes came to hers, dark and curious. "Didn't you know?"

"No, I—I suppose I was in Europe. What happened?"

"Long story." Caine began to walk again and was quiet so long Diana thought he'd refuse to tell her. "There'd been a bomb threat in Justin's Vegas hotel. When he went out to handle things, there was another threat, handwritten, addressed to him. He didn't like the feel of it. When he came back, he tried to convince Rena to leave, but..." With a quick grin, he glanced out to sea. "She's another stubborn woman. Justin was downstairs talking to the police about a second threat when the guy got to her."

The grin was gone, as though it had never been, and a look of barely controlled fury took its place. "He held her for almost twenty-four hours, handcuffed to the bed. He wanted Justin to pay two million in ransom."

"Good God." Diana thought about the small, violet-eyed woman and shuddered.

"It's the only time in all the years I've known Justin that I've seen him so close to losing it," Caine remembered. The look of cold fury was still in his eyes, but his voice was calm. "He didn't eat, sleep—he just sat by the phone and waited. It wasn't until the boy let him talk to Rena that we finally had a clue to who he was. In some ways, that was worse.''

"Why?"

This time Caine stopped and looked down at her. She wouldn't know, he thought. Perhaps it was time she did. "When Justin was eighteen, he was in a fight in a bar. The man who started it didn't care to be drinking in the same place as an Indian.''

The rich, dark eyes frosted over. "I see."

"He pulled a knife. During the struggle, Justin was ripped open—about six inches along the ribs.'' Caine saw her pale, but he continued in the same tone. "The man was killed with his own knife and Justin was charged with murder.''

Diana felt a sudden wave of nausea and fought it off. "Justin was on trial?"

"He was acquitted once the witnesses from the bar were subpoenaed and under oath, but he spent a few grim months in a cell.''

"My aunt never told me." Diana turned away to face the sea. "She never said a word.''

"You would have been around eight. I don't imagine you'd have been a great deal of help to him.''

She could have been, Diana said silently, thinking of her aunt's comfortable income, her influential connections. And I should have been told. *God, he was only a boy!* Squeezing her eyes shut, she struggled to clear her mind and listen. "Go on.''

"It turned out that the boy who had Rena was the son of the man Justin had killed. His mother had drummed it into his head that Justin had murdered his father and had been freed because the courts had felt sorry for him. He had no intention of hurting Rena, only Justin.''

The sea seemed louder somehow, more violent. "So Justin paid the ransom?"

"He was prepared to, but it wasn't necessary. Rena phoned just as he was leaving to make the final arrangements. She'd knocked the kid out with a skillet and cuffed him to the bed.''

Stunned, and amused despite herself, Diana turned back. "She did?"

Caine acknowledged her smile with one of his own. "She's tougher than she looks."

Shaking her head, Diana began to walk again. "And what about the boy?"

"His trial comes up later this month. Rena's paying his legal fees.''

Her eyes whipped up to his. In them was a mixture of anger and admiration. "Does Justin know that?"

"Of course."

She digested this in silence, walking again. "I'm not sure I could be so forgiving."

"Justin's more resigned than agreeable," Caine commented. "And when we had Rena back, safe, it was hard to refuse her anything. My first reaction was to get the kid locked up for the next fifty years."

Diana tilted her head to study his face. "I doubt he'd have much of a chance if you could prosecute. I've read some of your trial transcripts. You go for the jugular, counselor."

"It's cleaner," he said simply.

"Why didn't you run for state's attorney again?"

"Politics has too many walls." He sent her an off-center grin. "I imagine you've run into a few with Barclay, Stevens and Fitz."

"Barclay is the epitome of the dry, stern-eyed attorney. Dickens would have loved him. 'My dear Miss Blade,'" she began in a whispery thin voice, "'please try to remember your position. A member of our firm never raises her voice or challenges a judge in the courtroom.' Only on the golf course," Diana added in a mutter.

Still grinning, Caine swung an arm around her shoulders. "And do you challenge judges, Miss Blade?"

"Frequently. If Aunt Adelaide wasn't bosom buddies with Barclay's wife, I'd have been out on my ear by now. As it is, I'm a glorified law clerk."

"So why are you still there?"

"I have a deep supply of patience." His arm felt warm and friendly over her shoulder. Without thinking, Diana moved closer. "Aunt Adelaide wasn't thrilled about my choosing law in the first place, but she was instrumental in my securing a position at Barclay's." That rankled. Diana swallowed the light trace of bitterness. Her voice was low and even when she continued. "In her way, she was pleased that I was working for an old friend and a prestigious firm. If I hang in long enough, they might just give me something other than traffic."

"Afraid of her?"

Instead of being insulted, Diana laughed. The fear had been gone for years. Even the memory was vague. "Aunt Adelaide? I hope I've got more spine than that. No." She tossed her face up to the wind. "I owe her."

"Do you?" Caine murmured, half to himself. "My

father has a saying," he mused aloud. "There's no fee
for family."

"He doesn't know Aunt Adelaide," Diana remarked
dryly. "Oh, look at the gulls!" She pointed skyward
as a pair of them swooped overhead and out to sea.
"One flew close enough to touch when I stood out on
my balcony this morning. I wonder why they make
such a lonely sound when they seem perfectly content." When she shivered, Caine tightened his arm
around her.

"Cold?"

"Yes." But she smiled up at him. "I like it."

His breath was cool against her face, showing itself
in a thin white mist that was quickly snatched by the
wind. Diana was so entranced by his eyes that she
hardly noticed that the arm around her shoulders had
shifted, drawing her closer. Then they were face to face
and her arms had slipped up his back, over the cold,
smooth leather. Her heartbeat was a dull thud that
might have belonged to someone else. She heard the
wind echo off the water and surround them as if they
were on some lonely northern island. With one hand,
he cupped the back of her neck with cool, strong fingers. Diana felt the cold, wet drops land on her face
before she saw the flakes.

"It's snowing."

"Yeah." Caine lowered his lips to within a whisper
of hers, then hesitated. He heard her quiet shudder of
breath before she banished the distance.

Softly, slowly, his mouth roamed over hers. It was a
cool, lazy seduction at odds with the biting wind and
racing snow. He drew her closer gradually, until her

body fit tightly against his. She could feel those hard, seeking fingers run up and down the nape of her neck, teasing her mind with images of what they could do to her body. While she was distracted by them, his mouth became more greedy, pulling response from her before she was aware of the demand.

Her hands hooked around his shoulders and locked tight. Her passion seemed to rise like the wind, but it was hot, sultry, as he took his lips on a long, mesmerizing journey over her face. She heard the thick echo of crashing waves then nothing but the whisper of her own name as he traced her ear with his tongue. Diana pressed herself against him, searching and finding his roaming mouth with her own.

There was no teasing this time, no subtle greed. Now it was all flash, all fire. Neither of them was aware of the cold any longer as they demanded everything the other possessed. Diana felt all of her small, inner secrets slipping away from her, exposed, even as she felt herself being filled again with needs that were as much Caine's as her own. And the needs were deeper and more complex than anything she'd ever known.

Not just a hunger for the taste of a mouth, not just a desire for the hard, strong feel of a man's arms—it was a longing for a match, a mate. In her stirred the oldest, most primitive need to be completed physically and the oldest, most basic need to be fulfilled emotionally.

As if she felt herself drowning, she clutched at him but was suddenly unsure if he were anchor or lifeline. The will to survive smothered the yearning for pleasure, and she pulled away. Breathing jerkily, Diana stared at him while the wind whipped her hair and snow into her eyes.

"Well." Caine's breath puffed out in a long stream. "That was unexpected." When he reached up to touch her cheek, she backed out of range. His brows lifted and fell as he stuck his hands in his pockets. "A bit late to throw up walls now, Diana. The foundations already crumbled."

"Not walls, Caine," she said, calmer now. "Just basic common sense. I'm not your passion-in-the-bookstacks type."

Something flashed in his eyes, but she couldn't be certain if it was annoyance or amusement. "The statute of limitations on that misdemeanor must have run out by now."

"I have my doubts that you're rehabilitated," Diana returned mildly.

"God forbid." Before she could avoid him, Caine reached out to gather her tossing hair in one hand. "Diana." With a laugh, he brushed snowflakes from her cheek. "You belong in the desert, or someplace steamy with a white sun—wearing exotic clothes that would suit that face of yours."

She held herself very still to combat the desire to feel his skin against hers again. "I'm very well suited to a New England courtroom," she retorted.

"Yes." The smile remained in his eyes. "I think you are—or part of you is. Perhaps that's why you're beginning to fascinate me."

"I'm not interested in fascinating you, Caine." She met his eyes levelly and with the quick wish that she could knock the gleam out of them. "I am interested in going back in before I freeze."

"I'll walk you back," he said with such apparently boundless amiability that Diana wanted to deck him.

"That isn't necessary," she began as her hand was clasped by his.

"I suppose I could walk ten paces behind or ten paces in front." As she let out a frustrated breath, Caine grinned down at her. "You're not angry because we exchanged a friendly kiss? After all, we're family."

"There was nothing friendly or familial about it," Diana muttered.

"No." He lifted her hand to his lips, then lightly nipped at her knuckle. "Maybe we should try again."

"No," Diana said firmly and tried to ignore the thrill racing up her arm.

"All right," he said, a bit too agreeably for her taste, "let's have some breakfast."

"I'm not hungry."

"A good thing you're not under oath," he murmured. "You must have eaten all of three bites last night. Well," he continued before she could think of a comment, "have some coffee while I eat. I'm starving. We'll talk shop." He held up a hand, anticipating her protest. "If it makes you feel any better, I'll even put it on my expense account."

With a reluctant laugh, she climbed the beach steps with him. "It sounds to me as though you didn't get out of politics soon enough."

"You haven't the eyes of a cynic," he commented.

"No?" He was climbing the steps quickly now, so she had to jog to keep up.

"They're more like a camel's. Careful, it's getting slick."

"A camel!" Not certain whether to be amused or insulted, Diana stopped near the top of the steps. "Now that's a terribly romantic statement."

"You want romance?" Before she knew what he was doing, Caine had swept her up in his arms to carry her toward the back entrance.

Laughing, Diana pushed snow-coated hair out of her eyes. "Put me down, you idiot."

"It worked for Clark Gable. Vivien Leigh didn't call him an idiot."

"They were inside at the time," Diana pointed out. "If you slip on this snow and drop me, I'm going to sue."

"Some romantic you are," Caine complained as he pushed the door open with his back. "Whatever happened to women who liked to be swept off their feet?"

"They got dropped," Diana said flatly. "Caine, will you put me down?" She tried wriggling, but he only tightened his grip and kept walking. "You're *not* carrying me into the dining room."

"No?" For him it was a direct challenge, and he accepted it with a grin. She was light and carried the scent of snow. Her eyes held an indignant laughter that appealed to him. Caine decided then and there to put that expression on her face more often. She had a mouth that was meant to smile, and he had an urge to show her just how little effort fun could be.

"Caine." Diana lowered her voice as she caught a few interested glances. "Stop this nonsense. People are staring."

"It's all right, I'm used to it." Twisting his head, he kissed her briefly. "Your mouth's very tempting in a pout." As she made a frustrated sound in her throat, Caine stopped to give the dining room hostess a smile. "Table for two?"

"Of course, Mr. MacGregor." Her eyes swept up to Diana for only a moment. "Right this way."

Diana clicked her teeth shut as he carried her around tables scattered with breakfast customers. She watched a middle-aged woman tug on her husband's sleeve and point.

"Your waitress will be right with you," the hostess told Caine as she stopped by a corner table. "Enjoy your breakfast."

"Thanks." With a great deal of style, he deposited Diana in a chair, then sat opposite her.

"You," Diana began in a low voice, "are going to pay for that."

"It was worth it." Caine unzipped his coat and shrugged out of it. He'd already decided she needed to be hit with the unexpected from time to time. In his opinion, she'd been pampered, sheltered and restricted. As a MacGregor, he thought they were all one and the same. Absently, he combed his fingers through his hair, scattering already melting snow. "Are you sure you won't have something more than coffee, love?"

"Quite sure." Watching him, she began unbuttoning her coat. "Do you always get away with the outrageous?"

"Mostly. Are you always so beautiful in the morning?"

"Don't waste your charm." Diana slipped out of her coat to reveal a pumpkin-colored angora sweater.

"It's all right, I have more." While Diana gave a disgusted sigh, he smiled at their waitress, who returned his smile and offered them menus. "I'll have the pancakes," he told her immediately. "With a side order of bacon, crisp, and eggs over easy. The lady only wants coffee."

"Is that a normal breakfast for you?" Diana asked when the waitress bustled off.

Caine leaned back, observing she'd already forgotten to pretend she was angry. "I enjoy eating when I get the chance. There are days when I'm lucky to get more than a few gallons of coffee and a dried-out sandwich."

"Is your private caseload as heavy as it was when you were state's attorney?"

"Heavy enough, and I don't have a staff of assistants." He watched as she added a miserly drop of cream to her coffee. "That's one of the things I wanted to break away from."

"No law clerk?"

She had hands made for rings, he thought, but wore none. Caine had to force his attention back to her question. "Not at the moment. My secretary is disorganized, untidy and addicted to soap operas."

Diana gave him a mild smile as she lifted her cup. "She must have...other virtues."

Caine laid his elbows on the table and leaned toward her. "She's fifty-seven, sturdy as a rock and a hell of a typist."

"I stand chastised," Diana murmured. "Still, I'd

think with your reputation and background, you'd have one of the slickest firms in Boston.''

"I leave that for Barclay, Stevens and Fitz. Don't you like to get your hands dirty occasionally, Diana?''

"Yes.'' With a sigh, she set down her cup again. "Yes, damn it. I'd work for nothing if I could dig my teeth into something that wasn't cut straight out of a textbook. Traffic violations and property settlements,'' she muttered. "I'm not going to get anything else if I don't stick with the establishment for a while longer. The world of law wouldn't give me a standing ovation if I opened an office tomorrow.''

"Is that what you want? Standing ovations?''

"I like to win.'' The sleepy eyes became suddenly intense. "I intend to make a career out of it. Why do you do it?''

"I have a talent for arguing.'' For a moment, he frowned down at his coffee. "The law has a lot of shades, doesn't it?'' Caine lifted his eyes and locked them on hers. "Not all of them equal justice. It's a very thin rope we walk and balance is crucial. I like to win, too, and when I do, I like to know I was right.''

"Haven't you ever defended someone you knew was guilty?''

"Everyone's entitled to legal counsel and representation. That's the law.'' This time Caine lifted his coffee, drinking it black, strong and hot. "You're obliged to give them your best and hope that justice is the winner in the final analysis. It isn't always. The system's lousy, and only works part of the time.'' Shrugging, he drank again. "It's better than not at all.''

Interested, Diana studied him with more care. "You're not what I expected you to be."

"And what was that?"

"More hard-line, maybe a young, more fiery version of Barclay. Quoting precedents, a little Latin for effect, claiming that the law is carved in granite."

"Ah, an idiot." Diana burst into quick spontaneous laughter. He found it warm and wild, like her scent. "You don't do that enough, Diana—let yourself enjoy without thinking it through," he explained.

"My training." Even as she said it, it surprised her. Just what doors was he opening, she thought with a frown, before she had a chance to check the locks?

"Are you going to clarify that?"

"No." She shook her head quickly, then glanced up. "Here's your breakfast. I'm fascinated to see if you can really eat it all."

Secrets, Caine thought as the waitress arranged the plates. Perhaps it was her underlying mystique that had her crowding his mind. There seemed to be so many layers to her, and he couldn't resist the temptation to peel each one off to see what was underneath. Then there was the vulnerability…it wasn't often you found a strong woman with that soft, vulnerable edge. The combination, with those unmistakable hints of passion, was very…appealing.

Her manner, her speech, her style shouted Lady with a capital L, but there were those bedroom eyes and that wicked, promising scent.

He remembered her hot, unrestrained mouth on his and found he wanted her taste again…and to feel the skin she kept hidden beneath the discreetly sophisticated clothes. He'd always found women enjoyable puzzles to be solved. In this case, he could pick up the challenge, play the game, and do her the favor of showing her that life wasn't as full of boundaries and rules as she thought. Yes, he mused, Diana Blade was likely to keep him occupied and entertained for quite a while.

"Want a bite?" he said quietly and offered a forkful of fluffy pancakes.

"Afraid you've overdone it?" He only smiled and moved the fork closer to her mouth. With a shrug, Diana allowed him to feed her. "Oh." She closed her eyes a moment. "It's good."

"More?" Caine took a bite himself before offering her another. "Food, like other solutions to hunger, can be habit-forming."

With her eyes on his, she accepted the second bite, then leaned back. "I'm watching my intake at the moment."

"Oh, here you are." Serena swept up to the table, pressing a kiss to her brother's cheek, then Diana's. "Isn't that disgusting?" she demanded, gesturing to Caine's plate. "And he never gains an ounce. Did you sleep well?"

"Yes." Diana found herself at a loss in the presence of such easy kinship and offered a cautious smile. "My rooms are lovely."

"Want some breakfast?" Caine asked his sister.

"Going to share yours?"

"No."

"Well, I haven't got time, anyway." Serena made a face at him as he continued to eat. "I was hoping you could stop by the office a little later, Diana. Have you made plans for the day?''

"No, not yet."

"You might want to take advantage of the health club or the casino. I'd love to show you around."

"Thank you."

"Give me an hour." Serena shot Caine a look. "Only believe half of what he tells you," she advised, then was off again.

"Your sister..." Diana trailed off, then with a quick, wondering laugh accepted the slice of bacon Caine offered. "She's not what I expected, either."

"Do you always have a picture in your head before you meet someone?"

"Yes, I suppose. Doesn't everyone?"

Caine merely moved his shoulders and continued to eat. "What did you expect Rena to be like?"

"Sturdier, for one thing." Diana chewed the bacon absently as she considered. "She seems so fragile, until you really look and see the strength in her face. And I guess I was looking for someone more obviously intellectual, glossier. She's not the sort of woman I would have pictured Justin married to, though I had difficulty picturing him married at all."

"It could be," Caine said quietly, "that he's not what you think, either."

Her eyes lifted at that, instantly cool and remote. "No, I don't know him, do I?"

It was difficult not to be annoyed at how easily she could slip into her armor. Caine sliced through his eggs and continued mildly. "It's never easy to know anyone unless you want to."

"It isn't wise to lecture on a subject you know nothing about," she retorted. "You had a tidy little childhood, didn't you, Caine?" The futility began to rise in her, and with it, anger. "Mother, father, sister, brother. You knew exactly who you were and where you belonged. You've no right to analyze or disapprove of my feelings when you have no way of comprehending them."

Caine leaned back and lit a cigarette. "Is that what I was doing?"

"Do you think it's easy to erase twenty years of neglect, of disinterest?" she tossed back. "I needed him once, I don't need him now."

"Then why did you come?"

"To exorcise those last, lingering ghosts." She shoved the coffee cup aside. "I wanted to see him as a man so I'd stop remembering him as a boy. When I leave, I won't think of him at all."

Caine eyed her through a thin mist of smoke. "You can't pretend you're ice and steel with me, Diana. I was with you yesterday after you saw Justin."

"That's over."

"You aren't pleased I caught you being human, are you?" When she started to rise, he gripped her wrist, making no effort to keep his strong fingers gentle. "If you want to be a winner, Diana, you have to stop running away."

"I'm not running." Her pulse was beginning to pound. The polish had vanished and she had her first clear view of the man beneath—strong, threatening, exciting.

"You've been running since you stepped off that

plane," he corrected. "And likely long before that. You're hurt and confused and too damn stubborn to admit it even to yourself."

"What I am," she said between her teeth, "is none of your business."

"The MacGregors take their family very seriously." His eyes had narrowed, their color only more dramatic when seen through slits. "When my sister married your brother, you became my business."

"I don't want your *brotherly* advice."

He smiled, and his grip gentled abruptly. "I don't feel brotherly toward you, Diana." His thumb brushed across her knuckles in a long, slow sweep. "I think we both know better than that."

He could switch his mood with more speed than she. Rising, Diana gave him a coldly furious look. "I'd rather you felt nothing toward me."

Caine took a lazy drag on his cigarette. "Too late," he murmured, then smiled at her again. "The Scots are a pragmatic race, but I'm beginning to believe in fate."

Diana picked up her coat and meticulously folded it over her arm. "In the language of the Ute, Comanche means enemies." She lifted large angry eyes to his, and for the first time, he saw the full power of her heritage in her face. "We're not easily subdued." Turning, she walked away in her controlled dancer's step.

With a smile, Caine crushed out his cigarette. He was beginning to think it would be a very interesting battle.

Chapter Three

The Comanche, Diana discovered over the next few days, was as slickly run a hotel as any her aunt would have patronized. The food, the service, the ambience, all catered to the wealthy and the successful. It became obvious that though Justin might have started his career as a penniless teenager, he had made the most of the time in between. She told herself she could respect him for that, even cautiously admire him, without involving herself. She wasn't willing to take the risk of looking closely—Diana had never considered herself a gambler.

Justin was invariably polite when they met, but if she had been more open-minded, she might have seen he was as cautious as she.

Despite herself, Diana learned more about him—the ingrained integrity she would never have associated with a gambler, the shrewd, sharp brain he had honed on the streets, the flashes of vulnerability only Serena could bring out in him. Her brother was a man, she discovered, who would have held her interest and affection if it hadn't been for the years she couldn't erase.

Of Caine she saw little, deliberately. He had, in a very short space of time, been witness to too many of her private emotions. She could almost accept that he'd been there to comfort her when she had wept because he was sensitive and kind. But those few moments on the windy beach played in her head too often.

That kind of passion, the depth and suddenness of it, held its own special danger. She could remember it too easily, feel it again too effortlessly. If he could stir her by a look, or the mere speaking of her name when they were in a room full of people, Diana was well aware of what would happen if they were alone. She made certain it wasn't an issue.

Then there was the anger. How easily he strained her temper! Diana had always been pleased with her ability to control or channel her more violent emotions. She'd had years of practice concealing fury and frustration from her aunt in order to avoid the inevitable lecture. Somehow Caine could bring her to the boiling point with a casual sentence.

It wouldn't pay to dwell on it, Diana told herself as she finished dressing. They might run into each other in Boston occasionally, but that was her turf. His, too, she reminded herself. With a shrug, she ran a hand over the hip of her gray flannel slacks. In any case, Boston would be professional ground. She knew exactly who she was and where she was going. She'd never been a woman ruled by mood, she reminded herself. She was much too disciplined for that. Once she was back in

Boston, back to work, she wouldn't be so susceptible to these wide emotional swings.

She didn't want them, she told herself almost violently. She didn't know how to deal with them. What she wanted, what she intended to have again, was the calm order she'd maintained for herself. As long as she was here, she felt like something was tearing at her, ripping at her. Threatening her.

Justin, and all those memories, all those emotions he brought back to her—she didn't want to remember or to feel what she'd once felt.

Caine was widening an opening she hadn't been aware existed. He was playing on vulnerabilities she shouldn't have, on passions she didn't want. When she was near him she needed…needed what she couldn't afford to need.

On a long breath she fought back the rage and the confusion. She could still control it, she told herself. She *would* control it. And when she was back in Boston, she would go on with her life just as she had before.

Absently, she adjusted the cowl collar of her dark rose sweater. She was glad she had come. Now that she had seen Justin face to face, she would stop wondering about him and that part of her life would be at rest. She'd also grown to love Serena quickly. It wasn't characteristic of her, Diana admitted. She had learned to be very careful about sharing her affections. They had always been too easily tapped and, she felt, too easily rejected. For the first time in her life, Diana knew the pleasure of having someone who could be both family and friend.

Swinging her purse over her shoulder, she left the suite. She'd stop by her sister-in-law's office before she went for a walk on the beach. Caine invariably went out early, and Diana had timed her own outings around his. There was no point, she concluded, in tempting fate.

As she made her way through the casino, Diana was again impressed by the smart, informal decor. No glitter or chunky chandeliers. From what Serena had told her, the casino, like the rest of the hotel, reflected Justin's taste. It was a far cry from the tiny house with a rickety porch they had shared in Nevada.

But then, they'd both come a long way from there, Diana mused. She thought of her aunt's house on Beacon Hill with its strict, undisturbed elegance. Polished antiques and gleaming Georgian silver. Soft-voiced servants. She gave a last glance around the casino: silver slot machines and green baize tables, croupiers in crisply cut tuxedos, the faint wisp of expensive whiskey and tobacco. Yes, they'd both come a long way from a little box house with a parched yellow lawn. Yet, perhaps she'd been happier there than at any other time in her life.

Immersed in her own thoughts, Diana entered the reception area and nearly walked headlong into her brother.

"Diana." Justin took her arm to steady her, then dropped his hand to his side. She was so lovely, he thought. And the fleeting, polite smile she gave him tied his stomach into knots. He wouldn't reach her, he'd known it in the first instant. But seeing her made it more difficult to accept the loss he'd lived with all of his adult life.

"Good morning, Justin. I thought I'd stop in to see Rena, if she's not busy." How cool his eyes are, she thought. And how odd that that one mark of their white heritage should make him seem so wholly Indian.

"She's just going over the scheduling." When she continued to stare, he lifted a brow. "Is something wrong, Diana?"

"I just remembered that story about the settler one of Mother's ancestors captured." Her brow creased as she tried to recall a story told to a child so many years before. "She ended up staying with him freely. Isn't it strange that because of her, green eyes come out at least once in every generation?"

"You have our father's eyes," Justin murmured. "Dark, secret eyes."

Because she felt herself softening, Diana straightened her spine. "I don't remember him," she said flatly. She thought she heard him sigh, but there was no change in his expression.

"Tell Serena I'll be back in a couple of hours. I have a meeting."

Aching with guilt, afraid of rejection, Diana held herself very still. "Justin." He turned back, but she noticed his hand remained on the doorknob. "I didn't know about the trial...about your being in prison. I'm sorry."

"It was a long time ago," he said simply. "You were only a child."

"I stopped being a child when you left me." Without

waiting for his response, she turned and went into Serena's office.

"Diana." Smiling, Serena set aside the stack of papers in front of her. "Please, tell me you're dying to be entertained so I can get out from under this mountain of paperwork."

"I was afraid I'd interrupt you."

"There are days I pray for interruptions," Serena countered, then her brows drew together. "What's wrong, Diana?"

"Nothing." Turning, Diana faced the two-way glass and looked into the casino. "I'd never be able to work with this here. I'd always feel I was in the middle of a party."

"It's just a matter of concentrating on two levels."

"Justin asked me to tell you he'd be out for a couple of hours."

So that's it, Serena thought, and rose. Crossing the room, she placed her hands on Diana's shoulders. "Diana, talk to me. Just because I love Justin doesn't mean I won't understand how you feel."

"I shouldn't have come." On a long breath, Diana shook her head. "I keep finding myself going back, remembering things I'd forgotten for years. Rena, I didn't know I'd still love him. It hurts."

"Loving someone has its disadvantages." Serena gave Diana's shoulders a squeeze. "But if you love Justin and give yourself some time—"

"I resent him every bit as much," Diana countered as she turned around. "Maybe more. I resent him for every day of all those years I did without him."

"Diana, don't you see he did without you as well?"

"His choice; I never had one." The emotions began to push at her so that she swung away to pace the room. "He turned me over to my aunt and went his own way."

"You were six, he was sixteen." Frustrated, Serena tried to balance her loyalties. "What did you expect him to do?"

"He never wrote, never phoned or visited. Not once." As the words she'd held inside for years tumbled out, Diana whirled back. "I was so sure that if I did everything I was told, he'd come for me. Those first few years I was the picture of the model child. I minded my manners and studied my lessons and waited. But he never came. While I was waiting for him, he never gave me a thought."

"That's not true!" Serena said heatedly. "You don't understand."

"No, you don't understand," Diana fired back. "You don't know what it's like to lose everything that belonged to you and have to live on someone else's charity! To know every mouthful of food you ate, every stitch of clothing on your back had a price."

"Who do you think you owe for the food and the clothes, Diana?" Serena asked evenly.

"Oh, I know whom I owe," Diana retorted. "She never let me forget it, in her own discreet way. Aunt Adelaide doesn't believe in generosity without strings."

"Generosity?" Serena crossed the room as her temper snapped. "She doesn't know any more about generosity than you do."

"Perhaps not," Diana agreed with a faint nod. "But she gave me everything I've ever had."

"Justin paid for it all." The words came out on a crest of temper she couldn't control. "He sent her a check every month from the time she took you in until you graduated from Harvard. The checks might have been small in the beginning," Serena continued coldly. "He was living on little more than his wits then and dodging social workers. But they got larger—he's always been very good at what he does. She took his money, and you, on his word that he'd stay out of your life. He paid, Diana, with a great deal more than money."

She seemed to be frozen. Diana was afraid to move for fear that she would crack and scatter into a dozen irretrievable pieces. "He paid her?" Her voice was very quiet, very disciplined. "Justin sent Aunt Adelaide money, for me?"

"He had nothing else to give you. Damn it, Diana, you're a lawyer. What would have happened to you if he hadn't arranged for your aunt to take you in?"

Foster homes, she thought dully. An orphanage on the reservation. "She could have taken him in, too."

Serena gave her a long, steady look. "Would she?"

Diana pressed her fingers to her eyes. She didn't know when the headache had begun, but it was pounding mercilessly. "No." With a sigh, she dropped them again. "No. Later, when I was older, he could have contacted me."

"He thought you were happy, and certainly better off in Boston than you would have been trailing around the country with him. Justin chose his own life, it's true, but he did what he thought was best for you the only way he knew how.''

''Why didn't he tell me?''

''What do you think he wants, your gratitude?'' Serena demanded impatiently. ''Can't you see what kind of a man he is?'' She dragged a hand through her hair. ''He won't thank me for telling you. I wouldn't have,'' she added in a calmer tone, ''if you hadn't said you still loved him.'' As her temper cooled, Serena noted the wide, distressed eyes, the pale cheeks, the frozen expression. Without question, she reached out. ''Diana—''

''No.'' Diana held up a hand to hold her off. Her voice was frigid, her body stiff. ''You've told me the truth?''

Serena met her eyes levelly. ''I've no reason to lie.''

A brittle laugh escaped, but perhaps she wouldn't have bothered to suppress it. ''How odd, when it seems everyone else has, all of my life.''

''Let me take you upstairs, fix you a drink.''

''No.'' Gathering what remained of her self-control, Diana walked to the door. ''I appreciate you telling me, Rena,'' she said coolly as she turned the knob. ''It was something I needed to know.''

As the door shut quietly, Serena dropped into the chair behind her desk. Oh, God, she thought, rubbing her hand across her forehead. How could I have done that with so little compassion? Remembering the stricken look on Diana's face, she started to rise, then stopped herself. No, Diana needed some time, and Serena didn't think it would be she Diana would want to see in any case. Catching her bottom lip between her teeth, she lifted the phone.

"Page Caine MacGregor please."

Even after an hour had passed, Diana hadn't found her control. Her mind ran in circles, chased by her emotions. Everything she had believed was false. Everything she had was owed to someone she'd paid back with cold resentment. The only thing that was clear to her now was that she would have to face Justin once more, and she would have to leave. It was easier to prepare for the latter.

Taking out her suitcases, Diana began to pack, slowly, very meticulously, making the simple chore occupy her mind. If she chose, she could make it last for the better part of the afternoon. Perhaps by then the headache would be gone and the sickness deep in her stomach would have eased. Perhaps by then she wouldn't feel so utterly lost.

At first, she ignored the knocking at her door, then when it continued she reluctantly went to answer.

"Caine." Diana stood in the opening, showing clearly he wasn't welcome.

"Diana," he said in the same tone as he scanned her face. Seeing that her eyes were composed and dry, he moved forward until she was forced to give way.

"I'm busy at the moment."

"Don't let me stop you," he said agreeably as he wandered to the window. "I've always liked the view from this room."

"By all means enjoy it, then." Turning on her heel

she walked back into the bedroom. While she battled annoyance, Diana continued to pack.

"Change your plans?" Caine asked as he leaned against the doorjamb.

"Obviously." Diana folded a sweater and carefully laid it in the suitcase. "Rena must have told you about our talk this morning."

"She said she'd upset you."

Diana found it more difficult to keep her hands relaxed as she folded a blouse. "You've known all along," she said dispassionately. "You knew that Justin was responsible for my room and board and education."

"Rena talked to me about it after she'd written you. Justin never mentioned it." Coming into the room, Caine idly lifted the sleeve of a silk dress she'd spread on the bed. "Why are you running, Diana?"

"I'm not running." She tossed the blouse she'd been attempting to fold into the suitcase.

"You're packing," he pointed out.

"The words are not synonymous." Diana turned away from him again to give her attention to her packing. "I'm sure Justin'll be more comfortable when I'm gone."

"Why?"

Diana threw a tangle of clothes into the first case and slammed the lid. "Back off, Caine."

Her emotions were fighting to get out, he observed, and wondered why she felt they had to be suppressed. Healthier to let them out, he thought. Perhaps it was one more thing he could teach her. "Whom are you angry with?"

"I'm not angry!" Turning to the closet, Diana dragged clothes off hangers. "It was all lies!" Incensed, she slammed the closet door shut and stood facing him with her hands full of clothes. "All those years she made me feel as though I depended on her good nature, her sense of family obligation. She tucked me into pinafores and patent-leather shoes when I wanted to be barefoot. I wore them because I was terrified of her. Because I owed her. And all the time it was Justin."

Her hands gripped at the clothes as frustration overwhelmed her. "She wouldn't speak of him. She insisted I forget the first six years of my life as if they'd never existed. I was Comanche," Diana said with sudden fierceness, "but she allowed me no reminders of it. She took my heritage, my birthright, and still I felt I owed her. I learned about my blood in books and museums and had to struggle all my life to remember who I was—to remember in secret. I paid her, and while my brother was alone in prison I was taking ballet classes and eating off Sèvres."

Caine took a step toward her, watching the tears well up and be forced back. "Doesn't it matter that it was what he wanted?"

"No!" Diana tossed the clothes aside so that some landed on the bed and others fell to the floor. "I spent most of my life resenting him and catering to a woman who could never accept me for what I was. Now, I don't even know what that is. I thought I paid her for my education by dating the kind of men she approved of, by taking the kind of job she could accept. Balance the scales first, then do what you want." With a laugh, she dragged both hands through her hair. "But it wasn't her, and I don't know who I am anymore. Is it this?" She held up a white silk blouse, tailored, trim, elegant. "I thought I knew where I belonged." Crumpling the blouse into a ball, she hurled it to the floor. "I know nothing!"

He waited a moment while she stared at it, breath heaving. "Why should where the money came from make so much difference?"

"It doesn't to someone who's always felt entitled to it."

Caine grabbed her arms and gave her an impatient shake. "You're being a fool. You found out your aunt wasn't completely honest with you and that your brother hadn't forgotten you. Why does that change who or what you are?"

"Can't you see I was reared on a lie!"

"So now you know the truth," he countered. "What are you going to do with it?"

The fingers that gripped the front of his shirt relaxed abruptly as the anger drained out of her. "Oh, God, Caine, I've been so hateful to him. So cold. The more I wanted to reach out, the more I made myself back away."

He kissed her lightly, a quick, almost brotherly gesture. "You won't next time."

"No." Backing out of his arms, she stooped to pick up the clothes that lay on the floor. As if it were a symbol, she left the crumpled blouse where she'd thrown it. "I'm going to see him as soon as I've pulled myself together." With her back to him, Diana began to smooth out the skirts and dresses she'd wrinkled.

"You seem to be making a habit of being around when I fall apart. I don't think I like it."

"I'm not certain I do, either," he murmured, then found himself turning her to face him. "Vulnerability's difficult to resist." He ran a thumb down her cheekbone, following the movement with his eyes. She was soft in the way of a woman but with an underlying toughness he thought she hadn't even begun to tap. They were only two of the layers he was determined to explore.

"Don't." Diana whispered the word as his eyes came back to hers. In them she saw both desire and decision.

"I make a habit of touching what I mean to have, Diana." He ran both hands up her cheeks, combing his fingers through her hair until her face was unframed. "You stir something in me," he told her before his mouth reached hers.

She could have stopped it. As her arms drew him closer, Diana knew she could have pulled away and ordered him from her room. She still had the strength to do it. But his lips were so clever, so tempting. They whispered at hers, nibbling kisses, promises of endless delight as his hands slid beneath her sweater, up the smooth skin of her back.

He knew how to pleasure a woman. Perhaps the largest part of his appeal was that Caine wanted to give pleasure as much as receive it. He knew all the tricks, the slow subtle moves of seduction. But now, with her pliant in his arms, her mouth growing hungrier on his, he forgot them. Her scent was clouding his mind until he was crushing her against him with too much need for finesse. She was luring him, and it was he who was seduced before he knew the rules had changed.

He heard a moan, low with longing, and dimly realized the sound had been pulled from him. His hands were in her hair again, fingers grasping, unaware of their strength as he drew in all the hot, honeyed tastes of her mouth. And she met him fire for fire, touch for touch.

Diana knew nothing beyond the tide of sensation. The taste and feel of him dominated everything and still wasn't enough. Her tongue met his again and again, deeper intimacy, hotter passion, but she only hungered for more. For the first time, she fully understood the power and allure of greed.

His hands ran down her body, lingering at the sides of her breasts before they continued on over her waist and hips. He molded her like a sculptor learning the life and feel in his clay. And somehow she knew he understood her body as clearly as if she had been naked.

Caine tore his mouth from hers to stare down at her with eyes dark and fiercely intense. It seemed this time he'd been hit with the unexpected; aching desire when he'd have chosen careless, carefree passion. "I want you." His breath came fast as he smothered her lips again. "Now, Diana. Right now."

It was his anger that excited her—and that made her break free. "I…" Turning away, she pushed her hands through her hair. "I'm not ready for this. Not with you."

"Damn it, Diana!" Churning with needs, he spun her around.

"No." She shoved at him, gaining a few inches of distance. "I don't know what's going on inside of me right now. Everything's happening too fast. But I know I won't be one of Caine MacGregor's women."

His eyes narrowed, but he made no move toward her. "You don't stop putting people into slots, do you?"

"I'm going to put my life back together, Caine, I'm not going to let you complicate it."

"Complicate it," he repeated with soft, deadly control. "All right, Diana, you do what you have to do." He stepped toward her then but still didn't touch her. "But Boston isn't such a big town and this case is a long way from closed."

Though her throat was dry, she spoke evenly. "Is that a threat, counselor?"

He smiled then, slowly. "It's a promise." Cupping her chin, he gave her a hard, brief kiss, then turned and left the room. Diana didn't let out her breath until she heard the door close behind him.

This was all she needed, she thought as she looked at her tangle of half-packed clothes. He'd only gotten to her because her emotions were so confused and close to the surface. If there was one thing she'd learned to do over the years, it was to hold her own with men—in the courtroom and the bedroom. Caine MacGregor would have been no different if he hadn't been there when she'd already been vulnerable.

She wouldn't think of it now. Diana closed her eyes and waited for her system to calm. If they were to meet again in Boston, she'd be more steady on her feet. Now she had to face herself and her brother, and twenty years of deceit. Before she could weaken, Diana hurried out of the suite and down the hall toward the penthouse.

He might not be back yet, she thought as she lifted her hand to knock. If he's not, she told herself, I'll go down to his office and wait. It has to be now. Her hand hesitated and nearly dropped. I have to do it now. Straightening her shoulders, Diana knocked, then held her breath.

Justin opened it, bare-chested, a shirt slung over his shoulder and his hair still damp from a shower. "Diana? Were you looking for Serena?"

"No, I—" Her eyes were drawn to the jagged white scar along his ribs. Painfully, she swallowed. "May I come in?"

"Of course." After closing the door, he watched her fingers lace and unlace as she walked to the center of the room. "Would you like some coffee? A drink?"

"No, no, nothing." She gripped her fingers together again and let them fall in front of her. "You go ahead."

"Sit down, Diana."

"No, I…" Her voice trailed off and she shook her head helplessly. "No."

"What is it?"

It would be easier if she didn't have to look at him, she thought. Easier if she could be a coward and turn away as she said the words. Diana kept her eyes on his. "I want to apologize."

Justin lifted a brow as he started to slip on his shirt. "What for?"

"For everything I haven't done or said since I came here."

He watched her as he buttoned his shirt, but his eyes

told her nothing. He knew how to keep his thoughts to himself, she realized. That was why he was a gambler, and a success at it. "You have nothing to apologize for, Diana."

"Justin." His name came out in a plea as she stepped toward him. Stopping herself, Diana turned away a moment. "I'm not doing this well. Strange, I make my living stringing the right words together, but I just can't find them."

"Diana, you don't have to do this." He wanted to touch her, but thinking she'd only stiffen, he slipped his hands into his pockets. "I don't expect you to feel anything."

Gathering her courage again, she faced him. "I owe you," she said quietly.

Instantly, his eyes were remote and unfathomable. "You owe me nothing."

"Everything," she corrected. "Justin, you should have told me!" she said with sudden passion. "I had a right to know."

"To know what?" he countered coolly.

"Stop it!" she demanded and grabbed his shirtfront with both hands.

He thought as he looked down at her that there was more of the girl he remembered than he'd realized. Here was the verve and the fire. Lifting a brow, he studied her stubborn, furious face. "You always were a brat," he murmured. "Perhaps if you calm down, you might tell me what's on your mind."

"Stop treating me as though I were still six years old!" she demanded as her fingers tightened on his shirt.

It amused him to hear her shout, and wiped away the image of the cool sophisticate who had walked back into his life a few days before. "Stop behaving as though you were," he advised. "There've been things you've wanted to say to me since I walked into this room and found you here. Say them now."

Diana took a deep breath. She'd wanted to apologize, not to shout and accuse. But the control she'd practiced so scrupulously for so many years was lost. "All those years I resented you, even tried to hate you for forgetting me."

"I think I understand that," he said steadily.

"No." Shaking her head, she dug her fingers into his shirt in frustration. Tears began to gather and spill, but she didn't wipe them away because she didn't feel them. "How could you when I could never tell you? I lost everything so quickly, Justin. Lost everyone." Her voice trembled, but she couldn't steady it. "I thought at first all of you had left because I was too much trouble."

He made a soft sound and touched her for the first time—a hand absently passed through her hair as he had done from time to time so many years before. "I didn't know how to make you understand. You were so small."

"I understand now," Diana began. "Justin—" She broke on the word, fighting off a sob. She had to say it all, even if he turned away after she was done. "Everything you did for me—"

"Was necessary." He cut her off and was no longer touching her. "No more, no less."

"Justin, please..." She didn't know how to ask for

love. If she had one lingering fear, it was to try and to fail. While he watched, she struggled for words. "I want to thank you," she managed. "You've every right to be angry, but—"

"There's nothing I've done you have to thank me for."

She bit down on her lip to stop the trembling. "You felt obligated," she murmured.

"No." He touched her again, just the tips of her hair. "I loved you."

Her lips parted, but there was no sound. He was offering her love... He wouldn't accept gratitude. She wouldn't give him tears. Instead, Diana reached for his hand. "Be my friend."

Justin felt something unknot in his stomach. Slowly, he brought her hand to his lips, then spreading her fingers, he placed her palm to his. "We're blood, little sister. I've always loved you. From today, we're friends."

"From today," she agreed, and curled her fingers around his.

Chapter Four

It was bitterly cold. In defense, Diana had the car heater turned up full as she fought her way through sluggish Boston traffic. Oncoming headlights glared off her windshield so that she kept her eyes narrowed and tried not to remember that her ankles were freezing. By the time her car warmed up, she thought fatalistically, she'd already be inside the restaurant.

She considered it a wise move on her part to meet Matt Fairman for dinner. As assistant district attorney, he had his ear to the ground. In her current professional position, she didn't think it prudent to refuse the offer of a casual dinner date, even when she'd rather be home huddled in a warm robe drinking tea and watching an old movie. Diana didn't feel she could afford to offend anyone with Matt's kind of connections or to pass up the opportunity to make a few points on her own behalf. In any case, she was confident she could handle him on a personal level. She always had. And he was nice enough, she mused, shivering inside her coat, if you overlooked the fact that his mind worked on two levels. The law and women.

Matt was a good lawyer, she reminded herself. She thought, but couldn't be sure, that her feet were beginning to thaw. Pushing this aside, she concentrated on Matt. Besides being a good lawyer, and a shrewd politician, Matt had the inside story on every important case being tried or pending in the Boston area. He was also a gossip. If Diana wanted it known that she was now out on her own, she'd do better with a few words in Matt's ear than a full-page ad in the *Boston Globe*.

She'd resigned from Barclay, Stevens and Fitz the week she had returned from Atlantic City. It had been her way of making a stand against her aunt's manipulating. Diana knew she was taking a chance, both financially and professionally, and in the two weeks following the break she'd had her share of small panic attacks. Barclay was security, not only a steady paycheck, but a steady stream—well, at least a trickle—of cases. But Barclay had been her aunt's choice. She considered the abrupt termination her first real step toward independence. She didn't regret the decision or the twinges of doubt about the future.

On a bad day, she pictured herself sharing office space with another struggling lawyer, waiting for the phone to ring, hoping to defend someone over a speeding ticket. On a good day, Diana told herself that she was going to fight her way up the ladder, rung by rung.

If Diana had a regret, it was that she'd had so little time with Justin once they'd made peace—but she had felt it was essential that she get back to Boston and sort out her professional life. Resigning from Barclay had to be done while the heat of anger, the sting of betrayal, was still fresh—before, Diana had thought, she'd reasoned it out too well. It was too easy to be nervous, to think of all the consequences. Instead, she convinced herself that she was in a hurry to start carving out a place and a name for herself. And, she discovered, she was in a hurry to start exploring Diana Blade—all the parts of herself she had tucked away for so many years.

There'd been another reason for her leaving Atlantic City a few days ahead of schedule: Caine MacGregor. Diana acknowledged the fact that she had wanted to put some distance between them—particularly after that last emotional interlude before she had spoken to Justin. Caine was getting to her.

A man like Caine made an art out of getting to women, she mused. Smooth one minute, rough-edged and arrogant the next. It was a hard combination to resist, and she was certain he knew it. His reputation with women had been well circulated since his college days. Circumstances, or perhaps fate, had dictated that she had heard of his exploits through her years at Harvard, and then through their mutual associates in Boston. Diana had already known too much of Caine MacGregor before they'd ever come face to face—but it'd been then that the problem had jelled.

If it had been simply a physical attraction, Diana felt she could have handled it well enough. She was used to practicing self-denial, and an affair with Caine was out of the question. They had too many ties, both in business and now in family. He was, by choice and reputation, a womanizer. She was, by choice and reputation, cautious.

But it was more than desire. He kept reaching inside her and stirring emotions she couldn't define. She wasn't ready to define them. So Diana approached the problem logically—first by admitting there was one, then by removing herself from it. Now, she considered it solved because it was past.

Launching her own practice would take all her time and energy for months to come. The prospect unnerved her, excited her, though she'd yet to find suitable office space and her list of clients was still pitifully short. She'd been alone before, she reminded herself—alone and without resources. This time, there wouldn't be an Aunt Adelaide to trade security for obedience. This time, she'd make her own decisions, her own mistakes, her own triumphs. She knew exactly what she wanted: work, challenge, success. All she needed was the chance to find it.

When Diana found a parking space quickly in the crowded lot, she considered it an omen. Things were going to work out according to plan because she refused to allow it to happen any other way.

The cold bit through her coat as she hurried across the lot. A hard, icy rain had begun to fall, making the asphalt treacherous and oddly beautiful in the glow of streetlamps. She ignored her freezing legs by imagining herself already sitting near the fire in the lounge—a glass of white wine, the soothing notes from the piano, the scent of burning wood.

The rush of warm air as she opened the door brought out a sigh of pure appreciation. After checking her coat, Diana approached the maître d'.

"Diana Blade; has Mr. Fairman arrived yet?"

The maître d' glanced quickly at the list on his podium. "Not as yet, Ms. Blade."

"When he does, would you tell him I'm waiting in the lounge?"

Diana moved toward the large, comfortable room where sofas and armchairs were scattered around a huge stone fireplace. The flames were high, fed by thick oak logs that burned with a sweet forest smell. The lighting was soft, just flickering into the shadowy corners, while the hum of conversation and laughter lent an atmosphere of a large family party. Diana spotted an empty chair, and though it was farther from the fire than she might have liked, she settled down to wait.

I'd like to take off my shoes, she mused, and curl up right here for the next hour, just watching the fire. One day I'll have a house of my own, she decided, and a room something like this. No tidy little parlor like the one on Beacon Hill, with its sedate, well-behaved fire. I'd lie on the floor and listen to it roaring, watch the shadows and lights dance on the ceiling.

With a sigh, she snuggled deeper into the chair. I'm getting sentimental, she decided with a glance at her watch. Considering the weather and traffic, there was plenty of time for a drink before Matt joined her. Even as Diana scanned the room for a waiter, one wheeled a small table beside her chair. Diana glanced at the bottle of champagne as he drew the cork. An excellent year, she thought with a twinge of regret.

"I'm sorry, you've made a mistake. I didn't order that."

"The gentleman would like to buy you a drink, Ms. Blade."

"Really?" Diana turned her head as the waiter filled a glass. When she saw him, she felt a flare of excitement she couldn't quite convince herself was annoyance. He had, after all, told her Boston wasn't such a big town. "Hello, Caine."

"Diana." Taking her hand, he lifted it to his lips, watching her eyes over it. "May I join you?"

"It seems only fair." She gestured toward the champagne and two glasses.

It occurred to her that he looked every bit the smooth, sophisticated attorney in the slate-gray suit. Then she remembered how natural he had looked in the short leather jacket and jeans. It wouldn't be wise to forget the less genteel side of him. "How are you?" she asked, lifting one of the glasses.

"I'm fine." He sat back, studying her over the rim of his glass. He remembered her dress as one she had thrown onto the bed in a rage. It was thin turquoise silk and glowed against her skin. Her choice of colors, he mused, was very much like her choice of scent. Vibrant and daring.

Diana lifted a brow as he continued to stare at her in silence. "Are you here alone?"

"Mm-hmm."

Sipping, she allowed the champagne to linger on her tongue for a moment, cold and dry. The icy rain outside was already forgotten. "I'm meeting Matt Fairman. I suppose you know him."

"Yes," Caine returned with a hint of a smile. "I know him. Thinking about working for the D.A. now that you've resigned from Barclay?"

"No, I..." Trailing off, she narrowed her eyes. "How did you know I resigned?"

"I asked," he answered simply. "What are your plans?"

Diana frowned at him a moment, then deliberately relaxed. "I plan to open my own firm."

"When?"

"As soon as I take care of a few details."

"Have you located an office yet?"

"That's one of the details." With a frown, she ran a finger around the rim of her glass. She didn't want to discuss her problems with Caine, certainly not her doubts. Diana shrugged as though it were indeed only a detail rather than her entire life teetering in the balance. "It isn't quite as easy as I anticipated—if I want a good location and reasonable rent." Absently, she touched her damp finger to her tongue. "I have three possibilities to check out tomorrow."

Her unconsciously provocative gesture was arousing; Caine felt something warm moving through him but checked it. There'd be other times, he promised himself. Other places. "I might know of some office space you'd be interested in."

"Really?" As she shifted toward him, her hair swung to her cheek to be quickly tossed back.

"It's on the other side of the river, within a couple of T stops from the courthouse." He drank, noting that the silk clung nicely, draping down from snug shoulders. He'd been wondering for weeks what those strong shoulders would feel like under his hands. The trouble was, he'd also been wondering how she was doing on her own back in Boston, now that she'd learned about her aunt and Justin. He'd wondered particularly after he'd heard she'd resigned her position. The concern he felt worried Caine a great deal more than the desire. "A two-story brownstone," he continued. "It's been remodeled to accommodate a reception area, conference rooms, offices."

"It sounds wonderful. I can't think why the agent I'm going through hasn't mentioned it." Unless, Diana thought as she lifted her champagne again, it was a matter of the rent being as wonderful as his description. She wasn't going to touch the trust fund her aunt had set up for her. Her aunt, she corrected silently, or Justin? In any case, she wasn't going to touch a penny she hadn't earned on her own. "How did you happen to hear of it?" she asked him.

"I know the landlord," Caine remarked as he poured more champagne for both of them.

Diana caught something in the tone and studied him thoughtfully. "You *are* the landlord."

"Very quick." He toasted her.

Ignoring the humor in his eyes, she sat back, crossing her legs. "If you own such a marvelous building, why aren't you using it yourself?"

"I am. That color suits you very well, Diana."

She drummed her fingers lightly on the arm of her chair. "Why should I be interested in *your* office?"

"My caseload's packed," he told her, so briskly businesslike it took her a moment to make the transition. "I'm going to have to turn away some clients for the simple reason that I won't be able to give them my best in terms of time and energy."

She lifted a hand, palm up. "So?"

"Interested?"

Her brows drew together as she took a deep breath. "In your clients?"

"In making them *your* clients," he countered.

Interested? she thought. She'd stand on her head in a snowdrift for the chance at a few choice cases. Diana resisted the urge to kiss his feet. She had to be practical. "I appreciate it, Caine, but I'm not interested in forming a partnership at this time."

"Neither am I."

Confused, she shook her head. "Then what are you—"

"I happen to have some space in my building you could rent. I have some cases I'm going to have to refuse or refer. I prefer to refer them." As yet, he hadn't completely worked out why he wanted to refer them to her. She was family—that's what he told himself. He let the stem of the glass twist between his fingers. "It's a simple matter of supply and demand."

Diana was silent for a long moment. Caine knew that though her eyes had that heavy-lidded, sleepy look, she was thinking carefully. He almost smiled. He rather liked the way she plotted her way from point A to point B. By God, she was even more beautiful than he'd remembered, and it had barely been two weeks.

He'd resisted the urge to call her, until tonight when he'd finally accepted he wasn't going to get her out of his head. Still, he'd told himself he was just checking on her, one family member to another. Her answering service had told him where to find her. He'd come on impulse, with the offer he'd just made her already forming in his brain. If she accepted, he'd have the advantage—and the disadvantage—of being around her every day. That was business, he reminded himself. Once they'd settled that, he'd begin on the nights. If she was indeed going to begin a discovering of Diana Blade, he wanted to be around for it.

"Caine," she began, bringing her eyes back to his. "It's very tempting, but I'd like to ask you a question."

"Sure."

"Why?"

Settling back, he lit a cigarette. "I've given you the professional one. We might add that you and I are in-laws in a manner of speaking."

"Your family obligations again," she said flatly.

"I prefer the word loyalty," he countered.

Her face cleared with a look of surprised consideration before she smiled at him. "So do I."

"Think about it." Reaching in his jacket pocket, he drew out a business card. "Here's the address; come by tomorrow and take a look."

She couldn't afford to turn her nose up at a ready-made solution. "Thank you. I will." Diana reached for the card and found her hand caught in his. Their eyes met, his confident, hers wary.

"I like the way you look in silk," he murmured, "drinking champagne with just a touch of firelight in your eyes." His thumb skimmed over her knuckles and the buzz of conversation around them vanished. "I've thought about you, Diana." As his voice deepened, intimately, she felt a thick, enervating flow of desire. Her hand went limp in his. "I've thought about the way you look," he said quietly. "The way you smell, taste. The way you feel, pressed against me."

"Don't." The word was a whisper, the whisper desire itself. "Don't do this."

"I want to make love to you for hours, until your body's weak and your mind's full of me. Only me."

"Don't," she said again and pulled her hand free. Diana sat back quickly, her breathing unsteady. How could he make her feel as though she'd been ravaged with just words? Her body was throbbing as though his hands already knew it. He knew it, she reminded herself. It was a skill he had, one he'd honed to perfection. "This won't work," she managed at length.

"No?" Seeing her struggle against need gave him a small thrill of power—and of pleasure. "On the contrary, Diana, it's going to work very well."

Diana picked up her champagne again and drank. Steadier, she brought her eyes back to his. "I need office space, and I need clients." She took a deep breath, wondering if her pulse would ever slow to a normal rate again. "I also need an atmosphere of professionalism."

"The offer was and is strictly professional, counselor," he told her with a fresh gleam of humor in his eyes. "Whether you take it or not has nothing to do with other…aspects of our relationship, nor will it change what's going to happen between us."

"Can't you get it through your head I don't *want* any relationship with you?" she tossed back. "I don't intend for *anything* to happen between us."

"Then it shouldn't matter if we work in the same building, should it?" With another smile, Caine set his card on the table beside her. "I find it difficult to believe you're afraid of me, Diana. You strike me as a very strong-willed woman.''

Her eyes chilled. "I'm not afraid of you, Caine."

"Good," he said amiably. "Then I'll see you tomorrow. Fairman's just walked in, so I'll get out of your way." Rising, he brushed her cheek with a friendly kiss. "Enjoy your evening, love."

Annoyed, Diana watched him walk off. Damn the man for stirring her up! Snatching his card from the table, she ripped it in two. The hell with him, she told herself. He could take his office and his clients and jump in the Boston Harbor. *Afraid?* a tiny voice asked her. With a sound of frustration, Diana opened her purse and dropped the pieces of his card inside.

No, she wasn't afraid. And she wasn't going to cut off her professional nose because Caine MacGregor could drain a woman with a few soft words. She'd go to his office, Diana vowed, and drank the rest of her champagne in one impulsive swallow. And if the accommodations suited her, she'd grab them. No one was going to stop her from getting where she was going. Not even herself.

In the morning, Diana checked out two of the addresses given to her by the rental agent. The first was a positive no, the second a definite maybe. Instead of going to the third on her list, she found herself steering toward the address on Caine's business card.

She'd treat it exactly as she had treated the other potential offices, Diana reminded herself. She would be objective, consider the space and location, the rent and the condition of the building. She couldn't afford to let

the fact that it was Caine's building influence her one
way or the other.

With any luck, Caine would be out of the office and
his secretary would show her around. The decision, Diana thought, would come more easily without him
there.

She loved it the moment she saw it. The building
was rather narrow, old and beautifully preserved. It had
the quiet elegance found in Boston, snuggled in the
midst of steel-and-glass skyscrapers. There were
patches of snow on the lawn, but the tiny parking area
beside it was scraped clean. Pale gray smoke puffed
out of the chimney.

As she started up the flagstone walk, Diana glanced
around. There was a naked oak standing sentinel in the
yard, a long, trim hedge separating yard from sidewalk.
The courthouse was less than a mile away. So far, Diana reflected, it's too good to be true.

The door was thick and carved. Beside it was a discreet brass plaque: *Caine MacGregor, Attorney at Law*.
It wasn't difficult for her to imagine a similar plaque
below it with her name scrolled. Back up, Diana, she
warned herself. You haven't even seen the inside yet.
Still, as she opened the door, she remembered Caine's
comment a few weeks before about fate.

The reception area was done in rose and ivory. Duncan Phyfe tables flanked a carved arm settee. Diana
caught the scent of fresh flowers from the mix of
blooms in a thin cut-glass vase. The floor was hard-
wood, gleaming and bare except for a faded Aubusson
carpet. The mantelpiece was pink grained marble

topped by a long oval mirror. Below it a fire crackled eagerly.

Style, Diana thought instantly. Caine MacGregor had style.

Behind a satinwood desk, a round-faced, middle-aged woman had a phone tucked between her shoulder and ear as she pounded the keys of a typewriter. The surface of the desk was buried under stacks of files, scraps of paper and legal pads. She gave Diana a wide smile, then, hardly breaking rhythm, gestured toward the settee.

"Mr. MacGregor's schedule is filled through next Wednesday," she said into the phone in a surprisingly girlish voice. "I can give you an appointment Thursday afternoon." She stopped typing long enough to dig a thick date book out from under the wreckage of her desk. "One-fifteen," she continued, shuffling more papers until she found the stub of a pencil. "Yes, Mrs. Patterson, that's his first free slot. One-fifteen on Thursday, then.... Yes, I'll get back to you if he has a cancellation." She scribbled in the book, pushed it aside, then began typing again. With a faint lift of brow at the procedure, Diana slipped out of her coat and laid it on the arm of the settee. "Yes, I'll be sure to tell him. Good-bye, Mrs. Patterson." The secretary paused in her typing long enough to replace the receiver and smile at Diana. "Good afternoon, may I help you?"

"I'm Diana Blade—"

"Oh, yes." The woman cut into Diana's explanation and rose, revealing that the rest of her body was as round as her face. "Mr. MacGregor said you might be dropping by today. I'm Lucy Robinson."

"How do you do?" Diana found her hand taken for a firm, brisk shake. "You seem to be very busy," Diana began. "Perhaps it would be better if I made an appointment—"

"Nonsense." Lucy gave her a maternal pat on the arm. "Mr. MacGregor's with a client, but he gave me orders to show you around. I'll take you upstairs, you'll want to see your office first."

Before Diana could explain that it wasn't *her* office yet, Lucy was moving into the hall toward a staircase. She'd left her typewriter on, Diana noticed, and wondered if she should mention it. "Mrs. Robinson—"

"Now, you just call me Lucy. We're not formal here, it's more like family."

Family, Diana thought with something like a sigh. There seemed to be no getting away from it.

The staircase rose, uncarpeted and without a curve. The mahogany rail gleamed like satin. Thinking of the desk in the reception room, Diana decided the house-keeping wasn't Lucy's province. The woman glided up the stairs like a ship in full sail. A hairpin was dangling from the knot at the back of her neck.

"There's a conference room downstairs and a small kitchen," Lucy was saying. "There're plenty of times we don't get out of here for lunch, so it's handy. Can you cook?"

"Ah...not very well."

"Too bad." Lucy paused at the top of the stairs. "Neither Caine nor I are anything to rave about in the kitchen." She gave Diana a long look that was as friendly as it was assessing. "He didn't tell me you were so pretty. You're a connection of his, aren't you?"

Diana took a moment to work out the conversation. "I suppose you could say so. My brother married his sister."

"Knew it was something like that," Lucy said with a nod. "Caine's office is through there, used to be the master bedroom. Yours is just down the hall here."

With a glance at the door they passed, Diana continued down the hall. "It's a lovely house," she commented. "Caine doesn't seem to have made too many changes in the structure to turn it into offices."

"Only took a couple of walls out," Lucy agreed. "He said he'd had enough of working in four dull walls and brown carpeting. I say when a body spends most of their day in a place, it ought to be comfortable."

"Mmmm." Diana thought about her cubbyhole at Barclay, Stevens and Fitz. The carpet had been brown there, too, she remembered. "Have you worked for Caine long?"

"I worked for him when he was state's attorney," Lucy told her. "When he asked me if I wanted to work for him in his private practice, I packed up my desk and went. Here you are." Lucy pushed open a door, then stepped back to let Diana enter.

It was too perfect, Diana thought as she walked into the empty room. Small, but not cramped, with two sashed windows that faced east. Her heels echoed on the wood floor, bouncing to the high ceiling as she crossed to a neat, white marble hearth.

The wallpaper was silk, faded a bit but still beautiful. She could easily see the room furnished with a trim,

Federal desk, a few comfortable chairs, perhaps a small Victorian love seat with a low table. She could have a shelf on the north wall for her law books. If she wanted to begin her practice with style, she would never find anything more appropriate.

"I'm surprised Caine hasn't found a use for this room," Diana thought aloud.

"Oh, he had it furnished for a while. He'd stay here instead of going home when he was working late." Lucy discovered the pin trailing onto her neck and shoved it back into place. "Then he decided it was getting too easy to spend his life here. Caine's dedicated but he's not obsessed."

"I see."

"The law library's up here," Lucy went on. "That's where he had the walls taken out. There's a powder room downstairs and a full bath on this floor. It has the original porcelain taps. Oops, there's my phone. You just prowl around." Before Diana could say a word, she was bustling back down the hall.

Lucy, Diana decided, was nothing like the sharp young secretary she had shared with two other attorneys at Barclay. There everything had been done with quiet, unshakable efficiency. And the building had had all the charm of a tomb. An aristocratic tomb, Diana reflected, but a crypt was a crypt. This, she thought as she glanced at the faded wallpaper again, was much more to her taste.

Clients could relax here, assured of a personal touch. What few clients she could claim, she added with a rueful smile. Still, the location and the atmosphere would add to her caseload as much as her skill would.

When you were selling something, it paid to sell it with flair.

Mulling over the angles, Diana went back into the hall and wandered. Surely the mahogany wainscoting was the original, she reflected. No one paneled in mahogany any longer. Opening a door at random, she found Caine's law library.

Barclay's was no more extensive, she thought with a quick flash of professional interest. A long table dominated the center of the room on which a few books were stacked. Going to one that was left open, Diana saw it was marked *State v. Sylvan*. Murder one, Diana mused, recalling the case from her studies at Harvard. It had been a volatile, splashy affair in the late seventies. National publicity, packed courtrooms and a long, emotional trial. Just what, she wondered, was Caine working on that he was digging for precedents here? Intrigued, she bent over the book and began to read. When Caine came to the doorway ten minutes later, she was engrossed.

He didn't speak for a moment, realizing that it was the first time he had seen her completely self-absorbed. There was the faintest line of concentration between her brows, and her lips were slightly parted. She'd rested both palms on the table as she'd leaned over so that the jacket of her suit—a deep, vivid red this time— fit snugly over her back. Her hair was tucked behind her ear, revealing round, fluted-edged earrings of etched gold. He could picture her in court in that outfit—or at an elegant formal tea. He knew when he stepped closer that her scent would be there, making hundreds of dark promises. Cautious, he dipped his hands into his pockets and remained where he was.

"Interesting reading?"

Diana's head jerked up at his voice, but she straightened slowly. *"State versus Sylvan."* She tapped the open book with a finger. "A fascinating case. The defense pulled everything but a rabbit out of its hat over the three-month trial."

"O'Leary's a hell of a defense attorney, if a bit flashy for some tastes." Leaning against the jamb, he studied her. The light coming in the window at her back slanted across the hands that still rested on the table.

"Still, after two appeals, he lost," she pointed out.

"His client was guilty—the prosecution put together a very carefully structured case."

Diana ran a fingertip down the opened book. "Do you have a similar one, or is this just casual reading?"

He smiled for the first time. "Virginia Day," he said, then waited for her reaction.

The sleepy look in her eyes was replaced by quick interest. "You're defending her?"

"That's right."

Diana knew the story, from scraps in the news and speculation from other attorneys. A society murder. Unfaithful husband, jealous wife, a small, deadly revolver. "You don't pick easy ones, do you?"

He only gave her a shrug for an answer. "Lucy tells me she showed you the office."

"Yes. I saw evidence of her untidiness and disorganization," Diana began with a faint smile. "As well as an almost terrifying efficiency. The only thing I didn't catch was her addiction to soaps."

"She has a tape machine at home with a timer."

Diana laughed, turning toward him fully. "You're joking."

"No. Unless you've got the better part of an hour, I wouldn't ask her about any plots."

With a chuckle, she crossed toward him. "Your building is very impressive, Caine. I'm forced to admit it's better than anything else I've looked at."

"Forced to?" he countered, discovering he'd been right about her scent.

"I'd half hoped that it would be totally unsuitable so that I wouldn't have to make a decision. Did you buy the furniture yourself?"

"Yes. I've a weakness for auctions and antique shops. And then, I don't trust anyone else's judgment when it comes to something I have to live with."

"Very sensible. My aunt had her home redecorated professionally every three years. It never reflected anything. Tell me..." Diana steepled her fingers, pressing them against her bottom lip a moment. "If I don't take the office space, will you lease it out anyway?"

"Not necessarily." Again he found it almost sinful that such hands should be unadorned. "I'm not willing to spend so much time in the same place with someone I'm not sure is compatible."

Her brow lifted in amusement. "And you think you and I are compatible?"

"I think you and I will deal with each other well enough, Diana. Why don't we go into the office and sit down?" As they started up the hall, Caine glanced at her. "I can have Lucy bring up some coffee if you'd like."

"No, I'm fine...and she has more than enough to do."

His office was large, but craftily dominated by an antique oak desk. Like Lucy's, it was loaded with files and pads, but it reflected a scrupulous organization that hers lacked. Obviously, he hadn't been exaggerating about his workload.

The fire was lit here, too, burning greedily as though he'd just added fresh logs from the woodbox beside it. Rather than black framed degrees, Caine had hung a pair of vivid watercolors that picked up the faded tints in the wallpaper. Diana took one long look around before she chose a Sheridan chair.

"Very nice," she commented as he took the chair next to her. "I won't keep you, Caine; according to Lucy your schedule's full through next week."

"I think I can squeeze in a few minutes." Drawing out a cigarette, he allowed his shoulders to relax against the back of the chair. He'd just spent an hour with a hysterical client who was too close to jumping bail for comfort. It had taken Caine three-quarters of that time to calm him down. "Since you don't find the accommodations unsuitable, it seems you have that decision to make after all."

"Yes." Diana felt the warmth from the fire reach out to her and sighed. "I'd like to take it, Caine. Of course, there's the matter of terms."

Blowing out a stream of smoke, he named an amount that was within her budget but stiff enough to absolve her feelings of accepting charity. "Lucy's agreeable to taking on your work until you're settled. Then it'll be between you and her if you want to continue that way or hire your own secretary.''

Diana digested this with a nod, then took the next steps. ''All right, I think we can come to an agreement. As to the matter of your referring clients to me, I'm not sure I'm comfortable with that.''

''Why not?'' he countered. ''Weren't you hoping for a little quick advertisement by having dinner with Fairman last night?''

Diana glared at him a moment, smoldered, then settled back. ''I don't particularly like the way you put it, but yes. That's a bit different from what you're talking about.''

''If you don't want them, I'll send them to someone else,'' he said simply. ''At the moment, there are two I'd like to take, but simply can't. The Day case alone is going to require hundreds of hours.''

She itched to ask for details but made herself wait. ''Why would you refer them to me? You don't know if I'm any good or not.''

''On the contrary. I checked you out.''

''You what?''

He smiled briefly at her indignation. ''You wouldn't expect me to recommend clients to an attorney unless I knew they were competent, would you? You can't have it both ways, Diana.''

She let out a frustrated breath. She'd certainly backed herself into that corner. ''No. All right, what two cases am I considering?''

''The first is a rape charge. The kid's nineteen. Hothead, bad reputation. He claims the girl was willing— several times, in fact—then they'd had a blowup. The next thing he knew, he was being booked. The second is a divorce case. The wife's the plaintiff. When she came in here, her left eye was swollen closed and she was going to require extensive dental surgery."

"Wife-beating," Diana said with a surge of disgust.

"Apparently. According to her, it's been going on for some time, but she's reached her threshold. He's countersuing her on desertion charges. He has the power because he has the money and as yet she's reluctant to charge him formally with battery. It's going to be a mess."

"Never let it be said you're tossing me anything simple," she murmured. "I'd like to talk to them both next week."

"Good."

"You'll draw up the contract for the lease then?"

"I'll have it ready for you Monday."

"I'll let you get back to work." With a smile, she rose. "It appears I'll have to buy myself a desk." Diana saved the moment of excitement, of anticipation, for later when she was alone. "Thank you, Caine," she added, extending her hand. "I do appreciate you giving me first shot at this."

"I'll take the gratitude now. You might not feel so amenable after you've talked to these two people." Standing, he accepted her hand. "Business concluded," he stated. "Now..." Lifting a finger, Caine toyed with the wide bow of her blouse. "Have dinner with me tonight."

How easily his voice could take on that soft, intimate tone, she thought, feeling her blood heat in instant response. "I think it would be much wiser if we concentrated on the business, Caine."

"At the appropriate time," he murmured. She had a preference for silk, he mused as he ran a fingertip over the knot in the bow. Soft materials, flashy colors. "My mind begins to move toward other things on cold, windy Friday nights. There's a little place in the Back Bay where the fish is fresh and the cheese isn't. In a corner there's a table the light barely reaches. You can smell the candle wax and never see anyone you know."

He gently traced the line of her earlobe, idly fingering the gold she wore there. "I'd like to take you, drink wine, hear you laugh. Then later, I'd take you home and light the fire." Slowly, his eyes skimmed over her face, lingering on each feature. Yes, he'd like to do all those things and watch the changes in those features—the softening, the opening and the yielding. He was going to do those things, he vowed as something knotted in his stomach. He understood women, didn't he? And what they looked for in a lover. "I'd make love to you until the fire was only embers."

He'd stepped closer, but she hadn't noticed. Her unsteady breath feathered over his lips. He painted a picture with his words that she could see much too clearly. He'd be a terrifying lover—the kind women longed for, even knowing they might not survive the experience. And she wanted him, more than she had known she could ever want a man. Wanted him, knowing she would just be one more woman on his list. It was this that had her backing away.

"No." But the denial wasn't as strong as she would have wished. "That isn't what I want."

"It is," he corrected. Caine pulled her into his arms and kissed her with an anger his quiet words had hidden.

Deeper and deeper he drove her, ripping response from her, exploiting the panicked excitement that had her clinging even while she told herself to pull away. With one hand, he gripped her hair, drawing her head back so that he could have his fill of her.

He thought of what separated her skin from his hands—thin wool and fragile silk. The struggle built rapidly, almost painfully, to concentrate on her mouth alone and prevent his hands from pulling aside the trim, tailored suit to find her.

The days that he had gone without touching her crowded in on him, pushing him far beyond gentleness. He knew what it was to want a woman, but not to want one with a force that bordered on violence. It wasn't his way, yet he pulled her closer and ravaged.

Her mouth seemed fused to his, ignoring her mental commands to break free. Part of her, a part that seemed to be growing stronger, was driving her to submit—and more—to demand. Wild, passionate thoughts spun in her head, threatening to unleash something that might never be completely tamed again. It was tempting, so tempting to let it free, to let it sweep her wherever the current ran. Then, with a sound that was as much from fear as anger, Diana yanked out of his arms.

"No!" she said again and her voice rose with the words. "I'm telling you this is *not* what I want."

Caine's eyes lit with something closer to fury than desire, but his voice was calm enough. He wasn't used to having his desire mixed with anger and struggled to find his normal balance. "It is," he repeated, "but I can wait a bit longer for you to admit it."

"You'll have a long wait," she snapped, then snatched up her purse with a hand that wasn't steady. "You have the papers ready Monday and I'll have a check. If you can't handle things that way, then we'll forget it."

Caine said nothing as she stormed out, didn't flinch as the sound of the slamming door vibrated through the room. A log broke apart and fell with a shower of sparks. He needed a moment to get a firm grip on his temper. He hadn't meant to lose it. Indeed, he had promised himself he wouldn't. He'd been in tense courtrooms with the opposing attorney baiting him— he'd sat in grim conference rooms at the state penitentiary with clients cursing him—and he'd had perfect control. Diana could obliterate it with a word, a look.

Something unexpected was happening; he wasn't precisely certain what it was. If he were smart, Caine mused as his brain started to clear again, he'd do exactly as she demanded. They could be colleagues, discuss current cases, dissect points of law and complain about judges.

But he wasn't smart, Caine decided, waiting for the need that clawed in his stomach to ease. He was going to have her...and it wasn't going to be as long a wait as she thought.

Chapter Five

Why would anyone be hammering in the middle of the night? Diana asked herself as she pulled the covers over her head. The sound of thudding continued to come through loud and clear. She buried her face under her pillow as she promised herself she was going to lodge a complaint with the management.

It took less than thirty seconds for her to realize she had to give up or suffocate. Surfacing, Diana gave a disgusted sigh and opened her eyes.

Seven-thirty, she thought groggily as she glanced at the clock. Not the middle of the night, but close enough on a Saturday morning. And it wasn't hammering, she realized, but someone knocking on her door. Muttering curses under her breath, she rose and tugged on a robe.

"All right!" she shouted, belting the robe as she went. "I'm coming!" Diana pulled open the door so that it hit the security chain with a thud.

"Hi." Caine grinned through the crack. "Did I wake you?"

After one fulminating glare, Diana slammed the door in his face. There was a moment's consideration, then she unlatched the chain. He'd just start pounding again. "What do you want?" she demanded as she yanked the door open.

"It's nice to see you, too." Caine brushed a brief kiss over her lips before he walked by her.

Clamping her teeth together, Diana shut the door and leaned back against it. "Do you know what time it is?"

"Sure, it's...seven thirty-five," he announced after checking his watch. "Got any coffee?"

"No." Diana tightened the belt of her robe with a jerk. "It's seven thirty-five on Saturday morning," she added meaningfully.

"*Mm-hmm,*" he agreed in an absent murmur as he poked around the room.

It was far from finished. Diana was being very particular in furnishing what she considered her first real home—the first, at least, that no one could take away from her. There was an Oriental rug she'd bargained for in a secondhand store, an elegant rococo sofa that had taken a huge bite out of her savings and a French Provincial coffee table she had refinished herself in the basement of the apartment building. Her one good painting had been bought only that fall in Paris.

Caine slipped his hands into the pockets of his jeans as he studied these and the few other pieces she'd chosen. They were, like her, classy, individual and carefully placed. "I like it," he said at length. "You're putting a lot of yourself into this place."

"Shall I tell you just what your approval means to me?" Diana asked, not bothering to smother a yawn.

"*Hmm.* Touchy this morning," he murmured, giving her a brief glance. Three times on the brief trip from his place to hers he'd asked himself what the hell he was doing. He'd gotten three different answers, so he'd stopped asking. "Why don't I make that coffee?"

"You're not staying," Diana began as he headed for the kitchen.

"I'll be glad to. No problem."

"Caine." Be patient, she ordered herself. Don't lose your temper. "I was sleeping. Some people *like* to sleep late on Saturdays."

"Throws your whole system off," he told her as he began to root through cupboards. "That's why so many people have to drag themselves out of bed on Mondays." He found a can of coffee and began to measure it out. "Then just as they're getting the hang of it again, around comes Saturday and they blow it."

"That's very profound, I'm sure," she said as sarcastically as her groggy brain would allow. "I don't mind dragging myself out of bed on Mondays. Maybe I even *like* dragging myself out of bed on Mondays." She ran a frustrated hand through her sleep-tumbled hair. Seven-thirty in the morning was a perfect time to lose your temper, Diana concluded. "What the hell are you doing here!"

"Making coffee—unless you're hungry." Caine sent her an easy, amiable grin. "I'd fix breakfast, but about the best I can do is scramble eggs."

"No, I don't want any breakfast," Diana retorted rudely, then rubbed her fingers over her eyes. "I can't believe I'm standing here having this ridiculous conversation."

"It'll make more sense after you've had your coffee." After switching the pot on, Caine turned back to her. She was even lovelier now, he thought, with her hair mussed and the faint flush of sleep still in her cheeks. Her mouth would be warm and soft. "I think I've already told you once that you're beautiful in the mornings."

"Oh, sure," she muttered on a frustrated breath.

"Really." He cupped her chin in his hand as she continued to glare at him. "It probably has something to do with your skin." With his thumb he traced just under her jawline. There was sweetness there, and strength. He couldn't resist trying to draw out both. "Tell me, do you use some mystical Indian potion?"

"I don't know any mystical Indian potions," she managed as his thumb swept slowly back and forth. "And your coffee's ready."

"Is it?" Caine turned and poured a cup. "Are you having any?"

"I might as well, since it's obvious I'm not getting any more sleep." Gracelessly, she pulled open the refrigerator and found the milk.

Smiling at her back, Caine took his cup into the living room. He'd have to remember Saturday mornings the next time he wanted to have her at a disadvantage. "We have nearly the same view," he told her. "My apartment's only about a block away."

"Isn't that handy."

"Fate," he countered as he took a seat on the sofa and made himself at home. "Fantastic, isn't it?"

"One day very soon, I'm going to tell you what you can do with that fate of yours." She took the seat beside him, resting her elbow on the arm of the sofa and her head on her open palm. Letting her lashes lower, she yawned again.

Not bothering to conceal a grin, Caine settled back. "Lucy has the draft of the lease agreement. She should have it ready early Monday afternoon."

"Fine. I intend to do some shopping today. With luck I can have a few things delivered early in the week." The coffee was hot, and no better than she made herself. Diana resented knowing she'd be fully awake before she'd half finished it.

"Good idea. I'll go with you."

"Where?"

"Shopping."

"I appreciate the offer, but it's not necessary. I'm sure you have other things to do."

"Not really." Then he laughed, leaning over to tug on her hair. "Why is it I find it irresistible when you tell me to go to hell so politely?"

She gave him a long, cool stare. "I have absolutely no idea."

"I like spending time with you, Diana." At ease, Caine sat back again, but his eyes never left hers. "Why do you have such a difficult time accepting that?"

"I don't—that is, I do, but…" He's doing it to me again, she realized, and frowned into her coffee.

"There's three reasons," he continued, settling back. "We're family, we're associates…" Caine paused, watching her continue to frown in consideration. "And I'm attracted to you," he said simply. "Not just that rather fascinating face, but to all the quirks in your mind.''

''I don't have a quirky mind,'' she objected, then rose. Stuffing her hands in her pockets, she paced to the window. She could accept the associates. She was trying to accept the family without completely understanding it, but...

''You confuse me.'' With a sudden passion that surprised them both, Diana whirled back. ''I don't want to be confused! I want to know exactly what I'm doing, why I'm doing it, how I'm doing it. When I'm around you for too long, there's all these blank spots in my head.'' She gestured, then dropped her hand again. ''Damn it, Caine, I can't afford to have you popping up and making me forget things every time I start to work them out.''

Intrigued by the abrupt burst of temper, he watched her calmly, then took a slow sip of coffee. ''Have you ever considered letting things work themselves out?''

''No.'' She shook her head. ''I let my life drift for too many years. Not anymore.''

''In other words...'' He set down his coffee and rose, eyeing her thoughtfully. ''Because of a set of circumstances you couldn't avoid, you're going to shut yourself off from whatever feelings or desires you have for me because they don't suit your current plans?''

''Yes, all right.'' Knowing nothing was coming out as she wanted it to, Diana pulled a hand through her hair. ''All right,'' she repeated with a nod. ''That's close enough.''

''That's a very weak case, counselor,'' Caine commented as he walked to her. "I could poke all sorts of interesting holes in it."

"I'm not interested in your cross-examination," she began.

"We could settle out of court," Caine suggested, moving closer.

"Then there's your reputation," she added, deliberately stepping back. "You've hardly kept a low profile in your pursuit of women."

"You'll never get a conviction on circumstantial evidence and hearsay." He lifted his hands to her shoulders, massaging gently. "You've got to build your case on something stronger. Or..." Softly, he brushed one cheek, then the other with his lips. "You might try trusting me."

She felt the weakness creeping into her and forced herself to concentrate. "I might also try jumping out the window. Either way I risk a few broken bones."

Wishing he had some defense against vulnerability, Caine drew away. He'd meant what he'd said. He wanted her to trust him—even though he wasn't sure he could trust himself. "You want promises, guarantees. I can't give them to you, Diana. Then again," he added, "you can't give them to me, either."

"It's easier for you," she began, but he stopped her with a shake of his head.

"Why?"

"I don't know." She let out a long, weary breath. "It just seems it should be."

He clamped down on the need to just gather her into his arms until she'd forgotten she had doubts, forgotten to be logical. With an effort, he kept his hands gentle.

He wasn't certain what his own motivations were; perhaps he'd never had to dissect them before. He knew he wanted to introduce her to new things—excitement, fun, passions. The knight beating down the walls for the captured princess, Caine thought ruefully. In any case, he could work out the reasons tomorrow.

"Look, get dressed, spend the day with me. The circumstances when we met weren't the best. Why don't we take a little time and see what else we can come up with?"

"I'm not sure I want to know what else we can come up with," she muttered.

"Did Justin really get all the gambling blood, Diana?"

His eyes were so appealing when he smiled. She felt herself weakening again. "I don't know. I used to think so."

"What's a lawyer but a gambler figuring odds on the law?" Caine countered. The tension was easing out of her shoulders, so he resisted the need to do any more than keep his hands light and friendly.

"The problem might be I'm not thinking like a lawyer at the moment." Then, relaxing fully, she smiled. "If I were, I could probably cite several precedents that would establish, beyond a reasonable doubt, that I should toss you out the door and go back to bed."

Caine considered this a moment, then gave a sober nod. "We could probably argue that particular point of law for several hours."

"Undoubtedly."

"Diana, I'll be perfectly honest." Still smiling, he twisted a lock of her hair around his finger. "If you don't get dressed soon, I'm going to satisfy my curiosity and find out just what you have on under that robe."

She lifted a brow. "Is that so?"

"Of course, we could negotiate." Caine ran the lapel through his thumb and forefinger. "But I feel obligated to warn you I'm fully prepared to move on this point—in the very near future."

"Since you put it that way—I'm going to take a shower."

"Fine, I'll just finish off the coffee." Caine watched her walk away, letting his eyes roam down to where the robe swung across her hips. "Diana...just what *do* you have on under that robe?"

She sent him a bland look over her shoulders. "It's nothing," she said. "Nothing at all."

"I thought as much," Caine murmured as the door shut behind her.

Laughing, Diana pushed open the door of the shop. "I can't believe you did that. I just can't believe it!"

Caine followed her in, shutting out the cold. "It was a simple matter of truth," he said mildly. "I did see that identical lamp downtown twenty dollars cheaper."

"But did you have to tell that woman in *front* of the shopkeeper?"

Caine shrugged. "He'd be wiser to keep his prices competitive."

"He was about to have apoplexy," Diana remembered with another smothered chuckle. "I'd have died of embarrassment if I hadn't been concentrating so hard on not laughing. I'll never be able to go in there again."

"I wouldn't—until he lowers his prices."

Shaking back her hair, she narrowed her eyes to study him. "There's a great deal more Scot in you than shows on the surface."

"Thanks. Let's look around."

Diana began to browse through the antique shop, toying with a collection of pewter, loitering near a display of cut glass. "It's really your fault that we've been shopping for over an hour and I've bought nothing. I rather liked that corner chair," she mused.

"We can go back if you don't find anything you like better. Look here." He'd found a set of dueling pistols in a display case. Highland pistols, Caine reflected as he crouched down for a closer look. Yes, he was sure of it, noting the brass stock. The butt was designed as a ram's horn and there was Celtic strapwork, inlaid with silver. Eighteenth century, he calculated, seeing that the locks of both pistols were on the right. His father would love them.

"Do you collect that sort of thing?" Diana asked, intrigued enough to stoop beside him.

"*Mmm*. My father."

"They're exquisite, aren't they?"

Caine twisted his head, giving Diana as concentrated a look as he'd given the pistols. "Not many women would look at a weapon in that way."

She moved her shoulders. "They're part of life, aren't they? And you'll remember my people were warriors." She met his eyes now. "As yours were." With a half smile, she gave her attention to the guns again. "Of course, you wouldn't find a Comanche with elegant pistols like these. Do you know what make they are?''

"They're Scottish," he murmured, finding himself more fascinated by her than ever.

"That figures." Rising, Diana gave him an arch look. "And I suppose you'll buy them and I'll end up going home empty-handed." She noticed a clerk coming their way. "While you're haggling over the price, I'm going to look around."

She left him to stroll toward the other end of the shop. Who would have thought she'd enjoy spending her Saturday poking through stores? Who would have thought she'd begin to think of Caine MacGregor as both a pleasant companion and a friend? Shaking her head, Diana ran a finger over the surface of a highboy.

The more she was around him, the easier it became to be herself. There was no need to be Diana Blade of Beacon Hill. Oh, she was tired of that socially correct, polite woman! Yet twenty years of training had left its mark. How long would it be before she wasn't surprised to hear herself shouting? *A lady never raises her voice.*

Diana gave a wistful sigh. She'd worked hard to be a lady—her aunt's conception of a lady. All the strict little rules had been drummed into her head. Even when she had questioned them, Diana had obeyed them, rebelling sporadically—and, she admitted, discreetly. Those secret jaunts she had taken had been her safety valve, keeping passions and emotions under control. You can't change a way of life overnight, Diana reminded herself. But she was making progress.

Perhaps her drive to succeed in her profession was

another expression of the same rebellion. She couldn't—wouldn't—be some three-piece-suited attorney who only drew up contracts and wills. She wanted more than that. In court, she could let some of her passion slip through. There it was accepted, even considered eloquent. With words, she could fight for what she believed.

The law had always fascinated her. It was broad and narrow, succinct and nebulous. Yet she had always found it solid despite its infinite angles. She needed to succeed with it—wanted the excitement, the pressure and the glory of criminal law. Her mind came full circle back to Caine.

She wanted him, too. Diana would admit it for a moment, while he was a safe distance away. He made her feel, need—whether she wanted to or not. That sharp, sweet pleasure he could bring tempted her more each time. Perhaps that was one of the reasons she fought against it. It was frightening not to have a choice—Diana knew that better than most. She'd known desire before, and pleasure, but she'd always remained clear-headed. Not with Caine. And that's why she promised herself she'd be careful. Very careful.

She glanced back to see him examining one of the pistols. Strange that the old, beautiful weapon would look so right in his hands. There was something of the aristocracy about him, part scholar, part…wolf? Diana gave a quick shake of her head at the thought. She was becoming fanciful. Yet studying him, she thought she could see it. There was the intelligence in his eyes— and the danger. There was that lean, Celtic face with a mouth that promised to be fierce or gentle, depending on his whim.

A century ago he would have fought his duels with the pistols instead of words, she realized. And he would have won just as consistently. There was something not quite civilized under the polish his wealth and upbringing had given him. Diana recognized it because it was as true for herself as for Caine. The combination might equal something more savage than either of them bargained for.

Caine held the gun at arm's length, testing its weight. His eyes shifted and locked on hers—cool, dangerous. As the look held, Diana felt the needs building, experienced the violent, now familiar tug-of-war between intellect and emotion. The battle seemed longer this time, with the result less certain. By the time her intellect took control again she was shaken and weak— just as if his mouth had been on hers, with her body at last knowing the pleasure of his hands.

Be *very* careful, Diana reminded herself, and turned away again.

Still idly browsing, she examined a small upholstered chair. A lady's chair, she mused, with its pale blue brocade still in excellent shape. It had possibilities, she thought as she turned over its discreet price tag. After noting the amount, Diana decided it had definite possibilities. As she straightened to look for a clerk, she saw the desk.

That was it—perfect. With a low, pleased sigh, she began to examine it. Trim, elegant cherry, the desk had both the size and the lines she'd hoped to find. The border of the top was carved with cockleshells, frivolous enough to make her smile as she ran a fingertip over them. A far cry from the twentieth-century pine that was Barclay's standard for his staff. On the drawers were ornate brass pulls, and inside the scent of cherrywood lingered.

Mine, she thought quickly, possessively. Already, Diana could see it facing the fireplace in her office—hopefully laden with files.

"You found it, I see."

Beaming, Diana grabbed Caine's arm. "It's wonderful, isn't it? Exactly what I pictured." Her grip tightened as her other hand came to his. "I've got to have it."

He found it rather sweet that the practical Diana Blade would lose her head over a piece of furniture. Lacing his fingers with hers, Caine glanced down at the price tag on the corner of the desk, then back into her excited eyes. "Try not to look so eager," he told her dryly. "Here comes the clerk."

"But I—"

"Trust me." Bending his head, he gave her a quick kiss. "Sure it's pretty, love," he began in a different tone. "But you have to be practical."

"Caine—"

"May I be of some assistance?"

Caine turned a friendly smile on the clerk who had shown him the pistols. "The lady likes the desk." He gave a fractional shake of his head. "But..."

"An exquisite piece," the clerk began, turning to Diana. He hadn't been selling for over ten years without knowing whom to play to. "Just look at this carving. No one does work like this anymore."

"It's exactly what I've been looking for." She beamed at him, all goodwill. He could already see her writing out the check.

"Diana." Caine slipped his arm around her shoulder, squeezing a bit harder than necessary. Before she could protest, he brushed a kiss over her temple. "We're going to need several other pieces, remember? The desk is very nice, but so was the other one we looked at." She opened her mouth to tell him impatiently that they hadn't looked at any other, then caught the gleam in his eyes.

"Well, yes. But I do like this one..." Diana trailed off, struck with inspiration. "And that chair there," she went on, pointing at the little blue brocade.

"Another excellent choice, madam." The clerk began to think it would be a wonderful morning after all. "So right for a lady, as the desk is."

Diana sighed, letting her finger run lovingly over the desk surface. He better know what he's doing, she thought grimly, and shot a look at Caine.

With a smile, he patted her shoulder. "But you'll need a chair for the desk as well, and the right lamp. You'd almost be able to buy both of these with the difference in price between this desk and the other."

"You're right." It took effort, but Diana gave the clerk an apologetic smile. "I'm furnishing my office, you see. And there are so many things I need."

"I understand perfectly." He began to wonder if he would lose the sale of the pistols as well. The pistols, the desk, two chairs and a lamp... "We like to place the right furniture with the right people," he told her rather pompously. "Why don't you let me speak to the manager? I'm sure we could come to an agreement in terms."

"Well..." Caine pinched her arm to prevent her from agreeing too quickly.

Diana barely restrained herself from jabbing him with her elbow. "It won't hurt to listen, darling," she said in sweet tones that weren't reflected in her eyes.

"I suppose you're right." Caine gave her a smile as he met the killing look. "We'll just look at those lamps over there while you're talking to your supervisor," he told the clerk.

"If you lose that desk for me," Diana said under her breath as the clerk hurried toward the rear of the store, "I'll murder you."

"I'm going to save you ten percent," he said easily. "And you're going to buy me lunch." Caine stopped in front of a slim brass lamp with a fluted frosted shade. "They'll be more inclined to negotiate if they think they have to sell both of us. What do you think of this?" he asked, running a hand down the base of the lamp. "It goes nicely with the desk."

"Yes, it's lovely." She toyed with the delicate shade, then looked up at him. "You enjoy haggling, don't you?"

"It's in the blood. My father makes his living at it."

"And very well, too," Diana murmured. "I warn you," she added, "I'm going to have that desk whether he bargains or not."

"Did you want the chair, too, or were you making it up?"

"Yes, I want it." Diana laughed despite herself. "I'm not as devious as you."

"Stick around, you'll learn."

"Well." The clerk came up behind them, glowing with triumph. "I think we can come to very amicable terms."

Fifteen minutes later, Diana was outside, flushed with cold and pleasure. "How did you know he'd take off ten percent?"

"Experience," Caine claimed simply as he took her hand.

"I can see I'm going to shop with an entirely different outlook from now on." She tossed her hair back and grinned at him. "Thank you for the lamp, it was sweet of you to buy it for me. And I suppose the pistols will go to your father?"

"Mmm. He has a birthday coming up."

"You haven't bought a thing for yourself," she pointed out. "Isn't there anything you want?"

"Yes." Turning, he gathered her into his arms, pressing his mouth to hers.

The sidewalk was busy with shoppers who made their way around them with raised brows or muffled laughter. Diana noticed nothing. The air was sharp with winter, stinging her cheeks and ruffling her hair. She never felt it. Two women stopped to stare a moment. One of them sighed and said, "Isn't that lovely?" Diana didn't hear.

Her hands had gone to his face, and through the thin leather of her gloves she could feel the line of bone, the shape of jaw. A wolf, she thought again. You never know when they'll spring.

"Priceless," Caine murmured, drawing her away.

On a long, audible breath, Diana glanced around. "You enjoy having people stare, don't you?"

Laughing, he clasped her hands again and began to walk. "It really wasn't an issue. How about lunch?"

She searched for annoyance but couldn't find it. "I suppose I owe you that."

"You certainly do. There's a place around the corner."

"*Charley's!*" Diana exclaimed, surprised as Caine pulled her toward the door.

"Great chili."

"Yes, I know. I didn't discover it until I was in college." They shared too many tastes, Diana thought uncomfortably as they went inside to join the warmth and the noise.

Seeing her frown, Caine ran a hand through her windblown hair. "Don't you like it here?"

"Yes, I've always liked it here." She shook her head quickly, pushing away the discomfort. "I was thinking of something else." With the mood dispelled, she gave him a smile. "How do you like your chili?"

"Hot."

Laughing, Diana shrugged out of her coat. "So do I—so it stops just short of cauterizing my vocal chords."

The atmosphere was pure Victoriana with its gilt-edged portraits and long brass-railed bar. She'd stopped in from time to time during her college years, knowing she wouldn't run into her aunt or any of Adelaide's closer friends. They preferred the subdued elegance of the Ritz Cafe. As she took her seat across from Caine, a group at the bar began to sing lustily.

"How about some wine?" Reaching across the table, he took her hands. "It'll warm you up."

"Mmm. Something red and heavy." She allowed her hands to stay in his as he ordered. She'd enjoy his company, the closeness for the afternoon. Monday morning was soon enough to get back to business. "Tell me about your family," she asked abruptly. "The MacGregors have an almost mythical reputation in Boston."

Caine chuckled as he traced a finger over the back of her hand. "I suppose you'll have to meet the rest of them yourself to be certain how much was fact and how much was fiction. My father's a huge, redheaded Scot who'd probably still fight a Campbell to the death. He can drink a fifth of whiskey without blinking an eye, but he hides his cigars from my mother. He calls each one of us regularly to nag—for our mother's sake, he claims—about our not increasing the MacGregor line. 'Your mother longs to bounce a grandchild on her knee,'" Caine quoted with a perfect Scottish burr.

Diana laughed as the wine was brought to the table. "And what does your mother think about it?"

"My mother is a very relaxed kind of person, almost a negative of my father. He blusters, she comments. And in their own ways, they're both amazingly efficient." Unconsciously, he began to toy with the thin gold bracelet she wore on her wrist. Diana acknowledged, then tried to ignore as she had once before, the pleasure of having his hard fingers brush against her skin.

"I've only seen her lose that inherent serenity of hers a couple of times," Caine continued, half to himself.

"Once, I happened to be in the hospital when she lost a patient. I'd always thought she was strictly professional, almost cold about her work. After that, I realized she simply never brought it home with her. Then when Rena was kidnapped…"

Seeing the change in his eyes, Diana tightened her fingers on his. "That must have been hell for all of you. Those hours of waiting, not knowing if she was all right."

"Yeah." Caine shook off the lingering anger and lifted his glass. "Then there's Alan. He's more like my mother—very calm, patient. Even after growing up with him, I'm always surprised when he loses his temper. You forget he has one until it rips out and knocks you down."

Diana let the wine run warm through her system as she watched him. "Did you fight with him often?"

"Enough," he said with a nod. "More with Rena, I suppose. We're closer in temperament. And," he murmured reminiscently, "she has a hell of a right cross."

Diana caught the hint of pride in his voice and stared. "You didn't *box* with her, did you?"

Caine grinned at the astonishment in her tone as he poured more wine. "There were times I wanted to do more than just defend myself. And by God, there were times she deserved to be knocked cold." His grin widened as Diana continued to stare at him with a mixture of horror and fascination. "No, I never slugged her, but that was mostly because she was nearly four years younger and quite a bit smaller. I really didn't consider Rena as a girl until she was about fourteen. And that," he murmured, "was quite a surprise."

He loves them all, Diana mused, and it seems so easy for him. "You had a happy childhood," she commented, then looked down at her wine. "I was jealous about that before. You know, it was strange when I went to talk to Justin. The angrier I got, the less distance there seemed to be between us." With a wondering laugh, she shook her head. "Then when I wasn't angry any longer, the distance was gone. I was furious with you, too," she added, looking up again. "For interfering—and for being right. I really detested you for being right."

"It's a bad habit of mine," he said as their chili was served. "I can't seem to break it."

She gave an unladylike snort and lifted her fork. "I'm beginning to think I'd like to come up against you in court."

"Odd, I've had that thought myself. It would be," he decided after his first bite, "an interesting match." He sent her a slow, wolfish smile. "How's your chili?"

"Excellent." Diana kept her eyes level with his as she ate. "Tell me, counselor, are you so sure you'd win?"

"I rarely lose."

"Ah, the Perry Mason syndrome." When he laughed, Diana found herself more pleased with the sound than she should have been. It was too easy to forget her own rules when she was around him. Thoughtfully, she lifted her wine and studied its warm red hue. "Perhaps it's too bad I didn't go for a position with the D.A. after all," she continued. "If I were working for the state, we'd be bound to cross swords sooner or later."

"We will anyway," he murmured. "Though perhaps not in court."

"Perhaps," she agreed as she felt the little tingles of excitement begin. She fought them down, honest enough to admit them, too wary to allow them freedom. "But I wouldn't be too sure about winning."

"It could be," Caine said slowly, "that when the verdict comes in, we'll both have won."

"A hung jury?"

He smiled again, then brought her hand to his lips. The kiss was light and confident. "Justice."

Chapter Six

After spending an evening going over the police report and all the background notes Caine had given her on Chad Rutledge, Diana was no longer sure Caine was doing her a favor with the referral. It was a messy case, with several strikes against her potential client.

He'd been anything but a model of cooperation when he'd been picked up. In fact, Diana remembered as she glanced through the file again, he'd taken a swing at one of the arresting officers. Chad had denied the rape charges, then had claimed he'd been intimate with Beth Howard, the alleged victim, repeatedly over a six-month period. She denied anything but the most passing acquaintance.

Even before the medical reports had confirmed it, he had admitted to having sex with her the night of the alleged rape. When Beth's mother had brought her to the hospital for the examination, the girl had been bruised and hysterical. Chad's knuckles had been raw. Yet Caine seemed to believe his story.

With a sigh, Diana closed the file, then rubbed the bridge of her nose. She'd form her own opinion. They'd be bringing Chad to the conference room any minute. Glancing around at the dingy green walls, Diana thought that the frivolous Saturday morning she'd had with Caine only a few days before was light-years away. This part of her job had little to do with choosing the right desk.

The heavy door with its tiny thick window opened. Diana had her first look at Chad Rutledge. "I'll be right outside, Miss Blade," the guard told her as Chad dropped down in a chair at the side of the table.

"Thank you." She dismissed him without a look, giving her attention to her client. He looked younger than in his mug shots, but he had the same toughly handsome face and thick black hair. She glanced at his eyes. They stared straight ahead—sulky, disinterested. Then she looked at his hands. They clenched and unclenched slowly, as though he were working out a pain.

You can lie with your eyes, but not with your hands. Remembering Caine's words, Diana sat back. The boy was scared to death.

"I'm Diana Blade," she said briskly. Her own nerves, she discovered, weren't as steady as she might have liked. "I'll be taking over your case, if that's agreeable with you." Chad shrugged and said nothing. "Mr. MacGregor spoke with you, and with your mother before, but his workload doesn't permit him to give your case the proper time and attention it requires to insure you of the best possible defense."

"What kind of job's a woman going to do defending a guy for rape?" Chad asked the wall he faced.

"You'll get the best defense I can give you, regardless of your sex or mine," Diana returned evenly. "You told Mr. MacGregor your story, now I'd like you to tell me."

Chad hooked an elbow carefully over the back of the wooden chair. "Got a cigarette, babe?"

"No."

He swore halfheartedly and pulled one bent, unfiltered cigarette out of his shirt pocket. "At least he passed me to a looker." For the first time, Chad turned and faced her fully. There was challenge in his eyes as he skimmed them over her, lingering deliberately on the swell of her breast. Diana waited until his gaze came back to hers.

"Why don't we cut the crap and get down to business?"

The leer turned into a look of surprise, then annoyance. "Look, you've got the police report in that file there, what else do you want?" With a quick, nervous jerk, he lit a match, then drew greedily on his cigarette.

"Tell me what happened on January tenth." Diana drew a pad and pen out of her briefcase, then waited. "You're wasting my time, Chad," she said at length. "And your mother's money."

He shot her a furious look, then blew out a stream of smoke. "On January tenth, I got up, had a shower, got dressed, had breakfast and went to work."

Ignoring his belligerence, Diana began to take notes. "You're a mechanic at Mayne's Garage?"

"That's right." He sent her a lewd grin. "Want a tune-up?"

She could read the expression on his face by his tone

and didn't bother to look up. "Were you at the garage all day?"

"Yeah." He gave another shrug at her lack of reaction. "We had a Mercedes in for an overhaul. I do the foreign jobs."

"I see. What time did you get off?"

"Six." Chad shifted in his chair as he pulled in more smoke.

"Where'd you go?"

"I went home and had some dinner."

"Then?"

"Then I went out—cruising, you know." He smiled at her again, showing a slightly crooked front tooth. "Checking out the ladies."

"How long did you...cruise?"

"Couple hours." Chad drew hard on the cigarette so that the tip glowed red. "Then I raped Beth Howard."

Diana continued to write without breaking rhythm, though she felt the jolt down to the soles of her feet. "You've decided to change your plea?"

He slumped back in the chair, but his left hand was balled into a fist. "I figure I'm not going to get by with the bull I was passing before."

"All right, tell me about it." She glanced up when he remained silent. "Tell me about the rape, Chad."

"You get off hearing about things like that?"

"Did you pick her up in your car?"

"Yeah." The cigarette was no more than a fingertip in width when he finally snuffed it out. "She was walking home from the movies and I offered her a lift. We'd gone to high school together. She recognized me, so she got in. We talked for a while—just a lot of bull about what we'd been doing since graduation—drove around. I liked the way she looked, you know, so I gave her some story about needing to pick something up at the garage.''

"She went with you to the garage without protest?''

His tongue flicked out quickly to moisten his lips. There was already a sheen of sweat above them. "I told her I had to pick up some tools, you know? When we got there, I jumped on her.''

"And she resisted?''

"Yeah, I had to knock her around a little." He put his hand to his pocket and found another mashed cigarette. Diana saw that his fingers were trembling.

"And then?''

"Then I ripped off her clothes and raped her!" he exploded. "What the hell do you want? All the graphic details?''

"What was she wearing?''

He dragged a hand through his hair. "A pink sweater," he muttered. "Gray cords.''

"You're quite sure of that?''

"Yeah, yeah, I'm sure of it. A pink sweater with this little white collar and gray cords.''

"And you ripped them off of her," Diana persisted, still writing. "Tore them?''

"Yeah, I said I did.''

Setting down her pen, Diana met his eyes directly. "Her clothes weren't torn, Chad.''

"I said I tore them! I oughta know what the hell I did." He wiped at the dampness on his lips with the back of his hand, then moistened them again. "I was there, lady, you weren't.''

"Beth Howard's clothes weren't damaged when she arrived at the hospital."

His hand was shaking visibly now. "She changed them, that's all."

"No, she didn't," Diana said quietly, "because you never ripped them. Just as you never raped her. Why are you trying to convince me that you did?"

Chad put his elbows on the table, pressing the heels of his hands against his eyes. "God, I can't do anything right."

Diana studied the top of his head and listened to the sound of his labored breathing as it filled the tiny room. "You didn't put the bruises on her face, either, did you?"

Slowly, without uncovering his eyes, he shook his head. "I wouldn't hurt Beth."

"You're in love with her?"

"Yeah. Ain't it a hell of a mess."

"Start again," Diana ordered. "This time try the truth."

With a sigh, Chad lowered his hands and began.

He and Beth had gone through high school together each hardly aware of the other's existence. They'd run in different crowds. He'd been busy promoting his tough guy image, she'd been head cheerleader. Then one day six months before, she had brought her car into Mayne's for repairs, and everything had happened at once.

They'd started dating, her father had disapproved and ordered her to break it off. They'd continued to see each other secretly.

"It was like a game, you know?" Chad laughed

shakily as he tugged his hand through his hair again. "Even my friends didn't know—hers either. She'd say she was going to the library or the movies or shopping, and we'd snatch some time together. If she could get away for a couple hours at night, we'd go to the garage, seal up inside and talk, make love. I was saving up so that we could get married."

"What happened the night you were arrested?"

"We had a fight. Beth said she didn't want to go on that way anymore. She didn't care if we didn't have enough money or anywhere to live, she wanted to get married right away. She wouldn't listen. She started crying and I started yelling. Slammed my fist into the damn wall." He looked down at it as if he still expected to see the bruise. "Then she got in her car and drove off. I went out and had a few beers before I went home. Then the cops came. God, I was so scared at first, everything came pouring out."

"Why do you think she's accusing you of rape?"

"I know why." His eyes weren't challenging now, but helpless. "She smuggled a note to me through my mother. When Beth got home that night, she was still upset. Her father got on her and while they were arguing, she told him everything. He went nuts. Slapped her around, called her names. Scared the hell out of her. She says he threatened to kill both of us unless she did exactly as he said. Beth's scared enough to believe he means it." Chad let out a long breath as his hands began to work again. "Anyway, by the time her mother got home, Beth was hysterical. Her old man told the story and called the cops while her mother took her to the hospital."

"Where's the letter?"

"I got rid of it." Chad shook his head at Diana's expression. "My mom doesn't know what was in it, either, 'cause it was sealed. I don't think she'd have done it if she hadn't thought maybe something'd been going on between me and Beth for a while."

"If she writes you again, I want you to keep the letter."

"Look, I don't want her hurt anymore. When they first picked me up I was scared, you know. But I was mad, too. I thought she'd done it to punish me." He shook his head again, straightening his shoulders. "I'll take my chances on a few years in prison."

"You like your cell, Chad?" Diana demanded, pushing aside her notes to lean forward. "This is a picnic compared to the state penitentiary."

His mouth trembled as he swallowed. "I'll make out all right."

"They've got real rapists in there," she said coldly. "Murderers. Men who'd snap you in two without giving it a second thought. And how do you think Beth's going to feel knowing you're locked up in there, and why?"

"She'll be okay." A new trickle of sweat ran down the side of his face. "It won't be for that long."

"You want to risk twenty years of your life? You want her father to get away with setting you up? Grow up," she ordered impatiently. "This isn't a game anymore. You're going to go on trial for rape. The maximum sentence is life." Chad blanched and said nothing, but Diana could see the jerky workings of his throat. "You're going to have to sit in that witness chair and so is Beth. And you're going to have to tell the court exactly what happened that night. If you lie, the two of you face perjury charges.''

''If I plead guilty...''

Diana swooped the pad into her briefcase. ''If you want to play hero because your girlfriend's afraid of her father, get yourself another lawyer. I don't defend idiots.''

She started to rise, but Chad's hand shot out to take her arm. ''I just don't want to hurt her. She's awful scared.''

''She's been hurt,'' Diana said flatly. ''And she'll keep right on being scared until she tells the truth. Or maybe you don't believe she really loves you.''

His fingers tightened on her arm, but Diana didn't flinch. After a moment they relaxed. ''Tell me what I have to do.''

A portion of the tension in her shoulders eased. ''All right.''

When Diana walked into the office an hour later, she was drained. Lucy glanced up, took one long look, then stopped typing. ''You look like you could use some coffee.''

Diana gave her a weary smile. ''It shows?''

''Yep. Why don't I put some on and—'' Before she could finish the sentence, the phone rang.

''That's all right, Lucy, take care of the phone. I'll go fix some.'' As she walked back toward the kitchen, Diana slipped out of her coat. She could still see Chad's pale, frightened face, see his hand reach to his pocket for a cigarette after he had no more left.

And what was Beth Howard feeling? Diana wondered, tossing her coat aside as she turned to the stove. If I could get to her, she began, then let out a frustrated breath. That was the last thing the D.A. or her father would permit. Chad was going to have to wait for his day in court.

Rubbing at the ache at the back of her neck, Diana stared out the window over the sink, the coffee forgotten. With any luck, she could get the truth out of Beth Howard during the preliminaries. But if the girl was that frightened of her father...if she wasn't in love with Chad but merely playing games... With a sigh, Diana watched a bird peck at the lawn in search of food. So many ifs when a boy's life was at stake.

"Rough morning?" Caine asked from the doorway.

Diana turned. "Yeah." God, she was glad to see him, she realized. Glad to know here was someone she could talk to who would understand some of what she was feeling. "Busy?"

Caine thought of the brief upstairs on his desk but shook his head. "I could use some coffee." He slipped two mugs from their hooks and poured. "You saw Chad Rutledge this morning."

"Oh, Caine, that poor kid." Diana dropped into a chair at the small table while he added milk to one of the mugs. "He walked in doing an imitation of early Brando—some tough street hood—with fingers that trembled," she added in a murmur.

"Give you a hard time?" Caine set her coffee down as he sat across from her.

"He tried at first." With a sigh, she dragged her hair back from her face, holding it there a moment before she let her hand fall again. "Then he told me he'd raped Beth Howard."

Caine's mug paused on its way to his lips. "What?"

"He gave me a full confession," she began, warming both her hands on the side of the mug. "Very casual, like it was something he'd decided to do because he was a little bored. The more he talked, the more his hands trembled."

Sipping slowly, Caine shook his head. "It doesn't follow."

"I didn't think so, either." Diana tried to drink but found her stomach was still tied in knots. "I pressed him for details, and that's where he fell apart. He tried to convince me he'd lured her to the garage where he works, then knocked her around and raped her."

Caine's frown deepened. "That jives with the girl's story."

"Chad said he'd ripped her clothes off…torn them."

"Her clothes weren't torn."

Diana gave him a thin smile. "Exactly. It was all some smoke screen he'd dreamed up so that he could protect her."

Caine leaned back and drew out a cigarette. "Tell me."

Diana began, relaying the conversation exactly, point by point. As she spoke, Caine said nothing, but watched the play of emotion on her face. She was fighting not to get personally involved, he concluded, but it was already too late.

"If everything Chad says is true," he mused when she'd finished, "the girl'll fall apart on the stand."

"I believe him. He wanted to plead guilty and keep her out of it."

Caine's look sharpened. "What did you do?"

"I bullied him out of it." Diana allowed her eyes to close for a moment. "I don't know how the trial will affect him or the girl—if it gets that far. I've got a list of their close friends. Chad seems to think he and Beth kept their relationship secret, but the chances are something slipped to someone over the last six months. They're so young." Pushing back her hair, Diana rose to pace to the window again. "Oh, God, Caine, I was so hard on him."

The princess had stepped beyond the castle walls, he thought. He'd wanted her to—even pushed her to. Yet now, seeing the raw emotion in her eyes, he had conflicting needs to draw her further out and to urge her back to safety. When the shell cracked and opened, there was always pain. He spoke carefully, trying to fit back into the role of colleague.

"Diana, you know we can't always treat clients with kid gloves. It's no less than his life at stake."

"I know." She laid her forehead on the glass a moment. "It isn't easy to realize all at once that you can be cruel, that you can calmly sit there and whip somebody down with words. He was pale, sweating, shaking—I didn't give him a dram of sympathy."

"You gave him exactly what he needed." Caine had risen without her hearing, but he didn't approach her. This time, he wasn't completely sure how. "Now you're tearing yourself apart because you did what you had to do. His mother'll give him sympathy. You have to give him the best defense, whatever it takes.''

"I know." The bird was still there, bobbing along the grass determined to find what it was looking for. "Even if it means ripping up that girl on the stand. It's her father I'd like to get a hold of," she muttered. "Even when it all comes out—falsifying a police report—he's not likely to get much more than a slap on the wrist and a suspended sentence. And that nineteen-year-old boy's sitting in a cell, terrified."

Firmly, Caine suppressed the need to soothe and comfort. "He's not Justin, Diana."

She let out a long, shaky breath. "I'm that transparent?"

"At the moment."

"It was hard not to make the comparison." Lifting her hands, she hugged her arms as if seeking something solid. "He had that same tough, oddly attractive insolence that I remember in Justin as a teenager. And when I thought about him waiting in that cell, it was too easy to see how it had been for Justin. And I wondered…" She gave a small laugh. "I wondered if this could be another quirk of that fate of yours."

"You're going to lose your objectivity, Diana." His voice was tough and unsympathetic as the struggle went on inside him to be brother, lover, friend. "You've got no business in a courtroom without it."

"I know that." The words snapped out of her. She turned away with her jaw tensed and one hand balled into a fist. Objectivity, she thought, still unable to take those deep cleansing breaths that always kept her calm. She had no objectivity at the moment, but too many comparisons and too many regrets. She wanted to be held, soothed, and didn't dare ask because she needed to stand on her own. "I have to get it out of my system before I go back and see Chad again."

The words were low and tense, but they were the words he'd wanted to hear. Automatically Caine placed a hand on her shoulder. When the muscles there only tightened more, he increased his grip. He would have dealt with his sister the same way. That's what he told himself as he turned her around.

Wordlessly, he gathered her close, and though her arms came around him, she didn't cling. He knew she was looking for support, but not for answers. The answers she would find for herself.

In that moment, he discovered he'd never wanted her more; not just a warm, soft body against his, not just a mouth for tasting. He wanted her thoughts, feelings. He wanted to share what she was and feed back to her himself, so that there were no more boundaries and barriers. No more doubts. And while the tenderness enveloped him, his hands were gentle on her hair. Sensing something, Diana lifted her head.

His eyes met hers briefly, but she couldn't read them. He'd never looked at her that way before. Was there a question in them? she wondered. What was he asking her? Then his lips touched hers.

This had nothing to do with the other kisses they had shared. It might have been the first. His mouth was so soft. And careful, she thought dimly. Careful, as though he weren't so sure of himself. It ran through her head that he was kissing her as though he'd never kissed anyone before, this man who had known so many women.

His hands didn't press her closer but rested lightly on her back as though he would release her at the least movement. Diana was very still. Whatever magic this was, whatever reasons there were for it, she wanted it to go on. Yet it wasn't desire she felt, it was nothing so simple.

When he drew her away, they stared at each other—each as perplexed, each as moved as the other.

"What was that for?" Diana managed after a moment.

Caine dropped his arms slowly and stepped away from her. "I'm not sure," he murmured. Shaken, he walked back to the table and lifted his coffee. What the hell's going on? he asked himself, then drained the mug.

"Are you all right now?" he asked her as he turned back around.

"Yes." No, she said silently, but nearly managed a smile. "I think I'll go up and try to work out Chad's defense. Mrs. Walker's coming in tomorrow morning." When he gave her a blank look, she added, "The divorce case you referred to me."

"Oh, yeah." Caine stared into his empty mug and wondered what was happening to his mind. "They've hooked up your phone."

"Good." Diana remained at the window, not certain what she should do. "Well, I'll go on up, then," she said, but still didn't move.

"Diana…" Caine looked over at her, not sure what he was going to say. Feeling ridiculous, he gave a half laugh and shook his head. "Must be something in the coffee," he muttered. "Listen, do you have anything else tomorrow besides Walker?"

"Ah—no, no appointments. I have paperwork."

"I've got to drive up to Salem and see someone about the Day case. Why don't you come with me?" He continued before she'd worked out an answer. "It's a nice drive. You can clear your head and draft out your work while I'm tied up."

"Yes, I suppose I could," she considered. "All right," she agreed on impulse. "I'd like that, I might not have too many free afternoons."

"Good. We'll leave as soon as you're done with Mrs. Walker."

They stood for a moment in a silence Diana found unaccountably awkward. It was strange, she thought, that two people who had no trouble with words should suddenly have such a strained conversation. "I should be done by ten-thirty or eleven." She searched for something else to say but found her mind a blank. "Well, I'll go up, then."

Caine nodded as he walked back to the coffeepot. When he heard her footsteps drift away, he set his filled mug back down, untasted.

What the hell is all this? he wondered again, passing a frustrated hand through his hair. When he'd asked her to accompany him the following day, he'd felt like a gangly teenager asking for a date. With a half laugh, Caine went back to the table. No, he'd never felt that lack of confidence as a teenager. He'd never felt it at all—not with women.

After lighting a cigarette, he stared at the glowing

tip for several minutes. He'd always been sure of his ground when it came to the opposite sex. Enjoying women was part of it, not just as bed partners but as companions. That part of his life had always run smoothly. It was his firm intention that it continue to run smoothly. He knew, without conceit, that he didn't have to spend an evening alone unless he chose to.

Then why had he been spending so many alone lately? And when, he added thoughtfully, was the last time he had thought of any other woman but Diana?

Letting out a long breath, Caine began to sift the problem around in his mind—pull it apart, dissect it. He owed part of his success in his field to a synthesis of intellect and emotion. It had been that way since he'd been a boy: the quick, unexpected bursts of temper or passion, the long, quiet contemplations. He enjoyed puzzles—or the slow, meticulous solving of them. At the moment, however, he wasn't enjoying this one.

Uncomfortable. That was the first feeling he was able to clearly define. Thinking about Diana was making him uncomfortable, but why? He found her good company, enjoyed the flavor of their sparring matches. And he wanted her.

Caine drew hard on the cigarette, thinking of the sharp, turbulent passion he felt from her when he held her, when her mouth was avid on his. Desire didn't make him uncomfortable. He'd promised himself he'd be her lover sooner or later—and he always kept his promises.

It hadn't been desire moments ago, he reflected. Caine knew all the angles of that emotion. Neither had it been the brotherly type of affection he'd swung back to from time to time. It was Diana who didn't fit into any category, he told himself. She wasn't the easy sophisticate he was normally attracted to, nor was she the younger cousin he could show a good time.

Annoyed with himself, he rose and paced to the window. The light was thin—winter white. If she was making him uncomfortable, why had he asked her to drive to Salem with him? Because he needed to be with her?

Even as the answer ran through his mind, Caine made his thoughts back up and play again. *Need?* he repeated slowly. Now that was a dangerous word. *Want* was safer, and more understandable, but that hadn't been the answer that had sprung into his mind.

Very slowly, Caine walked back to the stove and lifted his cooling coffee. He drank, forcing himself to keep his mind blank for a moment. He thought of nothing but the faintly bitter taste of the coffee, saw nothing but the aged, exposed brick along the west wall. In the distance he heard the phone ring on Lucy's desk, then the quick rattle of the wind against the window behind him.

Good God, he thought, still staring straight ahead. Was he in love with her? No, that was ridiculous. Love wasn't a word he used, because love had repercussions. In an angry gesture, he dumped the remaining coffee down the sink. A man didn't go for over thirty years, then suddenly, without giving it a second thought, jump off a bridge. Unless…unless he'd woken one morning and discovered he'd lost his mind.

He'd been working too hard, Caine decided. Too many late nights poring over other people's problems searching for answers. What he needed was an evening with a compatible woman, then eight hours' sleep. Tomorrow, he promised himself, he'd be thinking clearly again.

Tomorrow, he remembered as he headed out of the kitchen, Diana would still be there. Swearing quietly, Caine walked up the stairs.

Chapter Seven

Diana would have enjoyed the ride more if she hadn't had the feeling something wasn't quite right. Caine was friendly enough—the conversation didn't lag or fall into awkward silences—yet she would have sworn there was something just under the surface of the camaraderie. Because it wasn't something she could define, Diana told herself she was imagining it—perhaps allowing herself to assign to Caine an echo of her own feelings.

There had been a tension in her since the previous day; one she attributed, at least in part, to her meeting with Chad Rutledge. It worried Diana that she couldn't shake it. An attorney—a good one—had to find that balance between callousness and emotional entanglement. The balance was as crucial for the client as it was for the attorney. Diana knew it intellectually but realized that the scales in this case were already tilting to one side. She could only comfort herself that the more involved she became in the technical points of the case, the less tendency she would have to compare Chad with Justin. For now, she would do exactly as Caine had suggested—clear her head and enjoy the ride.

"You didn't mention whom you're going to see in Salem," Diana began.

He had to force himself to gather his thoughts, to control the tension he was feeling. Like Diana, he told himself it was the case that had him tight, nothing personal. Personal relationships never made his stomach knot. He'd been telling himself that since the previous evening.

"Great-Aunt Agatha."

Diana let out an irrepressible sound of mirth. "You don't have to make something up," she said dryly. "You could simply tell me to mind my own business."

"Virginia Day's great-aunt Agatha," Caine said specifically, tossing her a grin. Discuss the case, he told himself. It might help him shake the feeling that he'd pried open a door for Diana, then stepped into quicksand. "She's reputed to be a very formidable lady and one who knows Ginnie better than anyone else. Unfortunately, she was ice-skating a couple of weeks ago and broke her hip. I'm going to see her at the hospital."

"Great-Aunt Agatha ice-skates?"

"Apparently."

"How old is she?"

"Sixty-eight."

"*Hmmm.* What are you looking for?"

Caine pushed the Jaguar forward in a burst of speed, passing a pickup before he answered. What was he looking for? he wondered. Even a few days before he would've been able to answer that with a shrug and a glib remark. The case, he thought with an annoyed shake of his head. Keep your mind on the case.

"The prosecution's going for murder one. The first thing I want to establish is that Ginnie carried that pistol with her habitually. If I'm going to prove self-defense, I have to get it into the jury's head early that Ginnie went to Laura Simmons's apartment to confront her husband with his current mistress, but not to kill."

"His current mistress," Diana repeated. "Apparently he had quite a number."

"The detective report Ginnie paid for a few months back indicates that Dr. Francis Day was a very busy man. He didn't do all his operating at Boston General." Caine punched in the car lighter. "If I can get the report into evidence, it should make the jury more sympathetic.... Then again, it gives Ginnie even more of a motive."

"So you're right back to the gun."

Caine nodded as he touched the lighter to the end of his cigarette. The conversation was easing the tightness at the base of his neck. Not quicksand, he thought now. He might've stepped into a puddle and gotten his feet wet, but he wasn't being sucked in. "According to Ginnie, she never left the house without it. She has a fixation about being robbed—not surprising, as she also has a penchant for wearing several thousand dollars' worth of jewelry at a time."

"Yes, and Ginnie Day hasn't endeared herself to the press or the public over the last few years," Diana remembered. "She comes across as a spoiled, selfish child with more money than class."

"True enough," Caine agreed. "But I can be grateful you won't be on the jury."

"I suppose I'm feeling a bit impatient with her type at the moment," Diana mused, shifting in her seat to face him. "Irene Walker," she said flatly. "She'd be the antithesis of Virginia Day."

"How'd it go this morning?"

"The bruises on her face haven't faded yet," Diana began, frowning at his profile. "I've never met a woman with less of a conception of her own worth. It's as if she felt she *deserved* to be beaten." With an impatient sound, Diana tried to push away the frustration she felt. "At least the friend she's staying with has convinced her to press formal charges against her husband, but..." Trailing off, Diana gave a quick shake of her head. "I have a feeling Irene Walker is like a sponge, simply soaking up the emotions of the people she's with. She's convinced herself—or her husband's convinced her—that she's a nonentity without him. I've recommended that she go into counseling. The divorce, and her husband's trial, aren't going to be easy for her." She let out a huff of breath that was as much astonishment as bewilderment. "She still wears her wedding ring."

"Taking it off would be the final break, wouldn't it?" he countered. "For a woman like Irene Walker."

"Do you know, they've only been married four years, and she can't remember the number of times he's beaten her?" Diana's eyes were hard and sharp for a moment. "I'm going to love getting him on the stand."

"As I recall, there were two witnesses to the last beating. You'd have him cold."

"That's exactly the way I want it. I'm hoping to get on the docket quickly, while Mrs. Walker still sees the bruises when she looks in the mirror. I think she's a woman who forgets too easily."

Caine glanced down at the briefcase next to her feet. "Is that what you're going to work on today?"

"I'm going to draft out interrogatories. I want to slap them on him right away. Between the divorce and the battery trial, I'm going to see that he gets nothing but trouble."

"Going for the jugular?"

She smiled then. "Someone told me once it was cleaner. Tell me…" Diana ran a fingertip over the back of the leather seat. "How long have you had this car?"

"The car?" He shot her a questioning look at the abrupt change of subject.

"Yes, I'd love to buy a new one myself."

The questioning look became a grin. Oh, she was definitely opening up, he mused. Breaking out. "A Jag?"

"One day." Diana arched a brow. "Or do you think they're reserved only for former state's attorneys?"

"I suppose I pictured you in a Mercedes—stately and elegant."

Diana narrowed her eyes. "Are you trying to insult me?"

"Certainly not," Caine replied gravely. "Can you drive a stickshift?"

"You *are* trying to insult me."

Without comment, Caine pulled over to the shoulder of the road. Curiously, Diana watched him get out, round the hood and open the passenger door. "You drive awhile."

"Me?"

He struggled with a grin at the half-incredulous, half-excited look in her eyes. Perhaps this, most of all, was what he couldn't resist—when the sophistication and intelligence were replaced by pure, simple pleasure. "If you're thinking about buying a car, you should get the feel of it first. Unless," he added slowly, "you can't drive a five-speed."

"I can drive anything," Diana stated as she climbed out.

"Fine." Caine settled back in the passenger seat as Diana switched places. "I'll tell you when to turn off."

Diana gripped the wheel with one hand and put the car into first. Under her palm, she could feel the light vibration of power, the promise of speed. After glancing in the rearview mirror, she shot back onto the highway. "Oh, it's wonderful!" she cried immediately. A check on the speedometer had her easing off the gas. "And tempting," she added with a quick laugh. "I'm afraid I'd end up defending myself in traffic court if I had one of these."

"I've always found it's just a matter of knowing you can press your foot down and go faster than anything else on the road," Caine commented.

"Yes, *knowing* you can, so that you don't." Tossing back her hair, she laughed again and passed a slower stream of traffic as the speedometer hovered just above fifty-five. "It would hardly be seemly for a public servant to zip down the road at ninety miles an hour, but it feels wonderful knowing you could." Diana shifted into fifth and kept the speed steady. "Is that why you bought it?"

"I like things with style," he murmured, studying her profile. "If they have enough power to challenge underneath the gloss." The hands on the wheel were confident, capable. Caine could picture her driving down an empty stretch of road on a summer night, the windows open, her hair flying. "You fascinate me, Diana."

She sent him a quick grin. "Why? Because I can drive a Jag without running into the median strip?"

"Because you have style," Caine countered. "Take the next turnoff."

While Diana settled into a corner of a waiting room to work, Caine walked down the hospital corridor to Agatha Grant's room. He found her in solitary splendor—pink lace bed jacket, white hair perfectly coiffed, thin cheeks tinted outrageously—with a bumper crop of magazines littering the bed. They ranged from gossip glossies to *Popular Mechanics*. As Caine entered, Agatha set down the sports magazine she'd been thumbing through to eye him appreciatively.

"About time they let someone with looks in here," she said in a raspy voice. "Come in and sit down, honey."

Caine's grin was spontaneous as he walked to the bedside. "Mrs. Grant, I'm Caine MacGregor."

"Ah, Ginnie's lawyer." Agatha nodded as she gestured to a chair. "The girl always did have an eye for a good-looking face. Looks like it's got her in a hell of a mess this time."

Caine took another pile of magazines from the chair before he sat. "I'm hoping you'll be able to help me with Ginnie's defense, Mrs. Grant. I appreciate you seeing me like this, so soon after your accident."

Agatha snorted and waved the words away. "I'll be up and around long before these doctors think," she told him, then gave a rueful smile. "Maybe I won't be doing figure-eights too soon. Okay, honey, tell me what you want to know."

"You know that Ginnie has been charged with murdering Francis Day." When Agatha gave a brisk, unemotional nod, Caine continued. "It's alleged that she went to Laura Simmons's apartment, knowing her husband was there and that Ms. Simmons was his mistress."

"The last of many," Agatha added caustically.

Caine only lifted a brow at the comment and continued. "Ms. Simmons left Ginnie alone with Day, at his request. When she returned to the apartment twenty minutes later, Day was dead and Ginnie was sitting on the couch with the pistol still in her hand. He'd been shot twice at close range. Ms. Simmons became hysterical, rushed to a neighbor's and called the police."

"Ginnie killed him." Agatha pushed at the magazines with gnarled, red-tipped fingers. "There's little doubt of it."

"Yes, she admits to that. However, she claims that Day became abusive when they were alone. At first, she says, they shouted at each other—something that had been habitual in their marriage for some time. Then she threatened to drag him through a messy divorce with all the trimmings—correspondents, detective reports—something he wanted to avoid, as he was next in line as chief of surgery at Boston General.''

Agatha gave a low, mirthless chuckle. ''Yes, he would have hated that. Ginnie's Franny guarded his reputation as a distinguished, dedicated man of medicine. It wouldn't have done for it to come out publicly that he was a lecher.''

Caine made a quiet sound that might have been agreement or speculation. She's a tough one, he concluded, noting Agatha's composed, painted face. ''During the argument,'' Caine went on, ''he lost control, slapped her. By this time they were screaming at each other. She claims he went wild, knocked her to the floor and picked up a lamp. He told her he was going to kill her. When he came toward her, Ginnie took the gun out of her purse and shot.''

Agatha nodded over the explanation, then leveled a hard look at Caine. ''Do you believe her?''

Caine returned the look for several seconds before he spoke. ''I believe that Virginia Day shot her husband in a moment of panic, and in her own defense.''

''Ginnie's a hardheaded girl,'' Agatha said with a sigh. ''Spoiled. We all spoiled her. And she has a mean temper, explodes easily without thinking of the consequences. But she's not cold-blooded,'' Agatha added with another level look. ''She would not, could not, systematically plan to kill.''

''In order to prove that,'' Caine returned, ''the first thing I have to establish is why she had a gun when she went to confront her husband.''

''The girl wouldn't step out of the door without that pistol.'' With a sound of disgust, Agatha shifted against the pillows. "Ugly little thing. I'd ask her what the hell she thought she was going to do with it and she'd laugh. 'Aunt Aggie,' she'd say, 'if anyone tries to mug me, they're in for a surprise.'" Agatha let out another impatient sound. "Stupid girl had to glitter—diamonds, emeralds. She'd think nothing of walking in the Back Bay or dashing around Manhattan, dripping with jewelry—as long as she had that damn pistol."

"You often saw her with the pistol in her possession?"

"I might be staying with her for a few days, stop by her room before we went out somewhere. I'd see her put the thing in her bag. Once at a party I saw it there when she went in her purse for a compact. I gave her hell about it," Agatha added. "For all the good it did."

"Then you'd swear in court, under oath, that Virginia Day habitually carried a twenty-two pistol in her possession? And that on numerous occasions you saw her with the gun and discussed it with her?"

"Honey, I'd lie in hell's face for her." Agatha gave him a thin, icy smile. "Never could stand that two-timing jerk she married."

"Mrs. Grant—"

"Relax," she told him with something like a cackle. "In this case I can swear to it without risking my mortal soul. If Ginnie *hadn't* had the pistol with her that night, I'd have wondered what was going on."

"Good." Caine allowed himself to relax. "And we might keep it just between you and me about lying in hell's face?"

"You got it." She sent him a crafty smile then, letting her eyes scan his face. "I don't suppose you and Ginnie…"

"I'm her defense attorney," Caine countered as he rose. Reaching out, he grasped Agatha's surprisingly strong hand. "Thank you, Mrs. Grant."

"If I were forty years younger and on trial for murder," Agatha said slowly, "you'd be a hell of a lot more than my defense attorney."

Flashing her a grin, Caine brought her hand to his lips. "Don't kill anyone, Agatha. I find you very hard to resist."

Pleased, she let out a lusty laugh that followed him down the corridor.

Caine found Diana where he had left her, a law book balanced on one knee, a legal pad on the other. She was busy writing, apparently not affected by the inconvenience. Without speaking, he took a chair and waited for her to finish. He always enjoyed watching her this way—when she was absorbed with what she was doing and cut off from her surroundings. No guards now, he thought. He'd wanted to help her accomplish that, just as much as he'd wanted to make love with her. Now that she was well on her way to the first, he realized he couldn't afford to do the second.

There were too many undercurrents in her, he decided. Undercurrents had a habit of pulling in the unwary. Perhaps it had been the sudden realization the evening before that he could conquer her, with time, with care, that made him now too cautious to attempt it. It was time to put their relationship on one balanced level and leave it there. For her sake? he wondered ruefully. Or for his own?

When Diana stopped writing ten minutes later, she closed the book and started to stretch her shoulders before she spotted Caine. "Oh, when did you get back?"

"Only a few minutes ago. You know, not everyone is able to block out their surroundings and work the way you do."

"One of my more basic skills," Diana claimed, slipping everything back into her briefcase. "I developed it out of necessity when I wanted to tune out my aunt. How did it go?"

"Perfectly." Caine rose, picking up Diana's coat to help her into it. "Just how much trouble did you have with your aunt, Diana?"

Immediately she tensed up, closed up. He saw it and wondered if his princess in the tower idea had been closer to the mark than he'd realized. "My aunt?" Her voice was cool and emotionless.

"Yes. How much trouble did you have?"

"She was fond of phrases like 'a lady never wears diamonds before five.'"

"A great deal, obviously," Caine murmured as he picked up his own jacket. "I wonder if I was a little rough on you in Atlantic City."

Surprised, Diana stared up at him as they walked toward the elevator. "There's no need to apologize." But her body was still on guard, her voice still on edge. "What brought that on?"

"I was thinking about Agatha." Caine pushed the button for the lobby. "She doesn't particularly approve of her niece, but she loves her. It shows." He released a lock of hair that was caught in Diana's collar. "I'm beginning to think it was just the opposite in your case."

"Aunt Adelaide approved of what she thought she'd made me." With a shrug, Diana stepped out of the elevator. "It was enough. As for love, she never loved me—but then again, she never pretended to, either. I can't fault her for that."

"Why the hell not?" he demanded, angry all at once with the clarity of the picture her limited words drew.

She gave him a steady look that clearly told him he was too close. "You can't blame someone for their emotions, or for the lack of them." When she turned away, it was a signal that the conversation was ended. Unable to stop himself, he grabbed her arm. Where she was cool again, he was heating.

"Yes, you can," he countered. "You damn well can."

"Leave it, Caine. I did." When he started to object, she turned again, then stopped. "Oh, my God, look!" Diana stared through the glass doors.

Still frowning at her words, Caine glanced over. Snow was falling fast and thick, already blanketing the ground. "So much for the weather forecast," Caine muttered. "This was supposed to hold off until tonight."

Diana drew on her gloves. "The drive back to Boston's going to be very interesting. And very slow," she added as they stepped outside into the full force of the storm.

"With any luck we'll be heading out of it." Caine took a firm grip on her arm as they walked across the parking lot. As he finished the statement, they looked toward the sky simultaneously. At Diana's arched brow look, he shrugged. Both of them were already covered with snow. "We could go back to the hospital and wait it out."

"Not unless you don't want to risk driving in it."

Caine looked toward the road as they stopped by the car. "We'll see how it goes."

For the first twenty minutes, they drove through the storm with relative ease. Caine was a good driver, and the car hugged the road confidently. Diana watched the snow hurtle down, building quickly on the roadside, coating naked trees. The farther south they got, the more the wind picked up, so that snow covered the windshield as quickly as the wipers cleared it. Catching her breath, Diana saw the car in front of them fishtail and skid into the center lane before the driver regained control.

"It's pretty bad," she murmured, casting Caine a look.

"It's not good." He kept the speed slow and even, with his eyes narrowed in concentration on the road ahead. With every mile, the visibility became shorter and the road slicker. He'd lived in New England long enough to know the makings of a blizzard when he saw one. It was falling too thick and fast. Caine was aware now that rather than heading out of the storm, they were heading into it. On the other side of the median strip, two cars slid into each other and stopped. Both he and Diana remained silent for the next twenty miles.

They'd reached the halfway point between Boston and Salem in nearly twice the time it had taken them to make the entire trip earlier. The light was failing, and when he turned on the headlights, the snow danced crazily in the beams. There were drifts of over a foot of snow on the side of the road, with more coming. An abandoned car sat crookedly where it had skidded off and stalled. Diana began to wish she'd taken Caine's suggestion of staying in the hospital more seriously.

A car passed them on the right, at a dangerous speed that had it sliding toward the Jag's front fender. Diana smothered a gasp as Caine swore ripely, forced to brake, then fight a skid. He was still cursing as he brought the car under control and took the first turnoff. "It's suicide to travel that road in this."

Diana merely nodded, busy trying to swallow her heart again.

"We'll stop off at the first hotel we come to, get a couple of rooms and wait until morning." He took his eyes off the road long enough to look at her. "You all right?"

Diana let out a deep breath. "Ask me again when I'm not praying."

Caine gave quick chuckle, then narrowed his eyes as the bluish glare of a neon light shone mistily through the snow. "I think we're in luck."

The last slash of the "M" in Motel had gone out, but the rest of the neon was garishly visible. "Ah, a *notel*," Diana said with a grin. "What better shelter from a storm?"

Caine glanced at the single-story compound before he pulled the car to a halt. "We won't get deluxe accommodations in this section."

"Will we have a roof?"

"Probably."

"That's good enough." She had to use both hands to push open the door against the wind. Standing outside, Diana sank to her knees, took a deep breath and burst out laughing.

"What's so funny?" Caine demanded as he began to pull her toward a tiny building marked "Office."

"Nothing, nothing!" she shouted back. "It just feels wonderful now."

"You should have told me you were frightened." He tightened his arm around her waist as the wind shoved both of them back two steps.

Diana lifted her face to the full fury of snow. "I would have when I'd run out of my repertoire of prayers."

The door jingled stridently as Caine shoved it open. The cold, clean smell of snow was immediately blocked out by the scent of cheap tobacco and stale beer. Behind a laminated counter, a grizzled man lifted his eyes from a magazine he was reading. "Yeah?"

"We need a couple of rooms for the night." One glance told Caine it was the sort of establishment that normally rented them by the hour. Amused, he reminded himself beggars couldn't be choosers.

"Only got one." The clerk lit a kitchen match with his thumbnail and eyed Diana. "Blizzard's good for business."

Diana looked at Caine, then back out the glass door behind him. He was leaving it up to her, she realized as a little nerve jumped at the base of her neck. She remembered that last long skid. "We'll take it."

The clerk dug under the counter for a key. "That'll

be twenty-two fifty,'' he told Caine, still holding the key. ''Cash, in advance.''

''Any place to get some food around here?'' Caine asked as he counted out bills.

''Diner next door. Open 'til two. Your room's out and to the left. Number twenty-seven. Checkout at ten, or you owe another night's rent. Room's got free TV and pay movies.''

Caine lifted a brow as he exchanged money for the key. ''Thank you.''

''Friendly sort,'' Diana commented as they fought their way toward number 27. ''You did mention food?''

''Hungry?'' Caine checked the number on a peeling gray-painted door.

''I'm starving. I hadn't realized it until…'' Diana's voice trailed off as her eyes widened in astonishment.

The room, what there was of it, was mostly bed. One bed, she noted, but even that didn't alarm her in her present state. The walls were a sizzling pink to match the wild-pink-and-purple sunburst pattern of the bedspread. There was one chair and an excuse for a table, both painted in glaring white. The rug, though worn and thin, picked up the purple tint all the way to the door of what Diana assumed was the bath. And on the ceiling over the bed was a round, dusty mirror.

''Well, it isn't the Ritz,'' Caine said dryly, struggling not to burst out laughing at her dazed expression. He set both their briefcases on top of a white plastic-topped dresser. ''But it does have a roof.''

''Hmm.'' Diana gave the mirror a last dubious look. Perhaps it was best not to think about that for the moment. "It's freezing in here." Turning, she saw that the drapes unfortunately matched the bedspread.

Catching her expression, Caine couldn't hold back the grin. "It's a room that's at its best in the dark. I'll see if I can get the heater working."

Ignoring what she considered his odd humor, Diana sat gingerly on the edge of the bed. The only bed, she reminded herself. The only room, the only hotel. "One might think you were enjoying this whole fiasco."

"Who, me?" Caine gave the heater a quick kick that sent it roaring into life. Enjoying wasn't the word he'd have picked. Even the thought of spending the night with her in this laughable room had the knot back in his stomach. For the next few hours, he'd have to concentrate on pretending he was her big brother again if he was going to remember his resolution not to touch her. "I'll go pick something up at the diner," he continued when Diana only stared at him. "There's no use both of us going out in this again. Want anything special?"

"Quick and edible." Remembering the storm he had driven through, she unbent enough to smile at him. If he was going to accept the situation with a shrug, then so would she. "Thanks. I owe you eleven dollars and a quarter."

"I'll bill you," he promised, then leaned over to give her a brief kiss before he went out.

Alone, Diana glanced around the room again. It wasn't so bad, really, she told herself...if you kept your eyes half-closed. And the heater was certainly working great guns now. She slipped out of her coat and looked for a closet. It seemed the room didn't run to such extravagances. Draping the coat over the dresser, Diana unzipped her boots.

The idea of a hot bath was appealing, but the prospect of undressing just to dress again had her vetoing the notion. She'd compensate by stretching out on the bed until Caine came back with dinner. Maybe some television, she thought idly, then noticed a black box attached to the side of the set. On closer examination, Diana noted it was some kind of timer fed by quarters. The pay movies, she remembered, and decided to try her luck. It might be wise to have a movie marathon; that way it'd be easier to remember they were both lawyers—a word without gender—rooming together through circumstances. She glanced over her shoulder at the bed again and felt a little bead of tension work its way up her spine. Resolutely, she turned away.

A search through her wallet found her three quarters, and what would amount to forty-five minutes of whatever movie was playing. Following the instructions printed on the box, Diana turned the set to the proper channel, fed in the quarters and twisted a knob not unlike one on a parking meter. She turned and went to the bed, stretched out in the center and gave a sigh of pure appreciation.

It was while she was busy arranging the pillows behind her head that the movement on the set caught her eye. After a classic double-take, she simply stared, open-mouthed. When the initial shock wore off, Diana lay back and laughed until her sides ached.

Good God, she thought as she hauled herself off the bed again, of all the motels in Massachusetts, they had to find one with pink walls and blue movies. Diana was just hitting the off switch when Caine walked back in.

"Do you know what *kind* of movies you get for a quarter on this machine?" she demanded before he'd shut the door behind him.

He shook himself like a dog, scattering snow. "Yes. Did you need some change?"

"Very cute." Though she tried, she couldn't keep her lips from curving. "I just wasted seventy-five cents. I wouldn't be a bit surprised to have the vice squad banging on the door."

"In this weather?" Caine countered and set two white bags down on the little table.

"Is that dinner I smell?"

"So to speak. I got quick, I won't guarantee edible." He pulled out two wrapped hamburgers. "You go first."

"Young attorney poisoned in notel," Diana murmured as she unwrapped one of the sandwiches.

"There's fries, too." He peeked into the bag. "I think they're fries. Anyway, I got some wine for now and coffee for later." He took out two capped foam cups and set them aside before he drew out a bottle. "The best I can say is that it's red."

"Oh, I don't know." Diana bit into the hamburger, taking the bottle in her free hand. "This was a great week. Does this place run to glasses, or do we swig straight from the bottle?"

"I'll check in the bathroom. No sudden stomach pains?" he asked as he went.

"No." She decided to risk the fries. "I don't suppose the storm's letting up?"

"If anything, it's worse." Caine came back with two plastic glasses. "Word over at the diner is more than a foot before morning."

Diana sat on the edge of the bed and took the offered glass. "I suppose we could watch the news," she mused with a glance at the set. "If you can get the news on that thing."

Laughing, Caine sat down and unwrapped his hamburger. "Poor Diana, what a shock that must have been."

"I'm not a prude," she said primly. "It was simply unexpected." She took a sip of wine, grimaced and sipped again. "It's really not too bad."

"Best in the house," Caine told her. "A buck fifty-nine a bottle."

"In that case I'll sip more slowly. Caine, there is one small detail we should discuss."

He took a swallow of wine. He'd known it was coming. While he'd trudged through the storm, he'd decided exactly how to handle it. "I'm not sleeping on the floor."

Diana made a face at his accurate reading of her mind. "There's always the bathtub."

"Be my guest."

"It's becoming painfully clear that chivalry is dead."

"Look," he began over a mouthful of hamburger. "It's a big bed. If you don't want to put it to any better use than sleeping—"

"I certainly don't."

The sharp answer was precisely what he'd been working toward. If they kept it casual, kept it up front, they both might survive the night. "Then you sleep on one side and I'll sleep on the other," he finished, telling himself it was just as simple as that.

"I'm not certain I like how quickly you agreed to that," she murmured.

"If you'd like me to convince you otherwise..." he began with a slow smile.

"No. That's not what I meant." Frowning, Diana finished off her hamburger. After all, she mused, he'd driven for nearly two hours in that miserable storm. She could hardly deny him a decent night's sleep. "You stay on your side and I'll stay on mine?" she repeated.

He leaned over to fill her glass again. "If you insist. I hate to repeat myself by bringing up Clark Gable again."

"Clark Gable?" Diana repeated blankly than gave a brief laugh. "Claudette Colbert—*It Happened One Night.*"

"Exactly," he said with an amused smile. "In a similar situation they imagined something along the lines of the walls of Jericho."

She gave him a long look. "How's your imagination?"

Caine shrugged and sipped his wine. "I told you once I could wait until you admitted you wanted me." Deliberately, he lifted his eyes to hers and deliberately he baited her, knowing she'd step back. He desperately needed her to step back. "I can be very patient."

Refusing to acknowledge the challenge, Diana merely nodded. "As long as you know the rules."

"I think I'll skip the coffee and have a bath before I turn in." Standing, he ran a casual hand down her hair. "You should get some sleep; it's been a long day."

She felt a quick sense of regret, which she firmly stemmed. "Yes, I think I will. Shall I leave the light on?"

"No, don't bother. It's impossible to miss the bed in this room." He wanted to kiss her, badly, and made himself walk away. "Good night, Diana."

"Good night." Diana waited until she heard the water running, then slowly rose. *You're being a fool!* a voice told her with sharp, surprising impatience. *You know there's nothing you want more than to make love with him. To lose yourself in him.*

That's just it, Diana thought with a sudden panic. I would lose myself, or a part I'm not sure I'm ready to lose. He's different, and I don't trust him. Or myself. Diana ran an agitated hand through her hair and listened to the sound. It wouldn't be the same with Caine as it might with any other man. He'd already broken down so many barriers, once the physical was down, he wouldn't stop there. She couldn't—wouldn't—allow him that kind of hold over her.

Oh, but she wanted him tonight.

Like Caine, Diana let her coffee sit, growing cold. She wanted nothing that might keep her awake and restless while she shared a bed with him. After a moment's struggle, she stripped down to her chemise. She wasn't going to be a fool and sleep in her clothes. Carefully, she climbed into bed, keeping close to the edge. She found this more difficult than she had anticipated, as the mattress sagged in the center. Swearing against what Caine would have called fate, Diana switched off the light and, gripping the side of the bed to keep from rolling out of her territory, firmly shut her eyes.

When Caine came out, the room was silent. He could see Diana's vague outline at the far side of the bed. He'd spoken easily enough about sharing that soft, warm rectangle with her, but the hot bath had done nothing to ease the need. It might be wise, he thought, to use the rest of the wine in lieu of a sleeping pill. God, he was going to need something knowing she was only an arm's length away. It would have been smarter, he told himself grimly, not to have given her his word he'd stay on his side. But he had.

Caine let the towel drop and got quietly into bed. Like Diana, he found himself sliding toward the center. Cursing silently, he shifted away.

With the habit of years, Caine drifted awake slowly and early. Something soft and warm was wrapped around him. Though still more asleep than awake, he knew by the scent it was Diana. Without conscious thought, he drew her closer, then heard her sigh as she snuggled against him. With lazy pleasure, he ran a hand down her, to where the silk gave way to skin, then back again. Diana pressed against him, her fingers sliding lazily over his back.

Murmuring her name, he touched his lips to her forehead while his hand slipped beneath the silk. They gave simultaneous sounds of pleasure, languid and soft. He thought it was no more than a dream—he'd dreamed of having her—but it had never been quite like this, so slow and easy. When he shifted, his leg slid intimately between hers while his mouth began a leisurely journey over her face. With an inarticulate murmur, Diana tilted her head back so that her lips found his.

The dream lingered...the kiss lingered, without pressure, as he continued to stroke and caress beneath the thin silk. There was no place for doubts in soft, drowsy light, no room for reservations on a soft, sagging mattress. He touched her, seducing both of them into sleepy surrender.

Warm, so warm, he thought, feeling the first real tug of desire as he found her breast. Diana moaned a little and arched against him. He thought he heard his own name whispered against his lips, and then her hands were moving over him.

Steeped in her, and the fantasy, he took his mouth to her shoulder, nudging the strap aside. They were as strong as he had imagined, and smooth. Following the gentle slope, he slipped the chemise down farther, pressing quiet, sleepy kisses along her arm.

He could hear her breathing now, a little fast, a little unsteady, and found that his mouth had fastened onto her breast to suckle and nibble. He was unaware of passion until the need was a hard knot in his stomach and his own breathing was labored. Her heartbeat was a hammer against his lips, which were now demanding more. And she was naked, although he wasn't fully aware that he had pulled the short length of silk from her.

Her fingers were digging into his flesh, her hips moving in a faster-growing rhythm. His name sighed from between her parted lips. For a moment, he tried to clear his head—separate dream from reality, but his body was in full command.

Then he was inside her, driven past fantasies and beyond reason.

Chapter Eight

The light was a dim, dark gray. Shuddering and stunned, Diana opened her eyes to see only shadows. She was cupped in the center of the bed, nestled beneath Caine and the thin blanket they had shared through the night. Though his face was buried against her throat, she could hear his unsteady breathing, feel the racing thump of his heart against hers. His skin was hot, and like hers, faintly damp. Her fingers were curled into his hair, and the taste of him still lingered on her lips. Her mind, like her body, felt heavy, as if wrapped in some thick, sweet honey. Tiny thrills of pleasure hummed over her flesh where she could still feel the pressure of his fingers. In one flashing explosion, her brain cleared.

With a quick sound of outrage, Diana struggled from beneath him, then rolled to the far edge of the bed. "How could you?"

Dazed, Caine opened his eyes to stare at her. "What?"

"You gave your word!" She began a furious search beneath the covers for her camisole.

Still throbbing from her, and equally stunned, Caine dragged a hand through his hair. "Diana—"

"I should have known better than to trust you," she said, pulling the brief covering of the camisole over her before she jumped out of bed. Her body tingled, her limbs felt weighted. In defense, her eyes grew stormier. "God knows why I thought you'd keep a bargain."

"Bargain?" he repeated blankly.

"You stay on your side of the bed, and I stay on mine," she reminded him bitterly. "You and your damn walls of Jericho."

He rubbed a hand over his face. "Are you crazy?"

"I must have been," Diana ranted, "to have thought you'd understand common decency."

"Now wait a minute." In the dim light, Caine could make out little more than her silhouette and the faint gleam of her eyes. But he could feel his own anger growing surely enough and pushed himself out of bed. His temper only increased as he felt a wave of weakness that came from a draining of passion.

"Don't tell me to wait a minute," Diana snapped, wrapping her hands around her arms as she started to shiver. "That was despicable."

Fury, and something he didn't recognize as hurt, sped through him swiftly. "Despicable," he repeated in an ominously low tone. "Despicable." In echoing the word, he fought for control. "You didn't appear to think so a few moments ago."

Her own fingers dug into her arms as she tossed back her head. No, she hadn't thought at all a few moments ago, only felt, only wanted. Caine had been right there—warm, gentle, seductive. "You had no right. No right!"

"*I* had no right?" he retorted. "And what about you?"

"I was half-asleep."

"Damn it, Diana, so was I!" Dragging a hand through his hair again, Caine struggled against a sensation of confused, frustrated fury. As he fought for calm, he grabbed his pants and stepped into them. Guilt was overwhelming, guilt that he'd taken her beyond the point she'd been prepared for. By doing so, he'd changed things between them just when he'd resolved to keep them stable. "Look, it just happened—I didn't plan it."

"Things like that don't *just happen*." Shivering, she whipped the garish bedspread from the tumbled bed and wrapped herself in it.

"This did," Caine said between his teeth as he pulled on his turtleneck. Even anger couldn't completely dissipate the feeling that he had woken from some hazy dream. "I don't even know how the hell it got started," he muttered. His eyes seared into hers. He might be guilty, but he wasn't alone. "I know when it ended, and before it ended, you were just as much involved as I was."

The truth stung—and frightened. "You expect me to believe you didn't know what you were doing?" she shouted at him. "That you didn't plan for this to happen?"

On an irresistible wave of fury, he swooped up his coat and marched to her. "Why the hell don't you blame me for the blizzard?'' he demanded. ''Or for the fact that this—this dump,'' he bit off with a violent gesture of his arm, ''only had one room? Or that the damn mattress sags in the middle?''

''I know exactly what to blame you for,'' Diana said. ''And what to regret.''

The room fell into deadly silence, broken only by the sound of angry breathing and the rumble of the heater. She saw something violent flash into his eyes, darkening them, narrowing them. In her own confused fury, she welcomed it—and a fight.

''You don't regret it any more than I do,'' Caine said softly. Without another word, he pulled open the door, letting windblown snow rush in before he slammed it behind him.

Alone, Diana gripped the spread tightly but still felt the icy chill on her skin. It was outrage, she told herself. Fury. She'd trusted him and he'd betrayed her, deceived her. He'd…made her feel wonderful, alive, desired.

A tiny, choked sound escaped her as she dropped onto the bed and huddled under the spread. No, no! she told herself as she balled her hands into fists. It shouldn't have happened. Once she had given in to him, and to herself, it would be only the beginning. Wouldn't she be right back to having her life dominated by someone who could pick up and leave at any moment? Not again, Diana swore, pounding her fist on her knee. Never again.

She'd barely begun to discover herself for herself. Everywhere, in every aspect of her life, there was Caine who'd been there, urging her to reconcile with Justin.

He'd been there, with an answer to her professional problems on her return to Boston. Now, he was here, tempting her to strip away her last defenses, expose the last of her emotions.

Would she be any different from Irene Walker if she allowed it? Diana wondered. When a woman was ruled by emotion, didn't she open herself to whatever a man chose to give her?

Closing her eyes, she bit down on her lip. No, she wouldn't—couldn't—allow it. All of her life she'd been forced to accept whatever someone chose to give her.

It had been a mistake, she told herself, and one she could have avoided if she hadn't dropped her guard. And she had every right to be furious with Caine. He'd exploited the situation, he'd aroused her when she had been drowsy and defenseless. Diana's shoulders slumped under the spread.

He'd been no more to blame than she'd been herself, she admitted. Hadn't she been half dreaming when she'd run her hands up his naked back? Couldn't she remember, if she allowed herself to, that misty, sleepy pleasure in pressing her body against his? Somewhere in the back of her mind, she'd known exactly what she was doing, and yet she'd made no attempt to stop it. Then she had blamed Caine because it was easier than admitting she'd wanted to love him.

Squeezing her eyes shut again, Diana pressed her fingers against her brow. Oh, how could she have said those things to him? How could she have acted like some outraged hypocrite when he'd been every bit as overwhelmed as she had been?

Pushing the hair away from her face, she stared around the empty room. What now? she wondered. Apologize. Though the answer had her shifting uncomfortably, Diana's conscience held firm. She'd been wrong—dead wrong—and admitting it was the only way she could live with it. Remembering her hard, accusing words, she knew she couldn't blame him if he told her to take her apology and go to hell with it.

With a sigh, Diana rose. She'd take a hot shower, dress and wait for him to come back.

Two hours later, Diana paced the cramped little room, caught somewhere between worry and annoyance. What *was* he doing out there? she asked herself for the hundredth time. A peek through the drapes showed her that the snow was falling with the same steady speed. Again she considered going out and looking for him, and again she reminded herself that Caine had the only key. Diana wasn't going to depend on the likelihood of securing another from the clerk.

He's hardly walking around out there, she told herself as she pushed the drapes apart again. Across the lot, cars were half-buried in drifts. She could see no sign of life, only the endless blowing curtain of snow. She imagined Caine sitting over in the diner, enjoying one of his enormous breakfasts and cup after cup of steaming coffee. She grew irritated at the picture, particularly as her own stomach insisted on reminding her it was empty.

He was doing it on purpose, she decided, twitching the curtains back into place. Punishing me. The flood

of guilt she'd felt earlier was now completely obliterated by resentment and basic hunger.

Infuriated, and undeniably trapped between four pink
walls, Diana snatched up her briefcase and flopped in
the center of the unmade bed. She wasn't going to
waste time worrying about Caine MacGregor. She'd
catch up on the rest of her paperwork and wait out the
storm. If he *never* came back, she told herself, it was
perfectly all right with her. Pulling out her pad, she
poured all of her anger and frustration into her work.

Nearly another hour had passed before Diana heard
the key rattle in the lock. Tossing down her pad, she
continued to sit cross-legged in the center of the bed
as Caine walked in. Covered with snow, and in no better frame of mind than when he had walked out three
hours earlier, he glanced at her, then shrugged out of
his coat.

Her initial intention of greeting him with an apology
was overruled, as was her second idea of ignoring him.
"Where the hell have you been?" Diana demanded.

Caine tossed his wet coat over the table. "The
storm's due to continue through the afternoon," he said
briefly. "There still aren't any other vacancies in this
place and the next hotel's ten miles down the road."

Diana felt another surge of guilt that slipped away
as Caine dropped into the chair and calmly lit a cigarette. "It didn't take you three hours to find that out,"
she snapped. "Didn't it occur to you that I was stuck
in here?"

He gave her a glance that would have been mild had
his eyes not been so dark. "Couldn't you find the
door?"

On a sound of fury, Diana scrambled off the bed. "You have the only key!"

With a shrug, Caine reached in his pocket, drew it out, then dropped in on the table. "It's all yours," he told her as he leaned across to pull a small bag from his coat pocket. "I picked up a couple of tooth-brushes."

She caught one as he tossed it at her. "Thank you," she said icily. She wouldn't apologize, Diana thought, if they were stuck in that dreadful little room for the next month. "Since it appears we're going to be marooned here for another night, we should discuss the arrangements."

Caine fought back anger as it boiled again. If he lost it this time, he warned himself, he would very likely strangle her. "Make whatever arrangements you like," he said coolly. "I'm going to shave." Picking up the bag, he rose.

"Just a minute." Diana pressed her hand to his chest as he started to walk by her. "We're going to get this straight."

The chill in his eyes turned quickly to fire. "Don't push me, Diana."

"*Push* you!" she retorted. "Do you think you can calmly walk back in here, announcing you're going to shave, after what happened this morning? Do you think I'm going to shrug this off as though it were a slight error in judgment?"

"That," he returned, taking her wrist and holding it aloft, "would be very wise."

Jerking her wrist free, she stood firmly in his path.

"Well, I won't. And you're not going to shave or anything else until you hear exactly what I have to say."

"I heard all I wanted to hear this morning." Giving her a none-too-gentle shove out of his way, Caine started toward the bathroom.

"Don't you dare walk away from me!" As the final hold over her temper snapped, Diana grabbed his arm.

"I've had enough." Pushed beyond endurance, Caine spun back around, grabbing her shoulders with enough force to cause her to gasp in alarm. "I don't have to take this from you!" he shouted. "I won't calmly stand here while you accuse me of resorting to some devious plan to get you into bed with me. I don't need any plan, do you understand? I could have had you last night and half a dozen times before without any need for ploys." He gave her a quick, hard shake. "We both know it. Damn it, I wanted you and you wanted me, but you haven't got the guts to admit it."

Eyes wide with fury, Diana pulled out of his hold. "Don't tell me what to admit! This morning I was asleep—"

"Are you awake now?" he demanded.

"Yes, damn it, I'm awake now, and—"

"Good." In one swift move, Caine dragged her back in his arms and took her mouth in a hard, savage kiss. He heard her muffled sound of protest, felt her frantic struggles for freedom, but only crushed her more tightly against him.

He thought of punishment, he thought of releasing the anger and the tension that had been building and building inside of him since that morning. Then he thought of how much he needed her and thought of nothing else.

With his fingers still digging into her shoulders, he pulled her away. Breathing hard, eyes locked, they stared at each other. Diana felt desire pounding in her, demanding freedom. She shook her head once, as if to deny it, but like an avalanche, it was already thundering its way down the mountain. Surrendering to all the needs raging inside her, she pulled his mouth back to hers and took what she wanted.

There were no gentle, sleepy explorations now. They were both awake, both ravenous, each feeding from the other's lips as though years had passed since they had tasted this kind of pleasure. Locked together, already struggling against the barrier of clothing, they fell into the bed. Now fury was all passion, and passion all urgency.

Impatient, Diana dragged the sweater over his head then made a deep, pleased sound in her throat as her hands found those tight ridges of muscle. Desperate for more, she shifted until she lay half across him, her mouth hot and avid on his. All the longings she had refused, all the desires she had suppressed, burst out in one violent explosion. She couldn't get enough of him.

She'd known almost from the first that he would be the one to unlock that last door she'd had so tightly locked.

Freedom. She moaned with the heady, painful thrill of it as she nipped into his bottom lip, wanting to drive him as she was driven. As she began to tug at the hips of his slacks, Caine groaned, rolling on top of her again, pushing her deep into the mattress.

As a lover, he was no less than she had expected—
terrifying, vital, exciting. The slow, dreamy loving of
the morning had been only a brief sample of what he
could bring her to. A wildness was growing in her—
some latent savageness she had once feared and now
reveled in. With it, there were no rules. Her body was
liberated, pulsing everywhere at once, arching, as fluid
as hot wine as he pulled clothes from her in a frenzy.
She heard a low throaty laugh that she didn't recognize
as her own as he swore at the last barrier of silk.

As if driven mad by the sound, Caine crushed his
mouth to hers again, probing deep as his impatient hand
tore the strap of the chemise in an effort to find her.
And her lips answered his with equal pressure, equal
turbulence.

It seemed akin to war, this desperate demanding, this
frantic challenging. His hands ran bruisingly over her
and she pressed him closer, daring him to take more.
She heard his ragged breathing match hers as his mouth
rushed down to her breast to ravage greedily until they
were both past the edge of control.

Passion was a blue-white fire now, searing skin to
skin. The silk ripped again as he dragged it down,
mouth and hands speeding after it, pausing only to find
new, surprising points of delight.

Diana cried out when he drove his tongue into her
center; but it was a low, smoky sound, trailing off into
a throaty moan. Her body was damp and agile, her
movements instinctive. Arousal came in titanic waves,
thrusting her up, tossing her back, cresting again and
again and remaining strong. As the musky scent of passion whirled in her head, she was unaware of the

breathless, wild demands she uttered. Reality had spiraled down to one man, one need. In a single cloudy moment, she realized they might be one and the same. His name trembled from her lips, but whatever words she would have spoken were only a gasp as he drove her to a staggering peak.

Then his mouth was fused to hers again, and even as her arms locked around him, he took her over the final verge of reason.

Lids heavy, body sated, Diana opened her eyes and found herself staring at their twin reflections in the mirror above the bed. Experimentally, she spread her fingers over his back and watched the movement in the glass. How dark her skin looked next to his, she thought hazily. And what a contrast the colors of their hair made when side by side.

It was odd to watch his body move with the breathing she could hear and feel. She ran her hands over his back again and watched the muscles ripple under them. Strong, she thought with another tingle of pleasure. Strong and reckless. And so, Diana thought with satisfaction, was she. Sighing, she let her fingers dive into his hair.

Caine made a quick, impatient sound and started to shift away. With a murmured protest, she tightened her arms. "Diana..." Lifting his head, he stared down at her, then with a brief oath he rolled away. "I didn't mean for that to happen. It sounds a little weak after this morning, but—"

"Caine." Diana shifted so that she lay across his chest again. "Don't." She pressed her lips to his until she felt resistance ease. "I'm so sorry for the things I said this morning. No." She laid her fingertips over his mouth. "I was wrong. I knew it even when I was shouting at you, but I couldn't stop. If I'd stopped, I would have admitted that I wanted you." Letting her head fall to his shoulder, she shut her eyes tight.

On a long sigh he ran a hand down her hair. "I didn't mean to touch you again when I came back here."

She gave a quiet laugh as she pressed her face into his shoulder. "And I was going to apologize when you got back."

"Somehow," he murmured, "I think this was a much better idea for both of us. Diana." He drew her away until their eyes met again. "I've never wanted anyone," he said cautiously, "exactly the way I want you. I don't want to hurt you. Will you believe that?"

She opened her mouth to speak but knew he would never understand the doubts, the lifetime of small fears. "No questions now," she said instead, touching her lips to his again. "No reasons. This is enough."

Fighting back the need to press her for more, Caine gathered her close to his side. "For now," he agreed, and found an astonishing surge of pleasure at simply having her lie beside him. "You know," he began as his eyes drifted toward the ceiling, "I'm beginning to like this room. After all, it does have a fascinating view."

Following the direction of his gaze, Diana gave a wry smile. "The next thing I know you'll ask me for a quarter for the television." In the reflection, she saw his brow lift questioningly. "No."

"Okay." He rolled on top of her. "I've always preferred doing things myself rather than spectating."

"Caine." As he nibbled at her neck she sighed, tilting her head to accommodate him. "I hate to bring up something so mundane...but I'm starving."

"Mm-hmm." He ran his lips along her jawline as he traced the shape of her shoulders.

"Seriously starving."

"How seriously?"

"As in willing to risk another one of those hamburgers."

"That sounds more like desperately," he murmured, and with a groan, he rolled aside. "Okay, I'll go buy you another slice of ptomaine."

"Thanks," she said dryly, but sat up as he did. The moment the contact between them had been broken she'd felt some of the tension return. Foolish, she told herself. She was a grown woman and lovemaking was part of life. Wasn't it as simple as that? "I'll go with you."

"It's nearly as bad out there as it was yesterday," he began as he reached for his pants. Why did he have the need to gather her to him again, reassure her, and himself, that nothing had changed? Everything had changed.

"I'd like to get out of this room for awhile." Diana let her eyes scan the walls. "The pink is beginning to close in on me."

Caine tugged his sweater on. "All right, we'll eat at the scene of the crime." He lifted a brow as Diana examined her torn chemise. "I suppose you're going to say I owe you one of those."

"I could take you to small claims court," she declared, slipping into her blouse without it.

Caine gave a burst of appreciative laughter and grabbed her around the waist. "It'd be worth it just to hear your opening statement." As she tipped her head back to smile up at him, he was drowned in a wave of emotion too strong to resist. Desire, he told himself almost desperately. Just desire, and desire was easy. "Oh, again," he murmured before his mouth found hers.

The fingers that had been buttoning her blouse stilled, her head tilted back in surrender, but her mouth met his aggressively. Through parted lips came a sound of quiet, lingering pleasure that seemed to skip into the core of him and expand. Once before she had felt that strange, soft texture to his kiss. It was infinitely gentle but seemed to demand more than passion. When he released her, Diana was forced to blink to clear her vision.

"Caine?" she said wonderingly. Was he telling her or asking her? Or was it something within herself that was questioning?

He took a step back, not quite comfortable with the feeling of uncertainty she could bring out in him. "I'm in the position of telling you to get dressed again." He smiled, but his eyes remained intense. "Otherwise, I won't be responsible if you go hungry."

With fingers that weren't completely steady, she finished buttoning her blouse. "I think you like confusing me," she muttered. "I'm not very good with moods, and yours never stays the same."

"Sometimes they keep me guessing, too," he said half to himself. When she looked at him, her eyes direct, her mouth unsmiling, he consciously fought off the tension. She was vulnerable, he was responsible. He wasn't at all sure he could handle the responsibility. Play it light, Caine warned himself. Keep it simple. "Maybe I like keeping you in the same mental state I'm in myself."

Diana gave him one of her long, deliberating looks before she smiled. "Do I confuse you, Caine?"

He met the look as he slipped into his shoes. Something vibrated in the room that both of them took great care not to notice. "I'm going to decline to answer that question at this time."

"Interesting." Diana pulled up the zipper of her skirt. "That leads me to assume that I do." She slipped into her coat. "I think I like that."

"You'll need your gloves," was all he said as he pocketed the key again.

The minute they stepped outside, Diana sucked in her breath at the force of the wind and the cold. The flakes were smaller, she thought as she hooked her arm firmly through Caine's, but the wind was going to make the drifts treacherous even after they stopped falling. Still, as she looked around, even the battered little motel seemed rather clean and picturesque in its coating of white.

"It's not such a bad little place," she decided while they struggled against the wind.

"It looks even better after you've been out in this for a while."

There was a path of sorts through the four feet of snow, where other tenants of the motel had fought their way to the diner and back again. Struggling through this, Diana still found herself buried up to her knees. When she stumbled, she tightened her grip on Caine.

"Sure you don't want to go back in and wait?" Caine shouted close to her ear.

"Are you kidding?" She lifted her face, squinting against the flying snow. "Is that it?" With her free hand, Diana pointed to the dim outline of a building with floodlights making an eerie glow against the unrelieved white.

"Yeah. The place's been doing a thriving round-the-clock business since the blizzard. Our 'notel' has all thirty-five rooms booked."

"You're a fount of information. God," she went on before Caine could retort, "I could eat *two* hamburgers."

"We'll discuss your suicidal tendencies when we get inside. Here, watch out." He tightened his grip on her arm to guide her. "There're steps buried somewhere under here."

Breathless, Diana stumbled through the door when Caine pushed it open. The heavy scent of frying grease hung in the air, overlaid by tobacco smoke and something that might have been bacon. Several scratched, plastic-coated tables were scattered around the long room, with vinyl-cushioned chairs and paper placemats. Along the rear of the room, was a counter, with many of its stools already occupied by diners, most of whom turned to stare at the newcomers.

In a covered dessert dish on the far end were a few tired-looking doughnuts, while behind the counter several signs announced the specials. It seemed the meatloaf dinner, with gravy, was only three forty-nine.

"Back again?" The chubby waitress behind the counter sent Caine a cheery smile. "And brought your lady. Come on in and warm up, honey," she told Diana. "You could use some coffee, I bet."

"Yes." The dingy atmosphere was forgotten in the face of the friendly greeting. "I'd love some."

"Coffee's on the house as long as it lasts," the waitress proclaimed, setting two cups and saucers on the counter. "I'm Peggy. Sit yourselves down and drink up. Hungry?"

"Starving," Diana said recklessly as she slid onto a stool beside a young, nervous-looking man with flyaway hair and glasses.

"We got fresh vegetable soup today," Peggy told Diana as she handed out thin, handwritten menus. "Been simmering all morning."

"Sounds fine," Caine decided with a glance at Diana.

"Mmm, for a start," she agreed, chewing on her bottom lips as she studied the menu.

"Two soups, Hal," Peggy shouted through the opening that led to the kitchen. "The BLTs are popular today," she added.

"Yes, all right, that sounds good." Closing the menu, Diana reached for a plastic container of cream as the waitress called out the rest of the order.

Caine leaned over, nuzzling at Diana's ear as he whispered into it. "Eat all you want. We're going to stock up on candy bars and canned sodas to get through tonight."

"You're so resourceful," she murmured, turning her head so that her lips met his.

"You folks from out of town?" Peggy asked as she refilled the coffee cup of the man beside Diana.

"Boston," Caine told her, taking out a cigarette. At the small sound of distress from beyond Diana, he glanced over.

"Charlie here was on his way to Boston, too," the waitress said, giving the young man's hand a sympathetic pat. "With his bride." She tucked a strand of tumbling blond hair behind her ear and sent Caine a quick wink.

"Supposed to be our honeymoon," Charlie muttered, staring into his coffee. "Lori took one look at the room and started to cry."

"Oh." Diana gave him an understanding smile. "I suppose it isn't exactly what she was looking forward to."

"We had reservations at the Hyatt." He lifted his head then, pushing his glasses back on his nose. "Lori's very sensitive."

"Yes, I'm sure." At a loss, Diana met the helpless stare. He looked, she thought, a bit like a little boy who hadn't found his bicycle under the Christmas tree. "Well, ah, perhaps you could make the room a little more—romantic."

"That room?" With a snort, Charlie turned back to his coffee.

"Candles," Diana suggested with sudden inspiration as the soup was set on the counter. "Maybe someone has some candles."

"Well sure, I got a few in the back room," Peggy

said helpfully as she gave the counter a swipe with a rag. "Your bride like candlelight, Charlie?"

"Maybe," he mumbled, but his frown became more thoughtful.

"Of course she does." Diana stirred her soup while she watched him. "What woman doesn't like candlelight? And flowers," she added. "Now where can we get flowers?"

"Got a few plastic poinsettias in the back," the waitress cut in, getting into the spirit. "We use 'em at Christmas, you know. Really brightens up the place."

"Wonderful."

"You think she'd like that?" Charlie asked Diana.

"I think she'll be very touched."

"Well…"

"I'm going to go dig them up." Wiping her hands on her apron, the waitress headed toward the back.

Charlie leaned forward to look at Caine. "What do you think?"

Struggling to keep his face grave, Caine glanced up from his soup. "I bow to a lady's opinion on matters such as this."

"Go ahead, kid," someone down the counter advised. "Give it a shot."

"Yeah." Abruptly decisive, he rose as Peggy came back, arms full. "Yeah, I will."

"Here you go, honey." She passed over three candles in plastic holders and several sprays of plastic poinsettia with large, glittered red bows. "You go fix up your honeymoon suite. Your little bride's gonna feel better."

"Thanks." He grinned at Diana as he stuffed as much as he could into his pockets. "Thanks a lot."

"Good luck, Charlie," Diana called after him, then swung back to her soup. Catching Caine's look, she arched a brow. "I think it's very sweet."

"I didn't say a word."

"You didn't have to, you cynic." When he only grinned at her, Diana turned back to her lunch. "Eat your soup. Some of us," she announced loftily, "appreciate romance."

"Should I buy another bottle of wine?" he murmured, raising her hand to his lips.

"Don't you dare." Laughing, she leaned over to kiss him.

Chapter Nine

Behind her desk, with the fire noisily burning, Diana worked at a steady pace. She'd given the Walker case meticulous research, careful thought and long hours. The story, Diana felt, was almost too typical. Irene Walker had been young, fresh out of college when she had married. She had never worked—her husband hadn't permitted it. Instead, she'd kept his home and fixed his meals, dedicating her life to his comfort. Now that their marriage was breaking up, Irene had no income, no training for outside work, and a small infant to care for. Diana was going to see to it that she was compensated for the four years she had worked as housekeeper, cook, laundress and hostess. The fact that Irene had been the victim of wife-beating only made Diana more determined that her client receive justice.

And I've got him, Diana thought with a sense of satisfaction as she closed a law book. I've got George Walker cold. Now if Irene would just stick with those counseling sessions…

Shaking her head, Diana reminded herself not to get in any deeper. She was already much too emotionally involved in the Chad Rutledge case; she couldn't afford to spread herself too thin.

Chad, she thought, pressing her hands to her tired eyes a moment. Things were not moving as smoothly there as they were for Irene Walker. Diana had already called over half the names on the list he had given her. So far, none of the people who knew him, or Beth, could give her any corroborating evidence. I need something, she thought, tossing down her pen in disgust. I have to go into court with something more than Chad's story and my own feelings. If I can't break Beth's story on the stand...

Leaning back in her chair, Diana stared up at the ceiling and thought through the case as it stood. A pretty, well-liked college student, blond, delicate— privileged family background. A tough, street-wise hood with a belligerent attitude and a quick temper. If it came down to his word against hers, Diana had little doubt what the outcome would be. Then there was the medical evidence—Beth's condition when she was admitted to the hospital emergency room, Chad's admission that he had been with her. No, she couldn't go into court with nothing more than a story about star-crossed lovers and expect it to work. Especially when she wasn't too sure of her client.

Oh, he was innocent, Diana mused, frowning. She didn't doubt that. But she was very much afraid that he'd lose his head if she started pressing Beth too hard. Diana wouldn't put it past him to stand up in open court and make a full confession.

With a weary sigh, Diana reminded herself that she

still had the last few names on Chad's list to contact. There were two Diana only had first names on, which meant a trip to the university and a bit of detective work. Who said law was all books and briefs? she thought, then managed a smile for the first time in more than an hour. This was what she wanted.

"Diana?"

Distracted, she glanced up. "Oh, yes, Lucy."

"I'm going to leave now, unless you need me for something." She found a thread hanging from the sleeve of her dress, wrapped it around two fingers and snapped it off. "Caine checked in about half an hour ago. His meeting ran over, but he said he'd be stopping in here before going home."

"Oh." Diana didn't notice Lucy's speculative look as she gazed into the fire. "No, Lucy, you go on home. I have some things I want to finish up here; I'll lock up."

"Want me to make some coffee before I leave?"

"Hmm? Oh, no." Smiling, Diana glanced back up. "No, thanks. Have a nice evening."

"You have one, too," Lucy told her with a last meaningful look before she walked back down the hall. "Tell Caine I left his messages on his desk."

"All right." Diana pondered the empty doorway for a moment. Lucy, she decided, was a great deal shrewder than that placid round face indicated. And I thought I was being so discreet, Diana thought with a rueful smile, working very calmly, very practically, day after day with Caine just next door. Keeping up the polite, friendly tone of colleagues in the same office building. But it seemed Lucy had caught something— a look, a gesture, a tone of voice. Diana wondered just how realistic she had been in thinking she could keep her relationship with Caine strictly between them. She wondered suddenly why she had felt it necessary.

Thoughtful, Diana rose to walk to the fire. It was burning low now, the coals piled high and glowing red. Stooping, she added a log and watched it catch with violent snaps and hisses. Perhaps her emotions had been like that: low and carefully banked until Caine had come into her life. Now she knew what it was to feel wild bursts of flame, fast, crackling heat. It was impossible, always impossible, to remain calm and controlled when she was with him.

It frightened her—he frightened her—Caine and his ability to make her want him with unrestrained and uninhibited passion. Caine and his ability to make her think of him at odd moments.

Emotion seemed to come so effortlessly to him, and the demonstration of emotion. She'd been trained for so long to suppress passions, control surges of feelings. Even now that she was freer with them, more comfortable with some of them, she was poles apart from Caine. She'd never have his spontaneity or his careless self-ease. Diana envied him while not completely understanding him. She did understand, however, that Caine had the ability to dominate by force of personality alone.

Perhaps that was why she had insisted that they keep their relationship on a firmly professional level during business hours. Diana was struggling to hold on to those hours, to keep them as a time where she still had complete control over her actions, her feelings and her thoughts.

I'm going to fall in love with him if I'm not careful,

Diana thought with a flutter of panic as she watched flames lap greedily around the new log. If I haven't already. Catching her bottom lip between her teeth, she tried to think clearly but found, as she found so often when she attempted to reason her feelings for Caine, that logic had no place there.

She wished there was a way to escape him. She wished he would come back so that she could be with him.

With a sound of annoyance, she turned away from the fire, then heard the phone begin to ring in his office. A glance at her watch told her it was nearly six and the offices were officially closed. Shrugging, Diana walked next door to answer.

"Caine MacGregor's office," she said as she fumbled for the switch on the lamp.

"Is he back yet?" a booming voice demanded.

"No, I'm sorry." Diana picked up a pen as she slipped into Caine's chair. "Mr. MacGregor's out of the office. May I take a message?"

"Where is that boy!" Exasperation came clearly over the wire—so clearly Diana held the receiver a few inches from her ear. "I've been trying to reach him all afternoon."

"I'm sorry, Mr. MacGregor's been in a meeting. Shall I have him return your call tomorrow?"

"Damn boy never could stay put," the voice muttered.

"I beg your pardon?"

"Hah!"

Diana's brow lifted at the exclamation. "I'd be happy to take your name and number, and any message you'd care to leave."

"This isn't Lucy," the man stated suddenly. "Where the devil's Lucy?"

Amused, and just a bit perplexed, Diana put down the pen. "Lucy's gone for the day. This is Diana Blade, I'm Mr. MacGregor's associate. Is there something—"

"Justin's sister!" the voice interrupted in a bellow. "I'll be damned. Now, I've been wanting to have a few words with you, girl. I'd heard you'd set up business there with Caine."

"Yes," she began, growing more bewildered. "Do you know my brother?"

"Know him?" There was an explosion of laughter. "Of course I know him, girl. I let him marry my daughter, didn't I?"

"Oh." As the light dawned, Diana sat back in Caine's chair. Hadn't she been warned about Daniel MacGregor? "How do you do, Mr. MacGregor. I've heard a great deal about you."

"Hah!" he snorted. "You don't listen to that son of mine, do you?"

She laughed, idly toying with the phone cord, not even aware that she was relaxing for the first time in eight hours. "Caine speaks very highly of you, Mr. MacGregor. I'm sorry you've missed him."

"Hmm, well..." He paused as the germ of an idea formed in his mind. "So you're a lawyer, too, are you?"

"Yes, I was at Harvard a few years behind Caine."

"Small world, small world. Rena tells me you favor Justin. Good stock."

"Ah...well..." A little nonplussed by the phrase, Diana trailed off.

"Good blood's an important thing, don't you know?"

"Yes." Brows knit, she shook her head. "I suppose."

"No supposing to it, girl, got to keep the line strong. I've a birthday coming up," he announced suddenly.

"Congratulations."

"I didn't want any fuss," he began breezily, "but my wife loves a party. Don't like to disappoint her."

"No," Diana agreed with the beginnings of a smile. "Of course you wouldn't."

"She misses the children, you know. Yes, off they went in every direction," he said in a pained voice, "and not a grandchild between them."

"Ah…" Diana said again for lack of anything better.

"A few grandchildren to spoil in her winter years," he continued with a sigh. "But when do children think about their parents' needs, I'd like to know?"

"Well—"

"Anna wants all the children here next weekend," he interrupted. "A family gathering. We'll want Caine to bring you along."

"Thank you, Mr. MacGregor, I—"

"Daniel, girl; after all, you're part of the family now." Back in Hyannis Port, Daniel gave a crafty, secret smile his careless words disguised. "The MacGregors look after their own."

"Yes, I'm sure," she murmured, then laughed. "I'd love to come for your birthday, Daniel."

"Good. That's settled, then. You tell Caine his mother wants him here Friday night. A lawyer, too, hmm? That's handy, aye, that's handy. Friday night, Diana."

"Yes." Baffled again, she stared at Caine's desk. "Good-bye, Daniel."

Diana hung up with the odd feeling she had agreed to something entirely different from a weekend visit to Hyannis Port. Sitting back in Caine's chair, she thought over the conversation. It seemed, she mused, that Daniel MacGregor was every bit as eccentric as his legend claimed.

I wonder how much Caine's like him, Diana reflected idly. Certainly, Caine had inherited his father's skill in dominating a conversation when he chose. And there was something in the laugh. If she hadn't been thrown off by the way he'd bellowed into the phone, Diana would have recognized the MacGregor patriarch by the faint Scottish burr. And what in the world was all that business about good stock?

Hearing the front door open and close, Diana rose from the desk to walk to the top of the stairs. "Hi."

As he tossed his coat over a hook on the hall rack, Caine glanced up. "Hi."

Recognizing the fatigue in the single syllable, Diana went down to him. "How'd it go?"

He flexed his back. "Three hours with Ginnie Day."

Diana needed no more. Lifting her hands, she began to knead at the tension in his shoulders. "You don't like her," she said as Caine let out a quiet sigh.

"No, I don't." He stretched under Diana's hands. "She's spoiled, selfish and vain. She has the courtesy of a nasty five-year-old."

"It must have been a very pleasant afternoon," Diana murmured.

Caine chuckled and lifted his hands to her wrists. "I don't have to like her, I just have to defend her. It would be easier if Ginnie herself wasn't the D.A.'s best weapon. There's no way to make a jury see her as a sympathetic victim. Most of the emotion'll be on the prosecution's side, while I'll have to stick with straight law.''

"You're going for a bench trial,'' Diana said as she studied her face.

A hint of a smile played on his mouth as he nodded in agreement. "I'd rather present this kind of case to a judge. When I told Ginnie, she had a temper fit and fired me.'' Laughing at Diana's outraged expression, Caine cupped her face in his hands, then kissed her. "For about five minutes,'' he added. "She might be rude, but she's not stupid.''

"It sounds to me as though it would have served her right if you'd taken her dismissal at face value and walked out.''

"Would you?'' he countered.

Her face relaxed into a smile. "No, but I'd have been tempted. Are you through for the day?''

"Yeah.'' His hand slipped to her waist to gather her closer. "Absolutely.''

"Then get your coat,'' she ordered on an impulse that would have surprised her even weeks before. "I'm going to take you to dinner. Then,'' she added as she took her own coat from the hook, "I'm going to lure you back to my place.''

"Really?''

"Really. Here.'' Gravely, Diana handed him his coat.

Caine studied her, noting that her eyes were as confident as her words. He touched her hair. "I like your style, counselor.''

"MacGregor," Diana returned as she buttoned his coat herself, "you haven't seen anything yet."

Flushed with cold and gripping an icy bottle of champagne, Diana opened the door of her apartment. Dinner had relaxed them, slowly nudging the demands of their work, the people whose lives and problems dominated so many of their hours, to the back of their minds. Now they were just a man and a woman with lives and problems of their own.

"I'll get the glasses," Diana stated, handing the bottle to Caine.

He glanced idly at the label. "I suppose you intend to fuddle my mind with champagne."

Coming back with two tulip glasses, she smiled. "I'm counting on it. Why don't you open that?"

Lifting a brow, Caine tore the foil from the top of the bottle. "I might not be as easily manipulated as you think."

"Oh, no?" Diana set down the glasses, then slid her hands up the front of his suit jacket, slipping it off him. This time, she would test her own strengths and his weaknesses. This time, she wouldn't be led, she would lead. "An open and shut case," she murmured, nibbling lightly on his bottom lip as she loosened the knot of his tie. When she felt his arms come around her, she drew back, keeping her lips inches from his. "How about that champagne?"

"Didn't we drink it already?"

On a low laugh, she caught the end of his tie between her thumb and forefinger. "No." Slowly she slipped the tie off and tossed it aside. She felt a quick thrill at her own action and wondered if he felt it, too. "Why don't you pour it?" she murmured, undoing the first three buttons of his shirt. "I'll put on some music."

As she crossed the room, Diana stepped out of her shoes. She turned the stereo on low, so that the soft, bluesy number was hardly more than a whisper. When she dimmed the lights, Caine glanced over to see her slip off her pine-colored blazer.

"I think," he said quietly as he filled the both glasses, "I'm in trouble."

With a laugh that was more of a sigh, Diana walked back to him. "You *are* in trouble." Taking a glass, she sat on the sofa and pulled him down beside her. "Deep trouble," she added, nipping at his ear.

"Maybe I should put myself entirely in your hands." Turning his head, he found her mouth with his, but she allowed him only the briefest taste.

"My thoughts exactly." She touched the rim of her glass to his, then drank. "Have I ever told you," she began while her fingers began to toy with the curls that fell over his ears, "that you fascinate me?"

"No. Do I?" Caine lifted his hand to draw her closer, but Diana caught it in hers.

"Yes." Slowly, she brought his hand to her lips, pressing them against his palm. Tonight she would be all woman, only a woman. "Strong hands." Watching him, she kissed his fingers one by one. "One of the first things I noticed was that they weren't the soft lawyer's hands I'd expected. I wondered how they'd feel on my skin." She laced her fingers with his as she brought the glass to her lips again.

Feeling desire sprint through him, Caine stared at her. She was mesmerizing him. He hadn't known she could, and the feeling left him burning and oddly weak.

In the dim light, her eyes were dark and mysterious with the seductively languid look that had stirred him from the first moment. "Diana—"

"Then there was your mouth," she went on, letting her eyes linger on it. "Such a clever mouth." She brushed her lips lightly over his. "The first time you kissed me I couldn't think of anything else. Exciting," she whispered, tilting her head back ever so slightly when he sought to deepen the kiss. "And at times indescribably gentle. I could spend hours and hours doing nothing more than kissing you." But she shifted away to watch him over the rim of her glass as she drank champagne.

"Diana." Caine's voice was low as he cupped his hand around her neck to drag her closer.

Diana kept herself a frustrating distance away with her hand against his chest. More time, she thought greedily. She wanted more of it to explore a power she'd just discovered. "I like your eyes," she murmured. She could feel his need—the tension of his need—in the fingers that pressed into her skin. He had always driven her quickly beyond control each time he touched her. This time, she thought, flushed with power, this time she would drive him, then revel in the consequences. "I like the way they darken when you want me. I can see it." She spread her fingers over his chest. "I love seeing it. You're tense." As she felt his heart thud furiously beneath her palm, her own speeded up to race with it. "You should drink your champagne and relax."

Throbbing, he met the challenge in her eyes. Through sheer force of will, he lightened his grip and fought back the first flood of need. She fully intended to drive him mad, and knowing it Caine determined to regain some control. "You know that I want you." Keeping his eyes on hers, he lifted the glass. "You know that I'll have you."

"Perhaps." She smiled again as she shook back her hair. Her scent seemed to drift out from it to wrap around him. The wine bubbled icily over her tongue, adding to the sense of power. "I think of storms when I think of making love to you." Leisurely, she ran a fingertip down his shirtfront, then back up to loosen the rest of the buttons. "That morning on the beach when I first kissed you—that little motel room in the blizzard. Storms and wind. Strange, I never get a picture of anything placid." She ran her hand over his naked chest, slowly, very slowly, moving down.

"If you want me to be gentle," he managed as the soft touch of her fingers tore at his restraint, "this isn't the way."

"Did I say that's what I wanted?" she asked with a low laugh. Watching him, Diana took his mouth again, this time allowing the kiss to linger.

His mind clouded—her taste, that wicked scent. Setting his glass aside, Caine plunged both hands into her hair and dove into the kiss. More, was all he could think. He had to have more and still more. Her mouth had softened seductively under his with a deceptive surrender he would have recognized had his mind been as clear as his need. Her quiet sigh seemed to race through him. With his breathing already labored, Caine reached for the zipper at the back of her dress.

Not yet, not yet, Diana ordered herself as her thoughts began to swim. Passion was lapping at her, as the flames had lapped at the log she had watched in the fire. But she wanted something more tonight. She wanted a few more moments of control, she wanted to prove to herself that she could erase every layer of the polish that lay over the dangerous inner man. She had once feared what would happen if the two of them came together without that safe gloss of sophistication. Now, she craved it. Feeling her dress begin to loosen, she pulled away.

"Diana..." Caine began on a half groan, but she evaded him and rose.

"Don't you want any more champagne?" she asked, pouring more into her glass.

In one quick move, Caine stood and grabbed her arm. "You know damn well what I want."

Another thrill of excitement sped into her, reflecting in her eyes even as she kept her voice low. "Yes." Impulsively, she drained her glass, then held it lightly by the stem. "Such a civilized drink. Take me to bed," she invited softly as she stepped closer. "And make love to me."

As the last thread of control snapped, Caine yanked her against him. The glass fell to the rug to roll across the room. "Here," he demanded. "And now." With his mouth crushed on hers, he dragged her to the floor.

His hands seemed to be everywhere at once, seeking finding, while his mouth stayed fused to hers. Diana gloried in it and, while her body wildly responded, sought to drive him further from reason. Her mouth was aggressive, meeting his with a hot, hungry fury that could only partially show the needs raging inside her. She would feed on his desire even while she stoked it.

She pulled the shirt from his back, and when his mouth freed hers briefly, nipped her teeth lightly into his shoulder. With a half-muffled oath, Caine crushed her roaming mouth with his again.

He peeled the dress from her, quickly, hands rushing to possess the soft, naked skin. Desire was stabbing at him, painful, forcing him to hurry where he would have lingered, driving him to take quickly what he would have savored. He thought he had felt need before, but it had never been like this: unreasonable, unmanageable. A rough urgency took the place of skill when he at last had her naked beneath him.

Her taste filled him, but he hadn't the patience to relish it. Her soft, rounded curves entranced him, but he hadn't the will to wait. The whispering music seemed to be all bass and drums now—pounding, taunting. And her scent promised no more and no less than the passion of the woman beneath him.

He swore once, with no knowledge of whom, of what he was cursing, then took her with a force that had her gasping out his name. Half-mad, he covered her mouth with his and swallowed the sounds. He drove her, drove himself, until there was only blinding heat and whirling colors. Caine knew nothing else; savagely he wanted nothing else. Caught in the vortex of the storm, they moved like lightning until, shattered, their strength drained. With something like pain, he felt sanity return.

Still, he couldn't move. His breath came in gasps he couldn't control as he buried his face in her hair. He was trembling, he realized with a small sliver of fear. No woman, no passion had ever made him tremble. What was she doing to him? he wondered as he tried to catch his breath. The last thing he clearly remembered was pulling her to the floor. All the rest came back as sensations. They might have lain there for ten minutes or for hours. He couldn't think—even now that the desperation had passed, he still couldn't think.

Had he hurt her? His mood had been close to violent when he had dragged her to the floor. There'd been something about the way she had looked at him when she'd told him to take her to bed. In that moment, he had lost all sense of time and place, and any tenuous claim he'd still held to being civilized.

Dazed, Caine lifted his head to look down at her. Her eyes were open, though those long, heavy lids were nearly closed. Her skin held that flushing glow of passion just spent. Incredibly, he felt fresh desire ripple through him. Dropping his face back into her hair, he took deep, steadying breaths. He needed a minute, he told himself. Good God, he needed a minute or he'd take her like a madman again.

Sighing his name, Diana ran her hands over his back. There'd been something in his eyes just then she'd never expected to see: vulnerability. She didn't feel power now, but wonder—and something else that made her touch gentle and soothing. No, she hadn't expected to see vulnerability, and even as she nestled closer, Diana wasn't certain she wanted to see it. Seeing it in his eyes only forced her to face her own weakness. Slowly, and with uncanny success, he'd scaled the walls of her defenses. And things weren't so simple any longer.

She could feel his heartbeat begin to level. The breath that feathered over her ear grew steadier. When Caine lifted his head again, his eyes weren't giving away any secrets.

"You're a surprising woman, Diana." He kissed her

but touched the lips still warm and swollen from his gently.

"Why?" she murmured.

"All that passion, all that…fire," he added as his lips continued to nibble at hers. "In a woman who takes such pains to be dignified…cool…unflappable. You wanted to make me crazy, didn't you?"

She sighed as his mouth began to feast at her throat. Triumph glowed through her. She'd discovered one more part of Diana Blade. "I did make you crazy."

His lips curved into a smile against her skin before he lifted his head again. "We'll have that champagne now before I take you to bed, as you asked." Caine poured more wine into the glass on the table, then offered it to her. "We seem to have lost the other glass— we'll share this one."

Sitting up, Diana drank, letting the champagne pour through her with its icy effervescence. "It's tastes even better now," she said with a smile as she passed it back to Caine.

"As you said…" He sipped as his eyes answered her smile. "A civilized drink. Diana…" Caine lifted his hand to her hair and watched his fingers comb through it. "Stay with me at my place this weekend. We can eat in, watch old movies." The grin touched his eyes again. "Neck on the sofa. We're both going to be under a lot of pressure these next few weeks with the cases coming to trial. It might be the last time for quite a while that we'll have the time to be together like this."

The picture he painted was tempting—and frightening. One more step into intimacy. Yet even as a part of her wanted to back away, she couldn't resist. "I

can't think of anything I'd rather... Oh!'' With a look
of comic dismay on her face, Diana paused in the act
of reaching for the glass. ''Your father.''

With a chuckle, Caine took another sip before he
handed her the wine. ''What does my father have to do
with it?''

''He called. I forgot completely.'' Her eyes laughed
at him as she drank. ''I believe we've received a royal
summons.''

''Oh?'' Caine traced a fingertip over the slope of her
shoulder, enjoying how dark and smooth her skin
looked in the dim light.

''For the weekend,'' Diana elaborated, laughing out
loud when his fingertip stopped.

''The weekend?''

''Your father's birthday.'' Leaning across him, Diana filled the glass again. ''He doesn't want a fuss, you
know, but your mother—''

''Of course.'' With a wry smile, Caine shifted so that
he could replace his fingertip with his lips. ''My quiet,
undemanding father would simply treat his birthday as
any other day of the year. He'll only go through the
noise and fuss and bother of a party for my mother's
sake. And naturally, he'll only accept presents because
she expects it. If it were up to him, the day would pass
without a thought.''

Chuckling, Diana struggled to concentrate on his
words as he began to lightly caress her. ''Well, it was
very sweet of him to include me in the invitation; I'm
looking forward to it. I enjoyed talking to him, even if
the conversation was a bit confusing.''

''How?'' He carefully traced her ear with his tongue,

taking the glass from her as it began to slip through her fingers.

"Mmm… He said something about Justin and I being from good stock. Caine…" As he caught the lobe in his teeth, Diana lost track of her own words.

"What else?" he murmured, pleased that her voice was unsteady and her body pliant against his. It wasn't often he could coax her into this kind of surrender. Sweet and complete. This time they would go slowly and he would savor every moment.

"Something—something about it being handy we were both lawyers." Somehow she was cradled in his arms, with his lips roaming her face, his hands roaming her body. And she was helpless.

"I see." And he did. With a sigh that was half-amused, half-exasperated, Caine continued to take her deeper. "Did Rena ever mention to you how she and Justin happened to meet?"

"What?" Drugged, her eyes already closed, her body already melting, she couldn't understand the question or the need for it. "No, no, she didn't. Caine, make love to me."

He wondered how she would react when she learned his father had engineered Rena and Justin's meeting in the hope of their making a match. He wondered how she would react when she learned Daniel MacGregor wasn't above applying a bit of genial pressure to secure what he might feel was a suitable mate for his youngest son. And that she would fit the bill very nicely. He wondered, as his lips toyed with hers, how he felt about the idea himself.

But it wasn't a night for thinking, Caine decided as her arms wound around his neck. It wasn't a night for thinking at all.

Rising, he lifted her and took her to bed.

Chapter Ten

Diana sat behind her desk, staring into the fire that crackled and spat in the hearth. In her hand she held Irene Walker's file. Numb, she stayed perfectly still as a log crumbled quietly in the grate.

She couldn't believe it—even running the conversation over again in her mind, Diana couldn't believe it. Charges dropped, divorce action canceled.

Glancing down, Diana studied the neatly written check that had been left on her desk. Paid in full— thanks, but no thanks. Irene Walker had decided to give her husband another chance.

He's so sorry that he hurt me. Diana could hear Irene's soft, apologetic voice as if her former client were still in the room. *And he promised it would never happen again.*

Never happen again, Diana thought, letting the file folder drop. No therapy, no counseling, but it would never happen again. Irene Walker lived in a dream world, Diana thought grimly, and the next nightmare might leave her with more than a few loose teeth and some bruises.

Damn! After pounding a fist on the folder, Diana sprang up. Damn, we had him cold! All that paperwork, all those hours of careful research for nothing. And sooner or later Irene would be back to go through the whole ugly mess again. Diana stared at the neat manila folder, knowing every word it contained. Yes, she would be back. It was inevitable.

Frustration drove Diana to whirl to the window to glare out at the frost-tipped branches. How could Irene love him after everything he'd done to her? How could she want to go back, take her child back, to that kind of life? It would be like living with an open keg of gunpowder. Dear God, Diana thought on a sigh of disgust, what a pitiful, wasted life.

At the knock on her door, she continued to stare out at the naked trees and frosty hedges. "Yes?"

"Bad time?" Caine asked, crossing the threshold but coming no farther into the room.

With her temper heating up, Diana turned. "Irene Walker," she said, moving to the desk to pick up the file. "She just reconciled with her husband."

Caine glanced at the file, then up into the smoldering fury in Diana's eyes. "I see."

"How could she be such a fool!" Diana put the folder back down and strode to the fire. "He calls her up, sweet-talks her into seeing him, then, with a few roses for good measure, convinces her he's a new man."

Caine walked to the desk, noting the check. "Maybe he is."

"Are you joking?" Diana demanded, spinning

around. "Why should a few weeks' separation make
any difference? She's left him before."

"She'd never started divorce proceedings before,"
he pointed out. "That and the threat of a criminal action
might make a man do some serious thinking."

"Oh, he's done some thinking," she agreed bitterly.
"No, he didn't want to face a possible jail sentence, he
didn't want to lose his wife and child *and* a good portion of his income, but what's he done to deserve clemency? Nothing!" Dragging a hand through her hair,
Diana paced the room. "He won't agree to therapy or
marriage counseling. She says he doesn't want to make
their problems public. *Public,*" she repeated, gesturing
broadly. "She burns the meat and he beats her in the
backyard in front of the neighbors, but he doesn't want
to discuss the problem with a professional. And she..."
Diana trailed off, dropping into a chair. "She's hope-
less. How can she love someone who periodically uses
her for a punching bag?"

"Do you think she loves him?" Caine countered.
"Do you really believe love has anything to do with
it?"

"Why else?"

"Wouldn't it make sense to say she's more afraid of
being on her own than she is of risking another beating?" Crouching down in front of her, Caine took Diana's hand. "Diana, love's a strong motivation, but it
isn't always the reason for staying with something even
when it hurts."

"Maybe not—I don't know." The feeling of helplessness swamped her again. Love. She didn't understand it, for most of her life hadn't had to deal with it.
But it seemed love was the one emotion that turned a

reasonably intelligent person into a fool. It was a maze, she thought in frustration, full of dead ends, wrong turns and potholes. "She thinks she loves him," Diana said at length. "Because of that she's risking everything."

"We're lawyers," he reminded her, "not psychiatrists. Irene Walker's problem is no longer a legal one."

"I know." On a long breath she squeezed his hand. "But it's so frustrating to know she could've been helped—even he could've been helped, and now—"

"Now you take her folder, file it and forget it." Caine gave her a long, steady look. "You don't have any other choice."

"It's hard."

"Yeah. But it's necessary. We can only advise in a legal frame, Diana. We can only work with the law. Once something goes beyond that, it's out of our hands. It has to be out of our hands," he added.

"Why didn't we choose something simpler?" she murmured. "And something less painful? It looks so basic from the outside—this is right and this is wrong, according to the law. And this is how we might get around it, legally speaking." With a sigh of frustration, she shook her head. "Then suddenly there're people involved and it's not so simple. I wanted to help her. Damn it, Caine, I really wanted to help her."

"You can't help someone unless they're ready for help."

"And Irene Walker isn't ready for help." Diana nodded, but her eyes still smoldered.

How could she explain that she saw the Walker case, her first case out on her own, as her first failure both professionally and personally? Diana had felt that free-

ing Irene from bondage would somehow have symbolized her own liberation from another kind of domina-
tion. Irene's was physical, hers had been emotional, and
neither had been healthy.

"I was ready to help her," she said after a long
breath. "I needed to help her."

He saw it then, the vulnerability that could creep so
unexpectedly into her eyes and bring him twin urges to
protect and to run for cover. Caine stayed where he
was while a quiet war raged inside him. "You can't
keep drawing parallels, Diana."

She closed down instantly. Her emotional withdrawal should have relieved him. He wished it had. "I
have to work my own way," she told him flatly.

"We all do," Caine agreed in the same tone. He
should have left it at that, but even as he told himself
to, he went on trying to reach her. "I defended a kid
once—drinking while intoxicated. First offence. I got
him off with the minimum. Three months later, he
wrapped his car around a telephone pole and killed his
passenger." His eyes darkened with the memory but
remained steady on hers. "She was seventeen years
old."

"Oh, Caine." At a loss, Diana could only reach for
his hand.

"We all carry around our baggage, Diana. We can
only do the best job we can and hope it's right. When
it's wrong, or when one gets away from us, we file it
away."

"You're right." The anger seeped out of her as she
rose. "I know you're right." Deliberately she took the
Walker file and dropped it into her desk drawer. "Case
closed," she murmured as she shut the drawer.

"Lucy tells me you have two other clients coming in next week."

Making an effort, Diana shook off the depression and looked back at him. "I handled them when I was with Barclay. They must have been satisfied."

Caine grinned at her expression. "Pleased with yourself?"

"Well, after all, they're coming to me, not Barclay, Stevens and Fitz."

Walking over, he lifted his hands to her shoulders. The tension was gone. "You're going to be very busy."

"I certainly hope so." With a smile, Diana slid her hands around his waist. "In order to become the best defense attorney on the East Coast, I require clients."

"It helps," Caine agreed and gave her a quick kiss on the nose. "In the meantime, it's..." He glanced at his watch. "Four forty-seven on Friday evening."

"So late?" Diana smiled ruefully. "I've been brooding for some time."

"Are you finished brooding for the day?"

"Yes, absolutely."

"Then let's go. My father'll carry on for an hour if we're late."

"Don't tell me you're worried about a tongue-lashing?" Diana asked with a laugh as she took her purse from the bottom drawer of her desk.

"You don't know my father," Caine told her, pulling her out the door.

Diana found the trip relaxing and quick. Caine had been right, she decided, in telling her to file and forget the Walker case. And for the weekend, she would slip

Chad Rutledge and her other cases to the back of her mind. It was time for the lawyer to ease off so that the woman could breathe.

She could look forward to seeing Justin again, with none of the doubts and pain she'd taken with her to Atlantic City. Perhaps this time they would be simply brother and sister. A family—though not on the same order as the MacGregor clan.

It was natural to think of them as a clan. Diana had already seen Caine's close relationship with his sister. Even if it hadn't been obvious from the way Caine had spoken of the rest of his family, the phone call from Daniel clearly showed just how much a family—in every sense of the word—the MacGregors were. Diana found herself intrigued, and a bit intimidated, with the idea. What she knew of family relationships was all secondhand. That, she mused, meant she knew virtually nothing at all.

In Boston, Caine MacGregor was a dynamic, successful attorney with a reputation for winning and women. In Boston, he was her lover, and her associate. In Hyannis Port, Caine was a son and a brother. Diana knew very little of that side of him. Would he be different? she mused. Wouldn't he have to be? In her aunt's house Diana had always been a different person following a different set of rules. Logically, she thought the same would hold true for Caine.

As the car climbed higher, Diana caught a few glimpses of the Sound, with waves tossing below. For a moment, she lost herself in it, appreciating the rocks, froth and energy. But when she looked up again, her impression of Nantucket Sound faded with a new image.

The house was gray against the cold winter sky. Huge and structured like a fortress, it stood with its back to the water. There was a fairy-tale aura about it, set apart, built high, standing against a dark, moonless sky with dozens of windows burning with light. It was ostentatious, a bit foolish and unapologetically pretentious.

"Oh, Caine, it's wonderful!" Diana leaned forward as the Jaguar sped closer. "What a marvelous place to grow up. It's the closest thing to a Scottish castle I've ever seen outside of a book."

"My father's going to be crazy about you." With a half grin, he glanced at her. "Not everyone has the same impression of it at first glance. My father has a few...quirks," he decided after a moment. "He built the house to please himself."

"I can't think of a better reason to build one." She tilted her head so that she could see the top of the tower. There was a flag blowing wildly in the wind. Diana didn't need to see the colors to know it would be a Scottish flag. "You must have loved growing up here."

"Yeah." Caine allowed his gaze to sweep from the tower to the sea wall. It was odd, he thought, that Diana's reaction brought him both pleasure and relief. Until that moment, he hadn't realized how disappointed he would have been if she'd been politely stunned. "Yeah," he repeated as his lips curved. "I guess we all did. It's huge and the devil to heat. Everything's done on a grand scale, wide, drafty corridors, high ceilings and fireplaces you could roast an ox in. Gothic arches, granite pillars and a wine cellar that's the closest thing to a dungeon I've ever seen. We used to play Spanish Inquisition down there.''

"Oh." Diana sent him an appalled look. "What lovely children you must have been."

"I like to think we were inventive."

Laughing, she turned her attention back to the house. "It must be difficult to stay away."

"No, because you know it's always going to be here, and you can come back. There're memories in every room." Caine swung the car around the circular drive and stopped. "Maybe I should warn you that the inside is exactly what you'd expect from the outside."

"Dungeons and all," Diana agreed with a nod as she stepped out. "I wouldn't have it any other way."

"We'll get the bags later." His hand linked with hers, Caine started up the rough granite steps.

On the door was a large brass knocker in the shape of a lion's head. Caine pounded it against the wood as he read the Gaelic inscription over it.

"Royal is my race," he translated with a grin.

"I'm impressed."

"Of course you are." Bending down, he touched his lips to hers, then with a quiet sound of pleasure, he drew her closer. "And so am I," he murmured before he deepened the kiss.

Instinctively, she wrapped her arms around him, pressing her body against the warmth of his as the night wind whipped around them. It was easy, always so easy, to forget everything but the feel and the taste of him. She felt his fingers brush over the nape of her neck as he tangled them in her hair. Her head tilted back, inviting more as her bones began to soften.

"That's one way to ward off the chill."

Diana's head whipped around at the voice. Leaning against the door was a tall, angular man with dark, brooding looks and a full, sculptured mouth that was curved in a smile.

"It's the only way," Caine returned and gave the man a hard, unselfconscious hug. "My brother Alan," Caine told Diana as he drew her inside out of the cold. "Diana Blade."

With her hand enveloped in the senator's firm, quick grip, Diana found herself quietly and thoroughly summed up. There was something about that dark, intense look, she thought a bit uncomfortably, that would brush away the nonsense and get right to the core. He was more like Caine than she had imagined, even though there was almost no resemblance between them physically.

"It's good to have you here, Diana." Alan's gaze changed so swiftly from intense to welcoming, she wondered if she had imagined that brief appraisal. "Everyone's in the Throne Room."

At Diana's lifted brow, Caine laughed and drew off her coat. "A family term for one of the drawing rooms. It's a barn." Carelessly, he tossed their coats over the carved lion's head that served as a newel post for the main staircase. "Rena here?"

"She and Justin were already settled in when I got here," Alan answered. Diana watched the silent, subtle look that passed between the brothers.

"Well, I guess that puts me at the top of the list, then."

Alan grinned—a quick, unexpected expression that lightened his features. "Yeah."

Caine swung an arm around Diana's shoulders as

they began to walk down the hall. "Bringing Diana should redeem me." He shot his brother another look. "You come alone, I take it."

"I've already had the lecture," Alan returned dryly. "Thirty-five years old and without a wife," he stated in a soft burr remarkably like his father's. "I'm in disgrace."

"Better you than me," Caine murmured.

"Should I know what you two are talking about?" Diana demanded with a puzzled smile.

Caine looked down at her, then up to meet his brother's amused eyes. "You will," he muttered. "Soon enough."

Diana opened her mouth to question, then was interrupted by the sound of a booming voice echoing off the walls. "The boy should come and see his mother more often. Children today are a disgrace. What do they think about the line—their ancestors and the generations to come? Where's the pride in the family name?"

"He's off and running," Caine said under his breath. He paused, his arm still around Diana's shoulders, at the entrance to the drawing room.

To say the room was impressive would have been an understatement. It had the dimensions of a ballroom with one huge, claret-colored rug spreading from wall to wall. At the far end was an enormous stone fireplace piled high with wood and flame. The windows ran from floor to ceiling along one side with stained-glass inserts along the top. The drapes were red and heavy but spread open so that the fire danced in reflection on the many panes.

Furniture was Gothic and oversized to suit the room.

A Belter table held an ornate urn and a porcelain casket box. The paintings against the thick, dark paneling were all in fussy gilded frames. Sitting on the stone hearth was a life-size statue of a jackal.

Though there were no less than a dozen chairs and sofas scattered about, the family was grouped in one section around a wide, high-backed chair, carved and curved like a throne and upholstered in the same red as the carpet and drapes. In it sat a barrel of a man, red-bearded, strikingly handsome in a bold, warlike fashion. It was a simple matter for Diana to imagine him with a kilt and dirk rather than the full-cut Italian suit he wore.

There was a woman to his right with fine-boned features and dark, slightly graying hair. As Daniel continued with his complaints, her expression remained serene while her fingers were busy forming a pattern with floss and needle in a cloth held taut on a standing hoop.

To the left, Serena was curled on a curved, overstuffed lounge, idly watching the colors of the fire reflect in a glass of kirsch. Justin sat beside her, his arm draped carelessly over the back of the lounge, his fingers toying absently with his wife's hair.

They're his court, Diana thought as her lips curved. And they've heard this proclamation hundreds of times before. What a magnificent man, she decided, watching Daniel drain the liquor in his glass before he continued.

"It seems a small thing to ask," Daniel went on, "to have your children pay their respect to their father on his birthday. It might be my last one," he added, shooting a look at his daughter.

"You say that every year," Caine commented before Serena could retort.

"It's his traditional threat," Serena stated as she sprang up to race to Caine. She hugged him fiercely, giving him a hard kiss before turning to hug Diana. "I'm so glad you came," Serena told her, then took both her hands.

Diana was as overwhelmed by the greeting as she was warmed by it. She found the MacGregors' unselfconsciously physical shows of affection appealed to her while leaving her uncertain if she were capable of returning them. "I'm glad to be here. You look wonderful."

With a laugh, Serena kissed her again. "I'll pour your drinks. Give me a hand, Alan, you need one, too."

"Diana."

Turning, Diana saw Justin standing beside her. Pleasure and a sudden sense of awkwardness ran through her so that while her eyes lit with the first, her hand reached for his with the second. Justin took it, then lacing his fingers with her drew Diana to him.

"Will you kiss me, little sister?"

He would ask, Diana thought as the clear green eyes stayed on hers, to give her the choice of backing away. Rising on her toes, she brushed his lips with hers and felt the awkwardness vanish. "Oh, it's good to see you, Justin." On impulse, she wrapped her arms around him and held tight. "It's so good to see you."

Justin kissed the top of her head, returning the embrace as his gaze drifted to Caine's. He felt something—the instinct that tells a person when two people close to him are intimate. The knowledge flashed into his eyes as Caine met his stare without faltering.

Caine read Justin's expression easily and kept silent. He remembered exactly how he'd felt when he had found Serena sharing Justin's suite at the Comanche. Annoyed, uncomfortable, possessive, protective—all the feelings an older brother has when he suddenly discovers his sister's grown up in front of his eyes. Their friendship spanned a decade, but fate had sent them a curve so that each had found himself attracted to the other's sister. Ties of friendship and ties of blood ran strong in both of them.

"Caine." Justin brought Diana to his side, holding her there a moment as he tried to sort out his emotions.

"Well, damn it, are you going to keep the girl in the doorway, or are you going to bring her in?" Daniel demanded, giving an impatient wheeze as he hauled himself out of his chair. "Let me have a look at that sister of yours, Justin. Rena, my glass is empty."

"It's nice to see you, too," Caine drawled as he crossed the room.

"Hah!" Daniel exclaimed as he gave him a stern look. Caine merely grinned at him until the folds on Daniel's wide face shifted with a bellowing laugh. "Disrespectful young pup." He gathered his son to him in a bear hug and gave him three hearty slaps on the back. "You're late, your mother was worried you weren't coming."

"As long as I haven't missed dinner." Caine unfolded himself from his father and went to Anna.

"So this is Diana." Daniel clasped her by both shoulders. "A fine looking girl," he decided with a quick nod. "You've a bit of your brother in you. Tall, strong," he went on. "Aye, blood will tell."

Diana lifted a brow at the greeting. "Thank you, Daniel. I appreciate you including me in your family weekend."

"Ah, but you're part of the family now, aren't you?" Swinging her around, he faced his wife. "A handsome girl, aye, Anna?"

"Lovely," Anna agreed, then held out her hands. "Don't let him make you feel like a thoroughbred at auction, Diana. It's just a habit of his. Come sit down."

"A thoroughbred at auction?" Daniel blustered. "Now what kind of talk is that?"

"Straight talk," Caine said casually as he sat on the arm of the sofa beside his mother. "Thanks, Rena." He gave his sister a wink as she passed out drinks.

Daniel harrumphed and settled back into his throne-like chair. "So, we have another lawyer in the family," he began. Caine shot him a long, deadly look, but he continued placidly. "I have great respect for the law, you know, having two sons who passed the bar. Of course, Alan's so busy with politics he doesn't take the time for anything else."

"You're top of the list now," Caine muttered under his breath, causing his brother to shrug.

"And you went to Harvard, too," Daniel stated between sips. "Now that's a coincidence for you. Small world, small world." His gaze skimmed briefly over his youngest son. "And now you two are partners."

"We're not partners," Caine and Diana said in unison, then shot each other a rueful look.

"Aren't you, now?" His father's smile, Caine thought, was entirely too bland. "Now I wonder where I got an idea like that? Well..." He gave Diana a paternal smile.

"Rena tells me you grew up in Boston, Diana," Anna interrupted tranquilly as she began to embroider again. "Do you know the O'Marra family?"

"My aunt was well acquainted with a Louise O'Marra."

"Yes, Louise, and what was her husband's name...Brian. Yes, Brian and Louise O'Marra. Odd people." Anna smiled as she finished another stitch. "They really enjoy playing bridge."

A chuckle escaped Diana before she could muffle it. Glancing up, she caught Anna's quick, knowing wink. "I hate the game myself," Anna went on, stitching again. "Perhaps because I'm so poor at it."

"No," Caine corrected, giving her hair a tug. "You're poor at it because you hate it."

"The O'Marra's have three grandchildren, if I'm not mistaken," Daniel put in, then narrowed his gaze as it swept around the room.

"Nice try," Caine murmured to his mother.

"How do you feel about children, Diana?" Daniel leaned back in his chair and fixed his clever eyes on her.

"Children?" She heard a muffled laugh from behind her, which Alan disguised halfheartedly with a fit of coughing. Caine muttered something under his breath that sounded suspiciously like an oath. "Well, I haven't had a great deal of experience with them," she began, sending Caine a puzzled look.

"Where would we be without children?" Daniel demanded, leaning forward again. "To give us that sense of continuity, of responsibility?" As he spoke, he punctuated his words with a thump of his finger on the arm of his chair.

"Your glass is empty," Caine said abruptly and rose. "Keep it up," he said under his breath as he took the glass from his father's hand, "and I'll dilute every bottle of Scotch in the house."

"Well now." Daniel cleared his throat and considered the possibility. "Dinner should be ready soon, shouldn't it, Anna?"

"I think," Serena whispered to Justin, "that we might take a bit of the pressure off our siblings."

"Go ahead." Justin brushed his lips over her cheek. "I'm dying to see his face."

"Speaking of children," Serena said, ignoring the fulminating look Caine shot at her, "I think Dad has a very good point."

"A good point," Daniel repeated, bouncing back to the topic with gusto. "Of course I have a good point. It's disgraceful, your mother without a single grandchild to spoil."

"Heartbreaking," Serena murmured, sending her mother a wink. "Well, Justin and I have decided to remedy that in about six and a half months."

"And about time," Daniel began, then stopped as his mouth hung open.

"Better late than never," Serena countered. Laughing at his stunned expression, she rose and went to her father. "Nothing to say, MacGregor?"

"You're with child?"

With a smile at his phrasing, she bent to kiss his cheek. "Yes. You'll have your grandchild before the leaves turn in September."

As Diana watched, Daniel's eyes filled. "My little girl," he murmured, then rose to cup her face in his hands. "My little Rena."

"I won't be little for long."

Daniel gathered her close. "Always my little girl."

Diana looked away, moved and strangely unsettled by the scene. She saw Caine, his gaze fixed on his sister, his eyes dark and intense as they were when he worked out a complicated point of law. He's trying to see her as a mother, Diana reflected. He's trying to picture himself as an uncle to her child. Justin's child, she realized with a jolt. Her brother's child. Something stirred in her—that old, buried need for family. Hardly realizing she moved, Diana stood and went to Justin.

"To your child," she said quietly and lifted her glass. "To the health and beauty of your son or daughter, and to our parents, who would have loved it." Justin stood, taking her hand as he murmured something in Comanche. "I don't remember the language," Diana told him.

"Thank you," he translated, "aunt of my children."

"We'll have champagne tonight," Daniel bellowed suddenly, and caught Serena close again. "Another MacGregor's on the way!"

"Blade," Justin and Diana corrected together.

"Aye, Blade." Flushed with good humor, he grabbed Justin in one of his bear hugs. "Good blood," he declared, then hugged Diana for good measure until she was laughing and gasping for breath. "Strong stock."

When he released her, the words played back in Diana's head. A glimmer of a notion flitted through her head, then fixed. Oh, my God, she thought, he was talking about me...about me and.... Stunned, she turned her head so that her eyes met Caine's.

He was watching her, his arm draped around his sister's shoulder. Reading Diana's glazed expression accurately, he gave her a crooked smile and lifted his glass.

He couldn't sleep. Caine didn't have to lie in bed and stare at the ceiling to know he couldn't sleep. Instead he sat in a straddle chair, smoking slowly as he watched the moonlight play on the bare branches outside his window. The house was quiet now, a quiet all the more complete after the noise and laughter at the dinner table.

Strange how right Diana had looked in the enormous shadowy room. Strange, he thought again, how right it had seemed for her to be here, in the home of his childhood. He'd managed—or nearly managed—to rationalize his feelings about her for weeks. He was attracted to her, enjoyed her company, liked to watch her laugh, found pleasure in her passion. It had been true of other women. Perhaps, Caine thought as he studied the tip of his cigarette, it had been true of too many other women.

Why couldn't he stop thinking about her, hour after hour, day after day? Why did he know, before he had even attempted it, that he wouldn't be able to walk away from her? And he wouldn't—by God, he wouldn't—let her walk away from him.

On a sound of annoyance, he crushed out his cigarette and rose. There were times when he couldn't rationalize his feelings. He couldn't quite convince himself he'd just enjoyed helping her along on her road to self-discovery. There were times when he knew—and was terrified—that he was in love with her.

Wanted, needed—those were easy words. Love wasn't—not for Caine. Love meant commitment, one to one. It meant giving and sharing deep intimacies when he'd been very careful never to dip below the surface with any woman...until Diana.

For wanting and needing the path was clear, but for loving it took all sorts of unexpected twists and treacherous turns. It sounded like an easy word—an easy word when applied to someone else, he mused. He loved and wasn't sure of his next step.

And how did Diana Blade feel about him? Caine wondered. He stared out the window, his palms resting on the sill. She was a woman who budgeted her affections meticulously. She wanted and needed him, but... With a short laugh, Caine turned away to light another cigarette, to prowl restlessly around the room. Love...how did a man go about coaxing love from a woman? That was something he'd been very careful to avoid. And somehow, he didn't think love could be *coaxed* from a woman like Diana. It was either there or it wasn't.

Or it was there, he continued thoughtfully, and she wouldn't admit it.

Suddenly, painfully, he needed her—the softness, the heat. She would be asleep in the high, huge four-poster in the next room. Without giving himself a chance to think, Caine crushed out his cigarette and went into the hall.

He knew every inch, every board. Without faltering, he found the door to Diana's room and stepped inside, closing it quietly behind him. There was only moonlight here, pale streams of it slanted over the bed. The fire had been lit but was down to embers that gave neither heat nor light.

She'd snuggled beneath the quilt for warmth. Her slow, quiet breathing barely moved it. Emotions flooded him as he watched her and altered the hunger to an aching tenderness. He knew at once how it would be to see her like this night after night, to know when he woke each morning she would be beside him. And he knew, too, what his life would be like without her. Bending, he brushed his lips over her cheek.

"Diana," he murmured as she sighed in sleep and shifted on the pillow. Whispering her name again, he began to trace kisses over her face, nibbling lightly at her lips until he felt her sleepy response. "I want you, Diana." Pressing his mouth to hers, he let his tongue wake her.

On a sound of pleasure, her response grew more active, then, coming fully awake, she let out a gasp of surprise and scrambled up.

"Caine!" she hissed, aware that her heart was pounding from a combination of fear and desire. "You scared me to death."

"It didn't feel like fear," he said quietly as he sat on the bed. Taking her shoulders, he drew her closer.

"What are you doing in here—it's the middle of the—" His mouth silenced her sweetly, effectively. Slowly, he slid his hands down, finding to his pleasure that she was warm and soft and naked. "Caine." Her mouth found a brief freedom as he tasted the curve of her shoulder. "You can't—your parents' house."

"I can," he corrected, and heard her breath catch as his hands moved lower. "Anywhere. I want you, Diana. I can't sleep for wanting you. Let me show you."

"Caine—" But his mouth was on hers again. There was no protest as he pressed her back against the feather pillow.

Had he ever loved her like this before? Diana wondered dazedly as he moved his lips and hands leisurely over her. Once—once in that first, dreamlike loving. There was no urgency, no hurry. It was as if they'd had years together and were assured of years more. Slowly, he savored the tastes of her mouth, the tastes of her skin, murmuring in approval as he went.

Steeped in him, she could find no will to rush. The blazing passion she had grown used to was banked, smoldering like an easy fire in a comfortable hearth. They moved at the same lazy pace, whispering requests, murmuring in pleasure while they lay flesh to flesh beneath the thick quilt.

She hadn't been aware he had so much tenderness in him—or indeed that she had it in herself. She wanted to please him, and to soothe. Her hands touched gently, as his did, but even gentleness aroused. As the lazy stroking continued, she seemed to become more and more aware of her body—every pore, every pulse. With a long, quiet moan, Diana surrendered to the next phase of passion.

He could hear the change in her breathing, the subtle alteration in the rhythm of her body. Her needs accelerated his own. He was dizzy from the scent of her, mixed with the faintest touch of woodsmoke from the dying fire. The linen sheets, worn smooth and thin through the years, skimmed over his skin as her hands pressed him closer. As her desire deepened, the taste of her seemed to grow darker and sweeter. He kept his mouth light on hers, toying with her tongue, nipping while her fingers dove into his hair.

He slipped into her slowly, aroused by the gasp of surprise that became a moan of need. Though she arched in invitation, he kept his pace easy, murmuring mindless promises against her lips as she shuddered for more. The greater his need, the tighter he clung to control. Hazy waves of passion rippled through him as she crested once, yet he guided her gently up again…and again.

Saturated with desire, she murmured his name over and over so that he quieted her with a long, luxurious kiss. He thought he could feel her melt, bone by bone, until her body was limp and he knew her mind was filled with nothing but him. It was then he gave his own needs their freedom.

The red smoldering flame became a blue-white flash that consumed them both.

Chapter Eleven

It would have taken days to explore every nook and
cranny of the house. The more Diana saw of it, the
more she wanted to see. She'd spent most of her childhood and adolescent years in proper drawing rooms and
parlors, admiring paintings by Reynolds or Gainsbor-
ough, Steuben glass and Queen Anne furniture—but
nothing had prepared her for the MacGregors' lifestyle. There were twenty-foot ceilings with arched
beams and gargoyles, carved mahogany doors, stone
fireplaces with spears crossed over the hearth—even an
occasional suit of armor. She might find an ancient
blunderbuss and a Favrile compote in the same room.
It was a hodgepodge, an Aladdin's cave, at once barbaric and sophisticated. If she chose, she could wind
her way down a shadowy corridor lit with gaslight and
enjoy a huge tiled swimming pool or steaming Jacuzzi.

As charmed as she was with the house, Diana was
equally fascinated by the MacGregors themselves.
Whether their environment had grown to fit them or

vice versa, she couldn't be certain, but they were an intriguing mixture of the worldly and primitive. Overlying it all was Daniel's fierce, innate pride in his heritage, his clan and his children.

And she'd been wrong about one thing. Caine was no different here than he was in Boston, than he'd been in Atlantic City. He was exactly who he was, having no need to put on different faces for different people. The security of his childhood, the strong, binding love of his family, had given him that gift. She wondered if he knew what a gift it was.

Because she wanted to think, Diana drifted away alone into what Caine had jokingly referred to as the War Room. Here Daniel kept his collection of weapons—daggers, swords, pistols, ornately carved rifles—and, to her amazement, a small cannon. The fire hadn't been lit, so the room was chilly. Sunbeams filtered through the leaded glass windows to fall in crisscross patterns on the thick planked floor. Diana's heels echoed hollowly as she walked idly from case to case.

So, she thought as she admired an Italian dagger with a jeweled handle, Daniel MacGregor was setting her up. Caine might have warned her—she'd meant to speak to him about it the night before, but they'd had no time alone. Then when he'd come to her room...

She couldn't—wouldn't—be pressured by people she hardly knew to make a decision that involved the rest of her life. She'd never thought of marrying Caine. Even as she realized that wasn't quite true, Diana passed over it. She'd never seriously thought of it, she amended. Marriage and children were things she'd never permitted herself to consider. Didn't marriage mean giving up part of yourself to someone else? For so long she had fought to keep that inner part private—so private, she admitted ruefully, that there had been times she herself had forgotten just what Diana Blade was made of.

And marriage meant risk—trusting someone to stay. No, there was only one person she could completely trust and depend on, and that was herself. She'd realized that years ago when she'd known the pain of loss, the fear of desertion. It wasn't going to happen to her again.

Love. No, she wouldn't think of love, Diana told herself as she stared at the empty hearth. She wasn't in love with Caine—she didn't *choose* to be in love with Caine. But something began to pull at her, threatening to cloud logic with emotions. Frightened, Diana forced it away. No, she wouldn't fall in love, she wouldn't consider marriage. In any case, it was academic. It wasn't Caine who was pressuring her. He'd asked her for nothing, given no promises, demanded none.

It's foolish to worry about it, she reminded herself. I've let his family get to me—that unity, that closeness. It appeals just as much as it frightens.

It tempted her to daydream, and she'd given up fantasies long ago.

"All alone, Diana?"

She turned, smiling, as Justin walked into the room. "I can't get enough of this house," she told him. "It's like something out of the Middle Ages, with unexpected touches of the twentieth century. The Mac-Gregors are fascinating people."

"The first time I walked in here I wondered if Daniel MacGregor was mad or brilliant." With one of his quick, charming grins, he scanned the room. "I still haven't made up my mind."

"You really love him, don't you?"

Justin lifted a brow at the serious tone of her question. "Yes. He's a man who demands strong emotions. All of them do," he added thoughtfully. "I don't think I fully realized until Serena was kidnapped that I'd made them my family for ten years. I wish you'd had that."

"I had other things." With a shrug, Diana walked to a slightly rusted suit of armor. "I was very self-sufficient."

"Was and are," Justin murmured. "Do you ever think too much?"

She turned back, lifting a brow in almost the identical manner of her brother. "You too, Justin? Have you gotten it into your head to match me up with Caine?"

His eyes remained calm and very cool. "It appears the two of you have managed that all on your own."

"That's my business."

"So it is." Dipping his hands into his pockets, he studied her. She was annoyed and, he suspected, a bit frightened. "I wasn't there for you when you were growing up, Diana. Perhaps it's too late to play big brother now, but I promised to be your friend."

She went to him quickly, pressing her face to his shoulder as she held him. "I'm sorry. It's hard for me—I'm afraid to need you."

"Or anyone?" Justin asked, tilting her face to his. Though she remained silent, the answer was in her eyes. "It's disconcerting to see so much of yourself in another person," he murmured. "Diana, are you in love with Caine?"

"Don't ask me that." Drawing away, she held up her hands as if to ward off the question. "Don't ask me that."

"All right." He hadn't expected to feel concern, or to feel this vague helplessness. "If I asked, would you tell me about the years you lived with Adelaide? Really tell me?"

Diana opened her mouth, then closed it again. "No," she said after a moment. "No, that's over."

"If it was over, you'd tell me about it. Diana," he continued when she would have spoken. "I'm not going to give you advice or tell you what you should do. But I'd like to tell you something about myself. I was in love with Serena, but I didn't tell her. I didn't," he continued with a rueful grin, "tell myself. I'd been in charge of my own life for so long. I'd never loved anyone—you, our parents—that was all too distant. Telling her was one of the hardest things I ever did. There are people love comes gently to. They're not us."

"What about Rena?" Diana wondered. "Was it easy for her?"

"Easier, I think." He smiled then and, sitting on the arm of a chair, lit a cigarette. "She's a great deal like her father—more than any of the others. She'd suffer all sorts of torture before she'd admit it, but when she came to me in Atlantic City, she'd already made up her mind that we'd be together. Daniel's little scheme had worked very well."

"Daniel's scheme?"

Justin blew out a stream of smoke and laughed.

"He'd thrown us together, very cleverly, by buying me a ticket for the cruise liner Serena worked on. Of course, he didn't mention to me that she worked there, or to her that he had a friend coming on board. He counted on chemistry—or on fate, as he puts it."

"Fate," Diana murmured, then gave a bewildered laugh. "The old devil."

"To put in mildly." Justin watched her through a mist of smoke. "He knows how to get what he wants. All the MacGregors do. And," he added slowly, "so do you and I—once we acknowledge what it is we want." She shot him a look, but Justin rose and slipped an arm around her shoulders. "Let's go find the clan or Daniel will send search parties."

There was something different about Caine. Diana couldn't quite put her finger on it, but she sensed it. At first, she wondered if perhaps the Virginia Day case was troubling him. He was to go to trial the following week, and Diana knew that he had been pumping his mother for every scrap of information she had on Dr. Francis Day.

On the surface he seemed relaxed enough—laughing with his family, teasing his sister. But there was something going on beneath, an edginess she'd never found in him before. There were times throughout the day that she caught him looking at her in his old direct, dissecting way. It was as if he were seeing her for the first time, as if they hadn't worked and talked together, as if they hadn't been as close as a man and woman could be.

While she felt herself being drawn into the circle of his family, Diana's thoughts of Caine kept her from being completely relaxed. There'd been a change—and if she was honest, she would admit she had sensed it in the way he had made love to her the night before. The road had suddenly developed a new surface. She would navigate cautiously.

"Well now." Mellow, pleased with himself, Daniel sat back in his thronelike chair with his gifts spread out on the floor around him. "A man's compensation for adding another year."

"Of course it has nothing to do with the basic greed or the love of opening presents," Serena commented as she crossed her bare feet on the coffee table.

"One of the trials of my life has been disrespectful children," Daniel told Diana with a sigh.

"The curse of parenting," she agreed, knowing him well enough now to play the game.

"The times I've been shouted at, aye, even threatened by my own flesh and blood." Daniel heaved a sigh as he flopped back in his chair.

"I'm getting pretty close to tears," Serena said dryly.

"I can overlook that in your condition." Daniel sent her a stern look. "But don't think I've forgotten how you yelled at me just because I bought that husband of yours a ticket for that boat. Yelled at me," he repeated, turning back to Diana. "And broke half a dozen of my best cigars."

"Cigars?" Anna said mildly.

"Old ones that were just—lying around," he said quickly.

"It must have been difficult, raising three...volatile children." Diana felt Caine's fingers squeeze the back of her neck, but she kept her expression bland.

"Ah, I could tell you stories…" Daniel smiled reminiscently and shook his head. "That one," he said, pointing a wide finger at Caine. "Hardly a moment's peace, Anna will tell you." Then he continued before Anna had a chance to. "That one was nothing but mischief when he was a lad, and then there were the females. A regular parade," Daniel announced proudly.

"A parade," Diana repeated. Turning her head, she started to smile at Caine but found him staring at her with that odd light in his eyes.

With their gazes locked, he cupped her face in his hand. "We're both grown up now," he murmured, then covered her mouth in a long, firm kiss.

"Well then," Daniel began with a wide grin as Diana sat silent and flustered.

"You haven't tried the piano yet, have you, Diana?" Anna asked calmly.

"What? I'm sorry?" Out of her depth, Diana turned to see a look of gentle understanding in Anna's eyes.

"The piano," she repeated. "You play, don't you?"

"Yes, I do."

"It's so rarely touched these days. Would you mind playing something, Diana?"

"No, of course not." Relieved, she rose to cross the room to the baby grand.

"You're pressuring the children, Daniel," Anna said quietly.

"Me?" He shot her an incredulous look. "Nonsense, anyone can see that they—"

"Why don't you let them see for themselves first?"

He subsided in a huff as Diana sifted through the sheet music.

She was grateful for the distraction. It was simpler

for her to remain outwardly composed when she had something specific to do. The notes came easily to her—a result of years of structured lessons and an affection for music. Music had perhaps been the only one of her accomplishments that had pleased Diana as much as it had pleased her aunt. She used it now as she had often in the past, as a curtain for her private thoughts and private emotions.

What had been in Caine's mind when he had kissed her? Diana wasn't accustomed to, or completely comfortable with, public shows of affection. Certainly not in the boisterous sense the MacGregors were. Yet even with that, she could have accepted a simple kiss. Was it her imagination, or had there been something possessive in the gesture?

Perhaps she was just letting Daniel's not-so-subtle machinations get to her. Those, and Justin's unexpected questions. Why should she feel pressured today when she hadn't felt so yesterday? Last night...hadn't it really begun last night?

Lifting her gaze from the keys, she met Caine's eyes. He was silent, brooding, Diana mused as her brows drew together. It wasn't characteristic of him to brood. Nor, she reminded herself, was it characteristic of him to be tense, yet he was. Could something have changed overnight without her being aware of it?

It might have been better if she hadn't come, Diana thought as she felt little fingers of tension probe at the back of her neck. She shouldn't have allowed herself to be charmed by the eccentricities of this family, the closeness, the camaraderie. It might not have been wise to have seen Caine in this kind of setting—away from Boston, the office, her own established apartment. If she wasn't careful, she might find herself forgetting her own goals and the rules she'd set up to accomplish them.

Success was first. It had to be, if she were to justify all the years she had danced to someone else's tune. And success, Diana knew, was a greedy god who demanded constant vigilance. Gaining it, then maintaining it, would require all of her skill and a large chunk of her time.

When she had chosen law, Diana had made a pact with herself. There would be no personal complications to interfere with her career. She had neither the inclination nor the patience for them. Again her gaze drifted to Caine. The knots of tension tightened.

Hadn't she told herself from the beginning that if she let him get too close, things would drift out of her control? She'd known, yet had somehow convinced herself that she could handle an intimate relationship with him without letting her emotions completely outweigh her logic. Had it been pride that had caused her to accept the challenge? Passion? It hardly mattered, since she had accepted and was now forced to deal with the consequences.

As the music built, her feelings intensified. She could feel them pour through her, hear the crackling snap from the blaze of the fire and sense somehow the varying emotions in play across the room. Why had she let herself get so involved? she wondered in quick panic. She had her life—a streamlined path she'd just begun to follow. There were all those promises to herself to keep, though she could remember, even when she struggled not to, the tenderness Caine had brought to her bed in the dark hours of the night.

Diana let the notes drift into silence, then gripped her hands together, finding they were not quite steady.

"Now that was a pleasure." Daniel gave a windy sigh from his chair. "Is there anything that brings a man more contentment than a beautiful woman and a song?"

Caine reluctantly took his eyes from Diana and gave his father a long, cool stare. "Did you have plans to survive until your next birthday?" he asked pleasantly.

"Now what kind of talk is that?" Daniel blustered, but then he hesitated.

He'd planted enough seeds for an evening...and he knew the value of strategic retreat. "We'll have another bottle of champagne and some more cake," he declared. "Caine, toss another log or two on the fire before you come along."

As the family swept from the room, Serena paused by the piano to squeeze Diana's hand. "He's an old meddler," she murmured, "but he has a good heart."

When the room was quiet, Diana rose and watched as Caine added fresh wood to the already blazing fire. The tension at the back of her head had built to an ache.

"Do you want some more cake?" Caine asked with his back still to her.

"No. No, not really." Diana linked her hands together and wished they were back in Boston. Would she be more certain of her moves there?

"Another drink?" Now this is a ridiculously polite conversation, Caine thought in disgust as he turned to her.

"Yes, all right." Moistening her lips, Diana searched

for some safe topic. "Did you get the information you wanted on the Day case from your mother?"

"Just a corroboration on Francis Day's character." Caine shrugged as he poured from the decanter to glass. "It was nothing that I didn't already have, but my mother has a way of getting to the heart of the matter without all the fuss. He interned under her at Boston General. Still, it's nothing I can use in litigation." As he handed Diana her drink, Caine brushed at her bangs in a habitual gesture. When she stepped back, he narrowed his eyes but said nothing.

"It always helps to get an objective viewpoint before you go to trial."

"Am I on trial, Diana?"

Her eyes came swiftly to his. "I don't know what you mean."

"You're hedging." Taking a step closer, he circled the back of her neck, then lowered his lips to hers. He felt the tension beneath his fingers, felt her initial resistance to the kiss. As he drew back, Caine lifted an ironic brow. "Yes, it seems I am. But I can't make my plea until I'm sure of the charges."

"Don't be ridiculous." Quickly annoyed, Diana lifted her drink and swallowed.

"Don't be evasive," Caine countered. "I thought we'd gotten past that point in our relationship."

"Stop pushing me, Caine."

He took a long hard look at the drink in his hand but didn't taste it. "In what way?"

"I don't know—every way." She dragged a hand through her hair as she walked away. "Let's just drop it, I don't want to fight with you."

"Is that what we're doing?" With a nod, he drank,

then set down his glass. "Well, if it is, let's do it right. You get the first shot."

"I don't *want* the first shot." Abruptly furious, she whirled back to him. "I'm not going to stand in your parents' drawing room and snipe at you."

"But you would if we were somewhere else."

"Yes—I don't know. Caine, leave me alone!"

"The hell I will." And the very calmness of his tone warned her of his mood. "Let's hear it, Diana. I want to know why you're pulling away from me."

"I'm not pulling away, you're imagining things." She took a quick, nervous sip of her drink and turned away again. When his hand touched her shoulder, she jerked, then cursed herself.

"Not pulling away," Caine murmured, trying to ignore the slash of hurt. "What's your term for it?"

"Look, it's late—I'm tired." Diana fumbled for the excuse, knowing it was a weak one. "Caine..." With a frustrated sigh, she moved away from him again. "Please, don't pressure me now."

"Is that what you think I'm doing, Diana? Pressuring you?"

"Yes, damn it! You, your family, Justin—all in your own separate ways." Setting down her glass, she leaned her palms against a table. She was overreacting but for once couldn't summon the logic to clear her mind. "Caine, can't we just leave this alone?"

"No, I don't think so." He would have gone to her, but somehow the distance she had put between them stopped him. He felt awkward, and close to furious with her for making him so. And he hurt—that was something he would think about later. "It's not my intention to pressure you, Diana," he said in a low, precise voice that had her digging her teeth into her lower lip. "But there are things that I think should be said now."

"Why?" she demanded as she spun back around. "Why this sudden urgency? There weren't any complications when we were in Boston."

"What kind of complications are there now?"

"Don't cross-examine me, Caine."

"You have an objection to that question?"

"Oh, you make me furious when you act like this." Seething, she dug her hands into the pockets of her skirt and whirled around the room. "I've felt like I've been under a microscope off and on since I walked through the front door. You might have told me I was top of your father's list as the proper mate for his second son."

"My father has absolutely nothing to do with you and me, Diana. I'd apologize for his lack of subtlety, but I don't feel responsible for it."

"I don't want your apology," she fumed. "But it would have been more comfortable if I'd been prepared. Damn it, I like him—and the rest of your family. It's impossible not to, but I don't like the quiet looks of speculation and the unasked questions."

"What would you like me to do about it?"

"I don't know. Nothing," she said as she moved to stand in front of the roaring fire. "But I don't have to like it."

"Did it ever occur to you that I might not particularly care for it myself?" Simmering with anger, Caine swirled his drink and stared at her back. "Did it ever occur to you that I might not care for the interference in my life, no matter how well intentioned?"

"They're your family," she tossed back over her

shoulder. "You're bound to be more accustomed to it than I. I spent twenty years trying to live up to my aunt's plans for me. I didn't get this far to follow someone else's."

"The hell with your aunt!" Caine exploded. "And with everyone else that isn't you and me. What do you want, Diana? Why don't you just spell it out?"

"I don't know what I want!" she shouted, shocking herself with the admission. "I knew yesterday, and now... Damn it, Caine, I can't deal with this. I can't deal with having my private life poked into—not by your father, my brother, anyone. It's my life, and I'll make my own decisions."

"You can't deal with it," he murmured, then gave a short laugh before he drained his glass. "Then deal with this. I'm in love with you."

Diana stared at him in utter shock, in utter silence. She wondered if her heart had simply stopped, and she didn't move a muscle as a log snapped loudly and sparks sprayed against the screen at her back.

They watched each other, both pale, their eyes dark with what seemed more like anger than any other emotion. How had it come to this? she wondered. And what in God's name would they do about it?

"Well, you don't seem thrilled about it." Furious with himself for having made the statement so baldly, Caine reached for the decanter. With studied calm, he poured a brandy. How could he have known that silence could bring this kind of pain? As he listened to the brandy splash against the glass, he wondered why he had waited more than thirty years to say those words to a woman to find only emptiness. "Would you like the statement stricken from the record, counselor?"

"Don't." Diana squeezed her eyes shut for a moment. "I don't know what to say to you—or how to handle this. It's easier for you. There've been other women—"

"Other women?" he exploded. He wasn't pale anymore, but his eyes were even darker, more furious than she'd ever seen them. Instinctively, Diana stepped back as he walked toward her. "How can you say that to me now? What do I have to do to make up for a past that happened before I even met you? And why the hell should I?" He gripped her by the shoulders, fingers digging into flesh. "Damn it, Diana, I said I love you. I *love* you."

His mouth came down on hers in anger and frustration, as if by that alone he could wipe out the hurt she brought him, the doubts he brought her. Something built inside her, threatening to burst. Diana dragged herself away with a cry of alarm.

"You frighten me." Her eyes swam with sudden tears as they faced each other again, their breathing unsteady. "I said that you didn't, but it was always a lie. From the very beginning—" She choked back a sob and pushed her hair away from her face with both hands. "You're what I've always avoided. I can't risk it, don't you understand? All of my life someone's played carrot and stick with me. Do this, fit into this mold and you'll have security, you'll have normalcy. I've just found my own mold, I won't fit someone else's expectations now!"

"I'm not asking you to fit anything," he tossed back. "I've never asked you to be anyone but yourself."

Perhaps it was the truth of that which frightened her more than anything else. She dragged a hand through her hair as the last lingering fear broke through. "How do I know you'll stay? How do I know, if I let myself love you, that one day there wouldn't be someone else, something else, and you'd just walk away? I can handle being alone now, I know how. But I can't—I *won't* be left again."

Caine struggled against fury, against the sense of his own impotence. "I've asked you more than once to trust me. It's not me that frightens you, Diana. It's ghosts, and your own self-doubt."

She swallowed, winning the battle of tears. "You don't understand. You've never lost everything."

"So you intend to go through your life never taking a chance because you might lose?" His eyes hardened as they swept her face. "I never took you for a coward."

"I *choose* the chances I take," she countered furiously. "*I* choose. I won't put myself in a position to be hurt, I won't take chances on my career—"

"Why do you automatically assume I'll hurt you? And what in God's name does your career have to do with my loving you? I have the same profession, the same demands. Who's asking you to make a choice between love and the law?"

"Did you have to chop down a tree, Caine? We're halfway through the cake and champagne, and…" Serena trailed off as she reached the center of the room. The waves of tension and hurt poured over her so that she stared in awkward silence from Caine to Diana. "I'm sorry," she said, knowing of no gracious way to cover up the intrusion. "I'll tell everyone you're busy."

"No, please." Diana met the banked fury in Caine's

eyes before turning to his sister. "Just tell them I'm a bit tired. I'm going to go up now." Quickly, without looking back, she walked from the room.

Caine watched her in silence, then turned to retrieve his snifter of brandy from the sideboard.

"Oh, Caine, I'm so sorry. It seems I couldn't have picked a worse time to barge in."

"It doesn't matter." He drained the remaining liquor, then poured more. "We'd said all we had to say."

"Caine..." Serena went to him, distressed by the controlled voice and stony expression. "Do you need a sympathetic ear, or solitude?"

"I need a drink," he answered, taking both the snifter and decanter to a chair. "I need quite a few of them."

"You're in love with Diana?"

"Right the first time," he said, and toasted her.

Ignoring the sarcasm, Serena sat beside him. "And you'd like to murder her."

"Right again."

"It's easy to be right when you've been through it. I don't know what went on in here tonight, but—"

"I told her, in the midst of a nasty little argument, that I was in love with her." He brought the snifter to his lips again and swallowed deeply. "It seems my timing—and my delivery—were a bit off."

"I'm going to do something I despise," Serena said with a sigh.

"Which is?"

"Give advice."

"That's my territory, Rena. Save it."

"Shut up." Firmly, she took the snifter from his

hand and set it down. "Give her some room, and some time. You're not an easy man to love in the best of circumstances. I should know."

"I appreciate the testimonial."

"Caine, a lot of things have changed in Diana's life very quickly. She's the kind of woman who needs to make her decisions a step at a time—at least she thinks she is."

He gave a quiet laugh as he leaned back in the chair. "You were always an excellent judge of character, Rena. You'd have made a hell of a lawyer."

"It comes in handy in my line of work, too." Reaching out, she took his hand. "Don't press her, Caine. There are storms inside Diana. Let her battle them out."

"I might have pressed her too far already." On a long breath, he shut his eyes. "Oh, God, I hurt."

Serena wanted to comfort and forced herself not to. "Love has to hurt, it's rule number one. Go to bed," she ordered briskly. "You'll have a better idea what to do in the morning."

Caine opened his eyes again. "It's a hell of a thing that I should be sitting here taking advice from the kid sister who sharpened her left jab on me."

"I'm a comfortable matron now," Serena said majestically as she patted her stomach.

"Hah!" Caine retorted in an accurate imitation of their father.

"Go to bed," Serena advised. "Before I take it into my head to see if that jab's still effective." Rising, she tugged him to his feet.

"You always were a bossy little busybody," Caine told her as they walked toward the doorway. "I'm still crazy about you."

"Yeah." Serena grinned up at him. "Me too."

Chapter Twelve

Diana sat in the empty courtroom, numb and nause-
ated. The hands she folded together on her briefcase
were ice cold and nerveless. She knew she had to pull
herself together—go out and get in her car, drive home.
Somehow she knew if she stood up at that moment, her
legs would buckle. She sat as still as a stone and waited
for the feeling to pass.

Logic told her she was being a fool. She should feel
wonderful—she should celebrate. She'd won.

Chad Rutledge was free, exonerated. Beth Howard's
father would face perjury charges. And so would Beth,
Diana added silently as she stared at the empty witness
chair. It was unlikely the girl would be convicted, not
when a dozen witnesses had seen so clearly that it had
been fear that had caused her to lie about the rape. Not
when a dozen witnesses had watched how pitifully she
had fallen apart under examination.

Not, Diana thought as a small pain rippled through
her, when a dozen witnesses had watched Diana Blade,
Attorney at Law, rip her to shreds.

Diana could hear the echo of her own voice in the now silent courtroom—cold, accusing, merciless. She could see the pale, fragile face of Beth Howard as it crumbled—and the tears, the near hysterical confession. She could hear Chad's loud, furious demands that Beth be left alone. Then there had been chaos in the courtroom as Chad had been restrained and Beth had wept out the entire story.

When the courtroom had been cleared, Diana had remained to deal with her victory and the cost of it in human terms.

She had never felt more alone or more lost than at that moment. She wanted to weep but sat dry-eyed. She was a professional, and tears had no place. Caine; oh, God, she needed Caine. Diana closed her eyes as the numbness faded into pain.

She had no right to need him or to use him as a lifeline when she felt she was sinking. Though two weeks had passed, she could still see the look in his eyes as they had faced each other in his parents' drawing room.

Hurt. She had hurt him, and now they treated each other like strangers. Each time Diana tried to tell herself it was for the best, she remembered that look in his eyes and the flood of feeling that had risen in her only to be forced back in panic.

Love. She couldn't afford to love him, couldn't afford the risk. It would be best if she found another office, perhaps left Boston altogether. *Running away?* a small voice asked her. With a sigh, Diana stared down at her hands. Yes, that's what she had in mind. If she ran fast enough, she might be able to escape Caine. But she wasn't going to be able to escape herself. And if she were honest, she would admit it was herself she was running from.

When had she started to love him? Perhaps it had been when he had shown her such gentleness and understanding after her first meeting with Justin. Or perhaps it had been on that snowy beach when he'd made her laugh, then made her ache with need. She'd known it was happening but had pretended otherwise. Every time her emotions had begun to take over, she had closed them off. Afraid.

She looked around the empty courtroom again, then slowly rose to her feet. It was twilight when she stepped outside. In the west, the sky was clumped with clouds that glowed with bronzes and pinks. The lengthening of days was the only sign of spring, as the wind was as sharp as a knife and the dark, leafless trees shimmered under a thin coat of ice. Diana saw Chad hunched in his coat, sitting near the bottom of the courtroom steps. She hesitated, not certain she was strong enough for a confrontation, then, squaring her shoulders, she walked down the remaining steps.

"Chad."

He looked up, staring into her face for a long five seconds before he rose. "I've been waiting for you."

"I can see that." With a nonchalance she wasn't feeling, Diana flipped up the collar of her coat against the wind. "You should have waited inside."

"I needed the air." He kept his hands in his pockets, his shoulders rounded against the cold as he watched her. "They wouldn't let me see Beth."

"I'm sorry." Carefully, she kept all emotion and all weariness out of her voice. I hurt, too, she thought in despair. For you, for myself. Must I always have the answers? "I'll arrange for you to see her tomorrow."

"You don't look so good."

Diana gave him a thin smile. "Thanks." As she turned he caught at her arm.

"Ms. Blade..." Awkwardly, Chad dropped his hand and stuffed it back in his pocket. "I gave you a hard time in there—I guess I've given you a hard time all along."

"It comes with the territory, Chad. Don't worry about it."

"Watching Beth..." He swore softly, then turned away to stare at the traffic. "I couldn't stand watching her cry in there. I hated you for making her cry like that. When I came out here to wait, I had a lot of things I was going to say to you."

Diana gripped her briefcase tighter and braced herself. "Go ahead, say them now."

He gave a shaky laugh and turned back to her. "I had some time to think. I guess I don't do enough of that." He took out a cigarette, cupping his hands around the match as he lit it. Diana saw that his hands were steady. "I've got something different to say to you now, Ms. Blade." Chad blew out smoke on a long breath before he met her eyes. "You saved my life, and I think maybe you saved Beth's, too. I want to thank you."

Unable to speak, Diana stared at the hand he held out to her. After a moment, she accepted it, then found hers clasped hard. "All I could think about in there was that you were hurting her. I couldn't see past that. Sitting out here, I started thinking about that cell, and what it would be like to be in one for the next twenty years. You don't know how good it is to sit outside and know nobody's going to come along and lock you back in a cage."

When his voice trembled, Chad swallowed but kept his hand tight on hers. "I'd have done that for her, and I guess, after a while, I'd have hated her. And she...she'd have lived with that lie crawling around inside of her. Beth wouldn't have made it. I know that."

"It'll be over for her soon." Diana lifted her free hand to cover their joined ones. Objective? she thought. Only a robot could be cool and objective when someone looked at them like this. He needed to give his gratitude, but he was also asking for comfort. "No court's going to punish Beth for being terrified."

"If they—if she has to go to court, will you help her?"

"Yes. If she wants me to. And you'll be there for her."

"Yeah. I'm going to marry her right away. The hell with money, we'll figure something out." His hand relaxed as he smiled for the first time. "I was always thinking I had to prove something, you know? To Beth, to myself, to the whole damn world. Funny, it doesn't seem so important anymore to prove that I can make it all by myself."

Diana gave him an odd look and shook her head. "No," she said slowly. "I suppose only fools think that way."

"It won't be so easy with Beth finishing school." He grinned now, as though the challenge appealed to him. "But we'll be together, and that's what counts."

"Yes. Chad..." She dropped her hand to her side. "Is it worth it? The risk, the pain?"

He tilted back his head and drew in the cold evening air. "It's worth anything. Everything." With a wide, brilliant smile he looked back at her. "You'll come to the wedding, Ms. Blade?"

"Yes." She smiled back at him, then gently kissed his cheek. "Yes, I'll come to your wedding, Chad. Now go home, you'll see your girl tomorrow."

Diana walked to her car, realizing the sickness had left her stomach. The dull threat of a headache at her temple had vanished. They were so young, she thought as she joined the long stream of traffic, with a dozen strikes against them. Yet that look of shining hope in Chad's eyes made her believe. They'd face the odds together, and if there was any justice, they'd make it.

And what about you? Diana asked herself. Are you determined to be a fool, or are you going to face the odds? Just how much Blade blood, gambler's blood, was there in her? Perhaps, like Chad, she had been flirting with spending her life in a cell. There was a certain safety there to compensate for the lack of freedom.

Words began to flit through her head—Justin's voice telling her that love came gently to some people, but not to them. Caine furiously telling her he loved her, demanding that she trust him. She could hear her own voice, edged with nerves, telling him she wouldn't risk being left alone. What was she now, Diana asked herself, if not alone? Alone and aching with love and needs, but letting those old fears—the ghosts, Caine had called them—rule her life. In doing so, she was breaking the most important promise she had ever made to herself. To be Diana Blade.

She'd intended to go home but now found herself pulling up in the drive beside the office. Instinct? she wondered, seeing that Caine's car was parked there. Her nerves began to jump again. What would she say to him? It might be best to go home, wait until she could think clearly and plan. Even as this went through her mind, Diana stepped from the car.

She could see the light in the window of his office. He's been working too hard, she thought. The Day case. The trial should be nearly over by now. Diana knew more of its progress from the press reports than from Caine. Had they spoken a dozen words to each other in the last two weeks? she wondered. What would she say to him now?

The first floor was dark and silent. She could hear the quiet creak of the door as she shut it behind her. Glancing up the stairs, she slipped out of her coat. Her timing was probably very poor, she thought, and caught her bottom lip between her teeth as she again considered going home. She walked up the stairs.

Caine's office door was open. Diana could hear the whispers from the fire as she moved toward it. Hesitating at the doorway, she studied Caine while he sat behind his desk. His head was bent over a stack of papers. His jacket and tie had been tossed in a heap over the back of the chair so that he wore the black vest unbuttoned and his shirt open at the throat. In the ashtray a cigarette he hadn't quite put out smoldered. As she watched, he dragged a hand through his hair, then reached up, without looking up, for his coffee cup.

She studied him, as she hadn't permitted herself to do since that night in Hyannis Port.

God, he looks tired, she thought with a jolt. As if he hasn't slept properly in days. Could the case be going so badly? Suddenly, he swore softly under his breath and ran his hand over his face.

Swamped with concern, Diana stepped forward. "Caine?"

His head jerked up. For an instant he stared at her with eyes that were dark and unguarded. She felt his need as a tangible thing, then, just as quickly, it was gone.

"Diana," he turned coolly. "I didn't expect you back tonight."

Maybe she had been mistaken. It might only have been surprise she had seen in his eyes, her own emotions she had felt. She searched her mind for all the things she wanted to say. "Chad Rutledge was acquitted," was all that came out.

"Congratulations." He leaned back and studied her with apparent dispassion. Was she more beautiful than she'd been yesterday? he wondered as the ache crept into him. Was he going to go mad seeing her day after day, loving her and not being loved in return?

"It was ugly," she said after a moment. "I'm not particularly proud of the way I treated Beth Howard on the stand."

Caine balled his hand into a fist, then flexed it. Her vulnerability would always tear at him. "Do you want a drink?"

"No, I—yes," she decided. "Yes, I'll get it." Moving to a cabinet across the room, Diana found a decanter and poured without having any idea what the liquor was. This wasn't happening the way it should, she told herself. All the words she wanted to say to him stuck in her throat. Self-doubts; hadn't he told her she was plagued with them? As usual, he'd been accurate. Now, she simply didn't know if she could find the right phrasing, the right tone, to tell him she wanted to do what he'd asked of her almost from the beginning. To trust.

Moistening her lips, she tried to break some of the tension hovering in the air. "Is the Day case giving you problems?"

"No, not really. It's nearly over." He sipped at his coffee and found it cold and bitter. It suited his mood. "The prosecution didn't have as tight a case as I'd imagined. I put Ginnie on the stand today. She was hard as nails, unsympathetic and perfectly believable. He couldn't shake her testimony an inch in cross-examination."

"Then you're feeling confident about the verdict?"

"Virginia Day will be acquitted," he said flatly. "But she won't get justice." At Diana's puzzled look, he pushed his coffee aside and rose. "Legally, she'll be free, but the public will look at her as a spoiled, rich woman who murdered her husband and got away with it. I can keep her out of jail, but I can't vindicate her."

"A lawyer I admire once told me a defense counsel has to keep his objectivity."

Caine shot her a look, then shrugged. "What the hell did he know?"

Diana set down her glass and walked to him. "Why don't you let me buy you a drink and some dinner?"

He needed to touch her. Caine could feel his finger-tips tingle with the need to stroke the softness of her skin. Rejection. The thought of facing it again had him slipping on his armor. "No." He moved back behind his desk. "I've got a lot to catch up on tonight."

"All right. I'll see what's in the refrigerator downstairs."

"No."

The single sharp word stopped her. The pain registered, pushing her back a step. Turning, she stared at the fire until she was certain her voice wouldn't tremble. "You'd like me to go away, wouldn't you?"

"I told you, I'm busy."

"I could wait." Unable to keep her hands still, she toyed with the handle of the brass fireplace poker. "We could have a late supper at my apartment."

He stared at her, the slim, straight figure in jade-green wool. She was offering him the opportunity to go back to the way things had been, the way it had always been for him with women before. Fun, games, no complications. Nothing had ever seemed so empty. With a sigh, Caine looked down at his hands. How many times in the last two weeks had he thought about her—about the way things had been between them? He'd considered begging; it wasn't a matter of pride. Once, in the early hours of the morning, he'd considered going to her apartment and using force for lack of anything better. Every possible angle from reason to abduction had gone through his mind, and every one had been discarded. He'd had to remind himself that love couldn't be forced or coaxed or pleaded out of a woman like Diana.

He wanted her, needed to lose himself in that mindless passion they could bring each other. He could almost taste her from where he stood, that not quite sweet, not quite sharp flavor of her mouth when it heated. It would have been simple once, but it would never be simple again.

"I appreciate the offer," he said curtly. "I'm not interested."

She shut her eyes at that, surprised again at how much pain words could bring. "I hurt you badly," she murmured. "I don't know if there's any way to make up for it."

He gave a quick, hard laugh. "I can do without the sympathy, Diana."

Distressed by his tone, she turned around. "Caine, that's not what—"

"Drop it."

"Caine, please—"

"Damn it, Diana, let it alone!" Struggling for control, he lifted his coffee again. She saw his knuckles go white on the handle. "Go home," he ordered. "I've got work to do."

"I have things I want to say to you."

"Doesn't it occur to you that I don't want to hear them? I stripped my soul for you," he tossed out before he could stop himself. "Made a fool of myself. I've already heard your reasons why you can't give me what I want. I don't need to hear it all over again. I don't think I can take it."

"Stop making this impossible for me!" she shouted at him.

"I don't give a damn about you at the moment." Enraged, he grabbed her arm and yanked her against him.

Before he could stop himself, his mouth was on hers, savagely, brutally. The hell with love, he told himself.

If this was all she wanted from him, then it was all he would give. He let the needs and frustration take him, oblivious to her response or protest until she was limp and trembling. On a wave of self-disgust, he shoved her away. Love, he realized helplessly, could not be ignored.

"Get out of here, Diana. Leave me alone."

Shaken, she gripped the back of a chair. "No, not until I've finished."

"All right. You stay, I'll go."

But she was at the door ahead of him, slamming it shut and leaning back against it. "Sit down, shut up and listen to me."

For a moment, she thought he'd simply yank her aside, throttle her for good measure. There was murder in his eyes as he glared down at her. Then he hooked his thumbs in his front pockets. "Okay, say your piece."

"Sit down," she repeated.

"Don't press your luck."

Her chin jerked up at the soft threat. "All right, we'll stand. I'm not going to apologize for the things I said two weeks ago. I meant them. My career is important to me—vital, because it's something I've done for myself. And trusting someone, trusting them with my emotions is the most difficult thing in the world for me. No one can make me do it, it's my own choice."

"Fine. Now get out of the way."

"I'm not finished!" She swallowed, then heard herself say. "I think it's time we were partners."

"Partners?" The fury in his eyes was replaced by blank astonishment. "Good God, you're standing there—now, after everything I've said to you—giving me a *business* proposition?''

"This has nothing to do with business," she shot back. "I want you to marry me."

She watched as Caine's eyes narrowed, sharpened, until she could read nothing in them at all. "What did you say?"

"I'm asking you to marry me." Diana kept her eyes level and wondered why her legs didn't buckle.

Brows drawn together, he stood where he was. "You're proposing to me?" he asked carefully.

She felt the color warm her cheeks but wasn't certain if it was embarrassment or annoyance. "Yes, I thought it was perfectly clear."

He laughed, quietly at first, then with more feeling. Running his hands over his face, Caine turned and walked to the window. Diana watched his reaction with a mixture of anger and anxiety. "I'll be damned," he murmured.

"I don't think it's funny." Diana crossed her arms over her chest and felt like an idiot.

"I don't know…" Caine continued to stare out the window as he tried to sort out his thoughts. After all the pain of the last two weeks, she suddenly appears on his doorstep and asks him to marry her. "Somehow it appeals to my humor."

"I'll just leave you alone to enjoy your little joke, then." She fumbled with the knob, but even as she jerked the door open, Caine was there, slamming it shut again.

"Diana—"

"Get away," she demanded as she attempted to shove him aside.

"Wait a minute." Taking her shoulders, he pressed her back against the door. "Are we always going to be at cross purposes?" he wondered. His eyes weren't laughing at her but were deadly serious and a bit wary. "I'd like to know why you asked me to marry you."

Diana glared at him a moment, then swallowed her pride. "Because I knew, after the things I had said to you, that you wouldn't ask me. I wasn't sure you'd forgive me."

He shook his head, and his fingers tightened demandingly on her shoulders. "Don't be ridiculous, it's not a matter of forgiveness."

"Caine..." She wanted to touch him but kept her hands at her sides, not certain she could accept that kind of unquestioning clemency. "I hurt you."

"Yes. By God, you did."

"I'm sorry," she whispered, but it wasn't pity he saw in her eyes. The first wave of relief washed over him.

"You haven't answered my question, Diana." He kept his hands firm on her shoulders, his eyes direct on hers. "Why do you want me to marry you?"

"I suppose I need a promise," she began, feeling the flutter of fear again. "I think when people just live together, it's too easy to walk away, and—"

"No." He shook his head again. "That's not what I want, and you know it. Why, Diana? Say it."

She swallowed as the slivers of fear grew to panic. "I—" Faltering, she closed her eyes.

"Say it," he demanded again.

Her lashes fluttered up so that she met his eyes levelly. Once the words were said, she knew there'd be no backing away. For her, they would be complete commitment. He knew it as well, she realized—and needed it. Why had she been so foolish as to think she was the only one with fears?

"I love you," she whispered, then let out a long, shuddering breath. With it went the fear. "Oh, God, Caine, I love you." She fell into his arms, clinging, and felt the release bubble up in laughter. "I love you," she said again. "How many times would you like to hear it?"

"I'll let you know in a minute," he murmured as his lips found hers. With a groan of pleasure, of relief, of joy, he drew her closer. "Again," he demanded against her mouth. "Tell me again."

She laughed and tugged him down until they lay on the rug. "I love you. If I'd known how good it would feel to say it, I would have told you before. Caine…" Framing his face with her hands, Diana looked down at him with her eyes suddenly serious. "Being with you, belonging to you, is worth everything I've known—I *have* known, but it seemed safer to pretend I could live without you."

Taking her hand, he pressed his lips to the palm. "I still can't give you guarantees, Diana. I can only love you."

"I don't want guarantees." She drew him down so that her cheek rested against his. "Not anymore. I'm going to gamble on you, MacGregor." Slowly, she ran her hands up his back. "And I'm going to win."

Caine slipped the jacket of her suit off her shoulders as his lips toyed with hers. "It's a night of firsts," he decided. "My first proposal…" He began loosening the buttons of her blouse. "The first time I manage to drag those three little words out of you…" His lips followed the trail of his fingers. "And the first time I make love with you in my office."

Diana sighed as she stripped his shirt from him. "There's a minor point of order, counselor."

"Hmm?"

"You haven't answered my proposal yet."

"Aren't you supposed to give me time to think it over?" He caught the lobe of her ear between his teeth.

"No."

"In that case, I accept." He lifted his head as a gleam of amusement lit his eyes. "Do we intend to add to the MacGregor line?"

With her lids half-closed, she gave him a lazy smile. "Absolutely. I come from very good stock."

Laughing, he pressed his lips against her throat. "Diana, you've made my father a very happy man."

* * * * *

NORA ROBERTS

Number one *New York Times* bestselling author
Nora Roberts is "a word artist, painting her story and
characters with vitality and verve," according to the
Los Angeles Daily News. She has published over a hundred
novels, and her work has been optioned and made into
films, excerpted in *Good Housekeeping*, translated into
over twenty-five different languages and published all
over the world.

In addition to her amazing success in mainstream, Nora
remains committed to writing for her category romance
audience that took her to their heart in 1981 with her very
first book, a Silhouette Romance. *The MacGregor Grooms*
brings back one of her best loved and most requested
characters, Daniel MacGregor, as he extends his
matchmaking proclivities to a new generation. With over
40 million copies of her books in print worldwide and six
titles on the *New York Times* bestseller list in one year—
including *The MacGregor Brides*—Nora Roberts is truly
a publishing phenomenon.

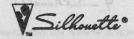